SWIMMING LESSONS

This Large Print Book carries the
Seal of Approval of N.A.V.H.

SWIMMING LESSONS

MARY ALICE MONROE

THORNDIKE PRESS

An imprint of Thomson Gale, a part of The Thomson Corporation

THOMSON
™
GALE

Detroit • New York • San Francisco • New Haven, Conn. • Waterville, Maine • London

LIBRARY OF CONGRESS CATALOGING-IN-PUBLICATION DATA

Monroe, Mary Alice.
  Swimming lessons / by Mary Alice Monroe.
    p. cm. — (Thorndike Press large print basic)
  ISBN-13: 978-0-7862-9414-5 (lg. print : alk. paper)
  ISBN-10: 0-7862-9414-0 (lg. print : alk. paper)
  1. Women — South Carolina — Fiction. 2. Turtles — Fiction. 3. South Carolina — Fiction. 4. Large type books. I. Title.
PS3563.O529S95 2007
813'.54—dc22   2007009467

Published in 2007 by arrangement with Harlequin Books S.A.

Printed in the United States of America on permanent paper
10 9 8 7 6 5 4 3 2 1

For Martha Keenan

I am a great lover of aquariums — and the South Carolina Aquarium especially. Their mission to educate, to preserve aquatic life and to support conservation efforts is an inspiration. I am impressed and in awe of the dedication, teamwork and enthusiasm I find in the staff and volunteers.
I thank each of you. In particular:

Heartfelt thanks to Kelly Thorvalson, Director of the Sea Turtle Hospital of the South Carolina Aquarium, for being incredibly generous with your time and for willingly serving as my mentor, teacher, model, friend and inspiration.
Truly, this book could not have been written without you.

Also at the S.C. Aquarium, my sincere thanks to an amazing team of professionals for your support and encouragement:

Kevin Mills, Jason Crichton, Kate Darby and Kim Rich, Tom Sheridan and Arnold Postell. And to dedicated turtle hospital volunteers Barbara Bergwerf, Beverly Ballow, Sherri Fox, Michelle Pate, Diane Lauritsen, Billy Warren, Pam Jones.

I am indebted to the incomparable Jean Beasely at the Karen Beasely Sea Turtle Hospital, Topsail Beach, North Carolina. Thank you for so generously offering me your valuable time to educate me and to share your stories, and for allowing me to join your amazing team of volunteers at the hospital.

The South Carolina Department of Natural Resources Marine Turtle Conservation Program has been a tremendous resource for me in the writing of this and other books on sea turtles. I owe great thanks to DuBose Griffin, Charlotte Hope, Tom Murphy and Joan Seithel — and special congratulations to Sally Murphy on your retirement! Thank you, too, to Meg Hoyle at the Botany Island Sea Turtle Program.

I am indebted to Micah and Daniel LaRoche of the Cherry Point Seafood

Company for their time in showing to me and explaining the workings of their fabulous operation.

Once again, the Barrier Island Eco-Tour, Isle of Palms, South Carolina, came through with another fabulous excursion filled with fun and facts to enrich my story. A fond and hearty thank-you to Shane and Morgan Zeigler, and to your great team.

My dear friends and fellow Island Turtle Team members are always there to help me ask the right questions and to research answers, edit for accuracy, support my work, inspire me and offer countless kindnesses too long to list. My love and thanks to Mary Pringle, Barbara Bergwerf, Tee Johannes, Beverly Ballow, Mary Ellen Rogers, Grace and Glenn Rhodes, Kathey O'Connor, Nancy Hauser, Brucie Harry and all the volunteers of the Island Turtle Team who walk the beaches for our beloved loggerheads.

Barbara Bergwerf has been a consistent and inspiring source of inspiration with her magnificent photographs of sea turtles and her work at the aquarium's sea turtle hospital. Now, as my coauthor of our children's book, *Turtle Summer, A Journal for My Daugher,* our collaboration grows. Thank you, Barb, for so generously sharing your talent and friendship with me.

For editing, advice and support in more ways than I can mention here, my love and thanks to Patti Callahan Henry, Marjory Wentworth, Patti Morrison, Jennifer McCurry, Tamar Myers, Nina Bruhns, Marguerite Martino and James Cryns.

I'm fortunate to have two brilliant editors, Martha Keenan and Margaret O'Neill Marbury. Thank you for your keen insights.

I am very grateful to my stellar agents, Robert Gottlieb and Kimberly Whalen, for your support, your enthusiasm and your guidance.

As always, for their unyielding love and support, and for making me laugh even while I am under deadline, I am forever grateful to my wonderful family, Markus, Gretta and Zack Kruesi, and Claire and John Dwyer.

ODYSSEY

The sea is thick and murky. Can you see me?

I am propelled forward, caught in a spiral of swift water. The Great Current carries me as it writhes along the coastline, swirling around the great gyre and through a vast spread of sargassum weed. It snakes from south to north, a supernatural force pushing me forward. Always onward.

I am a loggerhead. I've journeyed far in this vast ocean, a servant to my magnetic compass. Yet now I hear a voice that cries above the roar of the current. It is the voice of my ancestors, a voice that has guided mothers for generation after generation, for two hundred million years. I heed the call and spread my beautiful long flippers. Strange forces gain strength in my soul, compelling me eastward. Light shimmers above, then grows dark. Aqua to indigo, over and over on this odyssey.

I ignore the hunger that gnaws at my belly and swim through the living broth of drifting plankton. I push past gangly, gliding invertebrates and hallucinatory looking creatures, beyond the wreck fish and sea bream that share space beneath a gilt rock laden with pink coral and bright anemones.

I am riding a river of current, gliding in watery thermals, warmed by the sun, powered by the earth's rotation. I am soaring through liquid wind, reaching out to the place of my birth.

I am swimming . . . swimming . . . swimming home.

■ ■ ■ ■

PART 1

■ ■ ■ ■

*First get wet, get comfortable
in the water.
Let your skills develop naturally,
at your own pace.*

1

Last night, Toy Sooner dreamed again of the turtle. It was always the same dream, one so vivid that when she awoke she was tangled in her sheets, disoriented and filled with a great, nameless yearning.

Toy sat on the precipice of the sand dune looking out over the wave-scarred beach. Another day was ending. Around her the sea oats were greening and above, a night-hawk streaked across the slowly deepening sky. The tide was coming in, carrying sea-shells, driftwood and long-harbored memories tumbling to the shore.

She identified with the loggerhead sea turtle in her dream. Was it merely that the turtles were on her mind? She searched the restless sea that spread out to forever under the vast sky. Out in the distant swells, the sea turtles were gathering for the nesting season. Toy sensed the mothers out there, biding their time until instinct drove them from the safety of the sea to become vulnerable on the beach and lay their eggs.

It was an emotional time of the year for her. Each May when the sea turtles returned to the Isle of Palms, she felt the presence of her beloved mentor, Olivia Rutledge, returning with them.

She hugged her knees closer to her chest. This small dune on this empty patch of beach was her sanctuary. She came often to this sacred spot — to think, to remember, to find solace. She felt closer to Olivia Rutledge here — Miss Lovie to everyone she'd met. This dune had been Miss Lovie's favorite spot, and on some nights, especially when the sun lowered and the birds quieted, as now, Toy imagined she heard Miss Lovie's voice in the sweet-scented offshore breezes.

It had been five years since old Miss Lovie had passed. Five years spanned a good chunk of her life, she thought, considering she'd only lived twenty-three. After Olivia Rutledge died, Toy had worked hard every day of those five years to make a better life for herself and for Little Lovie, her daughter. That had been a vow made at Miss Lovie's gravesite and a promise to her infant daughter.

"I did my best to keep my vow," she said

aloud to Lovie Rutledge, feeling her spirit hovering close tonight. "I finished college, got a good job and I've made a nice home for Little Lovie. All tidy and cheery, with flowers on the table, like you taught me. I want so much to be a good mother." She rested her chin on her knee with a ragged sigh as the longing from the dream resurfaced.

"So, tell me, Miss Lovie. Why don't I feel that I am? Or content? I'm still like that turtle in my dream, swimming toward someplace I can't seem to get to."

A high pitched cry shattered her thoughts. "Mama!"

Toy's gaze darted toward the call. Her young daughter sat a distance from the shoreline surrounded by colorful plastic buckets and spades. Her long blond hair fell in salt-stiff streaks down her back as she bent over on hands and knees before the crude beginning of a sand castle.

"What do you want, Little Lovie?"

"Mama, come help me with my castle!"

Toy sighed, sorely tempted. "I'm working, honey."

"You're always working."

She saw a scowl flash across Little Lovie's face before she ducked her head and went back to her digging. Mingled in the muffled

roar of the ocean she heard Olivia Rutledge's voice in her mind. *Stop what you're
doing and play with your child!*

Toy desperately wanted to play with her
and enjoy each precious, fleeting moment
with Little Lovie. She felt an all too familiar
twinge of guilt and paused to allow her gaze
to linger on her daughter. Little Lovie was
carefully molding another tower with her
chubby hands.

That child was happiest when she was at
the seaside, Toy thought, her heart pumping
with affection. Whether collecting shells,
digging castles or rollicking in waves, as long
as she had her toes in the sand she was
content. She was only five years of age, yet
Little Lovie was so much like Miss Lovie
Rutledge that Toy sometimes believed the
old woman's spirit had returned to settle in
her namesake. For Toy, the sun rose and set
on her child. And it was *for* her child's
future that she gathered her discipline.

"Let me finish this report," she called
back. "Then I'll come help you finish that
sand castle."

"You promise?"

"I promise, okay?"

Her daughter nodded and Toy resolutely
brushed away grains of sand from her
notebook and returned to the report that

was due by morning. She was an Aquarist and had been placed in charge of her own gallery at the South Carolina Aquarium. It was her first break and she needed to prove that she was capable of the responsibility.

The noseeums and mosquitoes were biting in the sticky humidity and blown sand stuck to her moist skin but she worked a while longer, determined to finish in the last of the day's light. A short while later she closed her notebook and raised her gaze toward her daughter. Another lopsided tower had been added to the castle.

But her daughter was gone.

Toy's breath caught in her throat as her eyes wildly scanned the beach. "Lovie!" she cried out, leaping to her feet.

"Mama, look!"

Toy swung her head around toward her daughter's voice. Little Lovie was arched on tiptoe at the water's edge. The bottom of her pink swimsuit was coated with a thick layer of damp sand and she was pointing excitedly toward the sea.

Toy ran across the beach to grasp hold of her daughter's slender shoulders. "You know you're not supposed to go near the water," she scolded, even as her eyes devoured her child and her hands gently wiped sand from her face. "You scared me half to death."

The five-year-old was oblivious to her mother's concern. Instead, her large blue eyes were riveted to something in the surf.

"It's right there," she cried, wiggling her pointed finger urgently. "I see it!"

"What do you see, a dolphin?" Toy turned her head back toward the Atlantic to peer into the rolling surf. Then she saw it. A large dark object floated at the surface not more than fifty feet out.

It wasn't a dolphin. She squinted and moved a step closer. Could it be a turtle? The dark hulk appeared lifeless in the waves. "You stay right here," she ordered in a no nonsense tone, and this time, Little Lovie didn't argue.

Toy rolled her pants higher up on her slender legs, coiled her shoulder length blond hair in a twist at the top of her head, then walked into the sea for a closer look. She felt the chilly spring water swirl at her ankles, calves and then dampen the hem of her shorts as she waded forward, intrigued by the shadowy object bobbing on the waves.

It *was* a turtle! It had to be at least two hundred pounds — and it looked dead. What a pity, she thought and she wondered if this was a nesting female holding eggs. It was always a shame to lose an adult turtle, but to lose a nesting female was a tragedy. The loss was one of generations.

A wave carried the turtle closer and Toy's stomach clenched at the sight. It looked like she'd been floating for a long time. She was badly emaciated and the shell was dried and covered from tip to tip with barnacles.

"Poor Mama," she muttered. There'd been too many dead turtles washing ashore in the past few years. "Barnacle Bills" the turtle team called them, and this was another to add to the list. She'd call and have DNR pick the carcass up in the morning. Toy was about to turn back when she saw a flipper move.

"She can't be . . ." Toy bent forward, squinting. A breaker smacked her legs but she kept her eyes peeled on the turtle. A flipper moved again.

"She's alive!" she called out to Little Lovie.

The child jumped up and down, clapping her hands. Toy hurriedly waded closer to Little Lovie to be heard. "Honey, I'm going to need some help. Run up to Flo's house and tell her to come right quick, hear? Can you do that?"

"Yes, ma'am!"

The child took off like a shot for the dunes. Just beyond was the white frame house of Florence Prescott, the leader of the island's turtle team. Flo was very active in the community and always out doing something for someone, but she was usually home at the dinner hour. At least Toy hoped she was today.

She turned back toward the turtle. The inert creature was floating with her posterior up, like a lopsided rubber raft. She'd have to haul her in. She sighed and looked at her clothes. Well, they were half-soaked anyway, she thought as she began wading toward the turtle.

The pebbly sand suddenly dipped and sliding down, her toe was sliced by the sharp edge of a shell. White pain radiated up her leg and looking down, she saw the murky water stained red with blood. The turtle was drifting farther away in the current. Ignoring the pain, she kicked off to swim to the floating hulk.

The big turtle was in much sorrier shape than she'd first realized. As she drew near, the turtle's dark, almond eyes rolled in her large skull in a mournful gaze.

"Don't be afraid, big girl," she said to the turtle, feeling an instant connection. "I'll get you out of here in no time."

A small wave slapped her face as she swam around the turtle. Her eyes stung and she spit out a mouthful of saltwater. Once behind the rear flippers she could get a good handle on the shell. Then, using the carapace like a kickboard, she began kicking and pushing the turtle toward the shore.

She was making good progress when she caught a quick silvery flash of movement in the corner of her eye. Her breath hitched as she scanned the vista. The water's surface was turning glassy in the brilliant colors of the setting sun. She hesitated, not fooled by the serenity. Dusk was feeding time for sharks.

Toy knew she was in a vulnerable position. The predator would be curious about the sick turtle — an easy prey. With her toe bleeding she knew the smart thing to do would be to leave the turtle and get out of the water.

Then she saw it again. This time it was unmistakable. The slim, v-shaped dorsal fin broke the surface, heading her way in a lazy, zigzag pattern. Toy froze as the shark neared, then swiftly veered off. The turtle's instinct flared and her flippers feebly stroked in the surf. The shark surfaced again, but this time farther out by the inlet.

"Well, no one ever said I was smart," she

told herself, gripping the turtle's shell. With a grunt, she pushed with all her might, propelling the turtle forward. She repeated this twice more before her feet hit sand. The shark was closer again, circling in a pattern of surveillance.

That bull shark was four feet of sleek danger and she knew it could attack in shallow water. She hurried to the front of the turtle and grabbed hold. "We're not home yet," she muttered and began tugging the enormous turtle in. Behind her on the beach she heard Florence Prescott calling her name.

"Hurry, Flo!" she cried over her shoulder.

With athletic grace that belied her advanced years, Flo ran straight into the water, her tennis shoes still on.

"Drag her out of the water," Toy cried with urgency. "We've got company."

Flo looked over her shoulder. "God damn," she muttered.

Little Lovie ran into the surf, arms reaching for the turtle. "Let me help!"

"Lovie, you get back on the beach this instant!" Toy ordered.

"But I want to help!"

"Do as your mama says," Flo told her. "Sharks nibble hatchlings in ankle deep water and your toes are just the right size.

Go on now, git."

Little Lovie scrambled out of the ocean.

Flo grabbed hold of a side of the turtle's shell. Her deeply tanned arms spoke of many years spent in the sun. "On the count of three . . ."

With a heave-ho, they shoved the turtle up the final few feet to the edge of the beach. Out of the water, the full impact of the huge turtle's weight was felt. It was like pushing a boulder and it took all they had to get the turtle to scrape sand till only the tips of the incoming tide caressed her rear flippers.

The turtle remained motionless. Toy plopped down on the sand beside her and lifted her foot to check out her wound. She was shocked to see that the cut in her big toe was deep and bright red blood trickled in a steady flow. And it hurt like hell. It hit her how reckless she'd been to stay in the sea with a bleeding wound. Raising her gaze, she looked again out at the sea. The shark had already disappeared beneath the murky water. She started to laugh with re- lief.

"What are you laughing at?" Flo asked. "Is that a cut you've got there?" She swooped down like a mother hen.

"It's nothing."

"I'll be the judge of that. Those shells can be like razors. Let me see it."

"Really, Flo, I'm okay."

"Bring it here." Flo bent and, grabbing hold of Toy's foot, studied the toe closer. She clucked her tongue. Little Lovie hovered nearby, mesmerized. After a quick perusal, Flo released the foot and rose to a stand. "Put some antibiotic ointment on it and you'll live."

Toy looked up at her daughter with a reassuring smile.

"I can't believe you went out there with a shark trailing you," Flo said. "You know better."

Toy took the scolding with good nature. "I didn't see it when I swam out and I wasn't sure I was bleeding." She snorted and added smugly, "But I got her in, didn't I?"

Florence Prescott usually had something upbeat to say about most things, but she looked at the turtle with a frown and shaking her head said, "I'm not sure it was worth the risk. This turtle looks barely alive. And she's covered with gunk. I've buried strandings that looked better than this one."

"No, she's beautiful. That gunk is merely leeches, algae and barnacles. We just have to get her someplace where we can clean her up."

Before they could discuss this further, their attention was caught by calls coming from up the beach. "Well, thank goodness the cavalry's here," Flo said. She stretched her arm overhead and waved, calling out, "Cara! Brett! Over here!"

Toy turned toward the dunes and saw an attractive couple in khaki shorts and green *Barrier Island Eco-Tour* T-shirts. Toy's spirits soared and she grinned from ear to ear as she lifted her arm in a wave.

A tall, lean woman strode toward them in a long-legged, no-nonsense manner. Her glossy, dark hair whipped in the breeze and behind her smart, tortoise sunglasses, Toy knew Cara's brown eyes were sparkling with excitement at the prospect of a live turtle on the beach.

Behind her, Brett's broad shoulders and height towered even over Cara. Though he wore the same T-shirt of the tour company they owned, on Brett the clothes were faded and worn, giving him the disheveled appearance of an island boy.

Little Lovie yelped with excitement at seeing them and ran into Brett's arms for a quick hoist high up in the air.

"It's a turtle, see!" she cried out.

"I see it!" Brett's blue eyes brightened against his weathered tan as he grinned wide and swung Little Lovie around, her legs flying behind her. Then he tucked her on his hip with a hug of affection.

"What've we got?" Cara asked, walking directly to the turtle. She bent over the sea turtle to get a closer look.

"Probably a nesting female," Flo replied as she quickly moved to Cara's side. "She's covered with barnacles. And look, leeches too. Ugh, the horrid blood suckers are all over her."

Cara grimaced at the pitiful sight. "She must've been floating for weeks."

"Weeks? Longer than that," Flo replied. "These poor floaters can't dive to hunt and this old girl likely hasn't eaten in months. Her neck is so thin . . . she's all skin." She clucked her tongue. "I don't know if she's going to make it."

"She's not gone yet," Toy said, joining them at the turtle's side. She felt fiercely protective of the turtle she rescued. "I've been amazed at how resilient sea turtles can be. I'm not giving up on her."

"She's certainly a big girl," Brett said, drawing near with Little Lovie in his arms.

"Let's see how big she is." Cara pulled a measuring tape out of her backpack and made quick work of measurements. She called out the numbers to Flo who scribbled them down in her notebook. Little Lovie scrambled out of Brett's arms to hover closer, half curious, half repelled by the condition of the turtle.

Toy tucked her fingertips into her back pockets. The early evening's chill seemed to go straight through her wet clothes.

"From tip to tip of the shell, I've got forty inches," Cara called out. "I'm guessing she's well over 200 pounds."

Flo slapped the sand from her hands. "Well, that's that. I guess I'd better call it in to DuBose at the Department of Natural Resources to come get her."

"I could call the Aquarium," Toy piped up.

Cara checked her watch. "It's after six o'clock. DuBose won't be in her office."

"No, but there's the DNR hotline number," Flo replied. "Someone will come out."

"Tomorrow, most likely," said Brett.

"DNR doesn't do rehab," Cara said, zipping up her backpack. "What will they do with a live turtle?"

Flo shrugged. "Do you have any better ideas?"

"I could call the Aquarium," Toy said again, a little louder.

The two women turned their heads toward her in swift unison.

"The Aquarium?" asked Flo with doubt. "What will they do? They don't take in sick sea turtles."

"Well, actually, yes they — we do," Toy replied. "At least, the Aquarium took two in before. A few years back. They didn't do the rehabilitation, but they held the turtle until it could be moved to a vet. I don't know . . . it's just a thought," she added hesitatingly.

"Even so," Cara replied. "No one will be at the Aquarium at this hour either. Why do the emergencies always happen after business hours? It's like some unspoken law."

"But we *can* still call the Aquarium," Toy persisted. "We always have someone on call."

"Really?" Cara asked, interested. "Then, I suppose that is a possibility to consider."

"The DNR still has to be notified," Flo said with finality. "Anything to do with turtles is their jurisdiction."

"Sure, but then *they're* stuck with trying to find a place to rehabilitate it," Toy argued back.

Cara shook her head. "Flo, don't get worked up. We'll call DuBose."

While Cara and Flo argued the point

between them, Toy limped off, her heel digging half moons into the sand. She went to Little Lovie's lopsided sand castle, noticing the bits of shells and sea whip that Lovie had decorated it with while she stuffed the buckets and spades into the canvas bag.

"You okay?"

Toy turned her head surprised to see Brett standing by her side. His broad shoulders blocked her view of the women at the shoreline.

"It's just a scratch from a sea shell," she said and returned to stuffing her bag with toys.

"You know that's not what I'm talking about."

She tossed a sandy spade into the bag and rested her hands on her thighs, then she looked up again. He was standing with his hands on his hips and a calm and a patient expression on his face. It was so typical of him. Surrounded by volatile women, Brett was always a steadying force for them all. She'd come to look up to him as the big brother she'd always wanted and he'd steered her straight through some pretty rocky waters over the years.

"Do you really think the Aquarium will take the turtle in?" he asked.

She shrugged. "Honestly, Brett, I don't

know. I've heard talk of taking turtles in this season, but nothing's been decided. It's certainly not up to me." She hesitated then said with feeling, "But at least it's a possibility."

"And a good one. Do you know who to call?"

A smile twitched her lips as she nodded.

"So, what are you waiting for? Make that call. You sure don't need our permission. And it sounds to me like you've got the best idea going."

Toy pulled her cell phone from the canvas bag, dreading the task she'd set for herself. After all her bluster, she couldn't back out now. Brett crossed his arms and waited while she dialed the number of her supervisor at the Aquarium. She told herself it was the cold, not nervousness, that made her fingers stiff but the pounding in her heart was proof that it took nerves for her, a low-level staff member at the Aquarium, to be calling the Director of Animal Husbandry. She shivered as the wind gusted.

Jason answered the phone after two rings. The phone connection from the beach wasn't good and she had to repeat sentences, but she managed to quickly sum up the situation. After a few minutes conversation she closed her cell phone and looked up at Brett, eyes wide with triumph.

"Jason said to bring her in!"

"Well, hey! Good work, kiddo."

Toy felt a surge of satisfaction at the congratulations Cara and Flo gave her when she delivered the good news.

"The only problem is," Toy added, "the Aquarium is locked tight until morning."

"What are we supposed to do with the turtle till then?" Flo asked.

"When I interned at the sea turtle hospital at Topsail," Toy replied, "Jean Beasley told me about the first sick turtle they found. She was a big loggerhead, like this one. They found her floating, too. It was late in the day and they didn't have anywhere to take her, so they carried the turtle to Jean's garage on the island, washed her off, wrapped her in warm wet towels and watched her through the night. The next morning they drove her to a veterinary hospital. That same night the turtle was released back to Jean's garage." She smiled. "And *that* was the beginning of the Karen Beasley Sea Turtle hospital."

"You thinking of starting a hospital, now?" Flo chided.

Toy smirked and shook her head. "Maybe someday. But right now I'm thinking we need to stop talking and get this turtle off the beach. The sun is going down and Little Lovie is cold, I'm cold, and that means the turtle is cold, too."

As if to punctuate her statement, the turtle made an effort to take a labored breath. It was feeble yet enough to prompt the group to action.

"Well, if they could do it, so can we," said Cara. She bent over to grab hold of the turtle's shell. "Okay, everyone, grab a side."

Brett moved alongside the turtle and took hold. Toy followed suit.

"Whoa, gang. Where are we taking her?" asked Flo.

"Where else?" Cara replied with a crooked grin. "To the beach house."

2

Primrose Cottage was a quaint yellow beach house with mullioned windows and a welcoming veranda. It sat on a high dune across from the ocean and was surrounded by sweetgrass, sea oats and wildflowers that grew in a riotous display. Modest but comfortable, it was one of the few remaining original cottages left on Isle of Palms. Primrose Cottage was once the summer home of Olivia Rutledge. After her death, the beach house was passed on to Lovie's daughter, Cara, who then rented the house to Toy for a fraction of its worth. It was the kind of generous arrangement that a family member would make for another.

It was to this beach house that the turtle team decided to bring the sick sea turtle for the night. With Brett's strong back, the four of them managed to carry the enormous sea turtle up the beach, over the dunes, and along the narrow beach path to the house.

The sky was dusky and the yellow light streaming from the cottage windows was welcoming as they approached. Cara was panting hard and her arms strained like they were breaking by the time they set the huge sea turtle down on the sand and gravel in front of the beach house.

"I have a whole new understanding of what it takes for those mamas to crawl out from the sea under all that weight," Cara said, bent with her hands on her knees. "Look at my knees, they're shaking!"

"You think this was tough?" Brett asked her with a short laugh. He wiped his hands on his shirt. "Giving you a piggyback ride through the pluff mud makes this seem like a walk in the park."

While the others guffawed, Cara twisted her mouth into a smirk. "Ha ha ha, very funny," she replied. "Just for that I think I'll add a few pounds for the next jaunt to the hammock."

His brows rose. "I think my dreamboat has *already* taken on a little extra cargo."

This set off another round of laughs from Toy and Flo as Cara sauntered up to slap his arms, already raised in mock self-defense. Toy watched the teasing banter between husband and wife and wondered what it was like to have that kind of relationship with a man. The kind where slapping could be playful rather than hurtful.

"Save your energy. We're far from done," Flo called out, heading to the underbelly of the beach house's raised porch.

Primrose Cottage had endured years of salt air, blustery wind and blazing sun, and the old house was showing its age. It was an endless battle to keep the paint from peeling, the mold from peppering the wood, and any gravel on the driveway. The small area under the front porch was closed in on two sides by a wall of a wobbly, faded white wooden trellis weighed down with jasmine vines. This confined area was so stuffed, Toy could barely see the cement slab.

"We'll have to clean out this place if we aim to put this turtle here for the night," said Flo. She surveyed the area and muttered, "And I thought I had a lot of stuff."

"It's not all mine," Toy said defensively. "Most of it was Miss Lovie's and I don't figure we should move it."

"Why not?" Flo replied. "She won't miss it."

Toy looked dismayed at the comment but Flo only shrugged then moved a pink bicycle with training wheels and plastic streamers stemming from the handles. "If you ask me — and you didn't — I'd say both the elder and the younger Lovies have accumulated a mountain of stuff."

"Okay, okay," Cara called out as she surveyed the wall to wall clutter. "I admit, I'm not the best landlady, but you should've seen the mountain of junk I threw out already. You know what a pack rat my mother was. She couldn't bear to let go of anything. Every rusted tool and each cracked flower pot still had some life left in it. Every time I threw something out she was at the trash bin pulling it out again."

"That's just a reaction to the Depression years, child," Flo replied, rolling the tricycle out. "All of us tainted by it hang on to stuff longer than we should."

"Whatever . . . Because of her I hate to hold on to anything. Stuff just accumulates!" She shook her head and put her hands on her hips as she surveyed the assorted garden tools, turtle supplies, toys and pots crammed in the space under the porch. "See what I mean? In just five years all this stuff gathers. I guess I should've come over to clear this place out for you, Toy. It's mine to figure out what to do with."

"I don't mind," Toy replied honestly. "I hate to get rid of anything that belonged to Miss Lovie."

"Puhlease . . ." Cara said, raising her

hands. "I had to fight with my mother to throw anything out, don't make me fight with you."

"Well, let's just clear it out for now," said Flo. "Y'all can decide what to do about it later."

"I'll grab the car keys and move it out to the driveway," Toy said. "That'll clear a big space." She patted the gold, 1972 VW bug with affection before she opened the door. It creaked on its hinges. "This old girl has a few lapses, but this is one piece that I'll never toss away."

The VW Bug was once the pride and joy of Olivia Rutledge. Everyone who lived on the island knew that if they spotted "the Goldbug" parked along Palm Boulevard, the Turtle Lady was out on the beach tending to a turtle nest. Miss Lovie had left the car to Toy in her will, and at 103,000 miles, the Gold Bug was still going strong.

While Toy moved the car, the others worked together to shove the clutter to the lawn, leaving only Little Lovie's blue plastic kiddie pool. This was scrubbed, rinsed then filled to the half way point with water.

"I reckon this is as good as it's going to get," Cara said, surveying the cleared and swept space. "Let's bring her in."

"Easy now," Flo said as they each took

hold of the turtle and carried her under the porch. Gently, they slipped the enormous turtle into the kiddie pool. She landed with a soft splash, filling every inch.

"Snug as a bug in a rug," Brett said, rising.

"You ain't kidding," Flo added, drying her hands on her shorts. "She barely squeezed in. If that loggerhead was healthy, she'd use those powerful flippers to climb out from that ridiculous plastic bin and stopping her would be like trying to stop a tank." She clucked her tongue. "Poor thing. She's so weak and sick, she doesn't even try."

Toy crouched closer to the sea turtle that lay dull and limp in the pool. She looked more like one of Little Lovie's inflatable toys than a real loggerhead. She knew this noble turtle had survived against daunting odds to reach maturity. She'd traveled countless miles to the beach of her birth to lay her eggs. She didn't deserve to be in such a pitiful condition.

"I'm going to scrub her down," she said, rolling up her sleeves.

"Are you sure you're supposed to do that?" Flo asked. "Maybe we should just leave her be."

"Flo," she said, rising to a stand. "May I remind you that I work at the Aquarium and I've handled lots of sick sea turtles when I interned at the turtle hospital in Topsail. So, yes. I *am* sure we're supposed to wash her down." Her expression shifted to reveal the hurt exasperation she felt with the other woman.

Flo's brows rose in surprise at Toy's re-action. Then her shoulders lowered and her lips lifted to a thoughtful smile. "I reckon I can get pretty fixed in my ways at times."

Cara guffawed from behind them. "Who, *you?*"

Toy breathed easier and met Flo's smile.

"Well, kiddos," Flo said, slapping her hands together. "It looks like this turtle is in good hands. It's getting dark and I'm already late for my date. If you don't need me, I gotta go."

"Who is the lucky guy this time?" Cara asked.

Flo just waved her hand in a dismissive gesture. "You'll be fine without me for a while. I'll come back tomorrow morning to help with whatever you need done. What time do you think we'll be shoving off for the Aquarium?"

"Jason is getting there early to set up a tank for her. He said to bring her in around eight," replied Toy.

"Then I'll be here at seven. I'll bring coffee."

She leaned forward to give a quick kiss on Little Lovie's cheek then offered a wave to the others. "Take good care of our girl," she said as she walked off, her flip flops clapping against her heels. She disappeared around a gangly oleander.

The small space beneath the porch seemed suddenly quieter without her energy.

"So then," said Cara, breaking the silence. Her eyes turned toward Toy. "What should we do first?"

Toy scratched behind her ear, surprised to suddenly find herself in charge. She caught sight of Little Lovie standing by the steps of the porch wrapped tight in her beach towel, shivering. Her damp hair lay in clumps around her head. She was slight with no meat on her bones, as her mama would say. "The first thing I've got to do is warm up the little bug over there before she chatters away her teeth."

"Let me do that," Brett offered, walking toward Little Lovie. "I know you two ladies can't wait to get your hands on that turtle. While you scrub to your heart's content, I'll scrounge around the kitchen and fix up some hot dinner for all of us." He turned to the child. "What do you say to that?"

Little Lovie looked up at him with limpid eyes and her teeth biting the towel. She nodded.

"Come on then, before your lips turn any bluer," he said.

"Hey, darlin'," Cara called out to him. "While you're at it, I'd like a vodka martini with three olives." She winked when he glanced back at her with a smirk.

Toy enjoyed their banter and watched Brett place his big hand against Little Lovie's back, nudging her toward the door. They were so like what she thought a father and daughter should be. And she felt again a stabbing guilt that somehow she'd failed her daughter because there was no father for her.

"He's a pretty remarkable guy," she said to Cara.

"Don't I know it."

"He'll make a great father someday."

Cara's smile slipped. "God willing."

Toy caught the sudden shift in emotion and let the topic drop. Miss Lovie used to say that the island breezes softened the bones. In Cara's case, Toy saw that it was true. Marriage had sweetened Cara. And for sure, no one could have been nicer or more supportive of her and Little Lovie than Cara and Brett. They were like family

— the only family Toy and Little Lovie could count on.

"Let's get this show rolling," Cara said in an upbeat voice, wiping sand from her hands. "You're the boss here. You'll have to tell me how this is done."

"There's not a whole lot we *can* do here," Toy replied, unrolling the hose. "All the medical treatments will be done tomorrow at the Aquarium. But at least we can get all that slime and those leeches off. Even if she doesn't make it, I reckon she'll be happier for a bath."

"I hear that," Cara said, walking to the faucet. "Fresh water okay?"

"Yep. It's even better than sea water for cleaning her off. Kills those ol' barnacles."

"Well, here's a nice fresh water shower, baby," said Cara. Water gurgled from the hose and splashed onto the turtle's shell.

While Cara hosed down the turtle, Toy brought over a bucket filled with soft scrub brushes. Her stomach clenched as she knelt by the turtle. It was covered with stubborn barnacles and hundreds of thread-like, wiggly leeches.

"God, I hate leeches," she muttered with a shudder.

"You and me both," Cara said as she knelt beside her. Her mouth was a tight grimace.

Their eyes met, then with a mutual sigh of resignation, they both dove in and began to scrub.

They scrubbed and picked and rinsed until it seemed to Toy that she'd removed acres of the ocean's slimy bottom from the turtle. The bigger, gray, crusty barnacles were tenacious but the smaller ones were easily plucked off. Dozens more clung stubbornly to every inch of the turtle like boils. At least the horrible leeches were off and she had to admit the loggerhead did look better. The shell was spongy to the touch, but bits of its rich brown coloring could be seen between the dried, flaky bits.

The gentle turtle remained still and uncomplaining. She rolled her eyes back to stare at Toy with an almost human expression.

"Bless her heart. If I didn't know better, I'd think she was saying thank you."

"You're welcome, baby," Cara replied, patting her shell.

"I think we should name her."

"I thought you biologists didn't like to get personal with wild animals." Cara said the word *biologists* with a gentle tease.

Toy made a face, but secretly she thrilled to the title. It was hard earned. "It's true, but I confess I like to give names to the ones

I work with every day. It helps me remember one from the next and it's more personal. Besides, I have a hard enough time remembering names. Who can remember a number?" She paused to look with scrutiny at the loggerhead. "How about Caretta?"

Cara barked out a laugh and pretended to squirt Toy with the hose. It had long been a tender point between Cara and her mother that she'd been named after the Latin name for loggerheads, *Caretta caretta.* She'd spent a lifetime insisting on being called Cara.

"Don't even think about it. Besides, doesn't the Aquarium already have a turtle named Caretta? We have to come up with something more original for this big girl."

Toy sat back on her heels. "That's it! *Big Girl.*"

Cara nodded with approval. "Big Girl it is."

"Well, Big Girl," Toy said, tossing her scrub brush in the bucket. "I think that's about as clean as we can get you tonight. Let's wrap her up in wet towels, and then all that's left is to wait until morning."

"And pray she makes it." Cara added. "I don't know if turtles have expressions, but this poor girl even looks sick." Night was falling fast and in the dim gray light, the shabbiness of the under-porch area was apparent. "We can't just leave her out here by herself. What if she wanders off? Or some animal gets her?"

"No, of course not. I'll stay with her."

"Are you sure?"

Toy rose and put her hands to her lower back, aching from bending over the kiddie pool for so long. Her khaki pants were soaked and muddied, and her aching knees had dozens of tiny dents in the skin from kneeling on sand and grit.

"Yeah," she replied, stifling a yawn. "No problem. I'll just drag down the lounge chair from the porch. It'll be like camping." She snorted. "Kind of."

Cara grimaced. "I hate camping."

"Me, too."

They burst out laughing.

"I'll take the second shift," Cara offered. She stretched her long arms over her head, yawning loudly. "It's hotter 'n Hades down here. Lord help us." Then without saying more, she began rolling up the hose.

Toy began gathering up the brushes and emptying the bucket. They both moved with the silent, slow movements of exhaustion.

"One thing, though," Toy said in afterthought. "If I'm down here with the turtle, will you help get Little Lovie to bed?"

Cara's eyes lit up. "You don't have to ask

me twice."

Later that evening, they all headed for bed. While Cara and Brett settled Lovie, Toy dragged the old wooden lounge chair from the porch down the stairs to the cement slab, then went back up for a sleeping bag, a flashlight, a bottle of insect repellent and a bottle of chilled white wine. She slathered the contents of one bottle on her body and poured the contents of the other into a glass.

A vine of jasmine as thick as a python snaked in and out of the rickety lattice. Any breeze that might waft in from the ocean was blocked by the heavy foliage, but it provided a heady scent that helped over-power the dank smell of mildew and the fishy odor of turtle. Toy used the last of her energy to set the lounge chair at the edge of the concrete slab where the space opened up to the ocean's breeze. Then, without removing her clothes, she crawled into the flannel folds of the sleeping bag and lay facing the stars.

It was a steamy night on the island. From the darkness the insects were singing their lullaby. The moon was rising and from deep in the blackness came the soothing, omni-present roar of the ocean.

Not an evening passed that she didn't give

thanks to the Lord for being able to live here with her daughter in this cottage near the beach. Primrose Cottage was the only place in her entire life where she'd felt safe and truly happy.

The old wood lounge creaked as she shifted her weight. From somewhere a night bird called, and close to her ear she heard the high hum of a mosquito. Slapping her neck with a curse on all mosquitoes, Toy wrapped herself mummy-like in the sleeping bag and lay in her cocoon for several minutes while the heat sweltered.

It wasn't long before she couldn't breathe. "This is ridiculous," she muttered as she kicked off the sleeping bag. Instantly the breeze cooled her moist skin, and just as quickly, the pesky mosquitoes hummed closer. It was going to be a long night, she thought. She shifted on the creaking lounge chair to grab more repellent. Across the floor, the turtle remained unmoving under the towels. Often these turtles hung on to life by a thin thread. Toy sat very still, waiting for several minutes in the silence to hear a breath. None came.

Worried, Toy unwrapped herself from the sleeping bag to brave the mosquitoes and check on the loggerhead. She removed the towel from over its big head. The turtle was lying perfectly still.

"How are you doing, Big Girl?" she asked, squinting in the dark. She bent to gently touch the turtle's eyelids, seeking some response.

The turtle blinked and released a long exhale.

Toy exhaled, too, in great relief. "You had me worried there, old girl," she said, reaching out to place her palm on the turtle's roughened shell. She felt a strong bond with the mother sea turtle. "We single mothers have to stick together," she said and, though she had no logical reason for it, she acted on instinct and began to pat the shell.

She thought again of her recurring dream of the sea turtle. Of how Big Girl had traveled long and far to reach this bit of beach she called home.

"You made it home," she crooned softly. "All that way, through all those dangers. How many seasons have you survived out there in the ocean, huh? Are you forty years old? Fifty? More?"

No one knew for sure how long loggerheads lived. Some thought they lived to one hundred years or more.

"Don't you worry, Big Girl. You're not alone. I'm here for you."

■ ■ ■ ■

Upstairs, Cara closed the storybook and glanced over at the little girl on the bed beside her. Pale lashes rested on cherubic cheeks while soft puffs of air came out evenly through her rosy lips.

Cara's heart pumped with affection for the little girl she'd helped raise since she was born. Toy liked to say that the spirit of Miss Lovie came to rest in the heart of this child, and though it was Cara's nature to pooh-pooh such sentiment, in her heart she believed it was true. She caught glimpses of her mother's gentle spirit in Little Lovie. And certainly in her love of nature, the sea turtles especially.

Cara reached up to softly stroke the blond hairs away from Little Lovie's forehead, still damp from her bath. It was a gesture she remembered her own mother making. A surge of emotion moistened her eyes.

"You're thinking of your mother, aren't you?"

Cara turned toward the voice at the door. Leaning against the frame she saw the tall, broad form of her husband, his arms crossed at his chest, his eyes soft with concern. Brett's keen ability to observe even small details was what made him both a great wildlife guide and a great husband.

She nodded and let her gaze wander. "I always feel her presence keenly here at the beach house."

"It's not surprising. She loved it here more than anywhere else."

"Wouldn't she just love having a turtle under her porch?" She laughed lightly at the thought. "She sure loved the turtles."

"She loved *you*. Are you sure you won't be happier living in this house? She left it to you, after all. Maybe she wanted you to live here. I wouldn't mind moving."

"Someday, perhaps. But the memories are still too strong. Even after five years, the pain's too fresh." She shrugged. "I dunno. Maybe because she died so soon after our reconciliation. For so long we barely ever talked. And then when we finally started, she had to up and die. Hardly seems fair."

"At least you cleared the air. You had the chance a lot of other people miss."

"I know. I'm grateful for that, I really am." Cara reached up to tuck the pink sheet under Little Lovie's chin. "It's just, there's still so much I want to tell her. So much I would have liked to share with her. I feel robbed."

Cara rose from the bed and wrapped her

arms across her chest. She gazed around the room. This was once her bedroom, the room of a girl's dreams and heartaches.

"After she died, I tried sleeping in Mama's bed. The scent of her gardenia perfume hung in the air like a ghost. It was pervasive — in the closet, the curtains. It was like she was everywhere. I know it's crazy, but I missed her so much, I resorted to wearing her bathrobe to bed. I used to pretend that her arms were wrapped around me while I cried like a baby. Me!" She sniffed. "Pathetic, isn't it?"

"You never told me that."

Cara leaned back against him. "It's pretty silly, isn't it?"

"Not at all."

He slid his arms around her waist. They felt strong and secure, and closing her eyes, she caught the scent of the sea in his clothes. "I'd much rather sleep in our own bed, in our own house and have your arms around me."

He bent and she felt his cheek against hers and his muscle move into a grin. "That sounds good to me."

"Besides," she said, straightening. "It's been good for Toy to live here. She finds comfort in being surrounded by Mama's things."

"She loved her like a mother."

"In a lot of ways, she *was* her mother, the mother Toy never had. Remember the way she cried at Mama's funeral? Made me look like I didn't care as much. I got some strange looks, I recall."

"It's not your way to cry."

Cara wondered about that statement. It was the kind of thing people said about her and she used to believe it. Growing up, she'd worn her stoicism like armor against the slings and arrows of her father's anger. It had served her well as an executive in an advertising firm in the chilly north. Yet, she found that iron armor heavy to bear here in the softer air of the islands.

"Still, it's strange the way Toy doesn't want to get rid of anything of Mama's. I don't think she's changed a single thing in this house for the five years she's lived here. Not so much as a book has been moved from its sacred spot. It's like this house is a shrine to Mama's memory." She gave off a short laugh. "It would be annoying if she weren't so darn sincere."

"And insecure," he replied.

"What do you mean? I think she's doing great."

"She is. But all the responsibility of rais- ing Little Lovie falls squarely on her shoulders. Toy's still pretty young and she doesn't have a husband to help out. Or family to fall back on."

"She has us."

"That she does. But I'll wager she still feels alone."

Cara knew what it was like to live alone and not depend on anyone else for financial or emotional support. As empowering as it was, there were many lonely moments. Especially at night.

She looked around her old room — Little Lovie's room now. The rest of the house may not have changed since her mother's death, but Cara had insisted that this room be transformed from a grown-up's guest room with paintings of marshes and surf to all pink and frills with prints of mermaids on the walls. The only piece of furniture that had remained was the black iron bed that she had slept in as a girl. She'd always thought that one day her own little girl would sleep in it. Cara looked at the little girl in the bed now, and felt deep in her heart that this was the child meant to sleep here.

"It scares me how much I love this child. I don't want to be just some aunt in her life. Someone who sends her gifts on her birthday and on Christmas. I want to be someone special to her. The aunt she can talk to when she's angry with her mother. The one who gives her advice when she has her first crush on a boy, or when she gets her first period, or gets drunk and needs a ride home. I want to be that someone who takes her to special places, to expand her horizons. You know . . . the fun aunt."

"Honey, I've no doubt you can fill that bill."

Cara set the book on the bedside table and leaned far over to place a kiss on the child's forehead. She stayed a breath longer as she closed her eyes and inhaled the sweet scent of soap in Little Lovie's hair.

When she moved aside, Brett took his turn. His shoulders dwarfed the small girl as he placed a chaste kiss on her forehead. Rising, he smoothed the blanket and put her favorite stuffed sea turtle beside her. Then, placing his hand on the small of his wife's back, they walked softly from the room.

"I think God gives children that special smell to protect them," he said, closing the door behind him. "It's so sweet it melts you at the knees and you'd do anything for them."

"She *is* pretty special," Cara said.

"*Our* child will be special."

Cara leaned back against him, feeling the weight of that statement heavy in her heart. They had tried so hard for five years to have a child. "Brett, I'm scared to get my hopes up again."

"It'll work this time."

"It didn't the last two times. Let's face it, Mother Nature isn't very kind to women in their forties trying to have babies." She looked up and saw her pain mirrored in his eyes. "I just thought . . ." She sighed. "You know, that I'd be one of the lucky ones. I still fantasize that this time will be the one. You know, *the third time is the charm.*" She sighed and turned in his arms to face him. "Besides, we can't afford to keep doing the in vitros."

"Let me worry about that."

She patted his chest. "It's not just the money. I don't know if I can handle another round emotionally. The doctors might be able to say the embryo isn't a real baby yet, but for me, every time I lose one I feel that it is." Her voice hitched as she rested her head against his chest. "It just hurts too much."

"I know, I know," he said softly against her ear. "But remember, we're in this together. We'll be fine. Our baby will be fine. You have to have faith."

"I do," she said softly as he squeezed her tight. "In us."

3

Arising coastal sun sent piercing spears of light into Toy's eyes. She blinked lazily twice, then jerked her head up.

Her first thought was of Big Girl.

Clarity washed the cobwebs from her mind as she recalled in a rush all that transpired the night before. She'd stayed with Big Girl until the wee hours of the morning. Cara had crept downstairs to take the second shift, bumping into the clunky wood lounge chair with a loud curse. Toy had been in a fitful sleep, dreaming again of the swimming sea turtle and tangled up in the sweltering sleeping bag. She'd dragged herself upstairs to her bed, stripping off her sweaty clothes and flopping naked onto blissfully cool sheets. Under the gentle whirr of the ceiling fan, she'd fallen instantly into a deep sleep.

She felt groggy, like she could sleep for another few hours, but she dutifully rubbed her eyes and kicked off the sheets. She rose slowly and padded in bare feet across the wood floor to the small, white tiled bathroom, eager for the rush of cool water and minty soap to wash away remnants of the steamy night. She emerged a short time later, refreshed and eager to see the turtle. She dressed quickly in her Aquarium uniform of khaki shorts and the gray polo shirt with the SC Aquarium emblem, pulled her damp hair up in a clip and tied her tennis shoes.

Morning light poured into the small living room from a row of three windows that offered a breathtaking view of grassy dune, palms, blue sky and thousands of acres of sparkling ocean. In front of these were an old down sofa and two enormous armchairs slip-covered in the cabbage rose pattern that Olivia Rutledge had loved. Between the chairs sat a round ottoman in the same fabric. It had been a favorite spot of Miss Lovie's, and every time she looked at it, Toy thought of her sitting with her legs up, a book in one hand, sipping tea.

The tongue-in-groove walls and golden heart pine floors were typical of many of the old island houses. On the walls were oil paintings of the lowcountry, all by local artists, historical and contemporary: Verner,

Williams, Pratt-Thomas, Greene, Smith and others. It was a cozy, cheery room, and a world away from the shabby trailers Toy had grown up in.

From the main room, a narrow hall adorned with Rutledge family photographs that dated back to the turn of the century led to two small bedrooms. Toy went to the seaward room to gently nudge her daughter awake. Little Lovie groused and grumbled but eventually was lured from her bed. Next, Toy headed downstairs under the porch.

She found Cara stretched out on the lounge chair, one leg falling off it, gently snoring. She smirked, never having seen the usually sophisticated Cara Rutledge Beauchamps in that pose. The morning was already warm, hinting at the hot, humid day it would become. Toy bent close to the turtle and hesitated, wondering with sudden fear if the turtle had made it through the night. She removed the damp towels from its shell.

The turtle's eyes rolled up to look at her.

"Ah, Big Girl!" she exclaimed, relieved beyond measure. "It sure is nice to wish you a good morning. I'd be lying if I didn't tell you I was worried. But you're a survivor, aren't you? Just like me."

Her large eyes watched Toy with a sickly expression.

"You aren't feeling so good, are you? Don't you worry. We'll get you to the hospital in no time."

Toy heard a loud yawn behind her. She turned to see Cara squinting through half-opened eyes and scratching her wildly disheveled hair.

"I feel like I slept on a railroad track," Cara said in a hoarse voice.

"You look like it, too. A shower will improve your outlook."

"A shower, a massage . . . I need the whole spa treatment. How's Big Girl?"

"She's alive — barely. We can try to feed her once we get her in a proper tank."

"She probably just wants coffee." Cara absently scratched a mosquito bite on her arm. "Speaking of which, is Flo here yet? I'd kill for a cup right now."

"Not yet. Come on, sleepyhead. We'd better get a move on. It's going to be a busy day."

She went back upstairs to find Little Lovie back in bed. "You too?" she exclaimed as she tickled her stomach and toes, rousing her slowly. Reminding her of the sea turtle under their house did the trick and she laughed as Lovie scrambled into her clothes.

Next she began preparations for breakfast. She was putting bread into the toaster when Flo burst through the door like a hurricane.

"Morning, Turtle Team!"

"I thought you'd never get here with that coffee," Cara exclaimed, coming into the room. Her dark, damp hair was pulled back on her head and her brown eyes were more alive after her shower.

"Nice shirt," Toy said to her, looking at her own shirt that Cara was wearing.

"I can wear day old, wrinkled shorts if I have to, but I just couldn't put that stinky, turtle bombed T-shirt back on. You don't mind, do you?"

"Help yourself," Toy replied.

Cara stopped at the table where Little Lovie was eating cereal to lean over and nuzzle her neck. "Mmmm, gimme some sugar."

While Little Lovie squealed, Toy turned to reach for cups from the cupboard. Olivia Rutledge had stored the remnants of generations of mismatched collections of china in the beach house. One of Toy's morning pleasures was to choose a pattern to suit her mood. Today she chose the green and pink floral Wedgwood.

Flo poured the coffee while Cara poured the milk but no one took the time to sit at the table. They stood leaning against the counter and sipped as they arranged the day. Flo agreed to stay with Little Lovie while Toy and Cara escorted Big Girl to the Aquarium. This led to their favorite topic of conversation — the turtle nests.

"It's the end of May," Flo said with a sorry shake of her head. "We should have at least one nest by now."

Cara's face reflected her worry. "Last year's numbers were so bad, I was hoping we'd have a swell of girls coming to lay eggs this summer to make up for it. I hope our worst fears aren't realized and they just aren't out there."

"The hurricanes last year sure didn't help."

"It's early yet," Toy said with optimism. "After all, Big Girl was out there."

"I'll drink to that," Flo said, raising her mug. "May there be many healthy ones out there, just biding their time."

"Here's to their homecoming," Toy added, clinking mugs.

"Speaking of homecomings, I've got some news." Cara leaned forward, her eyes sparkling. "I heard from Emmi. She's sold her house in Atlanta and plans to move here permanently! She'll be here for Memorial Day."

"It's about time she got herself down here," Flo declared. "She usually blows in with the turtles. The season doesn't really start until we have one turtle nest *and* Emmi Peterson back."

Toy sipped her coffee and thought of the big-hearted, big-boned woman with a smile as bright as her fiery red hair. Emmaline Baker Peterson was the last member of the core Turtle Team started ages ago by Miss Lovie. Volunteers came and went, but the core team shared a bond that came from long hours spent together at the beach, mutual reliance and countless stories shared.

"I missed her last summer when she didn't come down," Toy said. "The whole season was weird. There were hardly any turtles and Emmi wasn't here. There must be a connection there."

"Last year was pretty tough for her," Cara said.

"Is the divorce final?" asked Flo.

Cara nodded. "She just signed the papers. Emmi sounded pretty beat up by the whole thing. To be honest, so am I. I still can't believe she and Tom are divorced. They were the poster couple for happy marriages. They'd loved each other since they were kids. Hell, I fell in love with Tom the same day Emmi did! How does love like that just end? If it can happen to them . . ."

"Tom was fooling around," Flo said in that matter-of-fact manner that brushed away any connection between Tom and Emmi and whatever Cara was brooding about. "When a man does that, he's throwing the marriage away. I'd like to give that boy the tongue lashing of his life. He was raised better than that."

"Be nice to Emmi when she gets here," Cara said. "No lecturing."

"Lecturing?" Flo sounded insulted.

"You know what I mean. Just take it easy on her. Despite everything Tom may have done, she didn't want the divorce. And their sons are taking it hard. It's going to take a while for her to get past this."

"All the more reason she should be here. With us," said Flo with certainty. "She needs her friends now more than ever."

Toy pushed away from the counter. "I know a turtle that needs us, too. Here comes Brett pulling up in the driveway. Come on. Let's move Big Girl to the Aquarium."

The South Carolina Aquarium is a proud, stunning structure of gleaming steel, stone and glass that captures the golden rays of the sun and the aqua blue reflection of the sea to sparkle against the watery horizon. It is the crown jewel of the Charleston harbor.

Toy felt a thrill each time she approached it. She still couldn't believe that she could walk through the gates every day and not have to pay for the privilege. The proudest day of her life was the day she got her job as a staff aquarist.

Toy was the manager of the Lower Ocean Floor Gallery exhibit. She oversaw the health and maintenance of over one hundred indigenous fish and reptiles. She directed their feeding schedules and the exhibit maintenance, managed the volunteers, gave tours to school children, and whatever else was called for. There was a team mentality at the Aquarium and she never knew when she walked through the doors what awaited her.

And never was that more true than today.

She glanced over her shoulder at the white crate in the back bed of Brett's pick-up truck. Big Girl lay quietly beneath a padding of towels. Toy chewed her lip, hoping the towels were still damp. Sitting shoulder to shoulder beside Cara and Brett in the front seat of the pick-up, she directed Brett to the rear loading dock of the Aquarium. She sighed with relief when she spotted two male volunteers in Aquarium logo shirts waiting at the black iron gate.

"Hey Favel! I sure am glad to see you," Toy called out as she hopped from the cab of the truck. Her gym shoes landed with a soft thud on the cement. "We had a heck of a time hoisting Big Girl into the crate for the trip in."

"Big Girl?" Favel's white hair was like snow on top of a tall mountain and made all the more striking by his deep tan. He was typical of the dedicated volunteers who spent as much time working at the Aquarium as the hired staff. Favel had been a diver since the Aquarium opened. Retired, he had to be forty years older than Irwin, a baby-faced college student majoring in marine biology.

"That's what we call the loggerhead. When you try and lift her, you'll know why." Toy turned and made quick introductions to Cara and Brett.

"Ethan isn't too happy that you're bringing this turtle into his domain, you know," Favel told her in a low voice.

"He isn't?" she asked, feeling a sudden stab of nervousness.

"You know how fanatic he is about cross contamination," he replied. "And, the fact that no one consulted him."

She swallowed hard, feeling her insecurity about bringing the turtle into the Aquarium as a lump in her throat. "Well, Jason approved it."

"Right," Favel said, acknowledging Jason as the last word. "So, let's give this turtle a room at the inn."

Brett helped the two men load the heavy crate onto a rolling cart. Toy followed them as they rolled it toward the lower dock entrance of the building. Toy didn't have much occasion to come to the cavernous port entry. Down here, enormous, monolithic cement pilings rose to form the underpinning of the Aquarium. Charleston Harbor flowed in and out of giant square bins, rising and falling with the tide and filling the air with the pungent scents of mud and salt. The raucous cry of gulls and the horn of the tour boat, Spirit of the Carolinas, sounded in the distance. The wild sea hovered at the precipice of the great Aquarium.

Inside the Aquarium the basement literally thrummed with power. Giant pipes and wires snaked along the ceiling. Red painted pumps, shiny black valves and rows of gray steel fuse boxes lined the walls. She followed the cart to the huge industrial service elevator and pushed the button for the third floor where Jason told her a holding tank would be waiting. She clenched and unclenched her fists as the elevator crawled slowly upward, worried about Ethan's reaction. She hoped that the others did not sense her nervousness. At last the elevator steel doors yawned open and they stepped out into another world.

The Great Ocean Tank, which the staff simply called the GOT, extended over two levels of the Aquarium and held 380,000 gallons of water and hundreds of animals and plants. From the public's side, the great tank provided breathtaking views of the sandy sea floor, the rocky reef, and the deep ocean to the public. Here at the top of the tank, however, behind the curtains, it was markedly different from the gleaming, light-filled rooms the public saw. Back here was the heart of the exhibit.

The top of the GOT was rimmed with ceiling-to-floor black curtains on one side, like a wall of starless night separating the exotic world that lived in the ocean tank from the utilitarian world of giant pumps and filters behind it. Pipes and valves connected to cavernous filtration tanks pumped salt water in and out of the tank like major arteries and veins to the heart.

Behind the GOT were several smaller

tanks. These held quarantined fish, hospitalized fish, and back-up stock to replenish the main exhibit. She knew most people didn't have a clue how much effort went into caring for a major Aquarium. It truly was manipulating a world for the animals.

And this world was the realm of Ethan Legare.

"Where is Ethan?" she asked, looking around as they rolled the crate onto the floor.

"He's usually in the tank first thing," Favel told her. "He dives to make sure all the animals in the tank are okay. And to check for floaters on the surface. He's got a big shark that likes to snack at night."

"And Jason?"

"Haven't seen him yet."

She exhaled, anxious that no one had been here to meet her. She turned to the group. "Could y'all just wait here for a minute? I'm going to go find someone who can tell us where to put Big Girl."

As she walked toward the top of the Great Ocean Tank, she couldn't help but notice how meticulous Ethan was in his care of the area. Every hose, pipe and brush was in place and the water in each of the smaller tanks was gleaming. He must have been here for hours already, she thought.

She came to the steel railing that surrounded the huge mouth of the tank and looked down. No matter how many times she experienced it, looking down into forty-four feet of crystal clear water teeming with giant fish was surreal. She spotted a tall, lean man standing on the metal dive platform inside the Great Ocean Tank. He was dripping water from his black dive suit and bent over a large dead grouper. He seemed focused on his task and she hesitated to disturb him. Looking over her shoulder, she saw the group waiting around the turtle. Deciding, she called out, "Ethan!"

He immediately lifted his head to look over his shoulder. Water cascaded from the tips of his brown hair down his face. He lifted his hand in a brief wave.

"I'll be right up," he called back then turned back to the half eaten fish at his feet.

She waved in acknowledgment and ducked away with a sigh of relief. He didn't seem too put out at having his third floor kingdom invaded by a sick animal.

She didn't know Ethan Legare all that well. He was a senior staff member and one of her superiors, thus he breathed the rarified air of management. Ethan remained an enigma to most of the lower level staff she worked with, as well. No one knew much about him, other than that he came from an old Charleston fishing family and had a sterling reputation as a marine biologist. She'd heard colleagues talking with a twinge of envy about the exotic places he'd traveled to while doing research.

It wasn't long before Ethan joined them at the cart, still in his black wet suit. He'd slicked his dark hair back with his palms but narrow trails of water still dripped down his face and lingered on the tips of his lashes.

"Ethan, this is Cara and Brett Beauchamps," she said, stepping up to make introductions. "They're members of the Island Turtle Team and helped bring the turtle in. You remember my talking about them, don't you?"

"I do," he replied, extending his hand. Though dressed in a wet suit, Toy noticed he had the manners of a man in a three piece suit. "Thanks for all your help."

The elevator doors opened again and this time, Jason stepped out. He grinned and waved in jovial welcome, shaking hands with the group and slapping Ethan's back.

Jason, too, was a source of feminine gossip at the Aquarium. Like Ethan, he was in his thirties, tall, great looking, and unmarried. Jason wore his dark hair neatly trimmed and his manner was more open and less reserved than Ethan's, despite the seniority of his position. Ethan and Jason were equally passionate about the Aquarium and their work, which prompted a lasting friendship and mutual respect between them. Avid fishermen, their expeditions to gather specimens for the Aquarium garnered them their nickname, "the saltwater cowboys."

"So, what do we have here?" Jason asked, moving to the crate.

Ethan removed the towels from the sea turtle, shook his head and said ruefully, "Looks to me like another Barnacle Bill."

Jason whistled softly. "She's in pretty bad shape." He lowered to inspect closely. "She's very thin and dehydrated. Her eyes are sunken, her skin is wrinkled. Look here," he said, pointing to the dry shell. "Even the keratin on the carapace is wrinkled."

"We didn't spot any outward signs of injury, other than a few minor scrapes and cuts," Toy reported. "From the looks of her carapace, we figure she's a floater."

"Floaters are tough to rehab without knowing what the underlying problem is," Jason said. "Our oceans are sick and these turtles reflect that."

"Where did you find her?" asked Ethan.

"Floating in the surf off Isle of Palms. At first I thought she was dead, but when she moved I swam out and brought her in."

"Aha. So you're a hero."

She shook her head. "Cara and Brett helped carry her in and once Jason gave us the okay to bring her in here, we kept her overnight in a blue plastic kiddie pool under my porch."

They guffawed at this image.

"I'm surprised she lived through the night," Jason added. "But these animals never cease to amaze me. They come in more dead than alive, yet still they manage to survive. This looks like another case of Floater Syndrome." He rubbed his jaw as he considered his options. "Okay boys, let's move her. Is there something I can use to set her down on so I can get a better look at her?"

"If it's okay with you, we have to get going," Brett interjected, putting his hand on Cara's shoulder. "Memorial Day is around the corner. It's one of our busiest times of the season. I've got more work than I can shake a stick at."

"You bet," Ethan said, going over to shake his hand. "Thanks for bringing her in."

"Take care of our baby," Cara said to Toy

before leaving.

"You know I will."

After they left, Ethan led the team toward the back section of the third floor. "I put the turtle tank as far from my other tanks as possible," he said to Jason. "I have to tell you, I'm not happy about keeping a sick patient from the outside without any diagnosis here with my healthy stock. If it is Debilitated Turtle Syndrome, that means we don't know what you're bringing into my space. No offense to the lady here," he said, indicating the turtle, "but I'm worried about any transfer of diseases into my tank. If there's a problem in there, it's a big problem. I hate to take any risks."

"I know," Jason replied as he followed. "Unfortunately, Ethan, there isn't anywhere else to put her right now. Let's take it day by day."

Ethan stopped. "For how long?"

"I don't know yet," Jason said, stopping beside him. "We'll begin rehabilitation here, then evaluate if she stays here for the entire rehab period."

"You're the boss."

Ethan resumed walking, taking the group to a corner in the farthest point from the Great Ocean Tank. He wiped his damp hair from his forehead. "Okay," he said with reluctance. "But I want sterilizing procedures in full force."

"Of course," Toy said, stepping up. She felt responsible for bringing the turtle in. "I'll use every precaution and be extra careful to keep all our supplies separate. If you have any problems, just let me know."

"You can count on that." His tone was direct but not threatening.

Toy was a little afraid of him, especially when his dark eyes flashed like they did now. Yet, she could sympathize with his position. The Great Ocean Tank was the most important exhibit of the Aquarium.

Jason did a brief exam of the turtle on a make-shift table of a piece of plywood on top of big cardboard boxes. The huge turtle lay on her backside, looking more dead than alive. When Jason finished, Ethan and Toy gently helped him to turn her to her plastron. Big Girl rolled her dark, almond shaped eyes back and cast Ethan a watery, baleful glance.

"Look at her," Ethan said, his deep voice softening. "She's emaciated, dehydrated and scarred. But despite all that I have to admit, she's beautiful."

Toy cast a quick glance to Jason. She saw a small smile of satisfaction play at his lips. No one could argue her case better than

Big Girl herself.

"Let's go ahead and give her fluids," Jason instructed. "The rest will wait until Dr. Tom examines her. He's on his way now."

"All right, boys," Ethan said with a tone of resigned acceptance. "We have a new in-patient. Bring her over and I'll fill the tank with fresh water. It will kill epibenthic growth and help her re-hydrate for a few days. After that, we'll return her to salt."

Ethan and Irwin carried Big Girl to the blue polypropylene holding tank. Then the four men gently lifted her into the freshwater bath.

"Who's going to be taking care of this turtle?" Ethan asked. When Jason looked to him, he lifted his hands. "Oh, no, don't go looking at me. You know how busy things get during the summer season. I won't have time."

"I did two rotations at the Karen Beasely Sea Turtle Hospital," Toy said, stepping forward. She could hardly believe she'd found the courage to plead her case to Jason, but she desperately wanted the job and believed she could do it. She couldn't imagine anyone but her taking care of Big Girl and she felt sure her desire burned in her eyes. "Jean Beasely personally trained me and I've had lots of experience with all kinds of sick and injured sea turtles. And I've been licensed by Department of Natural Resources to be on the turtle team for over five years. I feel confident I can handle the job. With your support, of course."

Jason's joviality vanished as he considered this decision with all seriousness. She knew he'd be taking a chance on a fairly new staff member.

"You brought her in," he said in conclusion. "Seems fair to give you the chance."

Toy's heart leaped at the opportunity. "Thank you, Jason. You won't be disappointed."

"I'm sure I won't be. But I want you to work closely with Ethan." He looked over at Ethan who was shaking his head with chagrin. "Just supervise, okay? And try to be nice." He smiled at Toy. "My door is always open." He looked at his watch and began walking off with purpose. "I leave her in your good hands!" he called out.

Ethan turned his head to look at her. Toy couldn't read his mind in his dark eyes, but she felt sure he could read the exultation in her own.

"I'll start a medical log," she said as she walked off, her feet not quite touching the ground.

Medical Log "Big Girl"

May 24

Received stranded female loggerhead sea turtle from Isle of Palms. Found floating in surf. No external signs of injury. Heavily encrusted with barnacles, algae, leeches. Put in a drop and fill tank in fresh water to eliminate growth. Very thin. Vet. to examine later.

Curved carapace: length 40″ width 36.5″

Weight: 240 lbs.

Condition: Floater

She's beautiful. TS

4

Toy woke while the sun was still rosy on the horizon. She quickly went through the motions of her morning routine, then went to rouse a sleepy Little Lovie from her bed.

She paused at the door of the pink bedroom, soaking in the vision of that sweet face swathed in frills and lace. Children looked like angels when they slept, she thought. She hated to awaken her. Moving to the bed, she sat beside her and showered Lovie's face with kisses, murmuring, "Wake up! Wake up, sleepyhead!"

Lovie rubbed her eyes and yawned. "Is it time to go to day care?"

"No. I have to go to the Aquarium to feed Big Girl. I'm taking you to Flo's, just for a little while. You can watch cartoons."

"It's Saturday?"

"Yes."

"But you promised me we'd go to the beach." Her voice was filled with reproach.

"I know. And we will. I'll be back as soon as I can. Now up and at 'em." She patted Lovie's bottom to get her moving, then drew back. Lovie's arms shot out to grab hold of her and tug her back.

"What, honey?" Toy asked.

Lovie's small hands reached up to frame Toy's face like blinders. Toy felt the gentle pressure on her cheeks while Lovie's blue eyes gazed at her, as though saying fiercely, *look at me!*

"I wanna be with *you*," Lovie said.

Toy's breath hitched. "I know," she said, knowing her answer fell pitifully short. "I want to be with you, too. I love you. You know that, don't you?"

Lovie nodded and dropped her hands.

Toy picked them up and kissed each one. "I'll be home in a jiffy and we'll build that sand castle."

Flo, bless her heart, was only too happy to mind Little Lovie for the morning, even at such an early hour. When they showed up at her door, Flo greeted them at her front door brandishing a neon green super-squirt gun and calling out, "Tawanda!"

"Oh, brother," Toy said with a light laugh. Flo was incorrigible. Toy thought the gun was a better toy for a boy than a girl, but Lovie lit up at seeing it. She grabbed the gun and tore out the back door to fill it at the spigot.

"I'll be back early so we can go to the beach," she called to Lovie's retreating back.

"Time for a cup?" Flo asked.

"I wish. But I'd like to get in and out of the Aquarium as early as possible. Lovie is giving me the cold shoulder for going in to work this weekend. She's so looking forward to going to the beach."

"Oh, for heaven's sake. I'll take her."

"I appreciate the offer," Toy replied with faint heart, "but I'd like to go with her. I've yet to keep my promise to help her build a sand castle. I've been so busy this week trying to set up a program for Big Girl at the Aquarium, my *little* girl is getting the short end of the stick."

"She doesn't look the worse for wear."

"I hope not. But this schedule isn't about to slow down any, at least not until I get a better handle on things."

"You know I'm here for you. Anytime"

She felt a rush of emotion. It had always been this way with Flo. "I know."

Flo narrowed her eyes in scrutiny, then pushed open the screen door and signaled with her hand that Toy should come into the house. "Come on, just for a minute. No whining."

Toy did so reluctantly. Flo closed the door and sat on the Chippendale wicker bench in the front hall. It fit two women comfortably.

"Now tell me. What's really bothering you?" asked Flo.

"Oh, nothing."

"Mmm-hmm. Nothing always means something."

Toy heard Lovie's high pitched laughing outdoors, no doubt because she pelted something with a super stream of water. The women chuckled and Toy felt her burden lighten.

"You look worried," Flo said.

"I am, a bit."

"Not about Lovie? She's fine, you know. No child could be loved more."

"Thanks to you and Cara. You're like surrogate mothers to her."

"More like favorite aunts. So, don't waste your energy feeling guilty about that. If not Lovie, what's the problem?"

"It's not a problem, exactly. I've been put in charge of Big Girl at the Aquarium."

"How wonderful! Isn't that what you wanted?"

"Yes," she said with hesitancy. "I volunteered for the task and would have been crushed if Jason hadn't given me the assignment." She threw up her hands. "What was I thinking? Suddenly I'm aware of everything I don't know."

"But that's normal, my dear. It happens to all of us when we start a new job or a new project. How do you think I got all this white hair?"

"Oh, great," Toy said with a rueful smile. "I'll be gray before I'm thirty. That's always a big help in attracting a husband."

Flo shrugged. "I never worried about finding a husband. Oh, sure, I thought about it when I was younger," she said. "It was the natural path for women. You married and had children. Folks were always after me about it, like my being single was a state of affairs I should be ashamed of. I never was in any big hurry. I surely never felt deprived. Just the opposite. Honey, *I thrived!*" She tossed back her head and laughed.

"After a while, heck, I just didn't want a husband. I got set in my ways, I reckon. I was fulfilled with my career as a social worker, I made a good living, had dear friends — male and female. I suppose I'd simply accepted that I'd live my life single. Not a spinster . . ."

She turned her head, eyes blazing, "Isn't that a horrid word? Spinster? It implies someone old and dried up. Unwanted." She frowned and shivered with disgust. "Unmarried men are called bachelors. I like that word. It conjures up someone debonair, even sexy. Freedom. Men have bureaus called 'bachelor chests.' Can you imagine ever wanting a 'spinster chest'? Women have 'hope chests', for hoping they'll get married." Her eyes flashed. "It's a conspiracy. Don't get me started on that. No," she said in conclusion, "I never worried much about finding a husband."

"I reckon I've always worried about it, but at the rate I've been working, I'll never find a husband, either. And lately, I'm too tired to worry about it. So, I guess you and I are alike in that." She sighed and, growing serious again at the mention of work, leaned back in the bench. She thought about Flo's life, her unconscious decision to remain single, and her satisfaction — even pride — of that path. Toy had always assumed her primary role as a woman was to marry and have children.

Yet life had taken her down another path. She had, in fact, not married. She had a child and now a career. It was possible she might not ever marry. Her acceptance of that possibility thrust her career as a provider for herself and her child into primary importance. She had to depend on herself.

It was a daunting realization, one that kept her up at night shivering in fear that she'd fail in her career or make serious financial blunders and end up in trouble. This was the dark shadow Flo had spied behind her eyes this morning.

She sighed and began to open up. "I'm afraid, Flo. The other day when Dr. Tom was examining Big Girl, he used medical terms I didn't know. I pretended I did, but in my notes I was madly writing the words down to look up later. Flo, I live in constant fear that my ignorance will be discovered and I'll be found out for the fake I am."

"Oh, Toy . . ." Flo said with a light laugh.

"Don't laugh! I'm serious. You can be sure Ethan knew the terminology. He chatted so easily with Dr. Tom, like he was a doctor, too."

"Well, of course he did. It makes sense, Toy. He has more experience. Isn't he your supervisor?"

"That shouldn't make any difference at all. I'm the one in charge of the turtle. But I'm always asking Ethan a question or having him double check most everything I do. I'm terrified of making a mistake. After all, this turtle's life depends on me." She wrung her hands. "But sooner or later I have to depend on my own abilities."

"And you'll know when that moment comes, my dear. Toy, I've been in that very same situation. Most of us have. When I started out as a social worker, the doctors came in and yammered on and on with their ten dollar words. I was shaking in my shoes, just like you are now. I felt downright stupid, completely out of my depth. But you know what happened?"

Toy shook her head. She'd been listening intently, not stirring in her seat.

"I studied hard, like you are now, and learned the words quicker than a hot knife through butter. Toy, every job has its own jargon, some more than others. But you're young, you're bright, you're enthusiastic." She smiled with great warmth. "You'll catch on."

Toy grasped this like a drowning woman. "*I am* studying every free minute, that's for true. Why, the other night, poor Lovie fell asleep next to me on the sofa waiting on me to read to her. She looked so cute with her storybook tucked under her arm." She sighed. "Of course, I felt guilty."

"Guilt is part of motherhood, my dear," Flo said archly. "Why would you think you'd be spared?"

Toy looked at Flo's leathery, deeply lined face and her bright, spectacularly blue eyes.

Ever since Miss Lovie had died, Flo had taken up the role of godmother to Toy and Little Lovie. Her advice, though often delivered with a velvet fist, was always heartfelt.

"You sure you don't want that cup of coffee? Maybe a sweet roll?"

"No, thanks," Toy, replied, rising. "I've really got to go. Thanks so much for listening. I truly do feel better."

"Go on then and make good your escape. And don't worry about that little ragamuffin. I got me one of those super squirters, too, and I'm dying to soak her good and proper. We'll be so wild with our new toys, she won't even notice you're not here."

What a pair, Toy thought but she walked with a lighter step to her car. With Flo's fiery tongue and Little Lovie's stubborn streak, they just might be good for one another.

Toy put down the ragtop of the Gold Bug and let her hair blow in the wind. The tide was high as she crossed the Ben Sawyer Bridge and the water of the Intracoastal Waterway reflected the brilliant blue, cloudless sky like a mirror. It was going to be a hot one, Toy thought. A lot of beachcombers were going to be happy and Brett's boat business was going to go through the roof.

Toy glanced at her watch. It was already 7:30 on the Saturday of Memorial Day Weekend. Traffic was blissfully light this early and she'd make good time. If she worked fast, she'd be home by lunch. Then she'd keep her promise and take Little Lovie to the beach. And *this* time, she thought as she tightened her hands on the wheel, she'd help build that sand castle.

Toy turned on the radio and hummed as she zoomed over the gleaming new Ravenel Bridge. She liked country music. Songs of unrequited love, broken dreams, fights in bars, life and death. Country music sometimes made her think of Darryl and how he used to sing to her the songs he'd written. She rarely thought of him anymore, and when she did, it was with detachment, like he was dead or from some other life, long ago.

Her future lay before her, she thought with a heady grin. Onward and Upward! Charleston loomed, its church spirals pointed heavenward. Traffic was light on East Bay Street and she make good time, parking in the empty lot just down the road from the Aquarium that would soon be another condominium. The city was changing along the waterfront at a pace that seemed faster than the one she walked as she made her way down the street.

Her Aquarium T-shirt was already beginning to cling to her skin by the time she entered the blast of air-conditioning inside. Her first stop was the compact, industrial food prep kitchen. Big Girl might be emaciated, but she was still a fussy eater. So far, she seemed to like squid best. Toy cut and weighed the squid and fish, thinking as she did so that trying to feed a thirtysome-year-old turtle wasn't all that different than trying to feed a picky five-year-old child. Toy cleaned up her kitchen mess and brought the food to Big Girl.

"You're here. Perfect!"

"Ethan?" She hurried toward his voice to find him cleaning Big Girl's tank with a skimmer. "What's happened? Is Big Girl okay?"

"She's fine. I got a call about another turtle."

"A turtle? Where?"

"At Cherry Point on Wadmalaw Island. The fishermen who found her are bringing her in to the fishery."

"How did you hear about it?"

"They called me."

"They called *you?*"

"Hey, don't get your panties in a wad. The

fishermen down there know me and that I work at the Aquarium. They wouldn't know who else to call. So, boss, is it okay with you to bring the turtle in?"

"Let me get this straight. You're asking *me* if it's okay to bring another turtle into the Aquarium. Into *your* space?"

She could almost hear the chuckle in his voice. "No. Jason has already given the okay. I'm asking *you* if you're ready to take on another one." He rubbed his jaw. "I don't seem to be on this decision tree, or you'd know what my answer would be."

The prospect of a second turtle was exciting, but the fact that Jason and Ethan had given the okay was thrilling.

"Yes, I do. And yes, I am. Bring it on in!"

"All right, then. I've already rustled up another holding tank. It'll be a tight squeeze, but we'll make it. Are you ready to go?"

"Go? Go where?"

"To get the turtle, of course. It isn't going to crawl in on its own."

"I thought you said that the fishermen were bringing it in."

"To the fishery, yes. But not all the way here. They're already doing us a favor by cutting their day short to bring the turtle to the dock."

"Oh, sure. Fine." She looked at the food

dish in her hand as her mind spun around all she had to get done. "I just have to feed Big Girl first, and clean out her tank."

"You feed. I'll sweep."

His enthusiasm was contagious. The corners of her mouth lifted to a smile as she felt the tension of the early morning bubble to excitement.

Cherry Point Seafood Company had been in business on Wadmalaw Island since the 1930s. It was a family business that once upon a time had transported passengers as well as seafood and local crops between the Sea Island plantations and Charleston. Back then, local folks could travel to Charleston by either water or horse, and most preferred a boat trip to a long, hot horse ride. Today, there were no more passengers. The long wooden structure with docks that stretched along Bohicket Creek was used strictly for commercial fisherman. It was home to the dozens of shrimp boats and fishing boats that brought in their daily catches.

"Sure seems quiet today," Ethan said, pulling the Aquarium's white pick-up truck into the parking lot. The bed of gravel and shells crunched beneath the tires. He cut the engine and the truck shuddered to a halt.

"Well, it is a holiday," she said, looking out the window. "Likely most folks took the day off." The fishery looked like a big, roughened wood shack. Along one side was a high loading dock fit for trucks, a smattering of heavy iron equipment, bales of rope, and farther down was the dock. She spied a burly man in jeans and white rubber boots leaning against a wood pillar, smoking.

"Usually the place is jumping, just swarming with fishermen and shrimpers bringing their catch in to be weighed and packed."

"It's not very big."

"Don't let the size fool you. On a busy day in the season, thousands of dollars of fish go through these doors, packed in ice and shipped out to restaurants and markets all across the country. Used to be there were a number of fish houses in these parts, but this is the only one left. Sign of the times, I guess."

Ethan wasn't dressed in his usual Aquarium uniform of khaki. On his day off he was slumming in olive green shorts, a stained white T-shirt and scuffed leather boots that had seen plenty of wear. His dark hair was an unruly mass and dark stubble coursed along his jawline. It occurred to her he looked right at home here on the docks.

"I've never actually met shrimpers before,"

she told him. "Should I be nervous?"

Ethan appeared puzzled. "They're just folks."

"Ethan, I've heard the stories," she replied with a roll of her eyes. "How they hate anyone connected with turtles. I've heard the names we're called, too — turtle kissers, turtle Nazis . . ."

His lips twitched but he only shrugged.

"I know there've been some pretty strong words between the two camps over the years. I just want to know if I'm going to have my head served on a platter in there."

"That was before — sure, there were some, well, unfriendly feelings between some shrimpers and those folks who were demanding that the boats put those TEDs on their nets." He scratched his neck and added wryly, "Time was, shrimpers called the Turtle Excluder Devices 'Trawler Elimination Devices.' Safe to say it was a touchy subject."

"To say the least."

"Hey, the bottom line is, those TEDs cost money."

"But it wasn't about the money."

"It was to the shrimpers who had to put out money they didn't have."

"Yes, I see what you mean. But, what's different now?"

"Well, for starters they've got the TEDs on every net they own now. And, those turtle shooters work. Hey, they never wanted to hurt the turtles and I think that's what riled them the most. They were painted as being bad guys when they were doing their best to make a living — a damned hard one — and not getting a break from anywhere."

"Why are you so defensive? You're a turtle kisser, too, you know."

He laughed. "I am. But I see their side of the story, too."

She turned to look out over the fishery and sighed. "So, no one's going to bite my head off out there today?"

She felt his gaze sweep over her.

"I think they'll be enamored."

A short laugh escaped. "Enamored?"

"Sure." He reached across her legs to lift the door handle and open her door. "Some of these guys have been out on the sea for weeks. You look a sight better than a turtle."

She pushed open the door. "Thanks a lot."

She followed Ethan into the dim, narrow halls of the fish house. Behind glass windows in the large room, the rusting machines lay still. Here and there she'd spy rubber boots but no man to fill them. Only when they neared the office did she catch the scent of burnt coffee and hear the hum of voices, punctuated by a woman's hearty laugh.

When Ethan stepped into the small, wood paneled office, all talk stopped. Two middle aged, deeply tanned men — one weathered and tall, the other short and paunchy — leaned against a Formica counter covered with stacks of paper. Both wore white rubber boots over their jeans. Across from them, sitting at an ancient wood roll top desk was a sweet faced, robust woman of the same age in a blue floral dress and shiny black flats. They turned to face him, and like lightning, their faces lit up.

"Lookee here! You son of a . . . sea horse," the woman sputtered. "Where've you been?"

She had to be at least sixty but she leaped up like a woman half her age to wrap soft, fleshy arms around Ethan in a bear hug.

"Shame on you for making yourself so scarce. If I didn't see you at church from time to time I'd think you'd gone off traveling again."

"I've been busy," he replied, accepting the rebuff good naturedly. "But you knew I'd be coming home for your barbecue tomorrow. I couldn't stay away."

"Your mama's been cooking pies all week so you'd better be there." The shorter of the men had eyes the color of sea glass and a thick gray beard that swaddled his cheeks like a wreath. He stepped forward to deliver a few good slaps on the back and mutter words of welcome.

In contrast, the tall man in a worn but ironed flannel checked shirt straightened slowly to his full height. His once dark hair was now mostly gray and his tanned, weathered face had deep lines coursing across his brow, at the corners of his brown eyes and from dimple to chin. He didn't smile but his dark eyes pulsed with emotion as he extended a callused hand.

"Hello, Ethan."

She looked at Ethan and saw that he was looking at the man with the same intensity in his stormy brown eyes. And then it struck her how very much alike the two men looked.

"Hello, Dad." Ethan reached out to take the hand. They held tight for a moment and the emotion in the room was palpable. Then the older man jerked his arm and drew his son into a quick, fierce embrace.

In another minute, everyone was talking and coffee was served, hot and bitter and loaded with sugar. Toy hung back by the door, peeking in. It was a cozy space, as worn and well used as the fishery itself. The paneled walls were covered with small, black framed photographs of the fishery and shrimp boats that dated back fifty years or more. She tried not to eavesdrop but she caught that the other man was Ethan's Uncle Will and the woman was his Aunt Martha and that Ethan was catching hell for missing church and not visiting his mother in the past few weeks.

His father, Stuart, was quiet in comparison to his sister and her husband, but his affection for Ethan was nonetheless obvious, as was the pride shining in his dark eyes. It was clear to Toy that the apple didn't fall far from the tree in the Legare family.

Ethan, while never boisterous, was as relaxed as she'd ever seen him. He clearly enjoyed being with his family. Smiles came readily, as did the laughter.

Then her name was called and she was brought into the room. Introductions were made and hands were shook. They couldn't have been nicer or more welcoming and she pretended she didn't see the suggestive eyebrow wriggling of Uncle Will to Ethan as he nodded her way. She ducked her head and took a swallow of her horrid coffee. There was a matchmaker in every crowd.

She was spared more chit chat when a gruff looking man with a cap over greasy hair shuffled over to poke his head in through the doorway.

"The Miss Peggy's coming in!"

"That'll be us," Stuart said and set down his coffee.

Immediately they filed out of the cramped office into the fresh, salty air. Toy lagged behind. Ethan looked back over his shoulder and catching her eye, waved her closer. When she caught up, he bent close to speak softly in her ear.

"That wasn't so bad, was it? No head chopping or bruises?"

She turned to him "Why didn't you tell me they were your family?"

"And spoil all the fun? Nothing I love more than to drop the bomb that I come from a long line of shrimpers after listening to a tirade from a Turtle Nazi."

"I owe you one."

He replied with a look that, had it not been Ethan, she would have sworn was flirtatious.

The long wooden dock was lined with tall cement pilings, and to these a line of boats, some seventy footers, some but twelve, were tied with thick, coiling rope. She read their names aloud as she walked by *Carson Elizabeth, Explorer, Tina Maria, Captain Andy, Miss Charlotte, Miss Georgia.*

"Most of the fishing boats are named for women," he explained. "Wives, daughters, mothers, sweethearts. It's an old tradition, meant to bring good luck to the men while they are away at sea."

"Do you have a boat?"

"Nothing big like these. Mine's about eighteen feet and just for fun."

"And do you have a name for it?" she asked, shamelessly prying.

"The Wanderlust." He cast her a slanted glance.

"Suits you," she replied.

Her attention was diverted by the sixty-two-foot Miss Peggy as it slipped into its watery square of real estate along the dock, growling and churning the waters. With the hanging nets on each side of the boat, she thought they looked like folded butterfly wings. The Miss Peggy was an old girl. White paint peeled from the wood and up close Toy could see the dread rust on metal. But she was still a graceful swimmer and slipped into her space as easily as a younger, smaller fishing boat.

Two men in jeans and white rubber boots climbed out off the high boat to the dock far below as nimbly as ship rats. On board, a wiry, weathered woman with dark gray hair pulled back in a ponytail waved them off, calling out something in a heavy drawl that Toy couldn't make out. While one of the men bent to tie the ropes, the other, a short, bald, barrel-chested man, came straight for Ethan and sucker punched him in the belly.

Toy gasped as Ethan doubled over. Until she realized that he wasn't grimacing in pain but laughter. The two men clung to each other, delivering velvet gloved punches like boxers in the ninth round while around them, the other men chortled, enjoying their antics.

"Don't mind them," Stuart said to Toy with a good natured grin. "They been fools since they were boys."

Ethan slapped the other man's back and turning, caught Toy gaping.

"Toy, come over and meet Bigger. He's the most conceited, ornery saltwater cowboy on the coast. He's also my cousin. We went to school together when we were kids, or at least whenever Bigger showed up. Bigger, this is my colleague, Toy Sooner."

"Colleague is it?" he said with a thick drawl. Bigger lifted expensive black sunglasses to the top of his slightly sunburned bald head and gave her the once-over with eyes as bright a blue as a torch. She felt scalded and knew his mind was up to no good. What he saw seemed to please him, however, because he stuck out his meaty arm emblazoned with a tattoo and took her hand, squeezing tight.

"What kind of a name is Toy?"

"What kind of a name is Bigger?"

Bigger turned toward Ethan, a smile pinching his lips. "She'll do."

"Daddy!"

A coltish young girl came running up the dock, all long legs and long black hair flying behind her like a mane. She leaped up to hurl herself upon Bigger, who grabbed her tight and gave her a whirl around the dock.

In a more leisurely manner, a tiny woman with black hair and almond eyes strolled up the dock to join them. On her hip was a little boy, no more than a year, with hair as black as his mother's. Bigger released his daughter and all bravado fled as, with something akin to reverence, he stepped forward to place a chaste kiss on his wife's cheek. Their eyes met, his passionate, hers knowing. Toy read more love in that greeting than if Bigger's wife had run like her daughter and hurled her tiny self into his powerful arms.

Bigger took his son in his arms, pride beaming on his face, and turned to Toy.

"This here's my wife, Lao. This wild thing is my daughter Lily and this hunk o' meat is my son, Bill Jr." He looked at Ethan with bluster. "What's the matter with you, any-way? Shootin' blanks . . . Look at me. I've got the Miss Peggy, a beautiful wife, two of the best children to roam God's earth. When are you going to stop wandering and get you some of these?"

"I don't know, Bigger. There's nothing like your family or the Miss Peggy, that's for damn sure," Ethan told him.

"You bet your ass."

"Bill . . ." Lao said softly, frowning at his language.

"Sorry."

"You've got a fine business sitting here just waiting for you," Aunt Martha said to Ethan.

Ethan cast a wary glance at his father. Stuart's face remained taciturn.

"We could use the help," Uncle Will added. "Bigger likes the sea too much to stay in an office and my Bill, he wants no part of the business. Moved off to Atlanta to be some banker." He said the last word like it tasted bitter in his mouth. "At least you didn't do nothin' like that."

"Ethan has a three-hundred-thousand-gallon fish tank to take care of right now," Toy said, jumping into the fray. "One of the largest in the country. And hundreds of fish. I'd say that's something."

All talk ceased and everyone looked at her like she'd spoken gibberish. All except Ethan. His eyes warmed as he looked at her.

"You and me," Bigger added, wrapping an arm around Ethan's shoulder. "We've got saltwater in our veins. At least you came back. I knew the tides would call you home."

"Daddy, where's the turtle?" the girl asked, impatient with all this adult talk.

Bigger hoisted his son and bent to face his daughter. "So that's what you come for? The turtle? Not to see your daddy?"

"But I gotta do a report for school," she whined with pleading eyes.

Lao laughed lightly and cupped her husband's cheek. "You're no match for a sea turtle. So where is it?"

Bigger snorted and waved her over. "Come on, sweet cheeks. Let's go get it. It's not looking so good, though." He looked back at Toy. "The faster you get her off our boat, the faster we can unload this shrimp."

"Yes, sir, captain." Toy climbed up the wall of the shrimp boat, surprised by how high off the dock it rose. The deck of the Miss Peggy stretched long before her. At first, it was confusing, there was so much going on. There were winches, chains, cables and ropes. Nets hung full from the riggers.

The wiry man she'd seen before stood at

the nets and was busy cleaning out the small fish and crabs. He turned his head when she passed and asked in a gravely voice, "You here for the turtle?"

"I am. Or," she nodded toward Ethan, "we are."

"Come and git her, then. She ain't lookin' so good. Don't wanna be blamed for killin' no endangered turtle."

"Where is she?"

He pointed a heavily tattooed arm toward the rear of the deck. Bigger led them there and lifted a canvas tarp. Under it, a juvenile loggerhead lay motionless.

Toy hitched her breath, stunned at the serious crack that ran across the length of its shell. All business now, she swung her backpack off her shoulders and knelt beside it. The good news was the turtle was alive. The bad news was the gorgeous reddish brown shell was split near in two.

"That's a nasty crack," she said in a flat tone.

"Propeller slash?" Ethan asked.

Toy measured the shell at three feet, noted it and a few other observations, then rose. "That's no propeller slash." She turned to Bigger. "What happened?"

Bigger cast a wary glance at his daughter. "We were pulling in the big nets, same as we always do. Damned if this turtle didn't fall right out of the net."

"You dropped the turtle?" Toy asked, shocked.

"Hell, no. I didn't drop it. It fell."

"Daddy, you would never hurt a sea turtle, would you?" Lily asked.

Bigger's face flushed and he shuffled his white boots. "No, I wouldn't. You know I wouldn't hurt no turtle. But folks like you," he said to Toy "just can't believe we care."

Toy felt tongue-tied.

"She's not saying that," Ethan interjected.

Bigger shook his head. "I got a turtle shooter on every net. But hey, it happened. And here she is. I could've just chucked her back in the sea. That's what some others might've done. But I brought her in. I called Ethan, didn't I?"

Ethan slapped Bigger's back. "You sure did. And I thank you for it. You did the right thing. We appreciate it. Don't we Toy?"

"Yes. Absolutely," she blurted out. "Thank you, Bigger. This turtle owes you its life. Any time you see a sick turtle out there, we'll come out here to fetch it and thank you each time."

Mollified, Bigger hoisted his son higher in his arms and smiled at his daughter. "Go get your pictures for your project. These folks have to move the turtle and I've got work to do. We're wasting daylight."

It was no easy task to maneuver the injured sea turtle from the shrimp boat into the crate in the back of the truck. With every move, Toy worried more damage would be done to the badly cracked shell. Ethan's family went out of their way to help in any way they could, and before leaving, Bigger had promised her a ride on the Miss Peggy, and Lily was beaming that Toy had named the sea turtle Cherry Point.

On the way back to the Aquarium, Ethan was quiet, seemingly lost in his own thoughts. Toy wondered about the family man that she'd seen at Cherry Point, a man in sharp contrast to the loner. With his family, Ethan had opened a window to himself she'd never seen at the Aquarium. There, Ethan seemed as mysterious as the twelve foot shark he swam with every day in the Great Ocean tank.

Toy cast a slanted glance at Ethan, eager to learn more about him before he shut the window completely.

"Your family seems very nice."

He nodded, eyes on the road. "They're good people."

"It sounds like you haven't been home in a while?"

"Never often enough to suit my mom."

"But you're a genuine local."

"Yep. Born and raised. You can't go anywhere near Wadmalaw without bumping into a Legare. The whole of Johns Island, really."

"It must be nice to have a big family."

"At times."

"Are you close?"

He cast a quick glance. "I guess you could say we are. We have our spats, like most families. But we've been in these parts since before The War. Most everyone's settled somewhere around Rockville or Charleston."

"Except Bill in Atlanta." She said "Atlanta" with the same sour tone Uncle Will had used.

That drew a reluctant laugh from Ethan. "Poor Uncle Will. He's worse than my mother. He never can tolerate any of us moving off. I reckon it's because we keep losing bits of our land and he's afraid we're losing the family, too. He holds on pretty tight."

"I find that endearing."

Ethan barked off a laugh. "I'm sure he'd like to hear that." He shook his head, muttering, *"Endearing."*

"Hey, it's better than *enamored.*"

"I don't know but I was right. My family was enamored with you. Especially Bigger."

"Your cousin is a real character."

A grin stretched freely across his face and affection gleamed in his eyes. "Yeah, that he is. One of a kind. You wouldn't want to mess with him, but he's got a heart of pure gold. Would give you the shirt off his back if you asked him. He's saved my sorry ass a few times, I can tell you. Guys like him are a dying breed."

"Did you ever want to be a shrimper, like him? Or run Cherry Point?"

His hands tightened on the wheel as the tires spun beneath them. "No," he replied at length. "I never did. It's not like I don't enjoy going out on the shrimp boats and lending a hand from time to time. Some of my best memories were on board the Miss Peggy. But it's a hard life. Long hours, tough work, hard men. The dock can be a pretty rough place at times. I used to work there in the summers coming up and some of the stuff I saw . . ."

He shook his head. "It's not for me. Never was. When I was a boy, I got a lot of ribbing for having my nose stuck in a book. I read about exotic places far away — *Treasure Island, Narnia, Forty Leagues Under the Sea.* If I ever dreamed of being a boat captain, it was Captain Nemo. My blood raced at the thought of getting in a boat and just . . ." He shrugged lightly. "Going." He stretched out his arm. "Sailing on and on and on. Seeing the world and not worrying about coming back."

"So, where did you end up going?"

"I went to Woods Hole in Maine for my graduate degree. It's beautiful up there, but way too cold for a Southern boy. Once I'd left home, I just kept traveling. Farther and farther away. I did marine research in Fiji, the Caribbean, the reefs off Australia, Indonesia, then ended up in Costa Rica. I spent six years there, the longest I've ever spent in any one place."

"I heard that you discovered some kind of bottom dwelling invertebrate?"

He nodded. "But I'm most proud of the work I did drumming up international support for sharks."

"When you add all that up, I can see how you were an ideal choice to run the Great Ocean Tank."

"You never know where the knowledge and experience you've gained is going to lead you in life. When I was chasing down black market shark poachers, I didn't think I'd be caring for sharks in an Aquarium. It's funny how life turns out sometimes."

"Did your father want you to take over the family business?"

"Yes, sure. It's only natural that he would. But I think he always knew I was more interested in studying the living fish, not the ones caught to be eaten. And between you and me, he's the one who inspired my interest. He was the one who taught me the names of all the fish, about their habitats and habits. He never let me keep an undersized fish and was mindful of our role as stewards of the earth and sea. When I went off to study marine biology I got some raised brows from some of the family, but he never once criticized my decision. He always encouraged me to carve out my own destiny." He chuckled ruefully. "Though he'll never understand why I ever wanted to leave a place as beautiful as Cherry Point. My greatest fear was that I never would."

"But you did."

He nodded. "Yep."

"And now you're back."

"I guess it's like what Bigger said. The tide brings us back, sooner or later."

"Sort of like the turtles. You came back home."

He turned his head to face her. "Sort of. Now, your turn. Where are you from?"

She shrugged nonchalantly, but inside she

cringed. In the South, asking someone where they were from was asking for a family history and church affiliation. Toy didn't have a family to brag on. She was ashamed to admit that her daddy had run off before she was born and the only siblings she had were two half brothers who were mean curs who'd as soon steal from her what little she had as say hello. One of them ended up in jail — to keep his daddy company, her mama liked to say.

No love was lost between Toy and her parents, either. Her mother and step-father had kicked her out of the trailer at seventeen when she got pregnant and never opened the door to her since. Not exactly the warm family bond that Ethan knew.

"I used to dream of traveling the world, too," she replied, guiding her answer in a different direction. "Like you did. But I never made it farther than Holly Hill, where I was born. My parents moved to North Charleston when I started high school. My life got complicated pretty fast. Now I have my daughter, my job . . . So much for traveling. I have this recurring dream of a turtle swimming in the ocean, trying real hard to get home. Go figure."

"Is your family in fishing or conservation or . . . ?"

Toy snorted and shook her head. "Hardly."

"Your husband?"

"My —" Her breath caught. "There is no husband," she blurted out.

"I thought . . . I know you have a daughter," he said in way of explanation.

There was an awkward silence during which Toy expected him to follow up with a question about divorce, or her being a widow. She tensed, not wanting to go into her history about Darryl and her being an unwed mother.

"So what got you interested in turtles?" he asked.

She silently blessed him for not prying. "That would be Miss Lovie, Cara's mother. I took care of her when she was sick. She used to live in this big ol' house in Charleston but she loved the beach house. When she got sick she wanted to live there — to die there, I reckon. Anyway, she wanted a companion, so I took the job. Her real name was Olivia Rutledge, but everyone on the island called her Miss Lovie. She was the island's first turtle lady and the dearest person you'd ever hope to meet." She looked at her hands. "She was real good to me."

"Is that how Little Lovie got her name?"

Toy brightened. "Yes. I called her Olivia

after her, but it was my neighbor Florence's mother, old Miranda, who gave her the nickname Little Lovie. It just stuck. It's a big name to grow into, but I think she'll manage it."

He smiled. "Well, if she's anything like her mother . . ."

She turned her head to look at Ethan. His dark brows gathered over narrowed eyes as he looked out at the road ahead. She could envision him steering the Miss Peggy, completely at home on the open sea. She thought of all he'd told her of his life and his travels. And looking out at the road ahead, she couldn't help but wonder what that kind of freedom felt like.

5

That afternoon was as glorious as a promise kept.

Toy said a hurried goodbye to Ethan after they admitted Cherry Point to the Aquarium, and forgetting all but her daughter, hurried home to build a sand castle.

The beach was drenched with sunlight and overhead a cloudless sky made the ocean a dazzling blue. Memorial Day was one of the busiest beach days of the summer but the densest crowd clustered near the pier where the restaurants played music and served icy drinks. Families gathered together on a menagerie of brightly colored towels and under umbrellas. Toddlers splashed gleefully in long stretches of tidal pool while grandparents proudly stood by watching. The kite boarders preferred the gusty winds near Breach Inlet and the blue sky was dotted with arched kites, like so many wildly plumed birds.

Oh, what a sandcastle it was! Toy didn't hurry the project but allowed Little Lovie to design however big a castle she wanted. Her daughter, she learned, could dream big. The moats were as long as Lovie was tall and at each corner they built an enormous turret, complete with sea shell decoration. There was a drawbridge across the moat and more turrets along the castle wall than Lovie knew how to count. By the time they were done, the skin under their nails was tender from digging, their shoulders were pink, and the sun was lowering in the western sky. Most of the other beachcombers had already left for home and barbecue.

After a rowdy day, the beach seemed very quiet, save for a few stragglers like them. Sandpipers returned to skitter along the shoreline and an unleashed dog trotted home. Their castle was done. Little Lovie ran off to the sea to wash the sand off her hands in the quiet surf. The tide was far out and the wet beach was gunmetal gray. It created a striking contrast to the pink streaks at the horizon. Toy hung back by the castle to watch her daughter at the waterline. Lovie gingerly dipped her toes in, testing the water, then treaded carefully a few inches into the lapping waves, stopping ankle deep. Her blond hair caught the last light of this precious day and it was like watching the sun spill over her shoulders as she bent to swish her hands in the waves.

Toy watched her daughter and all the yearnings for travel and adventure she'd felt listening to Ethan dissipated like the foam along the shore. Her own journey in life had brought her to this moment and she felt a sudden longing to capture it forever.

On the other side of the island, the Ecotour's tour boat was casting off for the sunset cruise. Cara stood on the dock and watched as Brett guided the big boat slowly back from the dock. The water churned loudly under the power of the engines, then eased forward toward the Intracoastal waterway. Every seat was filled with couples of all ages eager for a romantic cruise. While collecting the ticket money, Cara had overheard furtive whispers from couples worried that the sky was still so light that they wouldn't see a sunset. She assured them that the sun would indeed set, as it did every night, and the voyage was timed so that they would get the most breathtaking and romantic view possible.

Cara leaned against the wood railing to watch her husband at the helm of the long boat. Brett stood wide legged, his hands on the wheel. As the speed picked up, the water churned white wakes at the boat's sides, spraying droplets of water into the air. The wind tugged at the tips of his tawny hair escaping under his dark green baseball cap. His chin cut a strong silhouette against the sky while the tails of the blue chambray shirt, worn open over his T-shirt, flapped behind him like a flag.

As if he could sense her standing there, he turned his head toward the dock. Brett lifted his hand in a wave.

In that brief signal Cara understood at some profound level that his blue eyes had registered her standing there and his lips curved in a half smile. She knew, too, that his brief wave signaled his love and his intent to return home — to her — at the voyage's end. Cara swallowed deeply, moved that she understood all that in a quick flip of the hand.

She lifted her arm and returned the wave, feeling the connection. Then he turned and focused on the water ahead. She dropped her hand slowly, missing him as he disappeared from view, sensing how empty her life would be without him.

They'd been married for five years. Sometimes it seemed like five days, sometimes like five decades. In those five years they'd journeyed from the early days of naive and explosive passion to a deeper love derived from commitment, understanding and finally acceptance of each other's best and worst qualities.

Theirs had been a tempestuous love affair. When people thought of them, they usually compared them to apples and oranges — or Scarlett and Rhett. No two people could be more opposite. She'd loved the city life, the pace of her job as an advertising executive, the quick decisions and the thrill of the deal. Brett was a low-country boy in love with the salt marsh, the winding creeks and all the wildlife treasures that were hidden there. His pace was leisurely and his temper slow to ignite. But once he dug his heels deep in the pluff mud, he wouldn't budge an inch. This was in sharp contrast to Cara's quick, mercurial mind.

She might say that she married Brett against her better judgment, except that every instinct in her body had screamed that he was *the one.* Brett Beauchamps was the only man who had ever stood up to her, who continually surprised her, challenged her — and yes, loved her. Love had never come easily for Cara.

She turned and walked slowly down the

dock. She'd never envisioned her life the way it had turned out. When she was young, she'd dreamed of escaping the South forever, and all the expectations of her deeply rooted, South of Broad family. She grew up in an era learning the limits a woman could achieve outside the home and always desiring to surpass them. Everything she'd ever wanted was somewhere *off,* far from Charleston in cities where people moved fast, where the accent was harsh, and where a woman living alone was accepted as a norm, not viewed as someone to be pitied. Times had changed a lot since then, but back when she was a long limbed, skinny, dark eyed teen, all traffic traveled to points north.

Cara locked the door of the small wooden shed that housed the Eco-tour ticket office and walked past flashy, expensive fishing boats and across the open gravel parking lot to her car. The night was so quiet she heard only the gravel crunching beneath her feet, the dull thud of boats knocking against the dock, and the laughing cry of a gull.

She laughed back. What a hoot her life turned out to be. She had left her executive job in Chicago, her condo overlooking Lake Michigan, her beautiful wool suits and fine leather shoes to be the wife of a boat captain struggling to make ends meet on the Isle of Palms. Wouldn't her mother have just loved the way things ended up?

She chuckled at the thought, then sighed, missing her mother terribly, wishing she had lived to see her daughter happy at last, wanting to drive over to the beach house for a spot of tea with her and a quick chat. She would have told her mother that the only ingredient missing in her romantic saga was a child. She knew how much Brett wanted a baby and she felt a deeply rooted guilt that she, somehow, had let him down.

"Please, God, let this baby come," she whispered.

The car seat burned her thighs as she climbed into the compact sedan. The humidity and heat were so thick she could barely breathe. She quickly started the engine and rolled down the windows, welcoming the offshore breezes that whisked in. She didn't wait for the air-conditioning to cool things down. It had been a hectic day and she wanted to feel the cool water of a shower down her back. She guided the car around ruts in the lot, turned onto Waterway Boulevard and headed home.

A short while later she pulled off at the small, pink stucco house on Hamlin Creek that she called home. A sporty, blue BMW convertible blocked her entry into the garage. She cut the engine and checked the plates. She didn't recognize the sexy car but the license plate showed the orange peach of Georgia.

It could only be one person. She scrambled from the car and trotted along their winding front path, digging for her house keys. Just as she reached the door, however, it swung open. Standing before her was her best friend in all the world, Emmi Baker Peterson, arms wide and her flame colored hair a fiery wreath around her grinning face.

"Surprise!"

"Emmi!" she screamed, throwing her arms wide.

They squealed in unison like little girls as they threw arms around each other. Cara closed her eyes and instantly she was thirteen again and it was the beginning of summer and she and Emmi were arriving at Isle of Palms with their families for a whole, glorious season! Emmi's beach house was only a few blocks up the road, but both families lived the rest of the year in homes on the mainland.

They'd discovered each other early one summer morning while collecting sea shells near Breach Inlet. They couldn't have been more than seven or eight years old. Emmi was searching for an angel's wings shell and Cara had one in her bucket. Cara coveted an especially bright orange whelk in Emmi's bucket. That morning they'd traded shells — and they'd been trading secrets every since.

Cara leaned back, her hands still holding tight to her best friend.

"Emmi, there's nothing left of you to hug!" she exclaimed, blinking as she took in the dramatic changes. Emmi's body was long and lean and wrapped in tight, bleached jeans and a pink, form-fitting T-shirt. When she'd left Isle of Palms two summers ago, Emmi had been broad in the beam, all plump curves and full breasts. Looking at her, Cara guessed she'd lost over fifty pounds. And that wasn't all. Her short red hair was now as long as it had been in college, cut in layers that fell past her shoulders and highlighted with bold streaks of gold.

"You look incredible," Cara said, eyes popping. "So . . . sexy. Girlfriend, just how much weight did you lose?"

With a saucy shake of her head, Emmi placed her pink tipped fingers on her hips. "Sixty-three pounds," she announced. Then, her wide mouth stretched across her tanned face. "Can you believe it?"

Cara's mouth dropped open in a silent gasp. "Sixty-three pounds . . . Unbelievable."

"Ain't it, though." Emmi laughed in a way that indicated she was damned pleased with herself. "Divorce turned out to be the wonder weight loss program. Who knew? When you think about it, I really lost about two hundred and fifty pounds of dead weight. What a relief."

Cara shook her head. "I'm all amazement. And extremely jealous. In fact, I've decided to cast off our friendship of years and to hate you instead. It's just too inconsiderate of you to come home looking so good. You make the rest of us — meaning me — look like old crones." She skewered her eyes. "You look like you lost about ten years, too."

Her smile hardened. "I lost twenty-five years." Then just as quickly her face lit up again. "And I aim to make up for lost time." She winked and clicked her fingers. "There isn't a single man safe in the South today!"

It was a sassy gesture, even feisty, and though Emmi smiled her signature wide grin, Cara noted that the smile was not reflected in her eyes.

"Well, before you get too crazy," she said, "I'm desperate for a cool shower and a glass of white chilled wine. You pour while I shower. Then you can bring me up to speed."

Cara entered the tiled foyer of her compact house and dumped her purse on the small wooden table and her keys in a small sweetgrass basket. Over the years she'd carted out of the house Brett's old, battered furniture and sporting goods and decorated their home in the cool, pale blue tones she loved. Each piece of furniture was carefully chosen and the dark wood and glass were polished. She noticed a glass vase filled with white roses on the table and cast a glance of thanks to her friend. "Thank you, darling, I love them."

"No biggie." Emmi lifted a wine glass. It was nearly empty. "I hope you don't mind. I already helped myself. It was a long drive from Atlanta with my car packed to the brim. It's stuffed with every whatnot in this world I hold dear, including a goldfish."

She laughed, then coughed as wine went down the wrong way. "I'm fine," she rasped, waving Cara away. "I choked just remembering that trip. Thank the Lord I survived. On the highway I was fine, but every time I had to stop, the water in the damn fish tank went splish splashing all over the backseat. It's a miracle that fish made it here alive!"

She pointed to a three gallon Aquarium now sitting on Cara's kitchen counter. "Meet Nemo."

Cara saw a fairly large goldfish with beautiful fins doing a dead man's float at the top of the tank. "Good God, Emmi, I think it's dead!"

Emmi went to the tank and tapped it. The fish jolted to life and swam madly in circles. "Nemo, it's not nice to scare the guests," she said. Then to Cara, "Can he stay here for a couple of days? I think he really will die if he has to go back into that car."

"Sure, why not? Speaking of cars, that's a sporty one in the driveway."

"Like it?"

"What's not to like?"

"Exactly." Her green eyes glittered over the rim of her glass. "I traded my clunky old SUV in for a convertible. I'm done with station wagons, SUVs, big cars in general. No more schlepping kids and garden supplies around. This is the new me." She tossed her hair back again, a new gesture she'd picked up.

"Is it?" Cara looked at her friend through narrowed eyes. Emmi was slender and sexy, yes. But there was something off-putting about her aggressive youthfulness that she couldn't put her finger on.

"You're looking at me funny," Emmi said. "Sort of like the way you looked at me when I got my hair done for the prom. Remember?"

Cara burst out a laugh. Only Emmi could stir up memories that deeply stored. "How can I forget it? It was two feet of copper curls held together with a hundred bobby pins and two cans of hairspray."

Emmi threw back her head and laughed. "It *was* that high! I thought I was going to fall over with the weight of it. At five feet seven inches, plus heels and hair, I towered over Tom."

"My God, what were we thinking?"

"I was thinking I looked beautiful. Tom thought I did, anyway." Her smile slipped but she caught herself and shrugged. "At least he told me he did. That was probably a lie. Like all the other lies he told me."

Cara sensed a dangerous turn in emotions. "He wasn't lying," she hurried to respond. "You did look beautiful. And you look beautiful now."

Emmi lifted her chin and straightened, but the wine was beginning to affect her balance. "You bet I do. I look great. Tom was an idiot for letting me go."

"A first class loser."

"A cheating, lying, loser."

Too much wine, too little to eat. Cara went to the fridge to scrounge for cheese and crackers.

"Listen, sugar. Why don't you help yourself to some of this cheese while I freshen up. I'll be back in a flash."

In the shower she tilted her head back and let the cool water sluice away the day of selling tour tickets, answering the phone, and hopping on jet skis to help stranded tourists who stalled in the waterway. She was utterly exhausted, slightly sunburned and parched. She relished the idea of cuddling up with her best friend for a long chat over a chilled glass of wine. She emerged in minutes wearing a white terry robe and a white towel wrapped around her hair. She found Emmi curled on the couch like a sleek tabby cat. Her eyes were a telltale red, as though she'd been crying. On the coffee table was a new bottle of wine, uncorked, with two glasses. When she spotted Cara coming into the room, she forced a smile and held out a goblet of wine for her.

"Emmi, how long have you been here?" she asked, concerned.

"An hour at least. Maybe two."

Cara curled her legs under her as she sat beside Emmi on the sofa. Emmi was clearly one sheet to the wind. This was another change in her friend. Emmi had never been much of a drinker. Tom used to tease her about being a "cheap date."

"Did you eat any cheese?"

Emmi shook her head. "Not hungry, thanks."

"If you don't mind, I'm starving." She reached for a chunk of Brie, put it on a cracker and hungrily devoured it.

"So tell me what's going on with you," Emmi asked. "How are things in the wild world of ecotourism? Anything new with the infertility tests?"

"Same old, same old," she replied evasively.

"Which means . . ." Emmi prompted.

"Which means nothing much right now. We're in a holding pattern till the doctors advise us what to do next."

"Don't stay in that holding pattern too long. Your biological clock is ticking."

"Ticking? It's positively unwound! A baby now would be a miracle."

"Not with the miracles of modern science. Lots of women have babies late in life."

Cara sighed, silently sending off a prayer that what Emmi said was true. She reached for another cracker, busying her hands with spreading the brie.

"You okay with this?" Emmi asked gently.

"You still want a baby, don't you?"

"More than ever. It's just . . ."

"Just what?"

Cara couldn't put on a false front any longer to her best friend. She set down the cheese, fighting back tears she was determined not to shed.

"I never figured how hard it was going to be for me emotionally, is all."

"Cara . . ."

"It's insidious. No matter how I prepare myself, no matter how cool I appear, every time I go through the hormone therapy I get my hopes up. Sure, the hormones put one's emotions on a roller coaster, but it's more. When I get pregnant, the joy is indescribable. A dream come true. I'm in heaven. And then I miscarry." She released a plume of air to still her trembling lips. She felt tired, vulnerable. She didn't want to break down. Taking a breath, her voice held the old bravado. "I'm a realist. Always have been. I try to look at the situation as I would any project. If you take my age, the cost of in vitro, the doctor's advice . . ." Her shrug spoke volumes.

"What are your chances?"

"Not good. When I started trying at forty, I had a 15 to 20 percent chance. At forty-five, my chances dropped to 6 to 10 per-cent."

"Do the risks go up, too?"

"I don't think so, but with the hormone therapy there's always the chance of being swollen, bloated, nausea and having to pee all the time."

"That's called being pregnant." She raised her glass and took a sip.

Cara laughed. "Then sign me up."

"Are you going to try again?" Emmi asked more seriously.

Cara hesitated, taking a sip of her wine. Emmi had enough of her own problems to deal with, she didn't want to burden her. But also, Cara didn't want to tell anyone — not even Emmi — about this last round of hormone treatments about to begin and the next in vitro implant. Not until she was sure it took. It was one thing to deal with the pain of disappointment alone. She didn't think she could stand all the condolences again.

"Who knows?" she replied briskly. "If I do, I'd do it for Brett." She picked up the cracker and forced herself to eat it. "How's your house?" she asked, angling for a new topic of conversation. "I looked in on it as often as I could while you were gone."

"I don't know. I haven't been there yet."

"You haven't been to your house? Why not?"

"I came here first."

"But I wasn't even here. Why didn't you just run over and unpack first?"

Emmi shrugged and took a long swallow from her glass.

"Your turn. What's the matter?"

Emmi rose and went to the freezer and pulled out an ice tray. "I just couldn't go in there."

"Why ever not? You love that house."

"That's just it. I do love it." She plopped one, then two cubes of ice into her white wine. "Did love it," she amended, keeping her eyes downcast. Emmi's brows gathered as her bravado slipped from her face.

Emmi had always loved her family's beach house. She'd spent every summer there as a child and brought her children there after she was married. Her parents had left it to her when they retired to Florida. That small, white frame beach house with the tin roof had always been Emmi's touchstone. Cara couldn't imagine Emmi not hightailing it straight to her beach house to heal and regain her footing, especially now when she needed comfort the most.

She patted the sofa beside her. "Talk to Mama."

Emmi came and flopped down beside her. She slunk deep into the cushions, resting her head back. When she spoke, it was like a confession.

"I drove up and just sat in the driveway. The engine was off but I couldn't get out. I just kept staring at it. And while I did, a million memories came flooding back. Oh, Cara, so many memories. There's no part of that house I can look at and not think of Tom. I got my first kiss from Tom under the porch. I used to watch from the kitchen window as he walked up the porch stairs to pick me up for a date, his hair slicked back and a corsage in his hand. We made out on the front swing, made love for the first time in my room, groping on my twin bed." She choked back a tear. "We brought our babies there every summer, fried Thanksgiving turkeys out back, and hung lights on the palms at Christmas. Every happy memory I have there is with Tom . . ."

"Emmi . . ."

"I can't go back there. It's too hard. He even took that away from me." Her voice was bitter, laced with pain. "Now I hate my beach house."

Cara sighed heavily, fully realizing that it was going to be a long night. "Then you can stay here."

"Maybe just for a day or two. Until I get used to the whole idea."

"As long as you want or need."

"I'm fine," Emmi said forcefully. "Really I am."

"Of course you are."

Cara rose, gathered the two wine glasses and brought them to the sink. Then she went to the fridge to rummage for the makings of dinner. Brett had brought some local shrimp home from the market. She took these out and laid them on the counter. Taking a shrimp knife from the drawer, she began peeling. A minute later, Emmi was standing beside her at the counter, peeling shrimp.

They worked in the silence of old friends in a comfortable setting. Cara didn't have any answers for Emmi, nor, she suspected, did Emmi expect them. Or even want them. Sometimes, the best thing to offer was simply safe shelter.

Medical Log "Big Girl"

May 28

This turtle has major buoyancy problems. She's so full of gas her tail end floats high, making it hard for her to dive to eat. Endoscopy scheduled. We continue to debride, scrape and scrub. After days in a freshwater bath, the barnacles all came off but left pockmarked scarring. The outer scutes are so heavily dotted it looks like Big Girl is wearing a crochet sweater. Turtle is so emaciated there is a big void where fat flesh should be.

Even though she is underweight and dehydrated, she is the biggest rehab turtle I've ever worked with. Don't worry, Big Girl. Those scars will heal! TS

6

When the telephone rang, the room was filled with the metallic gray light of early dawn. Toy groaned and rolled to her stomach, dragging the pillow over her head. Who could be calling at this hour? Didn't whoever that rude person was know today was Sunday, the blessed day of rest?

Sleepily, she dragged her mind through possibilities. Favel said he would go to the Aquarium this morning to take care of Big Girl, and Irwin was covering the afternoon. She yawned lustily. She was so looking forward to sleeping late.

When the answering machine clicked on, she tugged the pillow from her head to listen. She heard Flo's strident voice on the machine.

"Hey! We've got a nest! And it's right smack in front of our houses. Toy! Are you there? Pick up. Pick up!"

Toy threw the pillow aside as she lurched

for the phone.

"Hello? Flo? Hello?"

But Flo had already hung up, no doubt to call Cara. Rubbing the sleep from her eyes, Toy sat up and scratched her head while adrenaline cleared her thoughts. A nest . . . In front of the beach house . . .

They're here! A smile dawned on her face. She hurried down the hall barefoot, tugging up the bottoms of her baggy cotton pajamas.

"Wake up, sleepyhead!"

"Go away," Lovie whined, turning her back on Toy and burrowing under the covers. Kiwi, the calico cat sleeping beside her, raised her head. Her yellow eyes regarded Toy with disdain at being disturbed.

Toy knew bringing Little Lovie to the beach would slow her down, but she wanted her daughter to share this, to be part of something that was important to her, as it had been to her namesake.

"Lovie, there's a turtle nest — right in front of *our* house!" She shook the lump under the blankets. "Come on, girl!"

Lovie pulled back the blankets, sending Kiwi leaping from the bed. "The nest is *here?*" When Toy nodded, Lovie scrambled from under her blankets as fast as a ghost crab from its hole in the sand. Toy went to her drawer and pulled out shorts.

138

"I can dress myself!" Lovie snapped.

Little Lovie pitched a fit when Toy tried to pick clothes out for her so rather than deal with a tantrum, Toy just called out, "Meet you in a few!" and trotted down the hall. Excitement bubbled in her veins. She grabbed her running shorts, sniffed the green Turtle Team T-shirt and deeming it acceptable, slipped it over her head. She then pulled her unbrushed hair back into a ponytail. Over this, she slipped on the Turtle Team cap. They met at the screen door where they both slipped on sand crusted sandals. Little Lovie had her pink T-shirt on backward and her golden hair tumbled in a mass down her shoulders. Toy held back a smile but wisely said nothing. Miss Lovie once told her to "choose your battles."

After a good push she got the wobbly screen door open. She'd have to fix that some day, she thought as she hurried to the old wicker basket on the porch. She found her long, thin, yellow metal probe stick and backpack. Just a week before, in anticipation of the season, she and Little Lovie had sat at the kitchen table and cleaned out the dusty green backpack of last season's sand and grit and put new batteries in the flashlight.

She'd watched as Little Lovie carefully

placed back all the turtle team tools: a red flashlight, a tape measure for measuring the tracks, orange tape, wooden shish kebob sticks for counting eggs, brochures for tourists, a magic marker and the lovely half shell that once was Olivia Rutledge's and now was her prize possession. Miss Lovie's probe stick and red bucket had gone to Cara, but Toy had purchased a red bucket of her own. In it were several thick wooden stakes and the bright orange federal signs that marked all nests.

"I think that's it," she said to Little Lovie, then had a sudden thought. "Wait one more minute." She ran inside to the kitchen junk drawer and grabbed a cheap instamatic camera. She tossed it into her backpack and hoisted it on her shoulders. Then going back out, she took Little Lovie's hand. "Let's go!"

They followed the narrow beach path like hound dogs on the scent. The tangy, salty morning air led them around white dunes that had shifted and grown tall during the winter storms. Now the dunes were dotted with yellow primrose and beach grass, and pocked by the small holes of ghost crabs. Toy looked over her shoulder to see their footprints in the sand — hers large, Lovie's small — side by side. Reaching the top of the dune, Toy paused, mouth open, her breath stolen by the sight.

The breadth of sand was aflame with the pink, orange and yellow light of dawn. Beyond, the vast blue ocean was glistening in the light, a rolling, breathing beast stretching out to meld with the horizon. She turned to look at her daughter. Little Lovie stood motionless, her blue eyes staring at the sunrise.

"I'm glad you brought me," Lovie said softly.

Toy squeezed Lovie's hand. In those few words, she knew her daughter's young spirit had fully awakened in the beauty of this dawn.

Scanning the beach, her heart quickened when she spotted the clearly defined turtle tracks that scarred the smooth sand from the high tide line up to the dune.

"Mama, look!" Lovie called out, pointing. Her voice was high with wonder. "The turtle walked *around* our sandcastle! Wasn't she nice?" Little Lovie clapped her hands and took off like a shot.

Toy laughed lightly, her amazement stirring her own childlike wonder. "You good ol' turtle," she muttered. The turtle tracks did, indeed, travel up to, then around, the sand castle seemingly not wishing to disturb it. Her gaze followed the turtle tracks up to a small circular mound on the dunes that was the turtle nest. Already a small cluster of people gathered around it. She recognized Flo's shock of bright white hair and Cara's glossy brown, Glenn's sun helmet, Grace's short dark curls, and . . . who was that lean, leggy redhead? She called out with a wave and began walking toward them.

"The turtles are here!" Flo exclaimed, raising her arms high in triumphant welcome. Her voice bubbled with the excitement they all felt. The joy was visceral. This nest signaled a beginning of their summer's vocation. Hopes were flying high that it would be a good season.

Cara turned and waved in welcome from her spot farther down the beach near the castle where she was measuring the tracks. Little Lovie came crashing into her legs, wrapping her arms around Cara. Grace and Glenn offered Toy hugs while accepting her congratulations for being the ones to find the season's first nest.

Turtle volunteers were a dedicated and loyal bunch. Toy knew all of the eighty people who took turns walking the beaches early in the morning to search for turtle tracks. Yet of all these, Grace and Glenn were special. In their late eighties, they put the young'uns to shame. They rose earlier, walked farther, and never missed a day. Toy thought it was divine justice that they found the season's first nest.

The redhead walked toward her. "Hey, no kiss for me?"

Toy looked at the tall woman again, and recognition clicked. "*Emmi? Is that you?*"

"In the flesh."

"Whoa, you look. . . ." She sputtered, trying to find words other than *so much better.*

"Don't go on about it," Flo said. "We've been paying her compliments all morning and it'll go to her head."

"You and the first nest, here on the same day!" Toy said.

"All's right with the world," Emmi replied.

Toy hugged her and felt the truth in that statement.

"If you're done chatting, can we get started here?" Flo called out. She was eager to find the eggs. She lifted her hands to cup her mouth and called, "Caretta!"

"Coming," Cara replied, tucking her notebook in her backpack. She brought Little Lovie up to the dune with her. "The tracks measured twenty-seven inches. That's a pretty good sized turtle. And the nest is high up on the dune. I think this mama picked out a very nice spot for her eggs."

"Yep, she done good," Flo confirmed, nodding with satisfaction. "We can leave this one right where it is. Now, let's find those eggs."

On cue, the four women brandished their probe sticks like swords. Toy felt the air tingle as they gathered at the turtle's nest. The hunt was on!

Toy used to believe finding the eggs was a matter of chance, but as the seasons passed and she gained experience, she came to realize there were field signs that pointed the way. The female loggerhead aggressively camouflaged her nest by throwing sand. But if Toy followed the inbound tracks, she could figure out in which direction the turtle lay when she dropped her eggs. The group studied the tracks as Flo put her probe to the sand and carved a circle around the large body pit.

Flo offered Toy the chance to take the first turn at probing for eggs. She chose a likely spot then carefully, oh, so gingerly, pressed her probe stick into the sand. She bent her knees, leveled her feet and took a breath. Steady now, she told herself as the probe slid into the soft sand. The first probe of the season was always like the first time she'd probed a nest. She remembered Miss Lovie guiding her through it.

"Easy now, child," Miss Lovie had said in her melodic voice. "Don't be in such a hurry. The eggs aren't going anywhere. Let the stick slide into the sand nice and slow. Bend your knees. If you feel the sand break away beneath you, stop! You can't be bumping into an egg!"

That was every turtle lady's greatest fear — to be in such a hurry that she poked through an egg. It rarely ever happened. For her, not one egg out of the thousands she'd found in five years. Nonetheless, breaking even one made a person feel hang dog contrite and it spooked you for the whole season. And, of course there was the not-so-gentle ribbing that came from the turtle team.

Toy felt the sand grow hard under her probe, a sign that the eggs were not there. She moved to another spot only an inch away. Then to another. Then another, seeking the soft spot. After her turn, Emmi began the same process. Then Cara, taking turns at probing. Ten minutes later, the mound of sand was dotted with small holes. The sun was rising and a tourist taking a morning's walk on the beach wandered over to see what the commotion was about, only to coo with excitement at her luck. Just when Toy thought this was going to be one of those tricky nests that kept them probing for hours, Cara's probe dipped sharply into the sand.

Collectively they gasped and leaned forward to watch as Cara went on hands and knees to dig with her fingers. Once the soft sand was found, probes were abandoned. Cara dug away the sand from the spot, going deeper and deeper, letting the soft sand sift through her fingers. Little Lovie leaned against Toy's legs, looking far into the hole, hoping to see eggs. Sometimes it was a false alarm and they all went back to probing. But they could smell the musky scent of eggs and were hopeful.

Cara's arm was in so deep her shoulder was almost touching the sand. Her face was turned slightly upward and her dark brown eyes were shining in anticipation as her hand followed the trail of softer sand.

Toy watched, envying Cara a little for her natural elegance, even in such an awkward position. Miss Lovie had always said that Cara looked more like her father, a tall, raven haired, chiseled man. But Toy thought that the older Cara got, the more she resembled her mother. Not that Cara would ever be the petite and blonde belle that Miss Lovie was. The resemblance was more in the softness of expression one moment, the elegant lift of the chin at another, the air of confidence, and the constant gracefulness that came, Toy believed, from generations of breeding.

Toy sighed, flashing back to her own mother's words. They'd been shopping on King Street and her mother had spotted a fancy-dressed woman walking down the street with an air of elegance.

"Can't learn that in no school," Toy's mother had told her. She'd clucked her tongue and pointed. "Look at her. Women like that, they're Thoroughbreds. It's in their blood." Her mother's husky voice had rumbled with belligerent admiration. It still hurt that she'd called Toy a "good work horse." Toy felt the same stab of shame she'd felt then and shook her head to expel her mother's voice. Why'd she always have to be so mean-spirited? Instead, she replayed Miss Lovie's words of encouragement in her mind.

"We've got eggs!" Cara exclaimed, retrieving a perfectly round, white egg out from the nest. Little Lovie was on it faster than a tick on a dog, begging for a closer look before Cara gingerly put the egg back into the nest and covered it back up with sand. It never failed to amaze Toy how a turtle egg looked exactly like a ping pong ball.

Glenn and Grace moved forward to put their names on the stake, claiming the nest as "their own." The hunt was over.

As Flo bent to put the markers on the nest, Toy stepped back and pulled her instamatic camera out from her backpack. First she took a photograph of the turtle tracks circling around Lovie's sandcastle. Then she went down on one knee and brought the little cardboard box to her eye. Through the narrow lens, she focused on the cluster around the nest, three adults and one child, shoulder to shoulder, laughing. It was a nice, standard group shot.

Zooming in, however, she discovered magic in the details — the wind tousled hair, bits of sand on the faces, and in all the eyes a childlike wonder and infinite hope for this, the first nest of the season.

■ ■ ■ ■

PART 2

■ ■ ■ ■

Hold your breath! Kick your legs hard and reach far with each stroke.

7

The following day, the Aquarium received a third sick turtle. The loggerhead was brought in by Department of Natural Resources from Kiawah Island. The local news stations were on hand and did a brief report on the rescue of the juvenile loggerhead from beyond the breakers. Toy laughed when she saw the clip because the men standing on the shore didn't want to get their feet wet. It took two slender women from DNR, DuBose and Charlotte, to wade out into the surf and pull the turtle in. This turtle had three glaring slashes across the shell from a boat propeller. Toy called this third patient turtle Kiawah.

Three days later, a fourth turtle was found by three young men who were out fishing for the day. They'd discovered a turtle trapped by the lines of a crab pot in Hamlin Creek. Being good ol' boys, they couldn't just leave him there. Every time the turtle brought his head up for breath, the rope tightened. They couldn't get the turtle unattached so they cut the crab pot loose and brought the pot and turtle both to the marina themselves. Their biggest worry was that they'd get arrested for stealing a crab trap.

Toy hurried to the marina and met the heroes at the dock. It was one of the saddest cases Toy had ever come upon. The rope from the crab pot had nearly cut clear through the flipper. Given the barnacle load and the emaciation, she guessed the poor turtle had to have been tangled up for several weeks. Toy called this turtle Hamlin.

Bringing two new turtles into the Aquarium caused a flurry of impromptu decisions. They couldn't put even one more turtle on Ethan's already crowded floor.

"It's just like in the bible," Favel had said as they measured the space for possibilities. "There's no room for them in the Inn."

"Well then, we've got to find a stable," Ethan had replied.

The stable turned out to be the cavernous basement of the Aquarium. It was being used for storage. Ethan and his dive team chipped in to move gear out and clean a corner of the area for the small tanks that Jason scrounged up for the initial fresh water baths. It was a temporary solution at best. By the end of the first week, with two tanks upstairs and two downstairs, Toy was exhausted at running up and down all day. Her supplies were tapped, as was her food budget. She didn't know how she was going to make it through another week.

Her prayers were answered by the kindness of strangers.

In the days following the television report, the Aquarium received an avalanche of donations from local people who had seen the program and wanted to help the poor sick turtles. Most of the checks and cash were in small denominations, tens and twenties, and each one was welcomed. There was the occasional $100 check and one for $500 from a Good Samaritan that sent the whole staff cheering. School children took up collections that totaled a couple hundred dollars. Other children wrote heartfelt letters and donated their allowances and emptied their piggy banks. Toy could hardly believe that strangers would care so much to send in their money to help, especially the children. Their generosity and care brought tears to her eyes.

Jason wrote a letter to the editor of the newspaper to officially express the Aquarium's thanks to the good people of Charleston for their help and support. Sure enough, that letter brought another flurry of donations.

Seemingly overnight, Toy found her small rehabilitation effort was the center of attention at the Aquarium. But she knew she really was in the limelight when the Aquarium's President called her up to his office for an impromptu meeting. It was the first time she'd been invited to a powwow in Kevin's office and her stomach fluttered as she brushed her hair in the bathroom and changed into a fresh T-shirt.

On the top floor, the administrative offices were sleek and polished. Toy stepped inside the president's corner office and was drawn to the huge plate glass windows that provided a spectacular view of the Charleston Harbor. Jason and Ethan had joined them, and across the room, Kate and Kim from the Development office were seated, dressed in dark power suits.

"Come in," Kevin said warmly, rising to a stand and waving her in. He was young, brilliant and in full possession of the gentlemanly manners that were appreciated in the South.

Ethan also rose to offer Toy his chair then crossed his arms and leaned against the wall behind her. Everyone was in an upbeat mood, buoyed by the public's support for the sea turtles.

"I've got some great news," Kevin said, opening the discussion. "The Board met and it looks like we now can consider building an official sea turtle hospital at the Aquarium. Kim, can you give us a brief report on the available resources for the hospital?"

After Kim's report they began to discuss how to handle any more turtles that were likely to be brought in.

"The first thing we need is more tanks," Toy said. "Ethan's been great to let us put Big Girl in his large holding tank. That freed up room for Cherry Point. We had to put the two new turtles in the basement. If and when we get another turtle in, I honestly don't know where we'll put it."

Jason leaned forward. "I've been thinking about this. The basement of the Aquarium is untapped for utilized space. With some redistribution and moving things around, we could actually build a credible turtle hospital down there. There's plenty of room."

"How many turtles do you realistically expect?" Kevin asked.

Jason looked to Toy.

She was silent a moment, working it out.

"It's hard to predict," she replied. "The sea turtles are nesting like clockwork now. We've already had eight nests on Isle of Palms and of course at places like Botany Bay there are lots more. The girls are out there. A lot depends on people spotting the sick turtles or bringing in those hit by boats. Naturally, we hope to find them before they end up dead on the beaches."

"Strandings are up," Jason reported. "And we're getting increased reports of Debilitated Turtle Syndrome. We don't really understand what the root cause of the illness is. The turtles are getting sick out there and the floaters are getting more common. It's timely for us to anticipate and gear up."

"The turtle hospital at Topsail Beach takes in around a dozen turtles each season," Ethan said. "I think we should aim for that number."

"Twelve?" Toy stared back with disbelief. "I can't find a tank for even one more turtle, much less that number." She puffed out her cheeks. She was barely managing both the gallery and sick sea turtles she had.

"I'm not complaining, but at the present I'm running between the third floor and my gallery on the first floor. Now adding the basement to that, I'll be going upstairs and down all day! My volunteers are borrowed from other departments, and our current examining table is a piece of plywood on a cardboard box." She paused then looking directly at Kevin said, "Frankly, sir, I don't know what I'll do if I run out of duct tape. We simply aren't ready for that number yet."

"What would it take to get ready?" Kevin asked.

Jason leaned back in his chair and clasped his hands across his flat belly. His eyes danced with possibilities. "If we could use the basement space, we'd need at least six to eight tanks with separate filtration systems, the additional husbandry supplies, a waterproof scale and a proper examining table." He winked at Toy.

"Dream on," Kate chided, shaking her dark hair. "Money is still very tight. We can't fund a whole hospital."

"Hey, you asked!" Then Jason shrugged. "But with the help of a few new volunteers, borrowed tanks, donated equipment and duct tape, we could make do."

"We have to try," Ethan said. "Those turtles are going to come in and we have to be prepared."

"Preparation is one of the things we wanted to discuss today." Kevin turned to Kate.

"Right," she said with alacrity. "I've found

out about a grant you can apply for." She began pulling out papers from a manila folder and passing them to each of the group. "It's potentially a great deal of money and would get this hospital off the ground. I'm excited about it because I think there is a very good chance of your getting it." She paused as she handed the packet to Toy. "The only problem is you'd have to write it fast."

Toy's hand stopped midair as she looked at Kate with alarm. "Me? But I've never written a grant before."

"I have," Ethan said. "Plenty of them. I could help Toy. And we'll get it done on time."

Toy turned to look at Ethan, surprised by his kindness. She offered a small, crooked smile of gratitude.

"Great. I'll put my stamp on it as well." Kate handed the papers over to Toy. "It's up to you two now."

"I think that gives us a working plan," Kevin said, summing up the meeting. "Jason, you're going to beg, borrow and steal tanks and supplies and set up a make-shift turtle hospital in the basement. Kim, you're to go to Shirley and line up volunteers for the hospital. Kate, you're going to pursue additional funding. Ethan, you're going to work with Toy to get the grant written."

He turned to Toy. "Toy, the hospital is your baby. Good luck."

The third floor deck overlooking the harbor was where the Aquarium staff could sit and chat, eat lunch, or take a break and just gaze out and watch the parade of pleasure boats, cruise liners and container ships cruise in and out of the harbor.

Toy often came out here to eat lunch and just think. After the meeting she came here feeling as though she needed to hold on to the railing to keep herself steady. Huge cumulus clouds were rolling in along the horizon. The wind gusted, flipping the ends of her blonde hair. She reached up to gather the wild strands in her hands.

"Mind if I join you?"

She startled and turned to see Ethan standing at the door.

"No," she replied, smoothing her hair. "I'd appreciate the company."

He closed the door and made his way toward her, his face expressionless.

"Want to sit down?"

"Okay."

They sat together on the wood bench, she clutching her knees, he stretching his long legs out before them. He pried open a bag of chips and silently offered her some. She took one. For a while they simply sat shoulder to shoulder staring out and munching chips watching ships pass through the harbor.

"We are actually putting together a *real* turtle hospital," she said, amazed.

"Feeling a little overwhelmed?"

"Yes," she admitted. "Happy, thrilled, excited . . . but overwhelmed, too. Did you hear what Kevin said in there? The turtle hospital is my baby. Did he mean the whole hospital is in my care? As in, it's *my* project?"

"You're the head honcho, the big boss. Aka, the one who gets the blame if something goes wrong."

"Oh, Lord." She lowered her head to her palms, feeling sick. When she raised her head again, she took great gulps of fresh air. "I used to have this nightmare. In it I'd find out that I had this major exam to take, only I'm in a panic because I didn't study for it."

"I know that dream."

"That's how I feel now. When Kevin told me it was my baby, I was honored by his trust, but it really hit home. The responsibility of those turtles is mine." She shook her head. "What about my fish gallery? I still have to take care of that, too. Ethan, I need some help! I don't know, maybe I'm not up to the task."

"He wouldn't have offered it to you if he didn't believe you were. And for what it's worth, I believe you are. And so does Jason."

She turned her head to look at him, half expecting to see teasing again in his eyes. She saw instead conviction shining in the dark brown and it took her breath away.

"I'll be there every step of the way," he told her. "And you know Jason will be hovering, and so will Dr. Tom. Everyone will weigh in. We're a team."

"A team, huh?" She helped herself to another chip. After a heavy sigh, she tossed the chip into her mouth. "Okay, then."

"Listen, about that grant."

"I'm sorry. I didn't mean for you to get roped into that, too."

"You forget I volunteered."

"I know and thanks. Really. But I know you never figured one sick turtle would blossom into a whole hospital."

"That's true, but I'm not surprised, either. The need is there. But about that grant . . ."

"You're backing out?"

"Toy, let me finish."

"Sorry. Go ahead."

"We're both too busy here during the day to write a grant. I hate to say it, but we'll have to find time to get together after work. I figure we'll have to get together most every night for the next few weeks if we're going to make the deadline."

She released a ragged sigh. "Ethan, I simply can't take any more time away from my daughter. I see her little enough as it is. That's where I draw the line."

He scratched his neck in thought. "How about if I drive over to your place? That way you won't have to leave her while we work."

"You'd do that? Every night?"

"It's no big deal."

She turned to look at him, weighing her decision. At times his intensity and focus could be intimidating. At other times, like now, his whole demeanor softened and his sincerity pulsed in his dark, intelligent eyes. Ethan was not the kind of man to make such an offer without due consideration. It was, she had to agree, the best possible solution.

"I suppose it would work," she agreed with reluctance. "I could cook dinner for you."

"Don't go to any extra trouble. I'll just grab carryout."

"It's no trouble, at least if you don't mind my cooking. I make a mean macaroni and cheese."

He grimaced. "I'll stick with carryout."

She bumped his shoulder in a companionable manner. "Hey, I can meet the challenge. A little shrimp, some grits. . . . Really, come for dinner. I have to cook anyway and it's the least I can do if you have to hightail it all the way out to the island every evening."

"Tell me again which island you live on?"

"Isle of Palms."

"Oh, right. In that beach house. Nice place to live."

"I love it. And you?"

"John's Island. Where else?"

She chuckled, thinking of the pull of his large family. "I don't believe you. I believe that you live right smack here at the Aquarium. You've got a bunk stashed in a closet somewhere, a change of clothes in one of the cubicles, and you shower and shave in the bathrooms. I figure that's the only way you can get as much done in a day as you do."

"Busted," he said. He crumpled the empty package of chips in his hands. "So, we're set then?"

"I guess so. I need at least one day to clean the house a bit before you come out," she confessed.

"Don't go to any extra trouble for me.

You're busy enough already, remember? Besides, I won't notice."

"That's what men always say, but they always do notice a mess when it's a girl's house. Speaking of busy, you're heading into the busy season with summer tourists. How are you going to manage the extra time to do this grant?"

"I just take it day by day."

She smiled, liking that philosophy enormously.

Ethan looked at his watch. "I've got to do The Show. I have a new diver in the big tank and want to see how he does."

"I'm embarrassed to say I've never actually watched the whole show."

"Come on, then, if you have a few minutes. You'll love it."

The indigo gray walls and carpeting of the arena around the base of the Great Ocean Tank gave it a Jules Verne, undersea mood. He led her to an area of wood benches arranged like stadium seating. They sat behind a group of school children, youngsters with parents, and older tourists. All eyes were on the two story tank and the great sea of fish that passed before them. While they were waiting, Caretta, the loggerhead sea turtle, swam by with its long, elegant flippers stroking. Several children jumped to their feet, pointing and squealing. Toy chuckled, feeling certain that the master show-turtle knew the commotion it caused whenever he swam by the exhibit glass window.

In contrast, the other star of the tank hushed the room when he glided by. The ten-foot Sand tiger shark's black, fathomless eye saw all. There were other sharks in the tank, but the big one drew the most attention.

Ethan stopped writing in his notebook to watch the great shark as it passed. She looked over and saw the fascination in his dark eyes, and the respect.

"You worked with sharks in Costa Rica, didn't you?" she asked him.

"For six years, with Randall Arauz. He knows more about sharks than anyone I've ever met. I was lucky to have him as my mentor." He pointed to the row of boys and girls craning their necks and pointing to the big shark. "See how they all get a thrill to see the shark? That's why the shark is such a big draw. He's dangerous. Scary, like the bogeyman. All most people know of sharks is what they've seen from *Jaws*. I'm trying to change that, to teach them the truth about sharks. Most shark bites are cases of mistaken identity."

He paused to watch as the Sand tiger

shark circled by again. "I'm not a fan of those folks who take tourists far out in the sea then stick them in steel cages. They chum the waters so the tourists can get a thrill of a close encounter. It's not natural. Tell me how that's any better than feeding the bears at Yosemite Park? Look what happened there. The bears learned to come close to the tourists and beg. Sharks are wicked smart. When we feed them in the tank we hit the wall three times and they come. Just like the bears in the parks, the sharks in the ocean will figure out that humans are feeding them — and they will come. It's not a good scenario."

"They'll start hunting us?"

"Not hunt us, but mistakes will be made. It's the sharks that are being hunted by us. To near extinction. Randall and I used to raid boats in Costa Rica and find hundreds of shark fins in the holds — some of them white, which is illegal."

"Why just the fins?"

"Because the Black Market pays a premium for shark fins, and even though it's illegal, the fishermen just cut off the fins and throw the rest of the shark back to sea so that they can make the weight limit at the dock. Each fin represents a dead shark. Thousands a year. We did our best with regulations, but money passes hands. It's an old story."

In the tank two divers slowly descended to the foreground. Immediately schools of fish began to circle them, some of the fish poking them aggressively. The sharks, however, circled past, seemingly disinterested in the humans.

"Well, *aren't* sharks dangerous?" Toy asked. "I'd be nervous to go in that tank with them."

"Actually, the sharks are the least of our worries in there. They're puppy dogs compared to some of the other fish. Sharks are predictable. They have defined habits and swim patterns. It's my job to stay up on those behavior patterns. I go in the tank every day, just to check things out. But I've also got eighty-five regular divers who are watching and I depend on their observations. If any one of them notices a tight turn, or if a shark snaps at a food bucket, I pull that shark out of there."

"So, you're responsible for the divers' lives?"

"And the lives of all the fish. I lost twenty fish last month to that big predator," he said, pointing to the tiger shark. "They're night feeders so I count the fish when I come in the morning. It's natural for him, but a problem for me."

He pointed to a diver who was tossing food from a plastic bucket. While he fed the fish, the diver was speaking on a microphone to the audience, explaining what he was doing and describing the different fish as they approached him. Several large ones swam close, pushing their way to the food bucket.

"That diver is more worried about being bit by one of those pork fish than a shark," he said. "But there's always a second diver in the tank, watching his back."

"What got you interested in sharks?"

"I've always been fascinated with them. They're ancient hunters. Perfect eating machines. We've got our share of sharks around South Carolina. You'd be surprised just how many. We used to pull them out of our nets all the time." He smiled. "You had to be careful or you'd lose a finger."

"How did you end up in Costa Rica?"

"I'd done some research there on plants, got involved with sharks. I taught diving on the side to the tourists to earn a little extra money. It was a nice life."

"Why did you leave?"

"You ask a lot of questions, don't you?"

"I'm just trying to figure out who you are. After all, we'll be working together."

"And what have you figured out?" His face

168

was serious but his eyes were mirthful.

"I can't say yet. You're hard to pin down."

"Precisely the way I like to keep it." He clicked his pen, put it in his pocket and rose. "Well, the show's over. I've got to talk to my diver."

"Thanks for inviting me to watch. I enjoyed it. Very much," she said, rising to her feet. "And thanks for your help with the grant. I feel like that diver in there swimming with the sharks. You've got my back."

He tilted his head at that, amused. Then he lifted his hand in a wave. "See you tomorrow."

Ethan arrived promptly at seven o'clock. He'd declined dinner but accepted dessert. Toy got the feeling that he was trying to maintain a professional relationship, and that having dinner together — even with a five-year-old chaperone — might be crossing some imaginary line.

They sat together at the kitchen table with coffee and a batch of iced, chocolate walnut brownies that Toy had made especially for him. Little Lovie was fascinated with this tall, dark-eyed man who came to their house. She joined the adults at the table with a book, some paper and a pencil, pretending that she was working, too. At times, she dropped her pencil and just sat with her chin in her palm staring at Ethan with her blue eyes intense, like the cat resting under her chair.

Eventually, Ethan put down his pen and folded his hands on the table. He looked at Lovie with a serious expression. "Do I have ink on my nose or is my hair sticking out funny?"

He'd meant it as a joke, but Little Love took the questions seriously. "No," she replied, shaking her head. "I'm just not used to a big man visiting in the house."

Toy put her head in her palm with a sigh.

Ethan tried not to laugh. "No?"

"Little Lovie . . ." Toy said in warning.

"Only the repairman to fix the fridge when it was broken. Mama didn't like him because he cost so much money."

"I see," he replied, all seriousness.

"And Brett, of course."

Ethan raised his brows. "Brett?"

"He comes here all the time. Sometimes we go to his house, too. We love him," she announced.

"Lovie," Toy said, her stern voice at war with her cheery smile.

"But we do!" she exclaimed.

A pregnant silence followed this pronouncement. Ethan nodded his head, then picked up his pencil and leaned back over the table. "We should get back to work."

For no one reason she could articulate, Toy felt the need to explain. "Brett is Cara's husband. He's like a father to Little Lovie and a big brother to me. She just adores him — we both do. We rent this house from them."

"Oh, yes," he replied, the pencil twiddling between his fingers. "I remember now. I met them when you brought Big Girl into the Aquarium."

"Right. Cara's mother, Miss Lovie, is the older lady I told you about. She passed away five years ago. I used to work as a companion for Miss Lovie. That's what first brought me to the beach house."

"Now the pieces are fitting together."

"Since we've lost the train of thought, do you mind if we take a short break? I need to put this little one to bed."

"Go right ahead. I'll help myself to these brownies. The scent of chocolate has been driving me crazy."

"Please, help yourself. If I have any leftovers, I'll be the one that eats them."

After Lovie was in her pajamas and brushed her teeth, Toy dimmed the lights in her room and tucked her into bed.

"I like him," Lovie volunteered. "He's nice."

"You think so?"

"Mmm-hmm. He likes you, too."

Toy couldn't help but ask, "Oh, what makes you think so?"

"He looks at you a lot."

Toy smiled in the darkness.

"Are you going to get married?"

"Don't be silly. We're just working together."

Lovie mulled that over in her mind. "But you could get married, right?"

"Good night, honey."

"But if you do get married, will he be my daddy?"

Toy reached out to stroke a hair from Lovie's forehead. "Hush now. Good night." Turning off the light, she gently closed the door.

When she returned to the living room it was empty. She spotted Ethan on the rear porch. He was leaning against the porch railing staring out at the ocean. She paused, struck by the novelty of seeing a man on her porch. It was a pleasant sensation, unexpected and surprising. She pushed back her hair and opened the screen door. It creaked loudly on rusted hinges. Ethan turned his head and his expression was relaxed and welcoming.

"I love the sound of the surf," he said. She thought his voice carried the same deep resonance of the sea.

"I do, too," she said, letting the door slip shut. She crossed the porch to stand by his side and look out. The sea was quiet tonight. It rolled in soft waves that were barely visible in the dusky night. "I leave my windows open at night and the rhythm of the waves lulls me to sleep like a lullaby."

"Do you live alone here?" he asked.

"Yes, just the two of us."

"What about Lovie's father?" he asked, sounding cautious. "Is he still in the picture?"

Equally cautious, she replied, "No. Actually, he never was in the picture. Darryl, that's his name, is a musician. He plays country rock. The guitar. He's pretty good, too. Time was he played at most of the local clubs, but he always dreamed of making it big."

She closed her eyes and breathed in the sultry, jasmine scented air. The emotions of that part of her history bellowed inside of her then waned, like the song of the insects singing in the night. Opening her eyes, she looked out into the darkness.

"I was young and he was ambitious. He

173

left right after Lovie was born and we've never seen him since."

He nodded in that easy manner of his yet he seemed pleased with her answer. He didn't press with more questions.

"We should get back to work," he said, reluctance in his voice.

"We really should," she agreed.

But neither moved to leave the porch. They stood shoulder to shoulder, content to listen to the waves roll in and out, aware that their breaths matched its steady rhythm.

8

Cara pulled her Jetta to a stop at the beach house, but she knew the bright light overhead was deceiving. She was, in fact, late for Flo's dinner party. It was a special "Girls Only" dinner that Florence had been planning for weeks.

She'd been held up at her doctor's appointment for the second in a series of hormone treatments. The therapy stimulated her ovaries and prepared her body for pregnancy. As she climbed from the car, her body felt too old and too tired to start this process all over again. She wasn't sure if her blossoming headache was from the drugs or the angst.

It was a long and arduous process. She'd already had blood tests and ultrasound scans of the ovaries so the doctor could pinpoint the optimal time to harvest the eggs. Then Brett would go in to make a deposit to the sperm bank. They had gone through the rigmarole of treatment twice before, and each time Brett shook his head and muttered, "Whatever happened to a good ol' roll in the hay?"

Whatever, indeed, she wondered, trying to recall the last time she and Brett had made love just for fun, without taking temperatures, drugs or checking charts. Lately, every aspect of her life seemed to be set by appointments on her daytime calendar.

She looked at her sides to see her hands clenched into fists. Every day she was so tense, her shoulders felt like they were held in a vise. She hadn't had a migraine in a long time, hardly ever since she'd made the move to Isle of Palms. What was it her mother had told her whenever she was in such a state? *You have to live on island time, child. You need to breathe in and out with the tides.*

Cara closed her eyes and breathed in, allowing the fresh sea air to flow through her lungs. Gradually her mind and body responded, like a dry sponge to water. She exhaled heavily, easing her hands open and releasing the pull of the dull ache in her head.

When she opened her eyes, she made a decision. If she was going to get through the ups and downs of trying once more for a baby, she might just as well be positive about it. No more nay saying and grousing. No more fists and frowns. She might be forty-five years old but she ate right, exercised and her body was primed. She set her chin, telling herself, *I'm going to have a baby.*

Behind her, a sporty blue BMW pulled into the driveway. The brilliant aura of red hair in the driver's seat could belong to only one person.

Emmi cut the powerful engine and waved. "Hey, girl, wait up!" Her long legs stretched out like a can-can dancer as she climbed from the low slung car.

Cara grinned widely. "How can you stand having to climb out of that little thing over and over again? My knees would give out."

Emmi grabbed her shiny gold leather purse from the side seat of the convertible and slung it over her shoulder. Her high heels wobbled as she made her way across the gravel driveway. Emmi was wearing sleek pants of soft sage green and a gorgeous top of matching silk that slid sexily over her body as she moved. Cara was always a smart dresser, but tonight when she looked down at her simple black cotton slacks and white, scoop neck shirt, she felt like a crow beside a painted bunting.

"Don't you look hot tonight. Why are you

so gussied up?"

"It's Friday night," Emmi replied with a tone that implied that was all the explanation needed. When Cara looked puzzled she added, "I have a date after dinner. A dream of a man I met at the Gastro Pub last Saturday." She cupped her mouth as though to whisper a secret. "He's thirty-five if a day."

Cara raised both her brows at that but didn't comment. This was Emmi's third date with a different man in as many weeks, and all of them younger.

"You're a flaming Mata Hari and I'm using words like *gussied up.* What's wrong with this picture? *I* used to be the one who wore great clothes and looked sleek and au courant."

"Darling, you're an old married now," Emmi replied, her eyes glittering with tease. "I'm on the prowl. Besides, all this . . ." Her hand indicated her body and clothes. "It's nothing a few hundred dollars at a salon and a boutique can't provide."

"Thanks. I feel so much better," Cara deadpanned.

"At least I'm not the only one late for dinner," Emmi said, slipping her arm through Cara's. "Which means, I won't be the only one scolded by Flo."

"You're always late. Flo will expect it from you. It'll be me she'll come after."

"You're right," Emmi said with a squeeze of the arm. "Oh, goodie."

"What held you up tonight?"

"I don't know, nothing in particular. Getting dressed just always takes longer than I think it will. I used to drive Tom crazy with waiting," she said with a short laugh.

"Even before that, remember how the nuns at Christ Our King gave you demerits for being late for mass? Your mama was fit to be tied."

Emmi laughed with a whoop. "I was the Queen of Demerits! If I could've collected demerits like green stamps. . . . You, on the other hand, would have been the darling of the nuns. Always punctual, probably the first in line. Too bad you weren't Catholic."

Cara loved the sound of her own laughter after such a trying afternoon. Emmi's ability to make her laugh — often at herself — was one of the things she loved most about her.

She opened the black, scrolled iron gate that led into Florence's front garden. The Prescott house was at one time the prettiest house on the island. Set back from the road by a formal front garden and a carriage house, it had been the biggest on the Isle of

Palms. Today, however, the newer mansions that lined Ocean Boulevard were easily double the size and twice as showy, a sign of the current affluence of the island. Yet, the Prescott house reflected the refined architecture and taste of an earlier era of beach dwellers.

Across the garden was the carriage house that had once been the domain of Flo's mother, Miranda. Though neither of them mentioned her name, Cara knew that both were thinking of the eccentric old woman who had charmed the girls as they grew up. Emmi linked arms with Cara as they made their way along the tabby walkway to the main house. Their thoughts were wandering back to the days when Miranda had invited the young girls into her studio to paint. Dressed in long flowing skirts and scarves, Miranda painted brilliantly colored land-scapes that Cara remembered as almost frightening. Sadly, the paintings were trea-sured by few besides Miranda. Nonetheless, she painted and gardened and lived life with a passion all found contagious. Her passing had left a void in Florence's life that was evident in the lifeless garden.

Florence Prescott had been Cara's moth-er's best friend and an adopted aunt to Cara growing up. Her father had rarely joined them at the beach house. There had been an unspoken understanding between her parents that this was their sacred time spent apart. Thus, summers at the beach were a bastion of female companionship — girlfriends and turtle ladies.

So many glorious summers were spent on Isle of Palms! Cara had spent nearly as much time in the Prescott house as her own. Flo and Miranda always had interesting people visiting, open cabinets filled with sweets, a fridge filled with Cokes, and closed mouths when it came to secrets.

As they climbed Flo's front stairs, Cara was saddened to see that the old house was not as spit-polished as it had been when Flo was younger and took pride in such things. Mold peppered the porches, spider webs lurked in corners and beside the door, a wooden planter box looked pitiful half filled with broken shells, dead insects and sand.

Emmi dropped her arm and looked around the porch with concern. "The place looks a bit shabby, doesn't it?"

"I was thinking the same thing."

"Is Flo all right? Her health is good?"

"She *is* getting older, I suppose. It's hard to think of Flo as anything but vibrant, but it's clear that she's slowing down. It takes a lot of energy to take care of a house like this, especially in this climate. One season goes by and bam! The metal rusts, the mold is back, and so are the weeds. It's a constant battle, believe me. And that's without the storms."

Emmi clucked her tongue as she looked across the front square of land that was fenced by a white picket fence stained brown in spots by well water. "Look at Miranda's roses. They're half dead and choked with weeds! This used to be Miranda's pride and joy. She adored flowers, especially roses. Do you remember the garden parties? How we all gathered in the garden for sweet tea and sandwiches?"

"Remember how Miranda declared that everyone had to wear a fabulous hat?"

Emmi laughed. "Oh, I'd forgotten the hats! How could I have? We spent days — weeks — dressing up our hats with flowers and ribbons. Did anyone take a photograph?"

"I don't think so."

"Then the memories are only in here," Emmi said, tapping her forehead with a finger.

"And here," Cara said, touching her finger to where her heart lay.

Emmi nodded wistfully. "Those were

halcyon days. Why is Flo letting her mother's garden go?"

'I don't think she cares much about gardening. The house was her thing. It was always Miranda who loved gardening."

"Is it old age, lack of money, or lack of interest that engenders this state of disrepair?"

"I guess it just depends. For my mother, it was her illness and budget. For me, it's lack of time." Cara looked over the railing at her own beach house. Though in better shape than Flo's, the trim was in need of paint and the trellis was being pulled from the wall by the weight of overgrown vines. When would she find time to work on it?

"I hear that. Speaking of time, it's time to face the music." Emmi raised the brass doorknocker fashioned in the shape of a sea turtle.

After three knocks, Florence swung open her front door, wiping her hands with a kitchen towel, looking as far from lonely as any woman could. Her white hair was trimmed short around her ears and a streak of flour branded her right cheek.

"Here you are! At last!"

"We're sorry we're late," Cara exclaimed.

"Oh, don't be. We're having a grand ol' time," Flo replied in a boisterous tone that swept away their apology. She stepped aside and impatiently waved Cara and Emmi inside. "Hurry up. We don't want to invite the bugs in."

Inside, Cara was assailed with the mouth-watering scent of freshly baked cookies. "Don't tell me we've missed dinner and you're already on to dessert!"

"No, no, no."

She followed Flo through the small front room crammed with antiques that had been in Flo's family for generations. Miranda's tasseled, paisley shawl was draped over the worn fabric of the sofa and countless figurines and photographs cluttered the shelves and table tops. Flo had complained bitterly about the clutter while Miranda was alive, yet after her death, Flo didn't have the heart to get rid of a single piece.

It was this deeply sentimental side to the outwardly unflappable and brusque Florence Prescott that endeared her to Cara. As she followed Flo into the kitchen, her nose tickled with the dust and musk that hung in the air like ghosts.

Flo hustled with purpose to the kitchen in a hurry to get back to the small baker standing on a wood chair in front of the kitchen table, rolling a ball of cookie dough in her palms. The child's head turned to reveal a gamine face, her wide grin exposing a missing tooth.

"Hi, Auntie Cara! Want a cookie? They're real good." Little Lovie's face was also streaked with flour, as was her shirt and most of the floor in a three foot radius around her.

Cara broke into a grin. "They smell heavenly." Her stomach was growling and it occurred to her that she hadn't had lunch that day. "I'm starving."

"Come on, then," Flo said, pulling out a white wooden chair from the table. "Sit yourself down. You too, Emmi. We're waiting on Toy so you're not late. In fact, you're early. Do you want wine or would you like to join Lil' Lovie and me and have a tall glass of cold milk?"

"I'll take that wine, thanks," Emmi replied, setting her large pocketbook on a chair.

"Coffee would be great," said Cara. "But I wouldn't mind some of that milk in it."

Cara sank into the chair beside Little Lovie with a soft groan. She felt strung out after the doctor's and it was the first time she'd relaxed all day. Beside her, Little Lovie was licking dough from her fingers.

"That's the best part," Cara told her.

"Want some?" Lovie stuck out her hand.

"I'll wait for my cookie, thanks."

Across the room, Flo was opening cabinets in search of dishes. "We're all running a little behind," she announced. "But who's watching the clock, anyway?"

Emmi looked at Cara, then her watch and shrugged. She reached into her purse and pulled out her cell phone, then walked to the foyer for a private conversation. After a few minutes she came back in. "No worries. I cancelled my date."

Flo was stunned. "You had a date? To-night?"

"Just drinks after dinner. Since things are running late, I don't want to rush my time here. I broke his heart, I'm sure."

Flo couldn't seem to get this straight in her mind. "But, you had a dinner date with us. It's already after six. When would you have met your gentleman? At eight? Nine?"

Emmi reached for the stack of plates from Flo's hands. "Who knows? Maybe ten. The night is still young. Besides, it's what happens after drinks I'm interested in."

Flo relinquished the plates in stunned silence, then cast a guarded glance at the child across the room.

Cara held back a grin and gave Emmi points for silencing Flo on any subject. Yet she felt again that sense of unease at Emmi's new aggressive attitude toward men and sex. She wasn't a prude but it was un-like *her* Emmi.

Emmi caught her watching. "What are you doing, sitting there like the Queen of Sheba? Aren't you going to help?"

"I should," Cara said, leaning back in the chair, "but I don't have an ounce of energy left."

"I've got enough pent up energy for both of us, so relax," Emmi replied. She sighed, pausing her setting of the table to let her gaze slide across Flo's kitchen.

Flo may have relinquished the rest of the house to her mother's tastes, but the kitchen was her own. She loved to cook and had completely gutted and rebuilt a kitchen to her liking. Light poured in from large windows and skylights overhead. The walls were white bead board, the cupboards were pine, and the counters were thick white marble, dotted at the moment with two dozen chocolate chip cookies. Flo scooped two of these with a spatula and placed them on a plate with neat and precise movements.

"I love this room," Emmi said wistfully. "Always have."

"Thank you, darling. You can have it," Flo replied flippantly.

"I'll take it," Emmi replied, only half in

jest. "I'm thinking of selling my beach house."

All conversation stopped as heads swung toward her.

"Why are you all so shocked?"

"Emmi," Flo began in a tone laced with scolding, "your folks have lived in that house near as long as mine have in this house. You can't sell it."

"Yes, I can," Emmi said, staring Flo down.

"Why do you want to sell?" Cara asked more gently.

"First off, I'm just thinking about it. But to be completely honest, I don't know that I want to live in it full time. It's always been more a beach shack than a full time home."

"You could redecorate. Add on." suggested Cara.

"I could," Emmi replied. "Or I could sell and move on. Look, I'm just thinking about it."

"Think some more," Flo said brusquely and turned her back on Emmi and the subject. Emmi tossed up her hands in frustration and walked back to the table to finish setting it. Flo carried over a plate of cookies and steaming coffee to the table. "*You* look terrible," she said to Cara. "No offense."

"None taken. I'm okay, just exhausted.

Busy day."

Flo slipped her hands into oven mitts, opened the oven door and pulled out a white casserole. Lifting the lid, Cara spied a dark, bubbling stew and her stomach started growling when she caught a whiff of garlic, spices and wine.

"Oh, Lord," she moaned. "That smells like a miracle! What is it?"

"Boeuf Bourguignon, and I hope you're hungry because I made enough to feed the multitudes. And there's a fresh-baked loaf of French bread and salad fixings in the fridge." She put the lid back on the casserole and closed the oven. "I hope it doesn't dry out before Miss Toy makes her appearance."

"When is she coming?"

"Soon. She got held up at work. Again. That's why I've got this little helper tonight."

And why dinner is a little late, Cara thought. The three women had worked out a system of childcare for Little Lovie that provided a loving, secure base for the child and support for Toy as a single mother during the years that Toy had gone to college. They'd agreed that Flo would cover Little Lovie in the morning and Cara in the afternoons. The system had worked well in the past five years, but lately with Toy's long hours and Cara working late with the Eco-Tour expansions, more of the child care time had shifted to Flo. Cara knew the time had come to revisit their schedule.

But not tonight, she thought wearily. She reached out to pick up a cookie. When she bit into the soft, warm loveliness of it, her toes practically curled.

"I don't dare eat any cookies," Emmi said, bringing her nose close to the cookies cooling on the counter and sniffing lustily.

"Aw, go ahead," Flo said, her brows gathering with disapproval. "You're starting to look a little scrawny."

"Scrawny? Really?" Emmi asked, delighted at the description. "You know what they say. Nothing tastes better than thin." She pushed herself away from the cookies and sat at the table beside Cara. "So, what's the latest gossip?"

"I got nothing," Cara said, averting her gaze. She was dying to tell the girls about the doctor's appointment, but she and Brett had agreed not to tell anyone yet.

"Well, I've got something," Flo said, coming to the table with her eyes sparkling. "Guess who's had a gentleman caller every night for the past week?"

"Who?" Emmi asked, eyes wide.

Flo looked over her shoulder at Little Lovie. The child was completely focused on rolling her cookie dough. She leaned forward and said in a whisper, "My neighbor."

"Really? She hasn't said a word," Cara said in a low voice. She huddled closer. "Are you sure it wasn't a repairman or something?"

"Honey, that was no repairman I've ever seen. This guy was tall, dark and handsome."

"Damn," Emmi said.

Cara leaned back in her chair, a small knowing smile curling her lips. "I hate to disappoint you, but that sounds suspiciously like a description of the man she works with at the Aquarium. Toy told me she was going to be working on a grant with him. I'll bet that's him."

Flo's face fell in obvious disappointment. "Oh."

"I met him when we brought Big Girl to the Aquarium," Cara continued. "He's the head of the Great Ocean Tank. Edward, Ethan, Nathan . . . something like that. You should've seen this guy in his black diving suit with those dark eyes," Cara added.

"In his *diving suit?*" asked Emmi.

"I swear to God! All lean muscles and dripping wet! He'd just come out from the big tank. It made for quite a sight."

"It's the best dive gig in town," Emmi added with a wicked smile. "Maybe I should volunteer."

Cara chortled and picked a bit of cookie and popped it into her mouth. "He *is* good looking," she added.

Flo leaned forward. "How old is he?"

"Thirty, maybe more."

"Is he married?"

"Uh-oh, your matchmaking antennae are popping back up."

"I just asked."

"I know what you asked. Save your breath. Toy isn't interested."

"How do you know?"

"Because Toy is never interested in anyone. The woman hasn't had a date in five years."

Flo frowned. "It's not for lack of my trying."

"Nor mine," Cara replied, sharing a look of commiseration. "No, our Toy may have a lot of male interest but as far as I can tell, she's a nun. She's taken vows of celibacy."

"Maybe not a vow of celibacy, but she's made a vow to your mother that she's hell bent to keep," said Flo.

"You mean about changing her life."

Flo glanced meaningfully over at Little

Lovie. "Maybe we should talk about this at another time. Little pitchers have ears."

"Are you talking about Ethan?" the child asked innocently.

Cara's eyes widened and she popped the rest of the cookie in her mouth.

"Who's Ethan?" Flo asked.

"Mama's friend. He comes over a lot."

"Is he nice?" Emmi wanted to know.

"Mmm-hmm," Lovie replied, licking her fingers. "He reads me stories. I like him."

Cara leaned close to whisper in Emmi's ear, "It's not nice to pump a child for information."

Emmi only smiled sweetly at Lovie. "Does your mama like him?"

Cara elbowed Emmi. "Best cookie I ever had," she said to the little girl, cutting off all further questions. Lovie beamed at the compliment.

She was reaching for a second cookie when the doorbell rang, and a moment later, Toy's voice sang out in the front hall. "Hello? Where are y'all?"

"Follow your nose," Flo called back.

"Mama!" Little Lovie cried out at the same time.

Toy entered the room looking as exhausted as Cara felt. Her skin was chalky, her gray-blue eyes were dull, her blond hair was falling from the elastic and her gray South Carolina Aquarium shirt and khaki pants were splattered with heaven only knew what. Yet the moment her gaze settled on her daughter, Toy's eyes lit up like sparklers and life sprang to her expression.

"Look at you!" Toy exclaimed arms out to Little Lovie as she crossed the floor. She wrapped her arms around the child and kissed her, oblivious to cookie dough and flour. "Are you being a big girl and helping Flo?"

"I made all these cookies," Little Lovie exclaimed, eager to impress her mother. "Want one?"

"In a minute," she replied, turning her head. "Thanks, Flo. This was real nice of you."

"Oh, stop. It's nothing," she replied with a scoff. "I think she ate more dough than actually made it into cookies."

"I think most of the dough is on her face and hands," Toy observed. In a swoop, she picked up her daughter and brought her to the farmer's sink that was big enough to bathe the child.

Cara watched with fascination as Toy hoisted the child under one arm while with her free hand she turned on the water. Then, using her palm as a cloth, she mopped her child's face and hands with a mother's speed and efficiency, all while Lovie remained motionless with her eyes and mouth clamped tight. Lickety-split and Little Lovie was washed and dry.

Cara wearily rested her chin in her palm, wondering when and where Toy had learned these maternal tricks of the trade. She came from the worst possible home life with a mother no better than an alley cat. But here she was, a model mother. Maybe it was something one was born with, Cara wondered. Something in the X chromosome. If it was, she hoped she had inherited that particular mothering gene as well.

"Mama, the big hand and the little hand are on the six," Little Lovie said, pointing to the wall clock. "Can I watch my cartoons?"

"Is it six-thirty already? Maybe you should eat dinner first."

"My tummy's full."

"She ate her weight in cookie dough," Flo said. "Before that, I fed her peanut butter sandwiches. Let her watch her show. Put your feet up and I'll get you a nice glass of wine while I serve dinner. We're dying to hear about Big Girl."

"Well, okay then," Toy said to her daughter. "Do you know how to turn on the T.V.?"

"Yes ma'am!" she called, running from the room.

"Let me get my own wine," Toy told Flo. "You've done enough for me today. And if you don't mind, I'll take some water first." She washed her hands and wiped her face with the dish towel. When she lowered it, she leaned against the counter and tilted her head, contrite.

"I'm really sorry I'm late," she told Flo. "You saved my life taking care of Lovie today. We had another turtle brought in at the last minute. Another one, can you believe it?"

"How many does that make?" asked Cara.

"She's number five."

Any talk of turtles brought Flo in close with focused attention. "Who brought her in?"

"Charlotte Hope from DNR brought her in from Fripp Island last night to Dr. Tom's clinic. The turtle spent the night there, then Tom brought it to the Aquarium this morning. This poor turtle . . . The lower third of the right front flipper was missing and it was very ragged with broken bone. There were large lacerations on the plastron and carapace above and below the flipper. Definitely looked to be a shark bite victim. Not to gross you out, but would it help to see pictures I took?"

"Sure," said Flo with eagerness.

"Uh, how about after dinner," Emmi said, and Cara readily agreed.

"After dinner, then," Toy continued. "Anyway, the flipper had to be amputated up to the joint. This was the first time I had fully anesthetized a turtle. When they are under you almost don't know if they are alive because you can't get a pulse or hear the heart beat like you can in mammals. I actually breathed for the turtle while Tom did the surgery! He's a great teacher." A grin of self-satisfaction spread across her face. "Very neat."

"You're learning so much, Toy," Cara said with honest admiration. She was beginning to see Toy in a wholly new light. It was like Toy was spinning fast into a glittering new galaxy.

"Speaking of learning a lot," Toy said, "the grant is going really well, too. We're making great progress. Ethan has worked on lots of grants in the past and he's very good at it. If we get this . . ." She crossed her fingers and sighed with anticipation of what she could do with all that money. "Just pray we do."

Flo narrowed her eyes, pouncing on this. "Is Ethan the young man who has been coming to your house most nights?"

"That's right," Toy answered as she reached for her wine. "We'll be working for a few more weeks so we can get the grant in by deadline."

"All work and no play . . ." Emmi chimed in.

Toy just shook her head at that. From the other room, the sing-song music and bumps and horns of cartoons blared.

"Five turtles," Flo said as she brought her own wine to join the girls at the table. "You'll be busy, that's for sure and certain. If you need any more help with that ragamuffin, just holler."

Toy swirled her wine in thought. "Thanks, Flo. Until I get more volunteers in there, I'll have to work later most nights. I don't know how long it will be before I can get a team working smoothly but until then —" she shook her head "— I just don't know. But I don't want to take advantage of your good heart. And Cara," she said, turning to her, "I realize this is your busy season, too." She exhaled a plume of air. "So, I'm going to look into hiring a babysitter."

Flo looked insulted. "A what? Now listen, sugar," she said to Toy. "I'll be happy to pick up my little darling from school, or camp or wherever — whenever. I've got time to spare. Don't you trust me to take care of her?"

Toy sat back hard against the chair. "Of course I do! I just thought, well, I hate to ask because you always seem so busy. You have your own life, too."

"Busy?" Flo looked astonished. "Honey, I'm retired!"

"But you're always running off doing something or other. You're involved in everything."

"I fill my days," Flo replied succinctly. "But that's different." Her brows gathered and she looked at her hands on the table. They were strong hands, tanned and with short, clean nails. They were hands that were no stranger to work. "I keep busy. But at my age, it's nice to still be needed. To have purpose. What with Miranda gone now, you and Cara and Emmi — and especially that precious child — you're my only family." She lifted her gaze and her blue eyes shone bright against her dark tan. "Don't you know that?"

Cara's breath held at this rare display of personal feeling from Flo. Across from her, the emotion of the day welled up in Toy's eyes. Even Emmi was silenced.

Flo brushed away crumbs from the table in staccato motions, as though trying to brush away the uncomfortable confession. "This house feels so empty. So quiet. I can't stand to hear myself patter around in it. The darn place echoes like a tomb. It's funny, but when Miranda was alive she used to watch her stories on the television all day. I thought back then that the constant noise would drive me batty. But now, why, I leave the television on most evenings just to hear another voice in the house. Isn't that silly? Truth is, I get darn lonely here all by myself."

She sighed and her gaze slowly swept the room. "To be perfectly honest, I love this house, but it's getting to be a little much for me."

Emmi gave Cara a glare that said *I told you so.*

"I didn't realize," Cara said at last, reaching out to put her hand over Flo's. "No, I didn't notice," she amended. "I've been caught up in my own world, my own problems. I should have realized that you might be missing your mother. Needing some help. But you have to admit, you put up a pretty good front."

"Yeah," Toy added with feeling. "What about all your gentlemen friends?"

Flo snorted. "What gentlemen friends?"

Emmi tilted her head in question. "You

always say you have a date."

Flo's smile slanted. "Ah . . . that. Well, I have a few friends I play cards with on Tuesday nights at the REC Center. Then there's bingo at the church on Thursdays. A movie club on Friday afternoons. I'm sorry to disappoint you, but I go out with men *and* women. We go out together. They're not *date* dates!"

Cara sat back in her chair, laughter bubbling inside. "Why you old fake!"

"Yeah," Emmi joined in.

Toy skewered her eyes and said in a scolding tone, "And you making me feel like a total loser for staying in on weekends while you waltzed out."

"You *should* go out more," Flo countered. "You're young! Pretty. You're shouldn't be hiding your light under a bushel like you do."

"Don't change the subject," Cara said. "It was all a cover-up. Why didn't you just tell us you were lonely?"

"It's not the kind of thing you just up and tell someone. *How are you? I'm lonely, thanks. How are you?*" She shrugged one shoulder. "Besides, I didn't want your pity. Don't want it now!"

"Not pity," Cara said gravely. "Never pity."

"After Miranda died, you were fussing

around me, treating me like I was the next to go. Girls, there's a lot of life left in this old mare. I'm not ready to be put out to pasture."

"We were just worried about you."

"Well, don't," she replied brusquely.

"I couldn't help but notice the garden has gone to seed," Emmi said, not beating around the bush.

Flo looked down at her hands as a faint blush crept up her cheek.

"Let us help," Emmi concluded.

"I can hire someone."

"Hey, wait a minute," Cara spoke up. "You just told Toy that she couldn't hire anyone because you wanted to help. Why can't you accept that we want to help you?"

"You've always been there for us all these years," Emmi said. "It's our turn now."

"If you won't let us help you, then I won't let you help me," Toy said.

"You girls are too much," Flo said. Her voice was low and her eyes averted.

Cara glanced across the table to meet Toy and Emmi's gazes and they shared a silent pact to be on better watch for Flo and her needs.

"You are not alone," Cara told her.

"Oh, honey, I know," Flo replied in a rush, obviously embarrassed for her position.

"You are not alone," Cara repeated.

"I know that darling," Flo said, pulling her hand away.

Cara reached out and took Flo's hand again, then looked into her eyes. In the fierce blue, she saw for the first time in all the years she'd known her, the advancing age and her new vulnerability. "You are not alone."

Flo opened her mouth to speak, then she closed her lips. The fight flowed from her shoulders as they lowered. Toy reached out to put her hand over the two. Emmi joined in.

"You're my girls," Flo said in a husky whisper.

Cara squeezed her hand, then let go, sitting back in her chair and averting her gaze. The others did likewise. She knew Flo would have been mortified for anyone to see the tear pooling at her lashes.

"How about some dinner?" Flo asked in a voice filled with false cheer, pushing back and rising to a stand. It was obvious to all that she was desperate to escape the tender moment.

"How about some more wine?" asked Emmi.

9

Summer on the Isle of Palms was in full swing. By the first day of summer children across the country were released from schools and families loaded up cars with gear and kids and headed for the beach. Cars with license plates from South Carolina, North Carolina, Ohio, New Jersey, Illinois and others were spotted all over the coast.

Cara didn't like to venture out on Palm Boulevard between four and five o'clock, especially not on the weekends. It was the hour of mass exodus from the beaches and cars lined up at the traffic light for the chance to get on the connector to the mainland. She glanced in the rearview mirror to see her niece, Linnea, and Little Lovie in the backseat, shoulder to shoulder, bent over Linnea's teen magazine. She'd taken the girls on a shopping spree at Towne Centre. They'd each found a swimsuit, flip-flops, beach hats and cute accessories for their hair and ears. She'd had so much fun watching them make their choices. Linnea was into the current fashions and was pushing the boundaries from girl to teen. Little Lovie liked anything that sparkled.

Cara had to work to keep the smile off her face as she listened to Lovie desperately trying to be grown up for Linnea. She was showing her the sparkly lavender nail polish she'd just purchased. Linnea never clucked her tongue or rolled her eyes when Lovie said something silly. What great girls, Cara thought, then made a quick decision. She turned off Palm Boulevard and into the parking lot of Acme Cantina, their favorite island restaurant.

"Aunt Cara?" Linnea asked, looking up from the magazine. "We're going out to eat?"

"Why not?" she said, letting loose the grin. "I'm not in the mood to cook and I thought we deserved something special."

"But will Daddy know where to pick me up? He doesn't like to be kept waiting."

"Let him wait. It'll do him good."

She cut the engine and turned to look in the backseat. Linnea's face was shadowed with distress. At thirteen, Linnea had lost the soft roundness of girlhood. Her long neck and high cheekbones under brilliant blue eyes gave hints at the beauty she would someday become. Though there was some of her mother, Julia, in her nose, Linnea looked remarkably like her grandmother, Olivia Rutledge.

Perhaps it was because Linnea looked so much like her mother, and that an expression of worry had been so common on her mother's face growing up, that Cara instinctively sought to erase it from Linnea's.

"Don't worry, sweetheart. I won't do anything to get you in trouble."

"It's just that Daddy gets so mad if I'm not ready."

"Does he?" she asked dryly.

Her brother, Palmer, though a dear at times, could be an ass at others. Since she'd returned home to the Isle of Palms they'd had their run-ins. Her brother couldn't stand it when she voiced *her* opinions, but that didn't stop him from voicing his — loudly and often. While she was living in Chicago, Cara hadn't had much contact with her brother and his wife, Julia, and their two children. She wouldn't have recognized her niece and nephew if she'd walked past them on the street. It wasn't a situation she'd been proud of. She'd made up for lost time in the past five years, taking the children to her house on weekends, spoiling them with gifts, and bringing the whole family out on Brett's tour boat to Capers Island for camping expeditions. Cara and Julia maintained a civil relationship but Brett and Palmer had struck up an unlikely friendship. Once they got together they were two wild good ol' boys, especially out on the water. Seeing it always made her laugh.

The one thing she couldn't tolerate about her brother, however, was his penchant for running his house with a firm hand, and especially the women in it. He liked being the king in the castle, a trait he'd inherited from their father.

"What time did your daddy say he'd pick you up?"

Linnea looked at her Swiss Army watch. "In about an hour."

Cara pulled out her cell phone. "No worries. I'll call him and let him know where we are. He can just as easily pick you up here. Okay?"

Linnea brightened. "Okay," she said as she set aside her magazine and unbuckled her seatbelt.

The back porch of the funky Tex-Mex restaurant was packed with folks getting a head start on the sunset happy hour. Inside the small, wood restaurant it was quiet and they were seated right away. Cara wanted a chance to talk to Linnea about the summer looming before them. June was almost over and Linnea usually spent the month of July with her and Brett at their house on Hamlin Creek. Linnea loved working on the turtle team with Cara in the mornings, and surfing and hanging out with her friends during the afternoons. Cara loved having kids hanging out at their house.

She ordered her usual chicken fajita salad. Linnea ordered a cheese burrito and Little Lovie ordered whatever Linnea did.

"Here's to a great summer," Cara said, raising her soda glass.

"I'm so glad you took us out to eat," Linnea said. "Mama and Daddy are going out tonight and that means Cooper and I will likely get stuck with pizza again." She wrinkled her nose. "I can't eat that stuff. So many calories."

Cara gave the slender thirteen-year-old a stern look. "Calories? Precious, don't even go there. You're so young. You can eat anything you want and burn it off. I remember those good ol' days. Wait till you hit my age . . ."

"You have a great figure, Aunt Cara," Linnea argued back. "You're so tall and thin.

Not short like me."

"Oh, Linnea . . ." Why was it young girls were never happy with what they had? They always thought what they didn't have was better. "When I was your age I was in agony because I had long legs, big feet and unruly dark hair. I wanted to look like my mother, like you do," she added ruefully. "Your grandmother was a real beauty, you know. She was the quintessential belle — petite, blond and graceful. I was a Rutledge from head to toe, which would've been great for a guy. But tall, dark and brainy wasn't so great for a young Southern girl back when I grew up. I was the proverbial ugly duckling."

"You grew up to be the swan, though."

"Did I tell you today that I love you? And keep on talking," she replied with a light laugh.

"Love me, too?" Little Lovie asked, worried. She climbed up on her knees in the booth to better sip her soda. Like her namesake, Little Lovie was destined to be another beauty.

"With all my heart."

Cara laid her right hand in the middle of the square wooden table. "Okay, first pact of the summer. Let's swear that we'll love each other forever. No matter what."

They loved to make secret pacts at the

beginning of every summer. Her heart pumped with affection when two small hands joined hers. "Forever," they all said.

Their dinners arrived in good time. After they swallowed the first bites, Cara brought up the topic on her mind.

"I was thinking about this summer. You're getting pretty old now, Linnea. What do you think about a job? Brett was saying he could begin training you on the tour boat. Nothing hard. You could go out on the boat with him, help haul up the crab traps and show the tourists the shells. Easy things like that."

"All summer?" Her voice took on that worried note again.

"Maybe not *all* summer." When she didn't reply, Cara added, "For a month, maybe?"

Linnea swirled her drink with her straw. "I dunno, Aunt Cara. It sounds great and all, but . . ." She looked up. "Here's the thing. I'm going away this summer. To camp. It's all arranged. There's this really great place in North Carolina. All the girls are going."

Cara was never popular as a girl, but even she knew that if *all the girls were going,* there was no use arguing. But all she could think was, *a summer away from the beach?*

Linnea took off on a long, rambling description of the camp in the mountains, the girls who were going, the activities, the boy's camp across the lake. Cara half listened over the inner roar of her disappointment. She had stored up years of knowledge to share with a young girl. She saw herself as Linnea's mentor as much as an aunt.

Looking at Linnea's face as she went on and on about the girls and the camp, however, Cara realized that this was her niece's first step away from her and toward independence.

"It sounds like heaven," she lied, trying to sound upbeat and supportive. "I guess I can understand. But I don't know how I'll tell your Uncle Brett. He was counting on you being here this July."

"I'll miss being here with you this summer, too," she replied with a woman's perspicacity.

Little Lovie looked crushed. "You aren't coming to our house this summer?"

"I'll come by after camp. After all, I can't spend a whole summer without the turtles."

"Looks like it's just you and me, kiddo," Cara said to Lovie.

"Auntie Cara, if Linnea isn't going to be on the turtle team, can I?"

Cara looked into the bright blue eyes of the child and realized that she, too, was growing up. At nearly six, she wasn't the baby any longer. Maybe it was the hormone treatment, maybe it was because she was due to have her eggs implanted, but Cara felt a sudden welling of emotion. Toy, Linnea, and now Little Lovie. All my babies are growing up, she thought, and her smile was bittersweet.

"Well," she replied, "I suppose the turtle team will have an open spot, won't we?"

Lovie nodded her head, eagerly.

Cara glanced at Linnea, who was also smiling in a very grown up way. She looked again at Little Lovie. "You'll have to go through basic training, of course. Early morning risings without complaints and nights slapping mosquitoes on the beach. Are you up to it?"

"Yes," Lovie replied as though making a vow.

"And you'll have to make sure no other children touch the hatchlings."

"I can do that."

Cara paused, pretending to scrutinize the child. Then she burst into a wide grin. "Okay then. You're on the turtle team."

Lovie was beside herself and grinned ear to ear.

Linnea hugged Lovie and Cara thought of all the little children her mother had taught to care for the sea turtles. She felt another surge of emotion, the kind that often comes with the passing of a torch.

Cara was about to launch into the turtle team's plans for the summer when from the corner of her eye she saw Palmer at the entry asking the waitress where they were seated.

"Oh, look," she said, changing the topic. "Your daddy's here."

Linnea took a final bite of her burrito then scurried from the booth to greet him.

"Take it easy, sugar," Palmer said in his long drawl as he hugged her. "There's no fire. Let me say hello to my sister here." With that he bent at the waist to kiss Cara's upturned cheek. "So, how're you doing, sister mine?"

"Good, thanks. You?"

"No complaints." He dug into his pocket and pulled out a few quarters. He gave one to Linnea and the other to Lovie. "There's a gumball machine over by the door. Why don't you girls find out what a quarter will get you?"

The girls took off giving Palmer room to slide into the booth. Middle age had given him a paunchy belly but he squeezed in and settled back against the wood stall. His face was ruddy and full cheeked, a common enough reaction to too much sun and bourbon.

"I see you're taking care of her kid again," he said.

He always knew exactly the right thing to say to get her riled. "Her kid?" she repeated in an icy tone.

"Yeah, Toy's kid. *Little Lovie,* right?" he said, stretching out the name. "I never understood how she named her after our mother. Kinda cheeky, don't you think?"

"It was an act of respect. And love. What's so hard to understand about that?"

He shrugged. "Just seemed odd to me. Like she wanted something for it, you know?"

"Oh, puhleese," Cara said, pushing her plate away.

On cue, the waitress showed up. "Can I get you anything sir?"

"Yeah, I'll have a Coke."

"Nothing more for me," she told the waitress. Then to Palmer, "I thought you had a dinner date?"

"I do. But not till later. If you've got a minute, I wanted to talk to you about something."

"Fire away."

"It's about that Toy Sooner girl, actually.

Well, not about her, but about the beach house."

Cara bristled. The beach house was always a touchy subject between them. Palmer had never completely reconciled that their mother had left her the beach house at her death. Her brother had already been given the family house on Tradd Street in Charleston, complete with the heirloom antiques, the cabin at Lake Lure and the family shipping business. But, as their mother had said, Palmer's hand was always in the cookie jar. Sadly, Cara had come to see that this was true.

"What about the beach house?" she said as evenly as she could.

"You do realize what it's worth today?"

"Not this again."

"Hear me out. Your taxes have shot up accordingly. I reckon . . ." He spread his palms. The broad gold wedding ring flashed. "What? Fifty . . . Sixty percent?"

"Forty. Ditto on the insurance. It's common knowledge. What's your point?"

He whistled softly and shook his head. "That's a hefty hike. I'm not talking out of turn when I tell you that Brett's talked to me."

Cara's eyes widened. She couldn't comprehend this. "About what?"

"We boys get together from time to time. We talk finances. You know that."

"Brother dear, I do the finances in our family."

He chuckled, low and rumbling. It was a sonorous sound that always had the power to lessen the tension between them.

"Sweetheart, I'm on your side. What I'm trying to tell you is that your husband is worried about keeping up the payments. He'd never say that in so many words, he's too loyal to you. But it's got to be hard going. You opened up two new locations of his business. That's a lot to undertake."

Cara felt a squeezing in her chest and stared out the window. Everything he said was true. Outside the window, The East Islands real estate sign advertised a three bedroom condo for just under a million, as though it was a bargain. And it was. The prices were shooting to the stars. Was Brett worried about money, she wondered?

The waitress brought Palmer's Coke and he took a lusty gulp. When he finished, he asked, "How much are you charging that lil' gal for staying in that house?"

Cara brought her attention back with a sigh. She was charging Toy the barest minimum that Cara could afford to let it go for, and the maximum that Toy could pay.

"She's paying what she can," she replied, deliberately vague. "For the last four years she's put herself through school and raised a little girl, all while working nights to make ends meet. Now she's got herself not just any job, but *the* job. Though it doesn't pay a lot, it's the long view she has to take now. She's really turned her life around and I'm proud of her. Palmer, you know it was Mama's final wish that I help her."

"And you have. No one can say you haven't. But it's been five years, Cara. Five years! I'm thinking about you, not her. I'll wager you could get three, four, maybe five times the amount of rent from tourists than you are from that gal."

"Maybe . . ."

He leaned forward. "How long are you going to let this go on?"

"I don't know," she replied, shifting uncomfortably in her seat. "We haven't set a timetable." Brett had brought up this very topic the other night after paying for Cara's expensive fertility treatments.

"It's costing you money to keep her in that house, plain and simple," Palmer said. "Think about it. That's all I'm saying."

She pursed her lips. "I have, actually," she replied. "I know we could be getting more in rent, a lot more. And I wouldn't be honest if I said the money wouldn't be welcome. But the truth is, neither Brett nor I have the heart to ask Toy to find another place. After all, she's only just started getting her life going. She's family."

"Family?" he said, his voice rising. "She's no kin to me."

"She is to me. Maybe not by blood, but in heart."

"You have Linnea. And Cooper. They love you. They need you."

"And I need them. But they also have you and Julia. Linnea is becoming a young woman right before our eyes. But Toy has no one. And Little Lovie . . ." She closed her mouth tight, emotion welling in her eyes. How could she explain to her brother the depth of her feeling for that child?

"Do you think it's a good idea to be so involved with another woman's child?"

"I may never have a child of my own."

Palmer let out a sigh. "I know. I'm sorry."

"It's okay," she replied, though clearly it wasn't.

"You ever think about adopting? Lots of folks do."

"Of course, I've thought about it. But I've been focused on having my own child."

"You aren't getting any younger, you know."

"Thanks a lot. I'll try to keep that in mind. But remember, brother, you'll always be older than me."

His grin spread like a shrimp net over the water, wide and full. "And you just remember, sister mine, that with age comes wisdom."

A few days later, when Toy walked out of the elevator onto the third floor of the Aquarium, she heard a loud splash and a man's muffled curse.

"Ethan?" she called out, hurrying over. But she didn't see him. Another splash and she stopped short in surprise. Ethan was hip deep in Big Girl's tank, his long arms outstretched, and he looked to be chasing the turtle. His head shot up when he spotted her.

"Thank God you're here!" he called out. "Grab a bucket. A clean one. Then hurry and bring it over here."

Toy felt a flutter of panic as she set down the turtle's prepared food and raced to grab a bucket. "What's going on?" she called over her shoulder as she rinsed a utility bucket at the sink. She was in such a hurry that water splashed all over her. "Is Big Girl all right?"

Ethan lifted his arms and in his cupped

hands she saw three perfectly round turtle eggs. Ethan released a proud father's grin.

"You've got to be kidding! She's laying eggs?"

"Either that or ping pong balls."

Big Girl started swimming slowly in the small fiberglass tank and Ethan continued following behind her, bent at the waist and with his hands outstretched. Toy couldn't stop the chuckle that escaped her lips.

"You look like a catcher waiting on the next pitch," she said.

"Hey, you come in here and try catching them."

"No, I wouldn't deprive you. It's clear you're having too much fun. Besides, you're doing a great job. Here," she said, stretching over the rim of the tank to hold the bucket out for him. "You can put them in here."

Ethan waded closer and gingerly laid the three eggs into the white bucket.

"Oh-oh," Toy warned. "Batter up! Here comes another."

He dashed back as Big Girl released one, then two more glistening white eggs. They floated down into Ethan's waiting hands. When he placed them in the bucket, Toy stared at the six eggs nestled in a circle at the bottom.

"This is nothing at all like helping a loggerhead on the beach."

He waded over to catch another egg then brought it to the bucket. "One more. Four hundred eighty-five to go."

"It's so sad that she's stuck in a tank and can't lay her eggs in the sand. I don't know what to do with them."

"Turtles are your bailiwick, not mine."

She carefully lifted the bucket to examine the eggs. What he said was true but she was completely stumped.

They waited and watched Big Girl awhile longer before Ethan shrugged and headed to the tank's rim. "That's it for me. I think that's it for Big Girl, too. At least for now. If not, it's your turn to jump in the tank."

"Seems only fair," she replied, gingerly placing the bucket on the floor so not to disturb the eggs.

Ethan grabbed hold of the rim of the tank and Toy couldn't miss the tightening of well defined muscles as he easily hoisted himself up and out. Water poured from his clothes and clung like a second skin.

Always until now, he'd been this person she worked with and respected — the way she would view a teacher or a doctor. But there was no denying he had a beautiful body, lean, taut and deeply tanned. When he stripped off the dripping T-shirt, she felt her face flame and spun on her heel at the first glimpse of hard chest muscles covered by dark hair. "I didn't want to see that," she muttered to herself as she hurried to the supply cabinet. She returned with two towels in her hand.

"You're soaked," she said brusquely, eyes averted while handing him one.

"If I had a dollar for every time I jumped in a tank, I'd be a wealthy man." He nonchalantly took the towel from her. "Thanks."

"Sure."

She went to the bucket to cover the turtle eggs gently with another towel, turning her back to him. "So few eggs . . ." she murmured. "I'm thinking I'd like to get these to the beach as soon as possible so I can bury them."

"Wishful thinking, I'm afraid," he replied, his voice ragged as he bent to dry his legs. "We don't know if those eggs are even fertilized." He straightened and fixed her with a level gaze. "They're probably not, you know."

"They probably *are*. Eggs won't calcify if they have not been fertilized. So, why shouldn't these be?"

"Well, she's been floating for a long time. I wouldn't get your hopes up."

"Even so. Putting the eggs in sand is the best solution I can offer. At least it's doing something."

"You're right," he said, surprising her with agreement. He tossed the towel to the floor. "Can't hurt to try. Seven eggs. That's got to be a record small clutch."

She nodded and wished he'd put a shirt on. "I wonder if she does have more eggs inside of her?"

"I wouldn't be at all surprised."

"I could bring a box of beach sand back to bury the eggs in."

"I guess that means we're on egg patrol. Come on, then," he said, his shorts dripping across the cement floor. "*Tempus fugit.* You see if you can get some food into Big Girl and I'll change her water. If we work together, we'll be done in no time. Then we'll head out to the beach and bury your eggs."

"*We?* You're coming with me?"

His crooked grin stretched out across his face, changing his serious demeanor to one of boyish charm. "I want to get some pictures of this for the record. If Big Girl does have more eggs — and with my luck she will — I reckon this will be the first of many trips."

■ ■ ■ ■

Hours later, Toy patted the sand then rested her palm on the dune. Beneath her hand, twenty inches down, seven turtle eggs nestled together incubating. She'd brought the eggs to Miss Lovie's dune. It seemed serendipitous to let the spirit of old Miss Lovie care for them.

The sand was toasty warm on her palm and above, the sun beat down relentlessly. Beside her, Ethan bent low to take pictures of each step of the process. He moved around the dune, his fingers snapping pictures so fast she heard the faint click click click, as rapid as a typewriter. They'd attracted a small cadre of tourists on the beach, all thrilled that they got the chance to see the turtle eggs. They'd come from all across the nation and had a million questions, which Flo was only too happy to answer for them. She was the consummate turtle lady.

Toy had but one question, and it was for Ethan. "Why do you take so many pictures?"

He was bent on one knee, aiming his camera at the cluster of tourists standing near Flo. After another click, he rose and came closer to her. "I don't know what I'm looking for," he replied. Then he lifted his camera to take a close-up of her. "But I'll know when I see it." His finger clicked again.

She stepped back, self-conscious at her photograph being taken. "But you only need one or two for the file."

He lowered his camera. It wasn't one of the compact cameras that the tourists were clicking as Flo put the familiar orange tape and wooden stakes around the nest to mark it. His was a black, professional Nikon digital with a zoom lens that stuck far out of the front. The relatively clunky camera hung from around his neck on a black leather strap.

For a moment he stood quietly, and she wondered if she'd offended him somehow. Then he began to speak in the manner of explanation.

"I started taking pictures when I began traveling. I didn't have any agenda, except to take pictures of where I'd been. Nothing more than any tourist might want to fill albums with when they're old and wanting to reminisce. But it was weird." He looked at her earnestly and his voice was laced with emotion. "The more pictures I took, the more I discovered how I could catch the essence of an image, or a moment, with a camera. I looked at the photographs I took with the same wonder that I'd looked at the stars or the ocean or some glistening fish at the end of my line when I was a child. I liked that sense of wonder."

"And you began to go after it."

"Yeah," he replied, encouraged that she got his meaning. "There are times when I look through the eyes of a camera that I feel a connection to the natural world that's closer, more intimate, than what I see with my own eyes."

He paused and shook his head. Toy sensed he was feeling self-conscious at having offered this zoom-in glimpse at himself. "I never thought about it quite like that."

Ethan snapped the lens cap to the camera. She watched his long fingers move adeptly on the camera and she could almost hear the debate going on in his head. "I might only need one or two photographs for the file, that's true," he said in a level tone. "But I take more to see what else I can discover. Sometimes I see things in the photographs that I didn't even know were there."

"Really? Like what?"

"Well, take the pictures I take at the Aquarium. During an exam, maybe my camera will catch a glimpse of an infection in the throat when the turtle opens its mouth for a squid. Or a lesion on a fish that I missed. And those are just the pictures I take for work. Here, take a look," he said, moving closer so that she could look at the small screen on his camera.

She was caught up in his enthusiasm as he flicked through several images in his camera of Big Girl — the scarring on her emaciated neck where bone had rubbed against shell, the way her rear floated upward in her tank, her huge jaw opened wide for a squid, the great turtle lying flaccid on her back as Dr. Tom did a procedure. There was a photo of the five round eggs in the red bucket, another of Toy on her hands and knees digging a hole in the sand with a half shell. When she saw the close-up of her hand curled neatly around the shell, her skin speckled with sand, she found it unexpectedly beautiful. Her attention was captured, however, by snapshots she had no idea he was taking.

There was Little Lovie, leaning over the nest with her hands on her knees, peering down into it, her face filled with wonder. One with a blond boy leaning against Lovie's shoulder, two children united by their obvious love of turtles. In another, excitement shone like the sun from Flo's blue eyes, her tanned arms and hands lifted in animation as she explained to the curious tourists the saga of the sea turtles. And finally, the close-up of her face, untouched by makeup, wisps of sandy blond hair across her pinkened cheeks, and in the pale blue eyes a vulnerability she knew too well.

"They're beautiful," she said. "You could be a professional."

"Oh no," he said with a laugh. "Technically I'm not that good. It's pretty straightforward with this camera."

"Maybe to you. I look at the camera and all I can do is push the button."

He lowered the camera. "Most new cameras are almost fool-proof. Anything I take for work, I just put the camera to my eye and click."

"But these other photographs," she said, persistent. "These ones where you've captured such expression. How do you learn to do that?"

Ethan looked out over the water, squinting. Toy thought he seemed as far off as the horizon. "It's all in the seeing, I guess."

"The seeing? What do you mean by that?"

He smiled, almost self-consciously. "You have to disappear behind the lens of the camera and see the world through different eyes. When I'm behind the camera I'm not looking at the big picture. For me, the story is in the details. I don't always know what I'm looking for. Sometimes you see it and you just know." He paused. "Does that make any sense?"

You see it and you just know. Old Miss Lovie had said that many times. Only she'd been talking about life. Toy suspected what Ethan was talking about was pretty much the same thing, too. *You see it and you just know.* Toy had felt that, many times — when she saw the sun rise over the ocean, when she saw her daughter sleeping. And it was how she felt when she looked at Ethan's photographs.

"It does," she replied, trying to contain her excitement. "Could you, I mean, is it possible for me to learn how to do that with a camera?"

"Not with *that* camera," he said with a short laugh, pointing to her instamatic.

She felt a rush of heat flash cross her cheeks and tucked the cheap cardboard camera behind her back. "Oh, this thing. I just picked it up . . ." She couldn't tell him it was all she could afford.

"You have to get a better camera," he said, matter of fact. "Nothing too expensive. At least not right off. If the bug bites you, you're hooked for life. It depends what you want and how many pictures you plan to take."

"I figure I should at least take pictures of the sea turtles. I can't keep asking you to do it for me."

She turned to look at her daughter. Little Lovie was on her knees in the sand, holding tight to a wooden stake while Flo wrapped orange tape around the nest. The nameless little boy was holding fast to another stake. Their expressions were very intent and serious.

"But that's not all." She smiled and pointed to the children. Ethan turned his head. She saw the flicker of a smile spark in his dark eyes and immediately he lifted his camera to his eye.

"I'd like to learn to . . . how did you say it? Capture the moment."

Medical Log "Big Girl"

June 23

Turtle passed whole eggs (7) and egg fragments. Brought eggs to Isle of Palms and dug a nest at standard 20 inch depth. We will continue to watch turtle closely. She's eating and defecating a lot. (good). Still buoyant. (bad). Culture results came back from Clemson —

negative.

Big Girl is certainly one for surprises! TS

10

In downtown Charleston, in the Medical University Infertility Clinic, Cara sat on a chair in the outpatient dressing room, buttoning her blouse. She stopped midway and let her hand drop to rest over her abdomen. She closed her eyes.

Beneath her palm, deep in her womb, her fertilized eggs had been planted. Her child was alive inside her body. Her and Brett's baby . . .

Embryo, she reminded herself, opening her eyes. The light of the overhead fixture was glaring. She raised her hand to continue buttoning her blouse. It was early yet. She mustn't allow herself to get too attached.

And yet, she couldn't help herself. The embryo would grow to become a fetus, she just knew it would. The transfer of the 2–4 cell embryos had been painless; she didn't feel any of the cramping she had the last two times. Surely that was a good sign?

She offered a tremulous smile to Brett when she stepped out into the waiting room. He rose from his seat like a shot, crossing the distance to her side in three long strides to take possessive hold of her arm. "Here, let me help you." His tanned face appeared pale with worry and his blue eyes were beacons trained on her.

"I'm all right," she said reassuringly. "Everything went like clockwork. Best ever. I just have to take it easy for a few days and wait for pregnancy symptoms. You know the drill."

"Nausea and swollen breasts. Got it."

She smiled again, a small tremulous effort, grateful for his humor at a time she felt weepy with maudlin sentiment.

He kissed her forehead. "Come on, little mama. Let's go home."

On the Isle of Palms, in her beach house, Emmi felt the walls closing in on her.

It was a dark, cloudy afternoon in late June. Roiling black clouds were heading toward the island from the mainland, swift and strong, providing a spectacular lightning show beyond the Intracoastal Waterway.

Emmi stood shivering in the middle of the dimly lit room. It wasn't that the air conditioning was set too low, or that the thin cotton sweater afforded her too little warmth. Emmaline Baker Peterson suffered the chill of memories.

Her grandparents had purchased the small, three bedroom beach house on Isle of Palms after World War II, then passed it on to her parents, who then passed it on to Emmi. She'd spent most of her childhood summers here and when she married, she brought her children here, too. She was attached to the old beach house with its white enamel appliances, hearty pine paneling, lumpy sofas and framed photographs of three generations of family members cavorting on the beach or proudly displaying fish on lines.

Her big, showy house in Atlanta had been decorated by professionals and was a show place for Tom's business entertaining. Here at the beach house, Emmi liked things the way they'd always been. She preferred to put her feet up, literally, on any surface she chose and just relax.

Only now, she couldn't relax. She no longer felt at home, or even that she belonged here any more. Everywhere she looked, a memory of a happier time jumped out at her.

On that blue floral sofa, she and Tom had made out while the television blared loudly.

She spied the frilly, black and white checked apron with ruffled edges, as old as the kitchen it hung in. Whenever Emmi had worn it, Tom came over to wrap his arms around her and nuzzle her neck. Under the front window was the scuffed and marred colonial table and chairs that she sat at as a girl. She could still see her sons, James and John, sitting there with their long legs curled around the spindled chair legs, shoveling cereal into their mouths, their hair sun kissed, their bodies tanned brown as berries. On the wood table by the sofa was an old black telephone that never rang. Her sons had not called once since she'd arrived.

She turned around, her eyes traveling from one object to another, from one memory to another. Emmi spun, her head getting dizzy, her eyes filling, her heart pounding harder. When she stopped short she felt her stomach continue spinning. She closed her eyes and put her hands over her ears, trying to shut out the echo of her family's voices reverberating in her brain, mocking the silence in the spinning room. Her blood felt as though it was draining from her face, her chest, her legs and into the floor. Dizzy, her knees buckled and she collapsed into a heap.

She didn't know how long she lay on the

floor, howling like a lone wolf. When she was done her throat felt raw and her voice was hoarse. Yet, her bellowing had drowned out the sound of voices in her head. Dragging herself to a sitting position, she felt shaky and weak, but oddly better, as though her violent crying had purged her body of all the heartache it had carried for far too long. Slowly she drew herself back up to her feet and took several long, deep, shuddering breaths. The crazy panic had subsided and her heart beat normally again. Only the chill remained. It encased her heart in ice.

When she looked again at the room and objects that had once been so dear to her, Emmi felt a strange detachment. The golden paneling, the worn sofa, the sepia family pictures . . .

She knew what she had to do. She went to the phone and dialed the number of an old friend of hers, one of the few that was close to only her and not to her *and* Tom as a couple. She hadn't talked to Cindi for a few years, but that didn't matter with old friends. After a few rings, she heard Cindi's rural southern drawl on the line.

"Hi Cindi! It's me. Emmi."

"Emmi! Well, hey girl. When did you come down?"

"A while ago. Sorry I haven't called yet. I've had a lot of sifting and sorting to do. You know how crazy that can get."

"I surely do. I'm just so happy you called. I was thinking about you just the other day. I drove by your house and saw the sweetest little car in the driveway. I asked Chip if he'd seen you then I got to wondering if you'd decided to rent your little beach house after all."

Emmi swallowed hard. "No, not rent it. I want to sell it."

Ethan's presence in Toy's beach house no longer was a novelty. At some point during the past month he had stopped eating take-out and begun to come early for dinner. Little Lovie had grown bored and stopped hanging around the table while they worked, preferring to play with her toys or read. In the past weeks, Ethan and Toy had made good progress on the grant, but in the past few nights as the grant neared completion, Toy got the impression that Ethan was in no hurry to finish. He took long breaks and they started taking their dessert on the porch. They also began talking. Not about the grant or the Aquarium, but about personal topics never broached at work.

Toy learned that Ethan loved sharks, sailing, surfing and anything that put him into salt water. She also learned that she looked forward to his coming over every night in ways that had nothing to do with his being a valued colleague. Ethan discovered that Toy loved poetry, old movies, sketching in her journal and taking photographs.

How Ethan had found out it was her birthday, she didn't know. She'd gone to great pains not to mention it to anyone at the Aquarium. He arrived at the beach house promptly at seven looking a little sheepish and carrying a box in his hands. He placed the gift-wrapped box with pink ribbon unceremoniously on the floor beside the table, then began pulling out the grant papers from his backpack.

Toy pretended not to notice the mystery box but secretly hoped Ethan noticed the fresh flowers on the table and, on the counter, the two-tiered carrot cake with cream cheese frosting that she'd baked specially for tonight. Her face was freshly scrubbed and void of makeup. She'd donned a clean, ironed white blouse over khaki shorts. She even spritzed a bit of the French lime and floral scented perfume that Cara had given her for her birthday, the expensive scent that she saved for special occasions.

It was also the last night of the grant writing effort. Tonight was merely a formality of checking the grant over before handing it in to Kate for mailing. They sat across from each other as they had most every night for three weeks and reviewed the grant page by page, making certain they'd crossed every *t* and dotted every *i.* Little Lovie hung close by, her radar on full alert that something was different tonight though she didn't know quite what.

Ethan and Toy ignored her heavy sighs and worked steadily until the last page was turned. The end of the project was nothing more than a whisper of paper on paper, but it sounded to them like a gong. They both leaned back in their chairs. They'd done it. In unison, they smiled with deep satisfaction and their eyes met.

In that moment, Toy felt a strong connection with Ethan. It struck deep and true and in that instant, she knew they'd crossed that imaginary line.

Suddenly an awkward silence surfaced between them. A tension she hadn't felt with him for weeks bubbled in her chest. Ethan must have felt it, too, because he quickly rose and began packing away the grant. The zipper of the bag hummed shut, and hearing it, Toy realized the full impact of the grant being completed.

Now there was no reason for Ethan to keep coming by the beach house in the evenings. That realization sucked the elation from the room like a giant vacuum. She felt hollow inside.

Little Lovie came to her side and hung on her chair. "Can we have some cake now?" She asked with a pleading tone. "Please?"

"It sure looks good," Ethan said, his gaze settling on the creamy cake.

"It's a carrot cake. I made it to celebrate the grant being done," she replied, thinking that in truth, she'd made it because he'd said it was his favorite.

"It's your birthday cake," Lovie corrected her. She turned to Ethan. "Mama bought flowers, too."

"They're real nice."

Toy rose to go to the kitchen. She reached up to the glass cabinet and pulled out three of her best china plates. "Don't pay any mind to my birthday," she said as she carried them to the table. Little Lovie leaned far over on her elbows when she carried the cake to the table. "It's just another day, and just a cake."

"Too late." Ethan bent to pick up the mystery box from the floor and held it out to her. Toy put the cake down and looked up at him, startled by the rare vulnerability she saw in the usually confident eyes.

"What's this?" she asked.

"I brought you something," he said. "To celebrate."

"A present? No presents allowed!"

"Don't think of it as a present. It's for your work." He set the box on the table and with his finger nudged the box closer. "Open it. You'll see."

Toy licked the frosting from her fingers then lifted the box, shaking it close to her ear.

"If you could see your face now you'd see how much you look like your daughter."

"A five-year-old, you mean?"

"Open it, Mama!"

"Okay, okay."

The box wasn't wrapped in frilly paper but the tape was indestructible. She resorted to using the cake knife to slice it open. Inside, nestled in the paper, was a camera. Toy's hands trembled as she lifted the camera box out then gingerly, as if it were made of spun glass, opened the package. Out slipped a slim silver digital camera no bigger than a deck of cards. Turning it in her hands she found it fit perfectly in her palm and weighed next to nothing.

"It has zoom," Ethan said, leaning forward

as eagerly as a boy while he pointed to a button.

She nodded, unable to speak.

"It's light, so you can carry it in your backpack on the beach. I thought you'd like that."

She nodded again.

"And look. You can preview your pictures on that screen to set them up."

The camera had all sorts of bells and whistles that she didn't know anything about but she wanted to learn. Oh, yes, she truly did. She coveted this camera.

Releasing a short whoosh of breath, she said, "Thank you. But, I can't accept this."

His face fell. "Sure you can."

She could hear her mother's voice in her ear. *Nice girls don't accept expensive gifts from men. Makes them beholden. Makes them expect something in return.* Toy shook her head. "No, it's too fine a gift. The nicest I've ever received. I appreciate the thought. But I can't." She was reluctant to put the camera back in its box.

"Toy . . ." He seemed to struggle with his words at the tip of his tongue, then said simply, "Think of it as a donation to the turtle hospital."

She gave him a slanted glance.

"Really, you need a camera. Now that the

turtle hospital made the move to the basement, I can't always be there to take a picture for you. I'll be busy on the third floor. And frankly, that instamatic just doesn't cut it."

"You're just being nice."

"I'm being practical. The more turtles you take in, the more you'll need to be taking pictures to monitor their progress. And if you get this grant — and you will — you'll need it. Take it, Toy. Please."

She gently, longingly fingered the camera.

"For the turtles," he urged.

Her lips twitched. "Well, when you put it like that . . ."

He smiled victoriously.

"Take my picture, Mama!"

Toy brought the camera to her eye and looked through the lens. First she aimed it at Little Lovie. The little minx posed with exaggerated flair then stuck out her tongue. Toy moved the camera to Ethan. He stood still, arms at his side, watching her, looking as if his heart had stopped. She felt again the pull of their connection and the air grew thick between them. She pushed the zoom button. The camera released a high pitched hum and in an instant, Ethan's face appeared inches from her own. She saw the coarse, late evening stubble along his jaw, the thick black lashes that framed eyes as rich and tempting as dark chocolate. Her breath stilled in her throat as she saw the truth evident in the focus of the camera lens.

You'll see it and just know.

Slowly she lowered the camera, lowering her gaze as well, sure that he could zoom in on every sensation and every longing she felt in her heart.

"I . . . I don't really know how to use it," she said.

"I'll teach you."

"You will?" she asked, looking up at him again.

He nodded. Then a half grin slid across his face. "Now that we're done with the grant, I find my evenings are free now."

She laughed out loud, a short, happy burst as if the vacuum she'd felt earlier had switched to reverse and suddenly all the elation that had been sucked from the room had been thrust back in with a whoosh, filling her with joy and unsurpassed giddiness.

Later that night, long after Ethan had left, Toy took Little Lovie's hand and together they walked out to the beach to sit on Miss Lovie's dune. She felt the need to spend a moment with Miss Lovie on her birthday.

It was high tide on an inky night. A storm

was blowing in over the ocean. The roaring wind was insistent and the waves were pounding the shore, creeping perilously close to Big Girl's nest. She cuddled her daughter on her lap and wrapped a thin cotton blanket around them both. The white corners flapped in the wind, snapping by their ears as they faced seaward, thrilling to the power of nature on display before them. She'd read somewhere that eighty percent of the human body was made up of salt water, and Toy knew it ran thick in their veins.

Toy could feel the electricity flowing in her daughter. Little Lovie thrilled to the wild, tumultuous power of nature. She shared her mother's love of the great sea in all its forms — serene, thundering, gentle, dangerous, roaring, lapping, solitary yet teeming with life. When a big wave thundered perilously close, Toy hugged her daughter, delighting in the innocent, full-throated joy of her laugh.

Oh, Miss Lovie, she silently cried to the spirit of her mentor. *This is the best birthday ever. I don't feel afraid any more! I feel so happy and hopeful.*

Toy felt buffeted by the brute force of her emotions tonight. Cuddling with her daughter, she found comfort here with the two

Lovies. One Lovie was her past, the other Lovie was her future. Yet here on this sacred dune, she felt the past and present swirl together, like the wind around them, to form this perfect now.

The following evening, Ethan came to the beach house as promised. When Toy opened the door, she immediately felt a difference in the air between them. All pretenses that he was here as a colleague to do work had dissipated like the day's light, leaving them in the sultrier, seductive mood of twilight.

Lovie ran to Ethan the moment he stepped into the house and wrapped her arms around his long legs.

"Ethan! We got a turtle nest today," she announced, craning her neck far back to look at his face.

"How many does that make?" he asked.

Lovie checked with her mother. "Twelve?"

"That's right. Twelve and still counting," she replied, delighted at her daughter's passion at being a member of the turtle team.

"The nest isn't far from here," Lovie went on. "Do you want to see it? Can I show it to you? Please? I helped put up the sign. That's *my* job. Come on, Ethan, you'll like it." She tugged at his arm, dragging him to the porch.

He looked up at Toy, his eyes filled with question. When Toy smiled and nodded, he replied, "Sure, pumpkin, let's go. Go grab the camera, Toy. We can start your lessons on the beach."

The breezes felt balmy and soft on her face as Toy followed Ethan and Lovie along the shoreline. The tide had gone far, far out. Where Breach Inlet was a churning sea mere hours ago, now it lay level as a floor nearly clear across to Sullivan's Island. A few fools ignored the warning sign and were attempting to walk across, but Toy knew better then to trust the swift changing tides and the rip currents.

At this late hour most of the shorebirds were resting, but a few peeps still skittered along the far shoreline in their comical, swift-legged run. Overhead in the far distance, an osprey searched for a final fish to bring back to his nest where his mate waited with two hungry young.

A thick, jagged line of sea wrack marked the high tide line for as far as she could see. Toy spotted an occasional ghost crab scuttling along it, silent as the wind and almost invisible against the sand, its dark, button eyes on the look-out for sand fleas that hid in the wrack.

Usually, Little Lovie was fascinated with the antics of the ghost crab but tonight her focus was on the sea shells that littered the sand. Toy watched as Lovie skittered along the beach not unlike the ubiquitous crab. From time to time she stopped to pick a shell up and carry it over like a prize to Ethan. One after another he patiently bent low to her level and examined it, then, carefully, handed it back to her.

"It's a pen shell," he replied, or "That one's a moon snail," or "a knobbed whelk."

Lovie repeated the name with utmost concentration, trying to set it in her brain.

Toy watched and wondered if Ethan could know how much his give-and-take with her daughter meant to them both?

When they reached the edge of a long gulley Lovie let out a squeal of delight and ran over to the shallow water. She called Ethan over, waving in excitement for him to hurry.

Ethan stopped before her and bent to look closer. "What have we got here?"

"Look, Ethan. It's a sand dollar!" She handed it to him like it was gold.

He took the sand dollar in his hands and inspected it. "It's a beauty, that's for sure. Why don't you walk to the shore and gently put it back into the water?"

Lovie frowned and shook her head. "No,

I'm gonna keep it."

Toy drew nearer, watching the exchange carefully.

Ethan lowered himself to her level and drew her near so she could look closely at the creature in his palm. "Look, Lovie. What color is this sand dollar?"

"Green."

"That's right." He flipped the sand dollar to its back. "See all those tiny feet waving at you? This sand dollar is still alive. They use their feet to dig or to eat. If we leave it here in the water, when the tide comes back in, it will carry the sand dollar back home again."

"But Ethan, I want to keep it. I love sand dollars."

"You don't want to kill it, do you?"

She shook her head, but without heart. He patted her back, and let her lean against his chest.

"Lovie, you're one of the lucky ones. You live here and can see the sand dollar on the beach where it belongs. Look at your pockets, all stuffed with shells to bring home. I'll bet you have lots of shells at home already, right?" When Lovie nodded, he laughed softly. "I thought so. Just pick the ones you love most, maybe two or three, and leave the rest here for someone else to find. If everyone is careful to take only a few, then there will be enough for us all."

Lovie thought about that for a moment, then hunched over her treasures. After some thought, she chose one half of an Angel's Wing for herself.

"This one is for you," she told him, handing him a moon shell. "You call it a shark eye, and I know you like sharks."

The rest she left in a small pile on the beach.

"I'll treasure this shell and every time I see it," he told her, "I'll remember how proud I am of you."

Toy hung back, deeply moved by the interaction. She wondered what her daughter was missing at not having a father in her life. She brought her camera up and began taking picture after picture of the pair, unsure of what it was she was seeking through the eyes of the lens.

Too soon, the sun slipped lower along the horizon and the sky darkened. Toy lowered her camera and called her beach scavengers home. Ethan held Little Lovie's hand and walked her back to Toy's side, their feet leaving deep imprints in the soft sand.

"Mama, I left the sand dollar in the sand," Lovie announced, testing out her mother's approval.

"Good for you! We'll have to tell the turtle ladies," she replied.

When Lovie shot forward toward the house, Ethan ambled to her side.

"She's a great kid," he told her.

"I know. Thanks."

He reached out and brought his hand up to gently sweep a wayward tendril from her face and tuck it around her ear. "She's a lot like her mother."

She felt her heart quicken and licked her parched lips. His gaze darted to her lips and she felt certain that he would kiss her. She held her breath.

He did not. She was surprised by the punch of her disappointment.

He tucked his hands in his pockets and they began to slowly walk in an angle from the shore to the dunes. "Toy," he said hesitatingly. "I was wondering . . . would you like to have dinner?"

"Well, sure," she replied. "I can fix us up something."

He chuckled. "No, not tonight. And not with Lovie. Toy, I'm asking you out to dinner. Just the two of us."

"On a date?"

He suppressed a grin. "That's the idea. You know, you put on a pretty dress and I put on a clean shirt and come by your house to pick you up."

"Oh," she said with a sense of wonderment. "When?"

He stopped and faced her. "How about Friday night?"

She turned and looked at him, squinting in the sun. "Okay."

He released a grin of pleasure. "Okay. I'll pick you up at six."

Medical Log "Big Girl"

June 30

Turtle is making good progress! We are moving her to a bigger tank to give her more room and see if she sinks or floats.

11

Friday crawled by slower than a turtle.

Toy counted the minutes of the day, because that evening, Ethan was taking her out on a date. She counted the minutes while she worked at the Aquarium, wondering if Ethan would come down to the turtle hospital in the basement, hoping he would yet praying he wouldn't. She counted the minutes driving home from work, cursing every red light along Coleman Boulevard. She counted the minutes as she washed her hair, soaped her body and rinsed in hot water, as she slipped into her sundress bought especially for tonight, styled her hair, applied makeup, sprayed a bit of scent, and as she drove Little Lovie to Cara's house for the evening.

By six o'clock she was pacing by the front door, pausing from time to time to look into the hall mirror. She saw in the reflection a fairly attractive, slender woman in her twenties with shoulder length blond hair in a stylish, green cotton sundress. Around her neck she wore a pearl necklace she'd borrowed from Cara. She reached up to touch them with her fingertips. They lay creamy against her tan skin. She'd always thought a string of pearls signaled sophistication. Girls of quality wore them for graduation photographs, on prom night, and on their wedding day. She had never gone to prom and she didn't wear a graduation cap and gown. This was the first time she'd ever worn pearls.

Toy's hand lowered. Looking deeper into her gray-blue eyes, she saw again the unsure, naive expression shining in them that, in high school, she'd tried to disguise with heavy kohl liner and a hardened, insolent gaze. The kohl was gone now, as was the insolence. Yet traces of the self-doubt lingered in the pale eyes that no makeup could disguise.

Drawing back, she told herself she was just feeling nervous. She hadn't been on a real date in years, though it wasn't for lack of invitations. She'd made such a mess of her life because of men in the past, she wanted to be darn sure she was feeling strong inside before she let any man back into her life. And she'd made the vow to

Miss Lovie before she died that she'd change her life for the better. Going out tonight with Ethan was, in a way, her first acknowledgment to herself that just maybe, she'd succeeded.

She turned away from the mirror. Certainly, Ethan was unlike any man she'd ever met before. He was strong yet gentle, opinionated yet open-minded. And he was kind to her daughter. That counted for a lot. She smiled, feeling certain that Miss Lovie would have approved of Ethan as well. For sure Cara did. It wasn't so much what she'd said. It was more the look Cara gave her when she'd clasped the pearls around her neck and told her to "have a wonderful time."

How silly she was to be nervous, she scolded herself. She saw Ethan most every day at the Aquarium. Yet in her heart she knew this anticipation and excitement came because tonight was different from the casual acquaintance relationship they shared at work. This was, simply, a man taking a woman out for dinner to get to know her better and to enjoy her company.

The doorbell rang, its two-note gong sending her heart pounding anew. She pressed her hand against her stomach while she steadied her breath, then gaining composure, walked to the door. Fixing a smile, she opened it.

Ethan stood at the door holding flowers.

Flowers. Her stiff smile bloomed with sincerity as she exclaimed over the gorgeous stems of pale, petal-pink tulips and fragrant freesia. The scent was overpowering as she lowered her face into the bunch.

"You didn't have to."

"I wanted to."

She raised her gaze over the tips of pink and was pleased to see that Ethan had dressed carefully for the evening as well. Though still in casual attire, his brown eyes seemed to glow over his coral polo shirt and khaki pants. There was about him an alertness that revealed he, too, might be a bit nervous.

"Let me put these in water. Come in." She was aware of his eyes on her as she walked ahead of him into the small kitchen. She reached on tiptoe to get a vase from a high shelf. Suddenly he was behind her grasping the vase.

"Thank you," she said feeling strangely formal as she filled the vase with water then put the flowers into it. She busied her hands, feeling self-conscious in her new sundress and Cara's pearls.

"You look beautiful," he told her.

Her hands stilled. "Really?"

"You should always wear pearls. They suit you. You know, in the East they say that pearls take on the soul of the person who wears them."

"I've never heard that." She smiled and thought to herself she was glad that she'd be carrying a little bit of Cara along with her tonight. Maybe some of her self-confidence and elegance would rub off on her.

"It's quiet without your little one around. Where is that minx?"

"I brought her over to Cara's. She hasn't been there much lately and was so excited. She was jumping around, begging me to hurry and hanging at the door like a dog that hadn't been walked in a week. Brett's going to take her fishing."

"I could take her fishing."

Toy thought she heard a slightly wounded tone in his voice, like he was jealous.

"Why, she'd just love that. Anytime."

"We'll go next week, then. I have to collect some specimens for the Aquarium and I won't be going all that far out. Speaking of which, we should get going," he said, looking at his watch. "I've a few surprises lined up."

"I like surprises," she said, grabbing her

purse and a summer sweater. "Are you offering any clues?"

"Just one. We're going to the Aquarium first."

She felt a charge of disappointment. "For work?"

"Nope. To pick up our ride."

An hour later Toy was speeding through the harbor on the Aquarium's sexy new fishing boat. The Scout was twenty-eight feet of unmatched, gleaming white power and she had to hold tight as Ethan let the twin Yamaha outboard motors roar through the harbor. She felt giddy at the rush and lifted her chin to laugh out loud as the wind streamed across her face like water. Hearing her laugh, Ethan turned from the wheel, his dark hair slicked back by wind and a grin stretching ear to ear. Yes, he was born to be on the water, she thought and grinned back at him, her eyes dancing with delight.

The water crossing the harbor was choppy but the boat soared through the green-gray peaks like a knife through butter. To her left she saw the great Ravenel Bridge, its two peaks looking like the masts of graceful twin sailing vessels. Over the roar of the engines he pointed in the direction of the enormous aircraft carrier at Patriot's Point. The Yorktown was permanently docked in the harbor as a tourist site and she'd seen it hundreds of times from the bridge. Yet the closer they drew to it, the larger it loomed until she felt dwarfed by the colossal size of the great ship.

Around them other pleasure boats were taking advantage of the warm weather for a sunset cruise. Several boats passed them, some filled with teens who whooped and hollered as they zoomed by, others with parents and children in life jackets, and still other couples like themselves who casually lifted a hand in a universal greeting. Several boats were headed for Patriot's Point. Every Friday the "Party at the Point" had live bands and dancing, a popular summer spot for Charleston. She thought that was where Ethan was taking them, but Ethan veered away from the Mt. Pleasant side and headed back into the heart of Charleston Harbor.

She was curious, but he'd told her he had some surprises and she didn't want to spoil them. She looked behind him to where a red cooler sat beside a large canvas bag stuffed with an old blue quilt. Her mind was spinning with questions about what was in the cooler when the boat hit the wake of a large tour boat and bumped the water hard. With a yelp her hold slipped and she lost her balance, tumbling to the side.

Ethan's arm shot out to grab her waist and pull her close.

"Almost lost you there," he said. Then looking down at her he added, "Wouldn't want that to happen."

She pushed the windblown hair from her face. As he negotiated the water, she negotiated the rush of feelings racing through her when he didn't release her. She fit neatly under his arm and leaned into him, relaxing in degrees, relishing the warmth and feeling in some strange way like she always belonged there. The engines roared as they picked up speed. A pair of dolphins raced alongside their boat, playing in the wake. Their gleaming bodies arced and dove in the churning water and Toy laughed aloud, feeling like she was riding atop their soft gray bodies. Her hair streamed behind her, water splayed her face in tiny droplets and looking up, she saw Ethan grinning wide, enjoying her reaction.

He steered the boat closer to what looked like a dilapidated old brick and mortar castle on a spit of land smack in the middle of Charleston Harbor. She'd read about Castle Pinckney in her history books, of course, but never went there. It wasn't a public park or a destination for tour boats, like Fort Sumter, and was off limits to all but licensed personnel.

Slowing down, Ethan released his hold on her and used both hands to maneuver the boat closer to the shore. The mighty engines growled low under churning water. Then the engines stopped and the world was instantly thrust into blissful silence. Her senses heightened and she could hear the gentle lapping of water against the boat, the creaking of rope and the sound of multiple birds crying out from the island.

"We're here," he announced. He moved with the speed of experience as he moored and set anchor.

"We're going ashore?"

"That's the plan." He turned to gather together the cooler and the canvas bag.

"But, I thought the island was restricted. Won't we get in trouble for trespassing?"

"Some people could," he replied. Then looking at her he cast a cocky smile. "But not me. I'm approved."

Of course he would be. She was silent a moment then looked down at her brand-new sundress and strappy sandals. Her hand reached up to touch Cara's pearls at her neck. "Ethan, I'm sorry. I didn't realize we were going to an island. I didn't wear the right clothes."

"You're dressed fine."

"But my shoes, my dress . . ."

"Well, the shoes might be a problem." He dug into the canvas bag and pulled out a pair of dime store rubber sandals that were bright neon pink. "So I brought these. I think they're your size."

She laughed as they dangled in his hand. "Great color. Perfect for my green dress. Speaking of which, is there a swimsuit in that bag for me? Or maybe shorts and a top?"

"No, but I've got a blanket for you to sit on so your pretty dress won't get ruined."

"I still have to get to the island from the boat."

"No problem there, either. I'll carry you. You won't get a drop of water on you."

Carry her? She stared at him while, in a flash, she recalled the story Cara had told her of her first date with Brett. He'd taken her to a remote hammock in the marsh and he'd carried Cara on his back like a pack mule all the way from the boat, through the pluff mud, to the hammock. It had all sounded so unbelievable and romantic when she'd first heard the story. Cara loved telling it and embellished the tale more and more as the years went by. Toy had always listened to the story with dreamy eyes, and now here was Ethan, offering to carry her ashore. She chuckled to herself and fingered Cara's pearls, wondering if the old saying about them was true after all.

"What's so funny?" he asked, his tone mildly hurt. "You don't think I can carry you?"

"No," she replied, quick to reassure him. "I mean, yes, I think you can carry me. It's just, well, so . . . unexpected."

His frown lifted and his smile turned smug. "That was the idea."

While she put on her rubber sandals, he rolled up his pants and climbed overboard into the water. It was only knee deep for him and she lifted the cooler and the canvas bag over the side of the boat for him to carry ashore.

"You're next," he said, when he came back.

"Do you want me to go piggyback?" she asked, thinking again of Cara's story.

"No. Just swing your legs over the edge and I'll catch you. It's not far."

The boat rocked as a wave hit it. She gripped the sides tight. "You mean, just let go and fall back?"

"It's easy, like catching a baby."

"I'll be the biggest baby you'll ever carry."

He looked at her and chortled. "Hardly. I've carried some big girls in my time without a problem. I'm pretty sure I can manage a little thing like you. Come on, Toy, trust me."

Trust me. If he only knew how big a deal it was for her to trust a man. She'd been disappointed by men all her life. She could think of one or two clowns who might actually step aside and let her hit the water and think it was funny. And here was this man, asking her to just fall back and let go.

She chewed her lip as she recalled how, whenever she was afraid, Miss Lovie had asked her, "What is the worst thing that could happen?" She thought of her new dress that had consumed every extra penny she'd had, of Cara's pearls. She looked down into the water and saw Ethan standing knee deep in the sea, the lapping waves dampening the edges of his rolled up pants. He was a tall man with strong, muscled arms. She'd seen him lift two-hundred-pound sea turtles, he could certainly catch her one hundred and fifteen pounds.

And this wasn't just any man, she reminded herself. This was Ethan. Besides, the worst thing that could happen to her was she'd get wet.

"Ready, set, go," he called to her.

"Okay, here I come." She gripped the side of the boat and gingerly lifted one leg over the side. "No peeking under my skirt."

"Scout's honor."

Next she put her weight on her belly then lifted her other leg over, leaving herself dangling on the side of the boat. Her arms shook with strain and once again she felt Ethan's hands around her waist.

"Okay, Toy, you're supposed to let go now."

Toy closed her eyes and let go. With a squeal she fell back and in an instant she found herself cradled in Ethan's arms. He'd caught her. She was so relieved she burst out laughing and swung her arms around his neck. "I did it!"

"Well, actually, *I* did it," he teased. "That wasn't so hard, was it?"

If he only knew. But she shook her head no.

Ethan carried her like she weighed no more than the canvas bag and she was sorry the distance to shore was so brief. He held her on the sand, smiling into her eyes.

"Ethan, you're supposed to let go now."

He let her down on the sand. "Like it here?"

She looked around, orienting herself to the small, marshy island. It was actually more shoal than island, lots of rocks and marsh and very little beach. Everywhere she looked there was bird doo and the shells of thousands of oysters.

"This is one of my favorite places," he told her. "It's so wild, yet so full of history. Not far from here is a bird sanctuary and, in fact, if you look around you'll see pelicans are nesting here, too. We'll need to be careful not to disturb them. The pelicans and gulls fly overhead and drop oysters down on the island. The impact of the drop pops the suckers open. Then the birds swoop down and gobble up their meal. Pretty clever, don't you think? That's why you see the empty shells all over."

She looked around the rocky island. Not far beyond were the walls of the tall masonry fort that looked to be holding back a burgeoning maritime forest. She pointed to a narrow path that snaked through and disappeared in the thick brush. "Where does that path lead to?"

"To Pinckney's Castle, where else? But it's not really a castle at all. Just an old fort. Here, take my hand. And mind where you step."

He held her hand and led her along the winding path to the crumbling brick walls of the historic monument. Nature was gradually succeeding in doing what no cannon or firepower could. Vines pushed through crumbling brick, creating huge holes in the structure. A steady breeze and the lowering sun cooled the air somewhat but the heat still brought a glow to her skin as they made their way through the tangled weeds to the deep shade of oak and palmetto.

They picked their way through the crumbling fortress. Toy imagined they were kids and playing in a make-believe fort, only this fort was real.

"I don't know much about Castle Pinckney, other than it was used in the war."

"After South Carolina seceded from the Union, Castle Pinckney was forced to surrender. That made it the first Union fort to surrender to the Confederacy. But there's a debate whether anyone actually ever fired a shot from Castle Pinckney. They used to hold prisoners down in there."

"In that dark and dank place? I can't imagine having to stay in there."

"I doubt many prisons were comfortable. But what a view they got. Come here, Toy. Look out there," he said guiding her view to the spectacular vista of harbor and sea. "From this point you can get a real sense of how important this harbor was during the war and how important it was to defend it." He pointed to the north. "To the left is Sullivan's Island with Fort Moultrie. And over there in the harbor is Fort Sumter, which is probably the most shot at and bombed fort in the country. And way over there to the south, Fort Waggoner was built on Morris Island. They had a big battle there, one of the major ones fought by a black regiment."

"I didn't know you were so interested in history," she told him.

"I'm not especially. But you can't grow up in Charleston without learning it. History is all around us. Wherever we turn we run into a monument, trip over a historical marker or face some bit of where we came from and what made us who we are. Living here, for me anyway, is like having one foot in the past and one in the present. Just look at this crumbling old fort. We're standing on over two hundred years of history. But all around the crumbling rocks, the wild is pushing up and through the stones, determined to survive. Someday the brush and then the sea will reclaim this island, just as it will a lot of the barrier islands. Probably that old lighthouse, too."

"That's kind of sad."

"I don't think so. It gives us a better perspective of our place. We hold our history so dear, our politics so tight. But in the fullness of time, all histories fade. Rome,

Ephesus, the Incan and Mayan cultures. The wheel of time turns round and round and proves change is part of nature. The problem comes in trying to interfere with nature or to think we know more than nature. Our failures are humbling. The more I learn, the more I see that, in the end, nature will prevail."

She turned to look behind her at the weathered gray stone fortress sinking in the marsh and thought of his words. *Change is part of nature.* Hadn't she changed, too? Lately, she could feel her old fears and insecurities crumbling as sure as that old brick and mortar.

She gazed far out to the watery horizon. The sun was beginning to set and the mood deepened with the skies. Ethan came to stand behind her and wrap his arms around her. She sighed and leaned once more into the warmth of his arms with a timeless ease. Together they watched the descending sun set the sky on fire.

To the south, Cara sat on her dock and watched the pink bloom over Hamlin Creek, slowly turning the glassy waters that unique, soft tint of lavender that always moved her to introspection. She sank deeper into the mesh folding chair and stretched her legs out along the dry, splintered wood. Across the dock, Brett sat at the edge, feet dabbling in the water, teaching Little Lovie how to fish. She was so small she had to hold the rod between her knees. Cara watched him patiently help Lovie hold the rod steady and how to swing the line to lure the fish.

Cara had offered to mind Little Lovie for the evening. She smiled. Toy was out on a date . . . at last! She felt like the proud mother of a fledgling. Cara approved of, and even liked, Ethan Legare. Not because he was handsome. Good looks had never meant much to her. She'd known plenty of handsome men who turned out to be empty-headed bozos. Ethan had that rare quality called character. She saw it in him when she first met him, as she'd seen it shining in Brett's eyes. That Ethan had brains was a big bonus. Toy would blossom with someone like him. Her mama had always told her to marry someone who raised the bar.

Yes, Cara was pleased as punch that Toy had agreed to actually go out with Ethan, just as she was happy to have Lovie for the evening. She'd missed having Lovie patter around and all her questions.

June had flown by. If all went well, July would be a quiet month of hope and prayer that the new life inside of her would thrive. She sighed deeply and looked out over the dusky creek. As the rounded, flaming tip of the sun slipped beneath the horizon, Cara laced her hands across her belly and made a wish.

"Well, we should roll her in. It's getting dark," Brett said to Lovie. On cue, the mosquitoes hummed annoyingly close.

"But I didn't catch a fish," Lovie complained.

"That's the lot of all fishermen," Brett told her. "You just never know." Then seeing her pout he added, "But let's see if we're any luckier with the crabs."

"Do you want me to help?" Cara asked, attempting to rise from her chair.

"You stay put," Brett replied, pointing his finger at her.

Cara sighed and sank back into the chair. Brett had been fanatic about her taking it easy since the implantation of eggs. He didn't even want her to attend the annual barbecue at the beach house on the Fourth of July. At first she'd been annoyed by his hovering and worry, but in her heart she viewed his concern as a sign of his desperation for a child. His face was set yet she saw the softness of concern in his eyes. So she obliged him and propped her legs up on the bait box.

"Happy now?"

He cracked a grin as he nodded, then turned back to Lovie. "Okay, now stand back from the edge," he said to the girl when she finished rolling up her fishing line. "I'm going to pull up the crab pot."

"Come over here, honey," Cara called, waving her over to her chair.

"I want to see."

"You can, just give him a chance to pull the trap up on the dock. You don't want him to bump into you and knock you into the creek, do you?"

Lovie leaned against the chair with a sigh. Cara put her arms around her slender body with bones as tiny as the egret's standing in the marsh. As they watched. Cara caught the scent of bug spray on Lovie's arms and shampoo in her wispy hair. She breathed in deeply, closing her eyes. Across the dock, Brett bent far over the edge, straining the fabric of his shirt as he pulled up on the thick rope, hand over hand, until a large, black iron cage emerged, dripping from the murky waters. Inside the trap, several crabs skittered noisily along the bottom, their claws waving in the air.

"You got some!" Lovie exclaimed, leaping from Cara's grasp to join Brett at the edge of the dock.

"Everybody stand back!"

Lovie halted in her tracks as Brett eased the trap onto the dock. Then she inched closer, hovering nearby, oohing at the crustaceans clicking madly.

"Lovie, go get me a ruler," he ordered.

The little girl ran to Cara who lifted her legs from the bait box. Opening it, Cara pulled out an old, splintered wooden ruler and handed it to Lovie, who raced back to Brett with her treasure.

"Okay then," he said, waving her closer. "Here's what I want you to do. Bring the ruler up close to measure. The crab has to be longer than five inches for us to keep it. That's from here to here on the ruler, see? If it's too small, we'll toss the crab back in. Ready?"

"Yes."

Cara smiled at Lovie's seriousness. Brett was a natural teacher. He loved his work as a naturalist and hated being trapped behind the desk. At every chance he shot off from the office like a kid excused from school to go out on the sea with the boats. He believed deeply that in teaching children — of all ages — he was helping to preserve the landscape he loved for another generation.

Brett pushed back his sleeve and reached

into the crab trap. The crabs scuttled sideways as far from his hand as possible, their pincers clicking menacingly. Moving with the speed of experience he dipped his hand in, grabbed a crab and pulled it out.

"How big is it?" he asked Lovie, holding the crab out for her to measure.

She shrank back, afraid.

"You don't have to do this."

"I can do it," she answered defiantly and overcame her fear to reach out her hand and bring the ruler close to the crab.

"Come on, slowpoke. This guy's gonna pinch me, not you."

"Okay, okay." She gathered her courage to bring the ruler close and measure carefully, though with excruciating slowness. "Six," she announced with relief.

"Good girl. That's a keeper," he replied and put the crab into the bucket. "I'm proud of you. Now here comes a big Jimmy," he said, holding up a large blue crab with beautifully blue tipped claws. "I can tell just by looking he's legal." He put this one into the bucket as well. He reached in again and pulled out another crab for Lovie to measure.

"It's five," Lovie reported with a hint of cockiness.

"Hmm . . . are you sure? Check again."

Lovie held the ruler closer to the crab.

"I don't think it's quite five," Brett said. "So, what should I do with her?"

"Put her back in the water?"

"Right. She needs time to grow up, just like you."

"But Uncle Brett, how do you know it's a girl crab?"

Brett turned the crab so Lovie could see the underside. "Girls have an apron, see?" he said, pointing to the rounded curve on the shell. "When she's grown up, we call her a Sook. But this one isn't grown up enough. So back to the water, Sookie." He gently tossed the small crab into the creek. Then he reached into the pot and pulled out another large crab with blue tipped claws snapping. This one he turned over so that he could show Lovie the underside.

"The boys have shiny blue tips on their claws and on the back of the shell they have a point. It looks like, uh . . . a pencil." He looked over at Cara and they shared a silent laugh. "We call the boys Jimmy. Into the bucket, Jimmy."

When he pulled the next crab out, Lovie leaned far forward, pointing excitedly. "Look, Uncle Brett. What's that? The big crab is holding on to the little one!"

Brett nodded while gently lowering the

crab to the dock. The larger crab remained immobile, carrying the smaller crab closely beneath him with its front claws mantled over it.

"We call this a doubler. Come, honey, look closer. This Jimmy is a daddy crab. When the mommy crab is carrying the fertilized eggs, the daddy mantles her for about three days until she can defend herself. He guards and protects her so nothing can hurt her."

Cara listened, never having known this about blue crabs. She was strangely moved.

Brett went on, "When the eggs grow, it will look like she has a big orange sponge on her abdomen. Then, when the eggs are ready they turn black and she'll release them into the water. Guess how many."

"A hundred?"

"Nope. Around two million. Can you even imagine that many eggs?"

Lovie shook her head.

"Neither can I. That's one big passel of eggs." He reached over to pick up the doubler. The male crab held tight to the female, cradling her when lifted in the air. "Only one egg in every million will survive to adulthood. And that's why," he said as he very gently lowered the pair of crabs back into the water, "we take care to put each and every mama crab back into the sea so she can produce more crabs for you in the future."

He reached into the creek to dampen an old towel with sea water then placed it over the crabs in the bucket. "That's all we'll collect this time. Let's bring the lot inside and we'll cook them up for the party."

"No, Uncle Brett! I'm not going to eat any crabs. They're my friends," Lovie said tearfully and got up to get her fishing pole.

Brett understood this sweet reaction and let her go, walking instead to Cara. He stood behind her to bend low and wrap his arms around her.

"Know what I'm doing?" he said in a low voice at her ear.

"No."

"I'm mantling you."

Her heart near spilled over with love for him. She closed her eyes, feeling safe in his arms and leaned far back. She turned her head to rub her cheek against his. "You Jimmies sure know how to talk pretty to a Sook."

"Yep. It's my job to guard and protect you."

"Sure. For three days."

He chuckled. It sounded low and rich against his chest. "For you, maybe a full week." He gently rubbed his palm across her belly.

She felt the lump in her throat about to choke her. "Well, come on, Jimmy. Help this old Sook up. Let's go inside before we become bait for the mosquitoes."

The Aquarium was a dark monolith against the harbor as Toy and Ethan approached the dock. Toy looked dreamily up at the sky and could have sworn the quarter moon smiled down on her like a Cheshire cat. It had been the most perfect, magical evening. Ethan had spread out a glorious picnic on the beach and they sipped chilled white wine with strawberries as the sun set in its fiery path to the sea. She'd never suspected he had such a deeply romantic side. When the blue sky deepened to lavender, he'd carried her in his arms back to the boat and they took off for Red's Bar, docking at Shem Creek. There they'd talked under the stars for hours.

It was after midnight when they slipped in the rear door of the Aquarium. He held her hand and led her through the dimly lit, hushed halls. Other than the security guards who waved at Ethan as he passed, the entire building was deserted, save for the animals.

"It's so mysterious at night," she said.

"But you've been to parties here at night."

"Yes, but those are grand affairs with plenty of people. I've never been here when it's so empty. It feels like another world."

"It's my favorite time to come. Some of the animals are nocturnal. Wait here. I'll drop the keys off and be back in a minute. I'd like to show you something."

The great entry hall gleamed like burnished silver in the moonlight that poured in from the enormous plate glass windows. Toy's heels clicked as she walked the hall, waiting. Curious, she pushed open the door to the Mountain Forest section. The heavy door clicked on closing and the metallic sound reverberated in the deep, shadowed quiet.

Stepping into the darkness, the air changed from the cool of the air-conditioning to the sultry, moist air of a summer night. This area was open to the outdoors and a light, moist breeze caressed her cheeks. As she walked the winding path she was enveloped in the earthy, green scents of woodlands and felt mesmerized by the pale light that cascaded through the foliage, creating a mosaic of shadows on the floor. She heard the eerie, rhythmic hoots of an owl and from deep in the green, crickets and frogs sang their night songs.

When she approached the pond, she saw

that the river otters had been alerted by the noise of her arrival. The pair stood on tiptoes with their large soulful eyes open and alert, curious as to why a human was walking by the pond so late at night. One bold one scampered close to investigate, pressing its nose close to the glass that separated them. His luminous dark eyes were like pools in the moonlight. Toy bent lower to his level, equally curious, but in a flash he pushed off the glass, somersaulting into the water. She laughed as the second otter dove in after him.

"Toy?" Ethan called softly from the main hall.

"Coming!" She left the mysteries of the forest behind her as she hurried to the shadowed figure in the hall.

"It's wonderful in there," she said when she came to his side. "I felt like I was walking alone in a forest."

"Come with me. Wait till you see this."

He took her hand and led her to the gallery of the Great Ocean Tank.

"Oh, Ethan," she sighed as she entered the dimly lit arena.

If the forest was exotic at night, the Great Ocean Tank was other-worldly. Moon glow shimmered from high above, created by one of the fifteen incandescent lights at the top of the tank. The glow cast eerie wave shadows on the surrounding walls. Standing at the ocean's bottom, she saw the water's color deepen in degrees. She felt as though she stood within an ocean at deep night. The coral glowed and she watched in awe the mysteries unfolding before her. Ethan wrapped an arm around her waist and they stood, linked, watching as fish schooled slowly by.

After a few minutes, Toy sensed awkwardness between them, a holding back after an evening where they'd talked about whatever came to mind.

She'd opened up and told him about her harsh upbringing, how she'd left home while still in high school to live with Lovie's father, and how Darryl had abandoned her after she'd given birth to their child.

Tonight had been an evening of revelation for her. Ethan had expressed himself in words and in experiences. He'd traveled the world, yet she'd learned that he felt more at home here, with the sharks and fish of the Great Ocean Tank, than he did anywhere else. This was the culmination of his life's work. This mysterious, exotic, erotic world was part of him.

Toy understood it all. She had no need or desire for more talk. Yet she didn't know how to move from this painfully stiff moment to where she knew — hoped — they were heading. Was it up to him to make the decision? His arm grew tense around her waist.

Deciding, Toy leaned into his arms. One smooth movement, yet one filled with significance. She felt her body slide and mold against his. Each point of contact along her skin thrummed and she thrilled at feeling like a woman again, one of real flesh and blood, after so many years of isolation. Then she turned, wanting to see his face.

His gaze locked with hers and his eyes spoke eloquently of his desire for her, of his hesitancy, of his understanding that she was not one to be rushed.

She raised her hand and delicately skimmed her fingers through his hair, beginning at the temple and trailing down to curl around his ear. A small smile lifted the corners of his mouth as he, in turn, lifted his own hand and repeated the familiar motion. This time, however, he let his hand linger to cup her chin.

Yes, her eyes pulsed to him. *Yes* . . .

As though he'd heard her, he lifted her chin slightly and lowered his head slowly. She counted his approach in ragged breaths.

His lips veered to the left, scorching a trail across her neck, to kiss her ear. Then again to the right, to kiss the other. Pausing before her mouth, their breaths mingling, he said her name in a deep, anguished whisper, "Toy." Then he lowered his head and she felt his lips on hers.

Closing her eyes, Toy felt herself swirling, going deeper and deeper, letting go, until, with a soft gasp, she slipped beneath the depths.

Medical Log "Big Girl"
July 3
Observed turtle sleeping on the bottom of the tank, completely submerged.
At last, Big Girl! TS

12

The American flags along Palm Boulevard were waving in the breeze as Cara and Brett drove to the beach house. Golf carts festooned with red, white and blue crepe paper paraded down the side streets by Breach Inlet, dogs were walked in flag T-shirts and here and there she spied a henna flag tattoo on the taut, tanned midriffs and arms of the beautiful youth. The festive mood of the island permeated everyone on this favorite holiday. Traffic crawled over the connector from the mainland with visitors hoping to watch the fireworks from the beach and the congestion on the streets brought driving to a snail's pace.

The Fourth of July Celebration at the Rutledge beach house began five years earlier during that final summer of her mother's life. Miss Lovie had told Cara that the gathering was to celebrate just being alive and sharing time with those they loved most in the world. Her mother had smiled and said, *If that wasn't cause enough for fireworks, then she didn't know what was!*

Indeed, Cara thought as Brett pulled up to the pale yellow beach house her mother called Primrose Cottage. It was in continuation of that very sentiment that everyone came to the barbecue tonight. She saw Emmi's blue sports car and Palmer's Volvo wagon already parked, and of course, Toy's Gold Bug. Brett hurried around the car to help her out of the car.

"Don't you think you're going overboard on this 'mantling' thing?" she asked as she gave him her hand.

"I told you that I was giving you the full week," he quipped, guiding her out of the car.

"A whole week? Lucky me."

"You just sit in a chair and put your feet up. I don't want you doing any dishes or serving any food this year. You already spent too much time standing up making salads and baking."

"Brett, I like to cook and we planned this barbecue for weeks. I'm supposed to take it easy, not be holed up like an invalid."

"You've been cooking up a storm. There's always enough food to feed an army in there, anyway."

"It wouldn't be a family barbecue if there wasn't a mountain of food. That's half the fun."

"Well you can eat all you want but just sit down while you're doing it. Please. For me."

She heard the seriousness in his plea and readily capitulated. "Oh, all right. But I'm already late showing up and if I don't help clean up they'll think I'm a slacker."

"I'll help clean up for you."

"See? You say something like that and it is impossible to deny you anything." She leaned over the pie she was carrying to kiss his cheek. Then sighed and said, "They'll still think I'm a slacker."

"Not if you tell them you hurt your back."

"And you think they'll believe you? Flo's antennae will be wagging. She'll ferret out the truth, you just wait."

"Leave Flo to me. I'll get her talking about turtles and she won't be thinking about you."

Cara laughed, knowing it was true. A nest was due to hatch tonight and Flo was on tenterhooks that those babies would boil out during the fireworks and get trampled in the dark by the multitudes.

Brett went to the back of the car to collect the steamed crabs while Cara carried her blueberry pie to the front door. She waited at the porch and took a moment to survey the little plot of property that her mother had left her.

The beach house had been spruced up in the past several weeks. Brett had eked out time to make repairs on both this house and Flo's next door. All the trim of both houses was given a fresh coat of white paint. Meanwhile Cara, Emmi and Toy had a "weed fest." That consisted of a weekend of backbreaking work putting Flo's disheveled garden back in order. She chuckled at the memory of the three of them pulling weeds, digging holes, spreading mulch and planting colorful annuals in pots. Emmi had groaned over breaking her nails, but Flo had wept tears of pure joy. Despite her claims that the garden didn't mean much to her, she had since been seen strolling through her mother's garden, tugging a weed, plucking a deadhead, or just sitting on the front porch gazing out at the blossoms.

Cara sighed, recalling how her own mother had loved the wildflowers that covered the dunes of her property. Their riotous color had diminished in the high heat of summer. Now, Miranda's roses took center stage and were showy against the soft green dune grasses of her mother's property. Both women were gone now, she thought with a twinge of sadness. How she'd have loved to share her secret with them both.

Brett came up behind her, his arms straining with the weight of the steaming crabs. "Open the door!" he called out. "Hot stuff coming through!"

When they stepped into the house everyone turned and called out their names in welcome, then fussed over the steaming crabs.

"Just set those babies right here," Palmer called out.

"Wait!" Toy cried as she ran to clear a space on the already burgeoning tables of food on the screened porch. Little Lovie followed, telling everyone that these were the crabs she helped to catch with Uncle Brett.

"Have room for one more pie?" Cara asked. She saw Emmi's cherry pie and Flo's banana cream pie on the table.

"Your pie completes our red, white and blue theme," Toy replied as she took the pie from Cara. "Our barbecue is now complete."

Cara looked around the beach house. The cottage gleamed with that party shine. The sun was still high but Toy had turned on the fairy lights around the porch ceiling. They were a dim glow beside the red, white and blue streamers and American flags.

"Everything looks beautiful. You've done Mama proud," Cara told Toy, knowing no compliment could have been sweeter.

"I think we've got all the favorite family recipes," Toy said, looking over the feast like a worried hen. "All except for your Aunt Rebecca's black eyed peas. No one wanted to make it this year."

"Honey, you couldn't squeeze another dish onto that table without the legs giving out. You must have ten pounds of potato salad." She walked along the table, her stomach beginning to grumble for the different bean salads, crispy corn bread, golden fried chicken, pulled pork with Granddaddy Clayton's barbecue sauce, Cooper's favorite brownies and every kind of pickle known to Southern man.

"It'll take the month to eat all this," Cara said, then looking around the room asked, "who's all here?"

"The usual suspects," Toy replied. "Flo invited a few friends. Ethan's coming after he makes an appearance at his own family's party. Oh, listen to this. Palmer actually skipped the business rounds of parties this year. He spent the whole day with Cooper on the beach."

"Really?" she replied, feeling a gush of

pride for her brother. She'd been begging him for years to spend more time with his kids. "Good for him. I'm thinking that's because Linnea went off to camp on Friday. It might be a good thing she went, after all. Palmer dotes on her, but Cooper needs a little father-son time. Where's Emmi?"

"She's here somewhere, sulking." She leaned in. "Her date cancelled on her."

"Oh. Too bad."

"I don't know. Not if it was the guy I saw her with the other night. Ethan and I stopped at Red's Bar on our date and I saw her with this sketchy guy. A real snake oil salesman. I don't know where she finds them."

Cara sighed, suspecting she was finding them at the bottom of the barrel. "Was she drunk?"

Toy hesitated, then reluctantly nodded. "Plastered. I'm getting worried about her. I've never seen her like this. Is she okay?"

"She's just having a hard time," Cara replied, loyalty demanding that she make light of the problem. But in her heart, she was worried about Emmi, too. "I'd better go find her and say hello."

"Maybe get her to eat something, too. She's already had two gin and tonics."

"Ooh, boy," she replied on a sigh. Cara

walked through the living room, saying hello to Flo and meeting her two male friends, then checked the porches, seeing Cooper playing a card game with Lovie, and leaning against the pillars Brett and Palmer were talking. She peeked in the kitchen to find Toy at the sink filling a bucket with ice.

"You seen where Emmi's hiding?"

"Check the bedrooms."

Cara went down the narrow hall to the two small bedrooms. Little Lovie's room was empty. Across from it, the guest room door was half closed. Peeking in, she found Emmi sitting on the edge of the bed, a drink in one hand, the other paging through a glossy women's magazine.

"There you are!" she said, pushing open the door and stepping in. "I've been looking for you."

"I've been hiding out," Emmi replied. She was wearing white shorts and a T-shirt with bright red poppies that looked like they were blooming over her full breasts. "Come join me."

Cara stretched out on the creaky double bed that had belonged to Palmer when they were kids. Other than the laptop on the ancient school desk, the small, dark paneled room with the nautical print curtains and paintings of sailboats on the wall was much the same now as it always had been.

"How come you're so late?" Emmi asked her.

Cara was relieved that Emmi wasn't slurring her words. "Work. Holidays are always busy."

Emmi nodded, accepting that.

"How come you're hiding out back here?"

She shrugged. "I don't know. I just couldn't face the merrymaking."

Cara felt a stab of irritation. "Just because some bozo cancelled your date?"

Emmi looked up sharply. "Oh, you heard. I guess that bit of juicy gossip is making the rounds."

"No, it's not . . ."

"Spare me, I could care less. But no, not because of that." She sighed and her bravado fled as she closed the magazine and set it aside. "It's because of two other bozos. My sons, James and John. They were supposed to come down this weekend, but canceled, as usual."

"Maybe they were busy. You know how boys are at that age. They're driven by their hormones. They've got girlfriends and parties to go to."

"I know all that. But they didn't even call to tell me they weren't coming. They don't call at all. Not once since I got here."

"You're kidding?"

"They're busy," she replied quickly.

Cara felt outrage for her friend. Emmi always catered to her boys, and this was how they repaid her? How could they treat her so abominably? She'd always found them self-centered and spoiled and this latest proved her right. After the divorce, Emmi needed the support and love of her boys more than ever and it pained Cara to hear her make excuses for them. Yet, knowing all this, she wisely kept her opinions to herself.

"Well, here's to independence!" Emmi raised her glass then brought it to her lips. The ice clinked against the glass, spilling liquid down her chest.

"Oh, damn," she cursed, jerking back the drink and dabbing at the front of her shirt. "Now I'll smell like a still all night. And I have to refresh my drink." She rose, tottering slightly.

Cara clamped her lips tight from the words she wanted to say, knowing none of them would get through to Emmi now, in this mood. Never get between a man and his drink, her father used to say, and apparently it was true for a woman as well. But she felt helpless as she watched her dearest friend stride out of the room, no doubt straight for the liquor table.

■ ■ ■ ■

Palmer was first in line at the table for crabs.

Cara walked across the room to give him a quick hug. "Hey, brother mine! I heard you've been on the beach all day. The tan looks good on you."

"You know me. One hour in the sun does it. Cooper has my genes. Look at him," he said, proudly pointing to the lean, ten-year-old boy who was standing at the serving table wolfing down a barbecue pork sandwich. "Julia can't keep that boy in clothes, he's growing so fast. Reckon he'll be taller than me in no time." He sidled a glance at Cara. "Might be he'll even be as tall as you someday."

"Very funny. I was just thinking if he keeps eating like that he might get to be as fat as you someday."

Now it was Palmer's turn to laugh his rolling belly-laugh that always set Cara to laughing anew.

"Where've you been all day?" he asked. "I thought I'd see you on the beach. We had a beauty of a day."

"Holidays are work days for us," she answered.

"Brett says you hurt your back?"

"I just strained it, nothing serious. I'm following orders, trying to rest it some."

"Well, poor invalid, come over here," Palmer said, leading her to a quiet corner. "Sit yourself down while I get you a drink. I wanted to talk to you about something anyway. What's your poison? Wine? Beer? Gin and tonic? I made a batch myself and they're good."

"Just water, thanks. I'm thirsty."

"Coming right up."

She lowered herself into the cushy armchair in the front room and put her feet up on the ottoman. From the corner of her eye she spotted Brett watching her, nodding his head in approval. She waved him away with a chuckle then turned to see her brother come across the room with a glass of ice water for her and a fresh drink for himself.

"Thanks, Palmer. So, what's on your mind?"

He took the chair next to hers but instead of leaning back in the cushions like she did, he leaned forward with his elbows on his knees. "First, what the hell business do you have to be riding out on those wave runners the way you do? You're getting too old for that. See what happened to your back? Why doesn't Brett hire some young buck to do that kind of work?"

"I'm touched by your concern, but I wasn't even out on a wave runner. Besides, Brett did hire a college boy to guide and retrieve folks. He also hired a pretty blond girl to take reservations. He's cute and she's a looker." She sipped her water. "Business has never been better."

"I'll just bet," Palmer said with a laugh.

"I happen to love churning up the water on a wave runner, by the way. Is that what you wanted to tell me?"

"Partly." He took a sip of his gin and tonic and sidled closer. He swirled the ice in his glass a few times. "Remember our conversation about renting the beach house?"

"Yes," she replied, but her tone was wary. "I remember clearly telling you that I wasn't interested in renting it as long as Toy and Lovie needed or wanted to live here."

"I know, I know. But here's the thing. Just by coincidence I heard about someone who's looking for a beach house to rent. She's an artist and wants to live near the beach to paint."

Cara doubted it was by coincidence. "Palmer, you know I don't want to mess with short term rentals. Everything in the house is just too precious. I'd be afraid some party or young children would get careless and something would get broken."

"That's what makes this lady unique. She's older, maybe fifty-something, and she is looking for a long term rental."

"Do you know how much I'd have to charge her for that location?"

"Honey, I'm telling you, this house is exactly what she's looking for. And she's got pots of dough and can afford to pay you what this location is worth. Not the paltry sum you're collecting from Toy."

"Palmer . . ." she said in warning.

"It's a perfect set-up. We both know that a long term rental like that is hard to find. Look, I know how tight things are for you right now and that money could come in handy."

"Brett shouldn't have told you that."

"Hey, I'm your brother. He didn't go out of house."

"Even still."

"If you don't want this rental, so be it. The point is, it's time to talk to Toy about finding a new place."

"We'll see," Cara said, then dipped her head to sip her water.

Toy stood in the kitchen with a butter dish in her hand. She didn't mean to overhear Cara and Palmer's conversation, but she'd heard her name and paused at the door in

297

time to hear Palmer tell Cara to rent the house for more money.

A faint prickling spread across her face and her stomach felt like it had dropped to the floor. She didn't have any idea that Cara and Brett were stretched for cash. They'd never let on, or even hinted that they needed to raise her rent. She slowly turned and went back into the kitchen. Setting the butter on the counter she looked out over the dunes to the ocean, feeling dazed. She knew the day would come when she would have to leave the beach house. But that day had always seemed so far away — some distant time when her life was settled. The white-tipped waves rolled into the beach, one after another in constant motion. She took a long shuddering breath and closed her eyes. In truth, she never saw herself leaving the beach house. She couldn't even imagine living anywhere else but here, where she felt safe, secure, loved.

Ethan's words of the day before came back to her: *change is a part of nature.* She'd thrilled to those words the other night. Today, those same words shook her world.

Flo brought a plate full of food to Cara then plopped down in the chair beside her. Her hands grabbed hold of a bun filled with juicy barbecue pork and brought it to her mouth. She closed her eyes and released a slight groan of pleasure.

"I think the barbecue pork is the best ever this year," she said.

"You say that every year."

"Every year it's good, but this year the red sauce has some serious bite to it."

"I'm partial to the fried chicken myself. You done good, Flo. It's as light and crispy as can be."

"Thank you," Flo replied in a tone that implied she already knew that to be the case. "I did a little something different with the batter. Miranda never let me change a whit in the past, but this time . . . Oh, never mind. I can tell you really care."

"I've never been one for cooking. But I'm real proud of my pie."

Flo dabbed a bit of sauce from her chin with a crumpled flag napkin then said, "Frankly, I'll be glad when the festivities are over and done with this year."

"Oh? Aren't you having a good time?"

"Sure, sure. A great time. It's not that. I'm just in a frazzle whether that nest will pop tonight with all those people out there."

Cara hid her smile, recalling Brett's comment.

Flo looked at her, assessing. "So, I guess

you're out of commission tonight?"

"Afraid so. Sorry."

"Your back, eh?"

"Mmm-hmm," she replied, biting into her chicken.

"No nausea? Tender breasts? Anything like that?"

Cara looked heavenward. "Just the back."

Flo shifted in her chair and took another bite from her sandwich. "Like I said, I hope the hatchlings don't come out tonight. If they do, we'll need all the help we can get."

"With all the noise out there, I doubt it will hatch anyway."

"You never know, those wily turtles. Who'd have thought a turtle would come ashore right where a bunch of tourists were partying? Remember the Fourth of July that crazy sea turtle crawled up right at Front Beach?"

"Oh, yeah, I do remember! When was that? Two years ago? Three?"

"Four," she replied in a know-it-all tone. "That turtle couldn't have picked a worse spot to land, but crawl ashore she did. I remember I was eating dinner when the police called me to come over. I dropped everything and ran but by the time I'd arrived the turtle was surrounded by tourists. They were clicking cameras and trying to touch the shell. Most didn't know better, but still."

"I remember. Thank heavens Brett was there. He had to push back a few drunken fools who wanted to ride the turtle back to the sea like they'd heard their granddaddy once did. He almost got into a fight with one of them. I was fit to be tied."

"Thank goodness the police came to *explain* the facts to them." Flo shook her head, sending her dangling earrings rocking. "That poor turtle, she was frantic. I've never seen a sea turtle hiss at a body before that. And I mean never to see it again."

"From your lips to God's ears."

"Well, let's hope nothing happens tonight. If it does, we'd sure need you out there."

"I can't, Flo. I could ask Brett to cover for me."

"No, don't bother him. He has precious few nights off. Well," Flo said rising like a bolt. "I'm going for seconds on this barbecue before Cooper eats it all. I swear that boy's been parked in front of that pork all night. He's growing right before my eyes."

Later that evening, when the sky began to darken and the food was cleared from the tables, Brett earned the accolades of the women and teasing of Palmer when he went into the kitchen to help clean up after the feast. All the focus quickly shifted from him, however, as soon as Ethan walked into the room.

Flo and Emmi were at his side faster than hungry swamp mosquitoes on a humid night. He was dressed in casual island attire — khaki shorts, a loose shirt and sandals. His dark hair was brushed back from his forehead to settle loosely along the collar of his shirt. He had a strongly featured face that was proud yet not aloof. His eyes were deeply set and he wasn't afraid to look someone straight in the eye while he fielded their questions with a polite evasiveness that impressed Cara.

She was sitting like a queen bee in her chair off in the corner, watching. This evening she'd discovered that she liked being invisible. People walked past her to join in other conversations and it afforded her the chance to simply observe.

She saw the speculation in Brett's eyes as he checked out this young suitor of Toy's. In contrast, Palmer was all handshakes and welcome, no doubt hoping this young man would marry Toy and carry her off someplace — anyplace — other than the beach house. The lady in question seemed coquettish when she went to greet Ethan and gently but firmly unwound Emmi's arm from his and replaced it with her own. As she made the introductions, Cara saw a spark in Toy's eyes that she had never seen before. When she saw Ethan turn his head to look at Toy, she saw that same spark in his eyes.

Very interesting, she thought as she rose from her chair. It was high time she got to know this man better. She took but one step when the first boom of a firecracker burst in the sky, startling them all. Cooper whooped and hollered for everyone to hurry up as he bolted for the rear door with Little Lovie in hot pursuit. En masse, they grabbed a drink or a sweater and marched to the rhythm of percussive explosions to the rear porch that faced the ocean, excitement bubbling for the big show to begin. To their right, they could see in the distance the finale of the Sullivan's Island fireworks. Then boom! An explosion of color burst straight ahead over the ocean in all its whistling glory. Brett came to stand beside her and wrapped his arm around her shoulder. Together they lifted their gazes to the sky.

It was a perfect night for fireworks. The weather was neither too hot nor humid and just a breath of breeze blew in from the ocean. A friendly family crowd sat on towels and blankets on the beach. They oohed, aahed and clapped after each aerial display of red, white and blue that thundered in the sky. When a series of great chrysanthemum patterns exploded directly overhead, lighting up the sky in gold, the neighbor's dog barked and Cooper brought his fingers to his lips and let loose a piercing whistle of approval, eliciting guffaws from his father and a "shhh" from his mother.

Turning her head, Cara caught sight of Ethan dipping his head to kiss Toy's upturned lips. They seemed to glitter in the golden light. Leaning against her husband, Cara smiled as the sky exploded once more with brilliant colors that bloomed across the sky.

13

Big Girl's rear was causing problems.

Toy, Ethan and Jason huddled around the tank discussing how to keep the turtle from floating.

"We're going to have to move her from the big tank," Ethan decided.

"No, Ethan, she loves the big tank," Toy argued. "She's been doing so well with the swimming and exercise. I hate to move her out."

"We've been going round and round with this problem and still no success," Jason argued. "I don't like the way her swimming is so labored. How many eggs did she release?"

"Fifteen total, but not any for a couple of weeks. Her shell is clean and she's eating well, catching food under water. Plus she's gaining weight. That's all good."

"But something's not right if she can't fully submerge."

They stood for a few minutes watching the turtle swim. Big Girl spent most of her time in an awkward head down, tail up position. Toy knew that Jason was right to make a new plan, but she thought the decision to move the turtle from the big tank and putting her back in a small one was the wrong one to make.

"Before we decide to take her out of the tank, I have a few ideas I'd like to try," Toy said. She glanced at Ethan. They'd discussed her idea and he nodded his head briefly, encouraging her to go on.

"Now, just think about this and don't laugh. What if we put a diver's weight belt on her?" she asked. "It would give her the boost she needs to stay under water."

"A diver's belt?" Jason asked, incredulously. "On the turtle?"

"Why not? It might just do the trick of keeping her submerged."

Ethan spoke up. "It's thinking outside the box, Jason."

Jason had a bemused expression on his face as he considered it.

"We could just give it a try," Toy said. "She's had the endoscopy, medications, and though she's improved, her rear still floats. We'd have to secure together two belts to get around an adult loggerhead, but hey!

This idea would give her the tincture of time she needs to heal. What have we got to lose?"

Jason watched the turtle as it swam in a circle around the tank, rear up. He shrugged. "Okay, we can try it. I don't know how your turtle is going to like the new fashion statement, but if it keeps her from floating . . ."

"We'll watch her closely and adjust the weight. If it doesn't work, we can do a second endoscopy," she countered. "I've read that if we limit the belt procedure to fifteen minutes, it shouldn't be stressful for her."

Toy noticed a sharper attention in Jason's eyes that spoke of respect for her opinion. When she first began working at the hospital, she went to Ethan and Jason with countless questions and for approval of her decisions. As the summer peaked and everyone became overworked, however, necessity forced her to trust her own decisions and not go to Jason or Ethan for approval. It occurred to her that Jason had come to this realization as well.

"Let's do it," Jason said enthusiastically. He liked innovative solutions.

Ethan immediately went to get a couple dive belts from his supply, eager to test out the theory. When he returned a short while later he was wearing his dive suit and was accompanied by Favel and a strange woman dressed in an Aquarium volunteer T-shirt. With her head of striking white hair Toy guessed her to be in her late sixties.

"Look who I found wandering the halls looking for a turtle hospital," Ethan said.

Favel greeted them with a brief wave but the woman walked straight for them with a smile that lit up her beautiful blue eyes.

"I'm Elizabeth," she said in a forthright manner and extending her hand. "Elizabeth Scrimgeur. I've been assigned to the sea turtle hospital as a volunteer."

Toy almost gasped aloud. She quickly took the hand and pumped it, afraid if she let go she'd lose her first full time volunteer.

"You're assigned to the turtle hospital?" she asked. "Nowhere else?"

"I'm all yours," Elizabeth replied with enthusiasm. "I'm a turtle team volunteer on Folly Beach and a self professed turtle fanatic. Just tell me what you want me to do and I'll do it."

"I like the attitude," Jason said, then stepped forward to introduce himself. "We all chip in where we're needed, but this program is growing fast. Welcome aboard."

"And just in time," Ethan said, stepping

up with the dive belts in his hands. "You're about to get an introduction to our first — and biggest — patient. Come on over and meet Big Girl, up close and personal."

As they walked past the tanks, Toy gave brief histories of the patients: Cherry Point, Hamlin, Sharkbite and Kiawah. The turtles swam close to the edges of the tanks, their almond eyes watchful as Toy passed.

"They seem to know you," Elizabeth said.

"Oh, these moochers. They're just hungry," she said, looking at the turtles with affection. "They each have their own personality. After we take care of Big Girl, I'll show you how to feed them. They do know who I am and are wary of strangers, but they'll warm up to you in no time. There's a lot to learn so we'll just take it one day at a time."

"I'm eager to learn," Elizabeth replied her eyes lingering on each turtle as she passed.

Toy smiled, understanding that fascination completely. Once smitten with sea turtles, it was a love affair for life.

By the time Toy and Elizabeth got to Big Girl's tank, Ethan had already climbed in. This large, 11,000 gallon tank had been Big Girl's home for the past few weeks and she swam quickly away with powerful strokes of her flippers, giving Ethan a hard time rounding her up. Toy climbed the platform of the large tank while Ethan tried to chase and maneuver Big Girl closer to her. Jason, Favel and Elizabeth stood at the ready, waiting for the chance to grab hold of the turtle and haul her out.

"Ethan, get a move on!" Toy called to him as she leaned over the edge of the tank. "She's getting past you."

"Hey, you come in here and see if you can do it better," he called back. He was chest deep in the water with his long arms outstretched, trying to herd the enormous turtle closer.

"Do you want me to get in there with her?" the new volunteer asked. "I'm not afraid of getting wet."

Toy turned from the tank to look at her. She had the agility of a woman half her age and was reaching for the turtle, not the least inhibited. "I'm sorry, what's your name again?"

"Elizabeth."

"Well, Elizabeth, watch your hand. Those jaws are powerful and I'd hate to see you bitten on your first day. You'll have plenty of opportunity to get in that tank in the future, but since this is your first day, we'll let you stay dry. We need all the help we can get on this side just to haul her out. She's one big turtle."

"But be careful," Jason chimed in. "Big Girl is wise to this maneuver and every time she comes near she gets her revenge by heaving water at us. If she looks you in the eye, duck."

Ethan herded the big turtle towards them. As Big Girl swam closer, she lifted her head out of the water with a noisy gasp for air. As her head skimmed just above the water, her dark, almond eyes looked at Elizabeth as if taking her measure.

"Duck!" Jason called.

In a swoosh, the turtle pushed the water with her flipper and a wave of water gushed from the tank, splashing Elizabeth from head to toe.

Dripping wet, Elizabeth sputtered with shock as Toy prayed Big Girl hadn't cost them her first volunteer. Elizabeth caught her breath then threw back her head and laughed. It was a hearty sound, contagious. Relieved, they all joined in.

"Hey, welcome to the team," Ethan called out from the tank. "You've just been baptized."

"Big Girl's gotten all of us at one time or another," Toy said. "If a turtle could smile, she'd be grinning from ear to ear right now, the stinker."

"Come on, Ethan," Jason called out.

"You're swimming like a girl in there. Be a cowboy and round up that turtle."

"Hee haw," Ethan called back and once again, tried to maneuver the wily, two-hundred-fifty-pound turtle closer to them. This time when Big Girl swam by Toy determinedly flung herself forward to grab hold of the carapace.

"Got her!" she called out.

In synchronized motion, Jason and Ethan lunged forward to grab the carapace and as a group they brought the huge, flipper-flailing hulk out from the tank. Elizabeth grabbed a side of the shell, and in a seal-like motion, Ethan pulled himself from the tank and again took hold of the shell. They maneuvered Big Girl to the scale where they weighed her, then moved her to a long stain-less steel table where they completed the procedure that secured a four-pound weight with a wrap.

As she worked on the belt, Toy tried not to laugh at the jokes flying fast and furious between Ethan and Jason, all having to do with fashion, the dive belt and unlikely scenarios. Even laughing they got the job done and had the turtle back in her tank in no time.

Big Girl was highly indignant nonetheless. Once she hit water she swam furiously to the opposite side of the tank, all flippers flailing. She took a few spins around the tank before she finally settled down. Toy leaned against the big tank, holding her breath as she watched and waited.

With relative ease, Big Girl dove to the bottom of the tank. Once there, she glided along the bottom in a slow sulk.

"It works!" Toy exclaimed and she clutched Ethan's arm. "Look, she's on the bottom!"

"Well, whaddya know," Jason said with a clap of his hands. His smile reflected both his approval and surprise that the belt had actually done the job. "Good job, team."

Ethan wrapped an arm around her shoulders. She smiled up into his face. Then she looked over to see Elizabeth standing, soaked to the skin, with a puzzled expression.

"You have to understand that this turtle's rear has been floating for weeks and we've been pulling our hair out trying to figure a way to help her dive," Toy told her. "She's had a litany of treatments. Now look at her! She's resting on the bottom. You came on a good day. To celebrate, how about I get you a dry T-shirt?"

"That'd be great, thanks," Elizabeth replied, relief etched on her face. "But before everyone leaves can I ask, who is in charge here? Who do I report to?"

There was a moment's hesitation. First, everyone naturally looked to Jason. But Jason's gaze was firmly, meaningfully, on Toy.

She felt his gaze on her but her own gaze turned inward. This was a defining moment. Her chest rose and fell as a calm certainty settled within herself. She'd worked hard for this position. She had earned it. The turtle hospital's creation and success was shared, and yet, at this moment, in the eyes of an outsider, she saw *herself* as its director. And that, she knew, made all the difference.

Toy turned to Elizabeth, her conviction welling up. "I'm head of the turtle hospital," she said in an unwavering voice. "You report to me."

Truth be told, Emmi had been a worry these past weeks. Cara felt she hardly knew her. Since she'd come to the island, Emmi's determined, single-minded focus had shifted from her family exclusively to single men. She was man hungry, there was no other way to describe her fervor in dating. And it was like she was trying to be young again, not only in the way she dressed but in the way she acted, too. It was plain embarrassing to witness.

And then there was the drinking. On the surface Emmi might look like she was living a good time but Cara had known her since she was eight and she'd never known Emmi to hit the bottle like she'd been doing lately. She'd tried to give Emmi her space, but friends didn't let friends wallow. It was time for a serious heart-to-heart.

Cara rode her bicycle from Seventh Avenue to Ocean Boulevard, thankful for the salty ocean breeze that stirred the soaring heat of midsummer. Theirs was a neighborhood of small, original beach houses, like her own and Emmi's, interspersed with the newer, bigger houses that seemed to be replacing them. It always annoyed her when builders referred to the original, small houses on the islands as "tear downs," as though the wrecking ball was only a matter of time. She pedaled past a charming, pink stucco house that had been at the corner for as long as she could remember. She worried that with the tearing down of the quaint original beach houses to build the mansions, the island would also be destroying its residential charm.

Hers and Emmi's houses were only blocks apart, too close to excuse the few times she'd stopped at Emmi's for a cup of coffee or dinner over the past few months. She rode up the cracked driveway, squeezing her hand brakes till they squeaked. The rusty bicycle finally stopped before a modest beach house. She swung her leg over the bar and rested the bike against the trellis. The house looked much the same as it had since they were children. She used to ride her bike from her beach house down the boulevard to the Baker's house to hang out, and if they got bored or were hungry for different snacks, they got on their bikes and rode back to the Rutledge house.

To Cara, the white wooden cottage on low wood pilings would always be the Baker House. Even after Emmi married Tom, no one referred to it as the Peterson house. She was relieved to see that the trim was freshly painted and that a pot of cheery red geraniums with trailing vines sat in a large terracotta pot on the porch. No one answered her knocks so she poked her head in, like she'd been doing this since she was eight.

"Emmi? Cover up, girl, I'm coming in!"

Stepping in, she almost stumbled over a pile of books. She caught herself, then looked around the front room, aghast.

Her first thought was that a hurricane had

hit the inside of Emmi's house. Cardboard boxes littered the floors, each half filled with the contents of the open cabinets and drawers. The counters were cluttered with more boxes, rolls of tape, papers and dishes ready to be packed.

Emmi came walking into the room carrying a pile of blankets in her arms. Her face was chalky with fatigue and her red hair was held precariously in place with a single plastic clasp. She wore a bright yellow apron dotted with red chili peppers over an orange spandex top and chocolate brown yoga pants. She stopped short when she spotted Cara in the foyer.

"Hey!" she exclaimed in surprise, her mouth stretching to a delighted grin. "This is a nice surprise. What brings you here?"

"I haven't heard from you for a while so I thought I'd stop by. What's going on?"

"Packing up. I swear, it's harder than I thought to pack up two generations worth of junk. Every closet was crammed full. I don't know what to do with it all."

"Call Goodwill?" Cara replied wryly. She'd been teasing Emmi for years that she ought to toss out all the old furniture and freshen up the place.

"I wish. But everything has some sentimental attachment. It's taking forever."

"You and Flo, both. You hang on to stuff forever." She looked around the place and thought how given one truck and lots of empty boxes, she could get the job done in a day. "Looks like you could use some help with the packing. Why didn't you call? And why the big hurry?"

It was an innocent enough question, she thought, but for some reason it had the power to unnerve Emmi. She dumped the blankets unceremoniously into an empty box, then, hands on her hips, stared out the window to regain her composure.

"I've found a buyer for the house."

Cara hadn't expected this. "So fast? Wow, that's great." When she saw Emmi's lip tremble she did a double take. "Isn't it great? Emmi, why are you crying? Isn't that what you wanted?"

"Not like this," she said, dropping her face in her hands.

Cara came closer, putting her hand gingerly on Emmi's shoulder. A box of tissue was on the table beside foam cups filled with cigarette butts. She yanked out a tissue and handed it to her. Emmi took it and blew her nose lustily then tossed the tissue in a box filled with trash.

"Are you having second thoughts? It's only natural you would. You've always loved it here. Emmi, you don't have to sell it if you've changed your mind. Do you want to keep the house?"

Emmi shook her head. "No. You don't understand. Cara, it's *Tom* who wants to buy the house."

Cara's mouth opened with astonishment. "Your Tom? I don't understand."

"It was a shock to me, too. He called the other day. James and John were with him, of course. Apparently, after I told the boys that I was putting the beach house on the market, they joined forces and went straight off to tell their father. Tom was livid. First he railed at me for putting the house on the market without consulting him. Can you believe his arrogance? Consulting him . . . We're divorced! I told him I wouldn't consult him on what color I should paint my toe nails much less anything to do with my life or my house, thank you very much. And this *is* my house. My parents gave it to *me,* not him. It's almost as if they expected this to happen."

"No, of course they didn't. You two were in love."

Emmi paused, as though letting that statement sink in. Cara wanted to get the rest of the story before she collapsed into a blubbering mess. "Go for the mascara while you're at it," she said, offering another tissue. "You look like a raccoon."

Emmi sniffed and made two swipes under her eyes then dabbed at her nose.

"So what happened then?" Cara asked, moving a box from a blue floral armchair and flopping into it.

"There was a row. Again. He brought up the same old argument about how he gave me the house in Atlanta so the boys could keep their home and how it was wrong of me to sell it. How that made things more difficult for them. When I told him how I had no choice but to sell the house because I couldn't afford to live in it on the measly amount of money he'd settled on me after twenty-five years, he had the nerve to tell me I needed to learn how to be frugal. I don't get any child support, you know. Trust me, that monstrosity of a house needed more cash than I could wrangle being frugal."

"I know," Cara replied, feeling her blood begin to boil. She couldn't believe Tom could be so heartless after so many years of marriage.

"And get this. He had the gall to tell me that he deliberately did not include the beach house in the divorce settlement because he knew how much it meant to the boys and he didn't want to see it sold for the settlement. So, he thinks it's like I'm cheating somehow to sell it now, after the divorce. As though I'm sneaky and planned the whole thing in advance. Like he did with that trophy wife-to-be.

"The worst part is that the boys think this, too. They took turns begging me not to sell it, telling me how much they love it and how they want to come here with their friends. Hello! Did they forget that if I kept it, it wouldn't be just a beach house anymore? That I need a place to live in, too?" She tore at her tissue, sending bits of paper floating in the air. "Or, maybe they just don't care."

"They're being incredibly selfish. You've spoiled them, Emmi."

She broke down into tears and this time, Cara let her cry. What a mess a divorce could be, she thought. She was there when Emmi and Tom had fallen in love, she'd been a bridesmaid at their wedding, a godmother to their sons. All that had been built together with hope for the future and love was now being ripped apart, piece by piece, leaving nothing in its wake but anger and resentment.

"And," Emmi cried, grabbing for another tissue, "here's the best part. Tom starts lighting into me that since I already sold the *family* house in Atlanta, how I ought not to sell the family beach house, too. How it means too much to the *family.* How we should keep it for the *family.* He kept using that word, *family.* I thought I was going mad and screamed back at him, What *family?* There's no family anymore. He broke up the family, didn't he remember that?"

"It sounds like he's trying to shift the blame on to you," Cara said. "That's a new low, even for him. If he'd managed to keep his family business in his pants none of this would have happened in the first place and his family would still be together."

"And now he gets to walk in and grandly tell me — in front of the boys — that he's going to make it all better by buying the beach house. Not for himself, he assured me. He was putting it in the boys' names. He's paying me the full asking price." She reached out and wagged her fingers in an exaggerated motion. "No more negotiating or haggling over money with the harridan. He wants me to FedEx the contract so he can sign the papers and get it over with, once and for all." She released a ragged sigh then repeated softly, "Once and for all."

Emmi shrugged, releasing a short, bitter laugh. When she spoke again, the anger had fled and was replaced by a softer, hurt tone. "So, there it is. Tom is buying my beach house." She sighed and turned to look at Cara, her green eyes reddened and wounded. "Ever since I was eight years old I had a crush on him. You should know. You were there. For thirty-two years he hung around this house. And now I find out that's what he wanted all along. The house. It was never me he cared about. He was in love with my goddamn house!"

"Emmi, first of all, that's just not true. Like you said, I was there. Tom loved you. He's an idiot for losing you and it breaks my heart to see how he's treating you. But once upon a time, he did love you. As for the house, you don't have to sell to him, you know."

"I know! Of course I know that," she exclaimed loudly, letting her frustration blurt out. Her lips tightened as she struggled for composure. "I sat all alone for hours and thought about it and thought about it." She shook her head with resignation and defeat. "And it all makes sense. If I want to sell the house, and James and John love this place and he's willing to pay me to give it to them, then I'd be a fool not to let him."

"You *would* get to keep the beach house in the family," Cara said, playing devil's advocate.

Emmi nodded, looking down at the torn tissue in her lap. "Except, I wouldn't be the one to pass it on to them." She looked up and her eyes were full of defeat. "Tom would get all the credit for that. He gets to be the big hero coming in to save the day, brandishing a check faster than a speeding bullet."

Cara rose to walk to the window. She remembered sitting on this porch when they were children, rocking back and forth on the porch swing while talking about their dreams. Cara was going to be a ballerina. Emmi wanted to be a marine biologist until she met Tom Peterson. Her dreams had changed then to wanting nothing more than to be Tom's wife and the mother of his children.

She turned and, crossing her arms said in her forthright manner, "Emmi, you don't have to sell. You could keep the beach house and live in it full time. The boys could visit you here. Maybe not with carloads of pals and booze, but nonetheless . . ."

"I thought about that, too," Emmi replied more soberly. Cara's matter-of-fact attitude was having its effect. "But that won't work for me. You see, for the past weeks that I've been living here, I've been haunted by the memories of us — the Peterson family. Everywhere I look there's a photograph on a table or a memento on the shelf. I don't know if I can get past the divorce if I stayed here. I'm having a hard enough time without a million reminders surrounding me of what's gone. It'd be like living in a mausoleum.

"No," she shook her head. "I need to start my new life. Without Tom. And I can't do it here."

Cara was fresh out of ideas. She came back to the chair and sat on the arm. "Well, then, Emmi, you've got to be realistic. If you don't want to live here, and you can't afford to keep it for the boys, then Tom stepping up to buy the house is the best thing that could happen. Consider it your way of getting the money that you should have in the divorce settlement. The Lord works in mysterious ways."

"Oh, Cara." She looked so crestfallen, so completely and utterly defeated, it shocked Cara to see it. "I didn't care about that big house in Atlanta. But why couldn't *this* house — my family house — have been *my* gift to the children? After all these years I'm suddenly nothing. I have nothing. I'm jealous of Tom and what he can buy for the boys. What do I have to give them?"

Cara came to sit on the sofa. She wrapped her arms around Emmi's shoulders and drew her near. "Did I ever tell you what my mother said to me that night we were holed up at our beach house during the hurricane? Right before she died?"

Emmi nodded. "She told you that she was leaving you the beach house. I remember because you were very emotional about it. You'd thought she was leaving it to Palmer."

"That's right. That night at the height of the storm, she told me that she'd always meant for me to have it, not because of any monetary value, but simply because she knew that I loved it. That meant the world to me. I felt then, as I do now, that it didn't matter if the hurricane came that night and took the house away. What she gave me that night was my sense of worth. I knew I mattered enough to have been considered."

"And that's supposed to make me feel better? That you felt worthy in your mother's eyes because she gave you the beach house? Great."

"You're not letting me finish. It wasn't about the house at all, don't you see? What Mama told me that night, what I've held close to my heart, is that in the end, the beach house was not so much a place as a state of mind. It's a sanctuary. The beach, the ocean, the solitude — these are only a means to help us travel to the true peace that lies deep inside of us. Mama told me to sell it if I had to. And maybe I will someday. But I'll always have the beach house because the magic of the beach house is not contained within four walls. The beach house is only a symbol of my mother's love for me."

She took Emmi's hand. "You are James and John's mother. Nothing will ever change that. You've been the rock of your family. *You* are the one who created the happy memories here in this house. *You* are the one who stayed up at night with them when they were sick, and the one who never missed a violin performance, a soccer game, or a photo op for the prom. *You* listened to their stories and bandaged their wounds. *You* are the one your boys will bring their wives home to meet, and their own families to visit. Because no matter where you are, Emmi, *you* are their home.

"Your duty now is to find that peace deep inside of you again so that you can welcome them with serenity and joy." She paused then asked, "Honey, I've got to ask you, what's with all this sexy spandex you've been wearing? And all that talk about wild sex and trying to be eighteen on the *outside* again? You need to find Emmi *inside* of you.

That wild, wonderful girl I grew up with who was afraid of nothing and believed she could be anything she wanted to be in the whole wide world. She's been hiding. Dig deep and call that girl back out! I miss her!"

Emmi released a half sob, half laugh. "So do I!"

Emmi had moved her head from Cara's shoulder and sat looking at her with eyes like two emerald flames in her face. Cara saw in them the hope that what she said might actually be true. Then Emmi took a deep breath, shuddered, and slowly straightened to an upright position. Releasing the breath, she scrubbed her face with a palm.

"I need a shower," she said. "And some dinner. I'm starved."

"Brett's bringing home some clams and I've got a crusty loaf of French bread and some fabulous green olive oil. We'll have a feast."

"Afterwards I'll finish packing and clean up this place."

"I'll help you."

She turned her head. "You realize I'm homeless. I'll need to find a place to live."

"You will. Again, I'll help you."

"Okay, then." She slapped her palms on her knees and stood. She brought her pink tipped nails to her head and raked the long red tresses, groaning loudly, like she was waking herself up from a bad dream. Then she dropped her hands and slanted a glance at Cara. Something wicked sparked in those green eyes.

"I'm gonna let ol' Tom buy this house. And just for him, I'll even jack up the price."

Cara laughed and clapped her hands. "She's back!"

14

July was arguably the busiest month for the turtle ladies. In the morning they were on call for the turtles that laid nests during the night, and in the evening they sat by the nests that were due to hatch. Some nights the moon shed its golden light upon a smooth beach, the tide was in, and the hatchlings scampered to the sea lickety-split. On such nights, Cara went home tired but fulfilled.

Other nights the sky was dark with clouds and the mosquitoes outnumbered the stars. Cara slathered on bug spray and sat huddled by the nest wearing a long-sleeved shirt and pants. These were the nights their dedication was tested.

It was on such a night that Toy went with Cara and Little Lovie to a sand dune to wait for a turtle nest to hatch. Little Lovie had proved to be a devoted turtle lady — or "Little Turtle Lady" as Brett had nicknamed her and had it printed on a T-shirt. Cara and Toy sat in beach chairs by the nest, their legs stretched out before them, and watched as Little Lovie walked the nearby beach and stuffed spartina into sand crab holes.

Toy had been hoping for some time alone with Cara ever since the Fourth of July party. Palmer's advice to Cara about renting the beach house still brought a prickly flush of anger whenever she recollected his words. Why couldn't Palmer just mind his own business? They were happy with the arrangement; things were moving along smoothly. Why did he have to go stirring up the mud?

But Palmer's suggestion had stayed in her mind, niggling her at quiet moments, demanding that she get past the affront and look objectively — honestly — at what Palmer was saying. She wanted to remain angry at him, but in truth, Cara *could* get a lot more money renting to someone else. The underlying question was how long could Cara continue to support Toy and Little Lovie?

Then Toy had thought about all of Cara and Brett's new expenses with the business expansion and how they'd been spending serious money on the in vitro processes. Cara and Brett lived in a modest house and lived a quiet lifestyle. Toy had always thought of Cara Rutledge as someone who was rich, without worries about money. Yet, what if she wasn't? What if that was merely convenient for Toy to believe? What if Cara was like so many people who had their money tied up in their businesses? What if she was pinching pennies and worrying about her bills, the same as Toy?

That image set root in Toy's mind and immediately she knew it was the truth. Seeing Cara in that light was an equalizer. Cara was not her mother or her aunt, not even her sister. Cara Rutledge Beauchamps was a friend.

And a friend did not take advantage of a friend.

Toy scooted her beach chair closer, dragging it through the sand.

Seeing her draw near, Cara leaned forward toward her. "Want some bug spray?"

"No, I'm fine."

"Water?"

"Yeah, actually. I finished mine."

Cara dug into her canvas bag, pulled out a bottle of water and handed it to her. While Toy twisted off the cap, she licked her dry lips, nervous about what she wanted to say.

"It's a hot night," said Cara after a long drink.

Toy nodded and clasped her hands together, feeling grit in her palms.

"Where's Ethan? I haven't seen him in a couple nights. He's becoming quite the fixture at the beach house."

"He's speaking at a fundraiser."

"I'll bet he's a good speaker. He's smart, his voice is low and rich — and if the women aren't interested in his topic, they can just stare at him for an hour. It's a win-win presentation."

"Very funny. He's actually very knowledgeable and interesting to listen to," Toy said, feeling a bit defensive of Ethan.

"I'm sure he is," Cara deadpanned. "Just as I'm sure he gets lots of contributions. Who could say no to him?" She slanted her gaze. "Not you, apparently."

"Cara . . ."

"Sorry, dear, but it was too easy. You know how we feel about Ethan. Brett and I like him very much. And Flo dotes on him. Not every fellow would spend most of Saturday helping Brett repair Flo's fence."

Toy's smile was spontaneous. "He is special," she replied, remembering how proud she'd felt watching him from the beach house window as he and Brett labored at Flo's house.

"The fence looks marvelous, doesn't it?

Do you think we could hoodwink that boy of yours into helping Brett build a fence for our beach house? Oh, by the way, Flo's cooking barbecue on Friday night and she wants us all to come, especially Ethan."

"Just say the word barbecue and Ethan will be there."

They chuckled at this common response in lowcountry men.

"Cara," Toy said, edging forward on her chair. "Now we're on the topic of houses, there's something I want to talk to you about."

Cara leaned back against the canvas chair and set the bottle of water on the sand. "Oh? What's that?"

"Well," Toy began hesitatingly. She took a breath and said in a rush, "I overheard what Palmer said to you at the party the other night. About the rent for the beach house."

"Oh, no," Cara replied, leaning forward. She rested her forearms on her knees shaking her head. "Damn that Palmer."

"No, he was being a good brother to you, looking out for your interests. And he's right. You could get a lot more money for that house from someone else."

"Toy, that doesn't matter. You and I have gone over this. I'm happy with our arrangement."

"But I'm not sure I'm happy with it." She saw Cara's stunned expression and, seeing that she'd misunderstood, hurried to add, "Cara, I'm grateful, of course. But I love you too much to take advantage of your and Brett's kindness. You've been helping me for five years, ever since Miss Lovie passed on. I never could have made it through school if it weren't for you. You're a second mother to Little Lovie."

"That's what I want, what I've always wanted."

"I know, truly I do. But I'm on my feet now. I've made it, thanks to you and Brett and Flo. I've a long way to go," she added with a light laugh, "but I can take care of myself more and depend on you less. That's all I'm saying." She took a breath. "And I can start by finding a new place to live."

"I don't know if I like that. I want you close by. I want that child near me. Where would you go?"

"Gosh, I don't know exactly, but not far. Mt. Pleasant, maybe? Little Lovie would be furious to be far from the turtle team. You're her life. And mine."

"Have you saved any money? That's the first thing. You'll need a down payment. And rents are high in Mt. Pleasant. Maybe I know someone . . ."

"Cara, listen to yourself. You're figuring everything out for me, like you've always done." Once again she felt a stabilizing calm within. "I can do this."

Cara didn't say anything at first. She just looked at Toy with a quizzical expression, like she was seeing her change before her very eyes. Then she leaned back in her chair. "Let's not decide tonight? Let's just agree to start thinking about it. We'll get through the summer and see where we are come fall. How does that sound to you?"

"Sounds good. It'll give me time to save some money and look around."

"Just don't go looking too hard. You'll find someplace and be gone before I can think this through. Just because my bossy brother thinks I can get more money doesn't mean I want it. I like having you in Mama's house. It feels right, and I know she likes it that way. She wanted you to live there, you know."

"Oh, Lord," Toy said, tearing up. "You had to go and mention your mother, didn't you? I was doing just fine but now we'll start to cry and I'll never be able to leave the beach house."

"I never cry," Cara said with a short laugh. "But I might get misty."

"One question," Toy said, wiping her eyes.

She had to ask and hoped it wasn't too personal. "I don't mean to pry, but how are you and Brett financially? Do you need the extra income from the beach house?"

Cara twisted her lips the way she did when she was wrestling with what she wanted to say. A myriad of expressions flitted across her face — surprise, vulnerability, sadness and finally honesty. She nodded her head slightly, barely enough for Toy to notice.

"Thank you," Toy said, her voice low with emotion. "For all you've done for Little Lovie and me, thank you."

Cara's cell phone rang, and Toy was relieved that the conversation ended on such a positive note. It was Flo calling from her nest on the other side of the island and she sounded frantic. Cara waved Toy closer to listen in.

"Y'all better come here right away!" Flo said in a strained voice. "We had a boil, but it's a disaster. When the hatchlings emerged from the nest, they began heading toward the ocean. But the sky's so dark tonight. Once the turtles passed the shadow of the dune, the darn lights from the city behind them were so bright that the hatchlings got all confused, turned around and headed back toward the street! Mary, Barb and Tee are here, and I called Bev, Nancy and

Kathey. I need the whole team here quick."

"We'll be right over." Cara hung up and turned to Toy who was waiting for the report. "It's a boil."

Lovie clapped her hands excitedly, saying, "Oh goodie!"

"Whoa there," Toy said, placing a firm hand on her daughter's shoulder. "It's getting late for you."

"But Mama . . ."

"You know the deal. We stay till ten o'clock at the latest and it's already almost ten. Way past your bedtime. No, don't get all pouty. You're lucky I let you stay up so late at all."

"But Mama, it's a boil!" The child was on tiptoe, pleading.

Cara was gathering her chair and supplies. She turned to Toy. "Is tomorrow a working Saturday for you?"

Toy shook her head. "No."

"Then let her come. Little Lovie can sleep late tomorrow. So can you. Flo really needs all hands on deck. The beach is flooded with hatchlings all going the wrong way. Lovie is part of the team, after all."

Toy slapped a pesty mosquito at her ear and knew there was no good argument against this. "All right." She turned to Lovie and pointed a finger. "But you must promise to stay close to the nest and not walk around the beach, got it? Flo needs our help as turtle ladies and I can't be worrying about you. Your job will be to monitor the nest on the dunes. The minute I see you walk off is the minute we go home."

"I will. I promise."

"Then let's get going," Cara said, grabbing her chair and taking off at a trot.

They arrived to find Flo knee deep in the ocean, holding a bright flashlight high in the air, mimicking the moon and hopefully guiding the confused hatchlings to the sea. The night was inky and it was hard to make out who was who on the beach. The women were mere silhouettes scattered across the sand, trying to steer the nearly invisible three inch hatchlings back toward the rolling surf using their feet as blockades. The small glowing circles of red light from their flashlights looked like low flying, rosy lightning bugs.

Toy settled Little Lovie at the nest high on the dune with the job of waiting to see if another baby turtle emerged. Then she began combing the nearby dune grass to rescue any hatchlings that may have wandered off to certain death. The hatchlings were completely disoriented, scrambling toward the lights on the pier, toward the street lamps and toward the porch lights of one careless homeowner who went out for the evening and left the ocean side porch lights brightly shining. Cara resorted to collecting the confused hatchlings in the red bucket and carrying them close to the shore where Flo's flashlight could compete with the bright lights.

By midnight they'd succeeded in getting most of the one hundred and eleven hatchlings safely into the sea and on their journey to the Gulf Stream. They closed up the nest, tidied the beach, then bid each other sleepy farewells, feeling tired but satisfied. It was one of those nights when they felt that their efforts truly did make a difference.

Toy carried a sleeping Lovie along the winding beach path to the street. She was petite and weighed little. Sometimes Toy still felt that Lovie was her baby. This summer, especially, she'd had to force herself to let her daughter spread her wings.

"I let her stay up way too late. I should be more mindful of her schedule."

"You're doing a fine job raising that child," Flo said as she followed in single file. "You should be proud. I've never known a child to care so much about nature. To *feel* nature as a child is much more important than just being able to list names of birds, or plants or animals. That kind of heart isn't something you can teach a child in books."

Toy hoisted her daughter to her hips, gaining a better hold. As a single, working mother, she couldn't hear compliments on her mothering skills enough.

"They say it takes a village to raise a child," she said. "In this case, it took a turtle team."

"I like that," Flo said emphatically. She didn't say more, knowing it flustered Toy to be praised too much. Flo figured it was because Toy grew up in a home with a paucity of kind words.

They reached their cars parked on a side street and loaded the sleeping child into The Gold Bug, along with sand covered backpacks and gear.

Flo kissed the warm cheek of the child, then closed the door to the car. "Sleep tight, little turtle lady."

When Cara arrived at her small, pink stucco house she saw that Brett had left the outside light on for her. Inside all was dark save for a stream of light shining from under the bedroom door. She dropped her sand encrusted backpack on the floor and slipped off her sandals. The night was so humid it had felt like she was wading through a mist. Sand clung to her sweaty skin from her scalp to cake in her toes. Sand was even in her teeth. She was sticky and smelly and couldn't wait to get into the shower.

Opening the door to her room she stepped into a wall of cool air from the window air conditioner. Brett was still awake, lying in his boxers on the bed against a bolster of pillows. The overhead fan was twirling, riffling the papers he was studying. He lifted his head when she came in and under his slightly damp hair, his eyes warmed at seeing her.

"At last. I was beginning to worry."

"I thought I'd never get home," she said, closing the door behind her.

"Did the nest hatch?" he asked.

She nodded, then stripped the sticky, sandy shorts off and pulled her turtle team T-shirt over her head. She dumped the damp clothes on the floor.

"Not my nest. The one on 27th and it was a nightmare. The hatchlings headed straight for the lights of the city. We had to carry them to the ocean, over and over again. They'd get right to the surf then turn around and head back toward the light of the street. Poor things. But I tell you, it was frustrating. I hope this doesn't happen all summer."

"Go take your shower. You'll feel better."

The cool water sluiced down her body, rinsing the sand off in sheets. Closing her eyes, she wanted to fall asleep right there in the pouring water. The air felt cooler when she stepped out from the shower. She dried herself quickly, feeling the lateness of the hour deep in her bones. Wrapping the towel around her breasts, she went to the fridge to scrounge for food. She was always hungry these days. Standing in front of the fridge, she ate a boiled egg, a chunk of cheese and poured herself a glass of milk.

"What are you working on?" she asked when she returned to the bedroom.

"The July report for the new site," he replied, looking up. He tossed the pencil on the bed. "Another month of summer gone. I don't know, hon. Three operations up and running . . . it's going to be tight."

"We're at the peak of the season. Things are picking up."

"They'd better be." He ran a hand through his tawny hair. He cut it short in the summer, but no matter what he did, it always managed to look unruly. "I wonder if we didn't expand too fast. The Bull's Bay operation is off to a slow start. We're barely making it."

She sat beside him on the bed. "Brett, I know this is tough for you to believe, but we'll be fine. Back when the property for the site in Bull's Bay became available we had to be aggressive or lose the chance of buying it."

"We spent every penny we had and we're in hock up to our necks."

Cara sighed. She knew Brett feared being in debt. He didn't have faith in the demographics she'd shown him. She'd spent years in marketing and advertising; she knew how to read the numbers. But he believed in her. He'd supported her business plan, put his business and house on the line, and worked like a bull in the harness seven days a week to launch the two additional operations. She hated to see the new creases carving across his broad forehead and the faint blue shadows under his eyes.

She moved to collect the papers from his hands and set them on the bedside table. Then she flipped off her towel, crawled across the mattress to his side and cuddled against his broad chest, wrapping one of his arms around her. His skin felt so hot against her own, which was cooled from the shower. She sighed and closed her eyes when he rested his chin atop her forehead.

"Toy talked to me about renting the beach house," she began. "She thinks we should start renting to someone else to collect more rent."

"What brought that up?" he asked sharply.

"She overheard Palmer saying something to me about it."

Brett cursed under his breath. "Tell her to forget about it. She can stay as long as she likes."

"I tried to, but she doesn't feel right about it. And we do need the money."

He sighed and it rumbled deep in his chest.

"Well, no need to worry about it anymore tonight," she said sleepily, gently patting his chest with her fingertips. "We've agreed to think on it for the summer. It's too big an issue to decide quickly."

He remained quiet and she knew he was working things out in his own way.

"We do need the money," he conceded. "But it's not just the cash flow that's wearing on me. Three locations means I'm working all the time. There's always something going wrong, some paperwork that needs doing. I never have time for myself. For us. We're always working, Cara. It's all we do. This is no way to live."

She opened her eyes and, leaning against one arm, lifted her face to him. She saw the intensity of his emotions in his eyes. Summer was his favorite time of year. He was a teacher at heart and loved taking boatloads of people out to witness the beauty of the lowcountry. He loved nothing more than to stand wide legged and grab the helm of his boat in two hands, to toot the big horn, to pull the throttle and hear the roar of his powerful engines as they churned white water. To put a man like that behind a desk was a crime against nature. And she knew that this man, her husband, did it all for her.

All her assurances were inadequate. They'd made their decision and had to stay the course. "We're just tired. It won't be this hard for long. Think of it as an investment in our future. It'll be tough this season, but when it's over, you'll have lots of time to spend with your child."

His eyes kindled at the words *your child.* This was their greatest hope, one worth struggling for.

Leaning forward, he kissed her lips. A familiar surge of emotion shot through her. He'd always had this power over her.

"What was that for?"

"Do I need a reason?"

"Never."

There followed a moment when she knew they were both considering kissing again and igniting the quick punch of lust that would lead to lovemaking. Fatigue settled the question. She lowered her head to his chest and was comforted by the three gentle pats he gave her shoulder. Brett reached over to flick off the light. Instantly the room fell into delicious, cool darkness.

"Good night," she murmured, feeling sleep descending quickly.

"I love you," he replied, then covered her bare shoulder with the sheet.

The ice clinked in the tumbler as Flo raised it to her lips. It wasn't often that she allowed herself to indulge in a sip of Jamieson's and water. She'd lived alone long enough to know that drinking alone was putting one foot on a slippery slope. Every once in a while, however, she indulged. And tonight was one of those rare nights. She wasn't depressed. She wasn't particularly happy, either.

She simply couldn't sleep. The long night on the beach had left her restless and when she'd looked at the small alarm clock on her bedside table for the tenth time and it still only read 2:00 a.m., she'd given up trying. So she'd come outdoors with whiskey in hand to sit on her porch and let the island breezes settle her some.

Flo rocked, soothed by the rhythmic creak of wood on wood and the scent of her mother's roses. Overhead she tracked a slow-moving cloud in the pewter sky until it thinned and became smoky wisps. The moody sky, the gentle roar of the ocean, the cries of the insects, the scent of roses. . . . Closing her eyes, she could have been the young girl who had rocked on this very porch while her mama and daddy slept upstairs. Her parents had built this house, she'd spent a lifetime here, her mother had died in it.

Miranda had believed that a spirit left part of itself behind in a beloved home. She claimed that the spirits were that unnamed *something* people felt when they returned to visit their childhood homes. The smells triggered memories, yes. The visual clues signaled recognition too. But it was the lingering love that elicited whisperings from the past.

Flo sipped her drink. She was not the romantic her mother was. To her mind, Miranda was gone, as her father had been for decades. And whether part of them remained in this old house or not, there was only herself left to bear the burden of its upkeep. Perhaps she came to her mother's garden tonight seeking absolution for her decision. Who knew? She brought the glass to her lips again and felt the gentle, welcome burn as it slowly slid down her throat.

The sound of a door closing across the driveway caught her attention. She stilled her rocking, and looking over, saw a man's figure leaving Toy's house. Her senses on alert, she sat up in her chair and leaned far forward, squinting.

My, my, my . . . if it wasn't Miss Toy's Ethan sneaking out of her house like a fox from the hen house. Hidden in the shadows, she watched as he quietly made his way down the stairs then walk across the gravel drive to the street where a pickup truck was parked. Moments later she heard a car door close, the roar of an engine and the crunch of wheels against gravel as the truck drove away. Flo held her wrist watch up to the moonlight. It was after three a.m.

A slow smile of satisfaction eased across her face. "Good for you," she murmured. Suddenly the world did not seem quite so sad or lonely. She chuckled softly and raised her glass in a solitary salute to youth and love.

15

Mid-August marks the end of summer along the southeastern coast and the beginning of the hurricane season. Visitors to the coast care only that the temperatures are hot and the sun shines bright over long stretches of ivory beaches. The locals, however, sense a subtle shift that begins soon after the children head back to school.

Officially the hurricane season begins June 1st when cyclones form in the western Caribbean Sea and the Gulf of Mexico. By late July, the storm formation shifts eastward and frequency increases. Still, most local residents don't pay much mind to the skies in July, though there are some that like to sit over iced tea and remind folks of those storms that blew in early, catching them unawares.

By mid-August, however, every storm that spins off the coast of Africa becomes the hot topic of conversation at every greeting, mealtime gathering or phone conversation. Most of these storms cross vast areas of the ocean before dying off somewhere in the North Atlantic. But those that earn a name and head toward the United States tend to be severe. When that happens, tourists head for the hills and the locals are tuned to televisions and radios as they track its progress and debate whether they'll leave at first warning or wait till evacuation is mandatory.

Cara never reconciled with the hurricane season. She tended to be nervous and short-tempered, even more so with her pregnancy. She'd never forgotten the terror of riding out a hurricane on the Isle of Palms with her mother, watching the water in the house rise foot by foot, hearing the wind howl like a banshee and sending them cowering in the attic, clutching each other and saying their prayers. She didn't care that Flo and Emmi teased her mercilessly. Cara remained staunchly in the "voluntary evacuation" group to leave the barrier island.

So on August 12th, when the officials announced a named storm in the Caribbean, she clicked into high gear. She stocked her emergency supplies and prepared her house for the storm. When all was in order she met Toy at the beach house and together they got the small house ready for a possible storm. The old beach house had withstood countless storms, as her mother often told her with pride. They were just putting away the plastic bins of supplies when Flo called out a greeting. She was dragging a wooden ladder from the garage and waved, leaning on the picket fence to catch her breath.

"Here we go again!" Flo called out. "Another hurricane season — and they say this one's going to be a doozy."

Cara and Toy waved and walked over to meet her at the gate.

"What are you doing?" Cara asked, pointing to the old wooden ladder that was splintered and splattered with paint.

"What everyone on the island is doing, checking my shingles and shutters!"

"You're *not* going to climb up on that ladder," Cara exclaimed. "It's ancient. The rungs are spindly and the whole thing looks like the worms have feasted on it."

"I am. This ladder has been through lots of hurricanes."

"Starting with The Great Storm of 1893, I'll wager."

Flo just waved the comment away as was her manner when anyone contradicted her.

"Seriously, Flo, you have no business

climbing ladders at your age."

"Maybe, but I can't reach the young fella who usually does it for me. It used to be I could call him and get on a queue for his services. But his number's been disconnected. I figure he's moved on to greener pastures and isn't waiting around for old ladies like me to ask him to do odd jobs. There's no one else, so it looks like *tag — I'm it.*"

"I'll get Brett to do that for you," Cara said.

"He's done enough already."

"He loves nothing more than to climb a ladder. He'll be furious if you deny him the pleasure, so it's no use arguing. Toy, why don't you help Flo carry that sorry excuse for a ladder back to the garage."

"How about to the curb for the trash," Toy said, then to Flo she added, "And you call me a pack rat."

"This old ladder has lots of life left in it."

Cara pulled her cell phone from her pocket thinking it was no wonder her mother and Flo had been such close friends. They looked at the world through the same glasses. "I'm going to call Emmi to meet us here. We can get your house ready for the storm in no time."

"Don't be silly, Cara," Flo said, slightly

flustered. "You're all too busy. I don't need you to do all that."

"I know we don't need to," Cara replied, dialing. "But we want to." She raised her palm at Flo's sputtering. "Don't bother, it's done. Emmi's on her way."

Three hours later, Flo's hurricane shutters were at the ready and on her floor lay piles of batteries, bottled water, flashlights, paper goods, tinned food and other paraphernalia on the list for hurricane preparedness. The evening had turned out to be an impromptu girl's night out. They poured glasses of red wine while Flo prepared the spaghetti sauce. The delicious scent of garlic and tomatoes filled the kitchen. As she stirred, Flo let her gaze travel across the room.

Toy sat cross-legged on the floor packing the supplies into big Rubbermaid tubs. Emmi was at the kitchen table checking items off the list, and Cara sat beside her organizing the evacuation route they all would take should evacuation be called. Flo never had children, but if she had, she couldn't have wished for three more dutiful daughters.

"The important thing about evacuation is that we all know each other's destinations," Cara said, wagging her pen in the air. "If any of us are held up by traffic jams or get detoured, we need to call. The key is for us to keep tabs on each other."

"Isn't that what we do all the time, anyway?" Emmi asked.

"Yes, smarty-pants, but at a time like this it's really important to be specific," Cara said. "I remember how terrifying it was to be caught in a hurricane and unable to find Toy when she was having the baby. Remember, Toy?"

"How could I forget? But it was different between us back then. When I left the beach house during that storm, I never imagined you'd come after me. I thought you'd never want to see me again since I'd gone off with Darryl."

"I'm still mad you went off with that man," Cara said. "I couldn't stand him or what he did to you. But not come after you?" She shook her head. "We loved you, plain and simple."

"I didn't even know where we were headed. I still can't believe how naive I was."

"And how stubborn," Cara added.

"You were eighteen," Flo reminded her. "Just a girl."

Toy shook her head with wonder. That period in her life when she was a pregnant teen desperate to hang on to her dream of a family with Darryl as her husband and her child's father was not a period she was particularly proud of. In fact, she was even ashamed of it.

"You know," she said, "sometimes I look back at that girl and I don't know who she was. But I swear to God, when I saw Brett walk into that emergency hospital looking for me, I knew what the word *rescue* meant. I never knew it could be such a relief to have someone care about you."

"You know now," Cara said and was rewarded with a grateful smile from Toy.

"I surely do. And so does Little Lovie. I guess that's why I'm not afraid of hurricanes. That storm brought me to the happiness I have now. You just never know how things will turn out."

"True. But even if you're not afraid of hurricanes, you don't want to be a fool and not prepare to get out of town, neither," Flo told her. "They don't call these *barrier islands* for nothing."

"Exactly," Cara said, passing out papers. "Take a good look at these and don't lose them. This is the evacuation route we all should take to Columbia, and the name and number of a friend of Brett's who has a big ol' house just outside of the city. He's agreed to let us stay there if we can't get a room elsewhere. He doesn't promise deluxe accommodations, but there are air mattresses and it will be clean and dry."

"I get spooked just reading this," Emmi said soberly.

"I confess, I do get a shiver," Toy agreed. "It makes the hurricane real, you know? Not just something that swirls out there in the Atlantic."

"It is real, all right," Flo said. "I went through Hurricane Hugo and just remembering it sets my heart to fluttering. Nothing like seeing a big boat parked in your neighbor's living room to put the fear of God in you." She set the paper down on the counter and shook her head. "I just don't know if I want to go through this over and over at my age."

"What choice do we have? It's the price we pay for living in paradise," Cara reminded her.

"Maybe for you. But I'm getting pretty old to pack up this house every year. I'm not sure that it isn't getting too much for me."

"Oh, get on with you," Emmi said. "You're ageless. I know women half your age who aren't in half the shape you are."

"It's catching up with me," Flo said and her smile faltered. She set down the wooden spoon with a soft sigh.

"Flo?" Cara inquired after her. She didn't care for the soul weary expression that sagged the corners of Flo's mouth, nor the lines that carved deeper in her face. She'd thought Flo had looked worn out in the past week or so, like she wasn't getting enough sleep. Flo was not one to complain or confide an ailment so Cara gently probed, "What's the matter?"

Flo cut the flame from the sauce and came around to join Emmi and Cara at the table. She pulled out a chair and slowly eased down into it. Her gaze traveled leisurely across the kitchen, thinking as she always did how much the airy, functional space suited her.

"I love this house," she said in a wistful tone. "Once upon a time, this was the grandest house on the island. But tough times took its toll on our family, as it does on many. Daddy managed to hang on to the house, but he couldn't afford to do much to maintain it. So by the time I inherited it in my forties, the old house had been a rental for years and was in a sorry state. Sea air isn't kind to wood houses, you know. Neither are most renters. I thought about selling it then." She sighed, shifting her eyes to her hands. "But I loved it too much to let it go. You know, of course, that I never married. I never had children. This place was my home.

"I had some money saved in the bank so I decided to bring this old house back to its former glory." She chuckled. "What a time that was. During the week I worked in Summerville, and on weekends I came here to work on the house. You only have that kind of energy when you're young. Later when I retired, I moved into the house permanently and brought my mother with me. I sank every penny I ever made into this house. At the end of the day, I think I did all right."

"You know you did," Cara said. "For whatever the reason, it was a right smart investment. Do you know how much this house is worth right now?"

"To the penny." She paused. "I guess now is as good a time as any to tell you."

"Tell us what?"

She took a moment then said in a strong voice, "I've decided to put the house up for sale."

This was met by stunned silence followed by immediate outcry.

"No! You can't!" Cara and Toy exclaimed in unison. Emmi sat drop-jawed and silent.

"We all have to move on at some point," she replied soberly.

"You'd say goodbye to us? To Isle of Palms? To the turtles?" asked Toy.

"I'm not saying goodbye to anyone, child. I'm moving, not dying!"

"Hold on," Cara said, palms out in an arresting motion. She appeared pale and shaken and needed a moment to take stock. "Let's talk about this."

Flo didn't expect Cara to respond so emotionally. She was the kind of woman who rarely cried and could always be counted on to think levelly in an emergency. Toy was tender hearted and her watery eyes reflected her emotions. Emmi, in contrast to both, sat far back in her chair with her arms crossed, deep in thought.

"You've got your brow all furrowed, Cara," Flo said. "Do you know you've done that ever since you were a little girl? Whenever anyone had a problem that brow would furrow and you'd try to fix it. Sugar, I'm not asking you to solve a problem for me. I'm just telling you what's what. I've taken care of myself all my life. I never depended on anyone. And I don't intend to start now. As I've said, I've given this a great deal of thought and I've consulted with friends and professionals. It's not uncommon, you know, to move somewhere more manageable at a certain age. It's much stickier when there is land and family involved." She smiled but there was no humor in it. "But in my case, there's just me. And all I've got in the world is this one house."

When she looked at Cara her gaze was steady and she spoke firmly to quell any arguments that were likely forming in her quick mind. "The value of this house has shot way up. It was a good investment, as you say." She shrugged. "The problem is, it's my *only* nest egg. It's all I've got in the world.

"Girls," Flo continued, "I'm an example of what each of you might face in the future. It's both a shock and frightening, after years of careful planning and saving, to come to the realization that you're running out of money. I thought I'd saved for my retirement. The problem is, the money hasn't kept up with inflation and isn't enough to keep me going. Frankly, I have less than $20,000 left in my bank account. So, don't ask me if I know how much the house is worth. The more critical question is how much my taxes and insurance have gone up. What good is the high rise in house value if I can't afford to stay in it?"

Cara was alarmed and looked across the table to see her expression mirrored in Toy and Emmi.

"Can you rent it?" asked Toy.

Flo shook her head. "I need the cash to move somewhere else. Nope, all my money's tied in to this house. I have to sell."

"Oh, Flo," Cara said, her dark eyes saddened. She was at a loss to add anything constructive. It wasn't that long ago that she was in exactly the same position as Flo — a single woman with a career, a good lifestyle, a nice house. No husband, no children. Cara looked at Toy and saw the stark fear etched on her face. She had to be thinking of her own situation. Single women had a lot in common.

The stunned silence was broken when Emmi said quietly, "I'll buy it."

The three women swung their head to look at her, their eyes round with surprise.

"I beg your pardon," said Flo.

"I said I'll buy the house," Emmi replied.

"Emmi," Cara said with a hint of warning in her voice. "Careful what you're offering. Are you aware of the value of Flo's house?"

"Of course. I squeezed out an exorbitant price for my beach house from Tom and have money in the bank from the sale of my house in Atlanta. I can afford it."

"But do you want this old house?" Flo asked, searching Emmi's bright green eyes for signs of jest, or worse, pity.

"Flo, I've *always* wanted it," Emmi replied plainly. "Don't you know that? When we were kids, Cara and I both used to wish we lived here and dreamed of owning it someday. Now, I can!" She turned to Cara with a tilted chin and a wry smile of victory on her face.

"You mean you'd have bought this house before?" Flo asked, incredulously.

"Honey, if I'da known sooner, we'd be in escrow by now."

"I'll be damned."

"This is like an answer to a prayer. I've sold my house and have been looking for a new place. It's been very hard to make this transition. But never in a million years did I think you'd ever part with this house."

"But, where will *you* live?" Toy asked Flo.

Flo opened her mouth to sputter something pat like she'd find someplace, most likely in Mt. Pleasant, but Emmi's voice interrupted.

"Flo will still live here, of course."

"Here?" Flo responded, dazed. "Here in this house?"

"Don't you want to stay in your house?" Emmi asked.

"Well, yes, of course. I . . . I'm just in a state of shock. I can scarcely believe this offer, that's all." She reached out to take a sip of her wine. She felt the red liquid flow down her throat, warming her senses. Feeling a bit more composed, she looked again at Emmi, who was engaged in a heated exchange of whispers with Cara. Something about being sure and not getting hopes up.

"Emmi," she said, interrupting them. They both turned their heads to give her their full attention. Sitting side by side, Cara with her glossy dark hair and Emmi with her flame colored hair, she could still see the bickering, laughing, joking eight-year-old best pals. Her own face softened, remembering.

"You're an angel to make this offer," she began. "An angel of Mercy, and I appreciate it. But, offering to buy my house is one thing. Offering to take me in is quite another. I've always managed to take care of myself and I'm not so old that I can't continue. Most of all, I can't take advantage of your affection for me, or this house."

"I don't expect you to," Emmi replied in her matter-of-fact tone. "And, Flo, I may be taking advantage of you. Let me lay my cards on the table." She spread her palms down on the table. "Simply put, I can't afford to buy this house and keep up the expenses on it all on my lonesome, either. The money I received in my settlement and the house sales is all I have in the world. I need to plan ahead so my money won't run out. The last thing I want to do is become a burden to my children or, God forbid, lean on Tom. So, here's what I'm thinking.

"I'll buy the house from you at a fair market price determined by an independent appraiser. Then I'll set up a rent you can pay me that's fair. That way, you'll have enough in the bank to live comfortably on and not have to move. And I'll have the help I need to keep up the payments. Plus, it's nice to have someone else in the house, isn't it? I've never lived alone and after these past few months, I've decided I don't like it. It gives me the creeps and I wake up at every bump in the dark."

"It just seems too easy."

"Life doesn't always have to be hard, does it?" Emmi asked. "I've done hard, and frankly, easy is better. Aw, Flo, the more I think about it, the more I realize it's not just a good plan, it's a great plan. Please, say yes."

"Best of all," Cara added, "I won't be losing my two best friends."

"And the turtle team won't be decimated in one season," Toy said with a wry grin.

"In that case," Flo said, "yes."

Flo lifted the bottle of Chianti and poured more wine into the glasses, noting as she did that Cara hadn't touched a drop of hers. Her hand was shaking a bit from all the excitement of the moment and she spilled a few drops. She raised her glass for a toast. Her gaze swept the women at the table and for once, she was short of words.

"What do I say? My heart's too full."

"To my new house," Emmi opened, raising her glass.

"To my new neighbor," Toy said, glass in the air.

Cara topped them all with, "Here's to the turtle team!"

The women raised their glasses, feeling the bond in the clinking glasses. As they sipped, Flo cast a surreptitious glance at Cara, noting that though she brought the glass to her mouth, she barely let her lips touch the liquid.

Flo set her glass down on the table. The color had returned to her cheeks and she felt for the first time in weeks that her feet were on terra firma once more. She took a deep breath, relieved, as a great weight lifted from her shoulders.

"Emmi, I just wish you'd have told me this plan of yours earlier. I haven't slept a wink in weeks, worrying about selling this place. My mother has been haunting me." She let her gaze slide to Toy and added with a sly smile, "It's amazing what wonders one sees sitting out on the porch late at night. Oh, the things that go bump in the night."

Toy's cheeks flamed and her pale blue eyes widened with wondering what possibly Flo could be referring to.

Flo chuckled, pleased that her comment had the desired effect of veering the attention away from herself. As she walked to the stove to set the pasta boiling, she heard behind her the relentless questions and ribbing of Cara and Emmi as they pried information from a reluctant, red faced Toy.

Medical Log "Big Girl"
Aug. 12
Removed the 4 lb. weight and dive belt from turtle. Buoyancy significantly better. Trim improved and swimming more relaxed. Turtle can easily submerge.
You go girl! TS

■ ■ ■ ■

PART 3

■ ■ ■ ■

Swim with a friend, never alone.
Confidence is good —
but too much can lead to danger.

16

It was a Sunday morning in the dog days of August and Toy indulged by sitting at the kitchen table lazily cutting coupons from the *Post* and *Courier.* She was exhausted and looked forward to a morning she could keep her jammies on and linger over a second cup of coffee instead of shooting out of the house in a blaze that wouldn't snuff until she came home again in the evening.

Kiwi, her calico cat, came in the room to meow piteously at her feet for breakfast. "Okay, okay," she crooned, stroking the silky fur. She put an end to the rising crescendo of meows by placing a bowl of kibble before the calico. While Kiwi was eating, Toy measured coffee beans in the grinder then started a fresh pot of coffee. With a little more time this morning, she skipped the cold cereal and put strips of bacon in the cast iron fry pan. Soon the air was filled with its tantalizing aroma, luring Little

Lovie into the kitchen, her stuffed turtle tucked under her arm, hair askew, and yawning.

"Good morning, sunshine."

No reply.

Little Lovie climbed into a chair and sat, blinking heavily, before the table. From the stove, Toy turned the bacon and watched her daughter slowly awaken like a flower blossoming in slow motion. It took a while for her senses to absorb the rays of sunshine and the smells of bacon and the world at large.

"May I be excused?" She was already climbing from her chair.

"If you eat two bites of bacon, you can watch your cartoons."

Lovie stuffed the bacon into her mouth and tore off to the living room to watch her television. It was a special luxury for Lovie to stay in her pajamas and not be rushed to school or to Flo's house in the morning. She yawned and lazily put the remnant of the bacon into her mouth, savoring the peace.

It didn't last. The doorbell rang, startling the cat. As Kiwi disappeared around the corner, Toy glanced at the clock, annoyed at the interruption of her relaxed morning. She wasn't even dressed. Who could be calling at nine-thirty on a Sunday morning?

"Mama, there's a man at the door."

Toy grabbed a towel and drying her hands hurried into the front door. "Honey, I told you not to answer the d. . . ."

Her voice vanished. She stopped dead in her tracks and felt her blood draining from her face. The seconds ticked on like hours as she stared.

He didn't look a lot different than when he'd left her nearly six years ago. He still looked sexy in a rough, cowboy kind of way. His dark hair was chin length and tucked behind his ears, only now he had a small gold loop in one lobe. She didn't care much for the long sideburns that traveled down the lines of his cheekbones like daggers. He wore dark jeans that belted with a large silver buckle and ended at a pair of scuffed cowboy boots. His brown T-shirt bore the image of a skull and crossbones swathed in fire, and over this was a thick black leather jacket that had seen a lot of wear. Around his neck was a leather strip holding a silver ring.

Her gaze swept across him, then landed at his eyes. Those sad, soulful eyes still had the power to hold her.

"Hello, Toy."

"Darryl."

She wasn't sure if she actually spoke the name or not. Her mind screamed at her to slam the door in his face, or to grab her child and run from the back door. But she felt rooted to the spot.

Darryl made the first move. He crossed the threshold.

Toy instinctively took a step back but clutched the door handle, barring his entry. He stopped awkwardly.

"What are you doing here?" Her voice was thick and raspy.

"I came to see you."

"What for?"

"What for? What do you think?"

"I don't know what to think. It's been over five years. I stopped looking for you a long time ago."

"Well, I ain't never stopped thinking about you."

They stared at each other in the thick silence that comment inspired.

"Mama, who is that man?" asked Little Lovie. She was standing by the door, her hand holding the flipper of her stuffed turtle.

Once again, she froze. What should she tell her?

Darryl cocked his head, his eyes piercing into hers.

"He's just someone I know," she replied over her shoulder. Then lowering her voice she said, "Darryl, there's nothing much for us to talk about. So why don't you just go?"

Darryl's gaze traveled to Little Lovie. "I think we have a lot to talk about."

"No, we don't." She blurted out the words.

"Your mama, she's just funnin' you," he said in an easy voice to Lovie. "Don't you know who I am?"

Little Lovie shook her head.

Darryl leaned close to Toy and said in a low whisper, "She favors you."

"Darryl, don't."

"What'd you tell her about me?"

"That her daddy was in California," she hissed in a whisper. "That's a world away to a child. Like France."

He snorted and stroked the small beard at the edge of his chin. "Well, least you didn't tell her I was dead."

"You might well of been."

"I've come back and I'm here now."

"It's too late. . . ." Toy said in warning against the conviction in his tone. But inside she knew it was like watching a twister coming, swirling fast and carrying in it all manner of old trash. It was a powerful force and there was nothing she could do to stop it.

Darryl turned to Lovie. "Well, what's your name, honey?"

"Lovie."

Darryl slanted an amused glance at Toy, telling her he realized that she'd named the child after old Mrs. Lovie Rutledge. "That's a right pretty name for a pretty girl."

"Thank you." Lovie was eyeing him with intense curiosity.

Darryl turned back to Toy. "Aren't you going to invite me in? It's only mannerly."

Resigned, Toy dropped her hold on the door and walked over to Little Lovie and placed her hand instead around her daughter's shoulders in a protective gesture. "Come on in," she said without invitation in her voice.

"I appreciate it."

"Do you want some coffee?"

"I'd kill for a cup. Black. No sugar." He paused. "Same as always."

The implied intimacy of that statement rattled her nerves. While pouring the coffee in the galley kitchen she kept close watch on her daughter in the front room. Darryl sat on one of the big upholstered chairs before the picture window and was looking out at the ocean, seemingly oblivious to the child leaning against the opposite chair, her eyes glued to him.

Of all the times she used to dream that Darryl would come back to meet his child . . . Today, Lovie was utterly disheveled. Her hair was unbrushed and her pajamas wrinkled and blotted with spots of juice. A coloring book and crayons littered the floor in front of the television that was still blaring. The beeps, bops and animated music of the cartoons sounded macabre in the importance of the moment.

Toy looked down at her cotton camisole and thin pajama bottoms. She knew she looked a fright with her hair loosely tied back in a pony tail. She hadn't even brushed her teeth. Why didn't he come calling when they looked decent, she thought? Then she scolded herself for caring one whit how they looked for the man who unceremoniously dumped them at a shelter and never looked back.

Carrying the cup in one hand, she walked into the living room, detoured to flick off the television and then gave him the coffee with a thrust that bordered on rudeness.

"Thanks," he drawled with appreciation and promptly took a swallow. "Best cup of coffee I've had in days."

Toy just bet that was true.

He took another sip while she stood awkwardly clasping and unclasping her hands. Then with another resigned sigh, she sat down in the chair opposite him.

"Isn't this cozy," he said, eyes crinkling. "The three of us sitting together."

"Don't get too comfortable."

He chuckled and put the cup down on the wood table. She reached over and thrust a coaster at him.

Darryl's brow rose at the gesture, but he took the coaster without comment and put it under the cup.

"Aren't you going to take off your jacket? It's kind of warm for leather."

"Okay then."

He was being too agreeable and it made her nervous. He slid out of his jacket revealing slender yet muscled arms. They were heavily tattooed, a signal of his wild past.

"I'll hang it up." She began to rise.

"Don't bother. I'll just set it here on the back of the chair."

"Suit yourself."

After laying the coat beside him he picked up his cup again and took a sip while his gaze traveled across the room. "Nice place you got here."

She saw the room as he did, saw the charm and pared-down elegance that defined Miss Lovie's distinctive Southern style. It wasn't that the room was showy —

just the opposite. The modest cottage reflected her personal, confident taste. Outdoors on the veranda, under a pale blue ceiling, wicker chairs and a rocker said, *come on out and sit a spell.* It was the kind of place folks like Darryl and she used to dream about.

"It's not mine."

"It's that old lady's, I know. Where is she?"

"Miss Lovie passed on, God rest her soul."

"Really? So you live alone here?"

Toy saw the speculation ignite in his eyes and immediately set up her guard. "I only rent here. For the time being. From Cara. It's her house now."

Darryl's eyes hardened. "Oh, yeah. *Her.*" He rose to stand, wiping his palms on his jeans. "Listen, I know I busted in on you unawares. It's a lot to take in. Tell you what. I meant to just stop by and invite you out to dinner. You and Lovie, of course."

The invitation took her by surprise. She stammered, "I don't know if that's a good idea."

"Sure it is," he urged in an easy drawl. "We can have a nice meal, catch up some. You can pick the restaurant."

She took a breath. "I . . . I suppose dinner couldn't hurt."

"Where do you want to go?"

"I don't know."

"How about Shem Creek? Lovie can look at the boats and the dolphins."

"No, not Lovie. Not this time."

"Mama . . ." Lovie cried out in disappointment.

"I said no." Her tone brooked no disagreement.

Darryl pointed playfully at Lovie and said, "You just wait, pumpkin. I'll take you out another time, when your mama says it's okay. You can wear your best dress."

"Ethan calls me pumpkin."

Darryl's face stilled. "Who's Ethan?"

"If you're going to start in on that, we can say goodbye right here and now," Toy told him.

He understood that she meant it and shrugged. "Hey, no problem. Shem Creek it is, then. I'll make a reservation. How about six?"

"I reckon that'll do."

"Don't forget, now," he said and tilted his head with a smile of promise.

"I won't." How could she forget, she thought as she woodenly followed him across the room and opened the door? He stepped close to her and she stiffened, drawing back from any physical contact. He paused, then only smiled and said softly,

"See you later."

Closing the door behind him, Toy slumped against it. She was trembling and had to close her eyes. Inside, she felt ravaged, like a twister had spun off, leaving nothing but wreckage in its wake.

Toy ordered coconut shrimp. Darryl had the grouper.

Not that it mattered. Her stomach felt tied up in knots and it was an effort just to swallow. Around her other couples leaned forward over their tables, sipping wine and allowing conversation to flow. Toy felt like a mannequin trying to smile and listen politely to Darryl across the table. In contrast, he wasn't the least uncomfortable and talked like he'd never left. The wine had loosened his tongue and he went on and on about the fancy gigs he'd played in California, the record producers who'd come within a breath of signing him to a big money contract, and the big name country stars he'd opened for. He was real good at name-dropping.

Toy quietly listened, barely touching her wine, watching the shadows on Darryl's face created by the flickering candlelight. As far as she could tell, Darryl had become a contest groupie. He'd spent the last five years traveling around the country entering one music competition after another, winning some, losing most, scraping together enough winnings to keep on going. As long as the dream was alive, he didn't see himself as a failure.

It struck her hard that she did. He'd always been the one with talent and brains, the great hope they'd both hitched their star to. He'd often told her how lucky she'd been to have him, and oh, how she'd believed him. Seeing him now, in the light of her own growth and experiences, she wondered how she ever could have been so naive.

And yet, he did still have his undeniable charm. His blue eyes, framed with a thick fringe of black lashes, shone in the candle light as he told his story. He leaned forward across the table.

"Do you know what's coming to Charlotte next month? Go on. Guess." When she shook her head, bewildered, he answered with great import, "American Idol." He smiled and slammed his palm on the table to drive home the impact of that announcement. "Yes, ma'am. American Idol is having auditions and you know I'm going to be there."

"That's real nice, Darryl."

His face fell in disappointment at her

lackluster reaction. "That's nice? Is that all you have to say? Don't you think I can make the cut?"

"Oh, I feel sure you can. I always thought you had talent."

He inclined his head and his gaze swept her face. "Yes, you did. I miss that, you know. Your confidence in me. It gets lonely out on the road."

Toy drew back and did not reply.

"Did I tell you how beautiful you look tonight?"

"Thank you," she replied, her hand darting to tuck her hair self-consciously behind her ear. She wasn't used to compliments.

He leaned forward again and reached for her hand. "Toy, I miss you."

She withdrew her hand and tucked it in her lap. "That's too bad."

Darryl's brows rose and he dug into his shirt pocket for a cigarette. His movements caused a silver ring on a chain around his neck to slip out from his shirt.

Toy released a silent gasp when she recognized the ring as the one he'd given to her when she was seventeen and had moved into his apartment. He'd told her then that it was silver but the next one he gave her would be gold when they were married. Toy had returned the ring to him at the shelter when she'd said goodbye to him before he left for California. It stunned her to see that he'd kept it.

"Damn, I forgot my cigarettes."

"I don't think you can smoke in here anyway," she told him.

He cursed under his breath, something about rules, regulations and America going to hell in a hand basket. Then he leaned far back in his chair with a pout. He had the look of a country rock singer, Toy thought as she watched him. A little bit edgy but handsome in his faded denim. Toy didn't miss the sultry looks the waitress was giving him.

"I thought you'd be glad to see me," he told her.

She released a short laugh. "You can't think I've been carrying a torch for you? I have a life of my own now. And that life doesn't include you."

"Huh. You used to be sweet. When did you get so cold?"

"Sometime in the past five years, I reckon."

"Toy, honey, I *had* to go to California back then. That was my big chance. You know how many years I sang at gigs in cheap bars waiting for one single break." He paused to look at his upturned, empty palms. "But it was all for nothing. That record producer guy up and went bankrupt before I could even cut a song. I tried a couple years more in LA, then I went to Nashville for a big contest that was gonna make me a star. I scored real high. I only lost that damn contest by a measly few points. The winner got twenty-five-thousand dollars. All I got was this here leather jacket."

He took a swallow of wine, finishing his glass. "Story of my life," he said, disappointment ringing in his voice. "But this boy ain't a quitter. I kept singing my songs and trying to get a break."

"So, why did you come back here? There's no big break waiting on you in Charleston. Oh, wait — American Idol."

"I came for you," he said plainly. "And Lovie."

She swallowed hard, willing herself not to believe him.

"You can let go of that poker face, darlin.' Your eyes give you away."

"It's too late," she replied icily. "I've moved on."

The confident smile slipped from his face, replaced by a flash of jealousy she was quick to recognize.

"Is it that Ethan guy?"

"What business is that of yours?"

Now it was his turn to swallow hard. She could see the struggle he had to keep his emotions in check. There were days when she'd have shivered in fear at seeing that flash in his eyes and poised to duck. She looked at her hands, pleasantly surprised that she no longer trembled. Or cowered. In fact, she lifted her chin a notch, as if to dare him to cross the line.

He ran his hand through his hair. "I expect I deserve that."

She didn't reply.

"Honey, try to understand. The life I led was no place for a woman, much less an angel like Lovie. I've spent too many nights holed up in some cheap motel that smelled of must and urine, with nothing but a broke down TV and a King James bible. But I'll tell you, being that low makes a man look up."

"That sounds like a line from one of your songs."

He scratched the back of his neck and smiled ruefully. "It is. But I wrote it and it's real." He leaned forward again over the table, his mood serious. "Hell, I'm running my mouth here, but what I'm trying to say plain and simple is that I've changed. You're all I have that matters in this world. You and my music."

He sounded so sincere that the words had the power to wound her. She closed her eyes and shook her head. "No, Darryl."

"Just let me meet my daughter. That's enough for now. Let me meet her and tell her who I am." When Toy hesitated he said with feeling, "Toy, she is my daughter!"

"You might be her birth father, but you're not a real father, the one who was there for her every day of her life. Darryl, I'm not sure it's best for her to meet you. You're not part of her life. You're not her family."

"I suppose you think that Cara is her family."

"Don't you be saying anything bad about Cara," she said, warning in her voice. "She's been real good to me and Lovie. I don't know what we'd have done without her after you dumped us at the shelter. Yes, she is family."

"Your family, huh? Well, I'll say this for you, you've come up in the world." He stretched out his long legs. She noticed the heels of his boots were worn clear down to wood. "Do you ever see your real family?"

"Cara and Brett *are* my real family."

"I'll take that as a *no.*"

"Take it any way you like. There's no love lost between them and me. You know that better than anyone."

"Have they met our daughter?"

"*My* daughter," she amended and crossed her arms across her chest. "And no, they haven't."

"You haven't brought her over to see my mother, either."

"*Your* mother? Why would I do that?"

"She's real hurt she's never seen her own grandchild."

"You've got to be kidding! Maybe you can ask her why she — and her son — never came by to see his child. Why should . . ." Feeling her temper about to blow, she exhaled slowly. "Darryl, I don't think we should argue about your mother or my mother right now. They're the least of our concerns. In fact, I think this conversation is over." She gathered her purse and tossed her napkin on the table to leave.

Darryl shot his arm out to grasp her hand. "I didn't come back for trouble," he said in earnest. "Hear me out. Please."

She stared pointedly at his hand, his long, tapered fingers wrapped around her wrist. Feeling them again on her skin triggered a maelstrom of emotions inside of her. Those fingers had elicited pleasure in her past — and pain. She must never forget that, she told herself.

"I'll listen," she said, pulling her arms to

her side. "For a little while."

He drew his hands back to rest on his side of the table. He stared at them a moment before speaking. "I know there's nothing I can say or do to make you forget what I done. I was damn stupid and thoughtless. I had everything a man could want and I walked way."

"Yes, you did. And you didn't look back. Not once in more than five years."

He looked up to meet her gaze. "I'm sorry."

She blinked, surprised by the apology. She cleared her throat of the emotion welling up in it. "You made your choice."

"Toy, please. Let me make it up to you. Give me another chance."

"It's too late."

He closed his eyes with a grimace and sought to regain control. Opening them again, he was calmer. It disarmed her.

"All right, then. It might be too late for us. I have to accept that. But it's not too late to get to know my daughter. You might not want to know me, but she might. Don't you think it's high time for her to get to know her daddy, too?"

"I can't be having you hurt her like you hurt me, Darryl."

"I won't. I would never. I know you have

reason to doubt me. I treated you bad and I'm sorry. But I was young. We both were. But we're older now and I've come to understand what I've missed. I want to be in Lovie's life, in any way you'll let me. And maybe, God willing, you'll let me back in your life. But I ain't asking for that now. All I'm asking for — begging for — is a chance to know my daughter. Just to let her know she has a father. Me," he said, jabbing at his chest with emotion. "I'll make you proud, Toy. I swear I will."

She turned her head, not wanting him to see the emotion in her face. Isn't this what she'd always hoped would happen? Her dreams when she was pregnant that Darryl would somehow change and acknowledge that he was a father came rushing back, leaving her awash in indecision. Could she really deny either Darryl or Lovie the chance to get to know each other?

God help me, she thought as she took a breath and released her answer.

"I'll think it over. For Lovie's sake."

Later that evening, Toy tucked Lovie into bed. Her daughter's breath smelled of peppermint toothpaste and her skin of sweet soap. After she finished reading the bedtime story, she turned off the bedside lamp and lay back in the bed for what Lovie called her "chat with the lights off." It was only in the secrecy of darkness that Lovie shared her innermost thoughts.

"Did you have a nice dinner?" Lovie asked Toy.

Toy laced her hands across her belly. "It was okay. I had shrimp. How about you?"

"Auntie Flo made hamburgers," she said in a ho-hum tone. "Did you see a dolphin?"

"No. I didn't sit by the window."

"Oh, too bad." She paused and made steeples with her fingers. "Did you go out with that man?"

"Darryl? Yes, I did."

"Not Ethan?"

"No." Toy waited for Lovie to say something more and when she didn't, she closed her eyes and they lay side by side in the darkness. Toy struggled with what she'd come to tell Lovie. How do you ask your child if she wants to meet her father, she wondered? She'd never read this in any parenting book.

Yet, every instinct in her body was telling her what to do. Toy had spent a lifetime wondering who her own father was, what he looked like, what his personality was, whether she took after him in any way. There were no photographs of him, no mementos of him growing up. Whenever she'd asked about him her mother had curled her lip and spat out a dismissal. *"Him? That lazy, no-count mongrel. I bless the day he left me. Don't talk to me about him. Ever!"*

Eventually Toy learned to stop asking but the emptiness remained to fester in her heart. She still harbored the uneasy belief that the reason her mother had been so cruel to her was because she was her father's daughter. There had never been any discussion, or honesty, about him. Instead, her father had been clouded in mystery. Even now she wondered about him. Sometimes, when she looked at Lovie, she wondered if her daughter's eyes, her smile, her quick temper — any part of her — resembled that man she'd never met. She would rather have known all about her father, the good and the bad, than know nothing at all.

Darryl was right. He was Lovie's father, warts and all. Toy had always been honest and true with her daughter. She could not back down from the truth now.

Toy opened her eyes and tried to form her words. "Honey, there's something I need to tell you about that man you met this morning. About Darryl. Are you listening?"

"Yes."

"He is an old friend of mine. A very

special friend." She paused, garnering her courage. "Honey, that man . . . Darryl . . . is your daddy."

Lovie didn't move or speak and Toy tensed in the darkness, waiting.

"Did you hear what I said?"

"He's my daddy?" She said the word *daddy* slow, like she was playing with the feel of it in her mouth.

"Yes."

"But my daddy is in Cafonia."

"He was in *California* but he came back here to see you."

"To see me?"

"Yes. And me, too." Toy turned on her side to closely watch her daughter's expressions. Her eyes were accustomed to the dim light and she saw that Lovie's eyes were opened and staring at the ceiling. Toy couldn't read any emotion in her expression.

"Is that okay with you? Because you don't have to see him if you don't want to. I could tell him to go away and that would be the end of it. It doesn't matter to me if you see him or not. I just want you to be happy. You get to decide." She paused. "Do you want to see him?"

"I guess."

Toy was surprised by Lovie's lack of enthusiasm. She thought she'd be all over the chance to meet her father. For so long she kept asking about him, where he was, when he was coming back. She'd embarrassed Toy countless times trying to draft any man who was even nice to them into the role of her daddy.

"You don't seem very happy about all this."

"Does it mean you're going to marry him?"

"Darryl? Oh, honey, no."

"But he's my daddy."

"Yes, but that doesn't mean I'm going to marry him."

"But then we could be a *family.*" Her voice rose with a pleading note.

Hearing it near broke Toy's heart. "It's confusing for a child, I know. And I'm sorry. I know you want a daddy and a family. I do, too. But not in that way."

"If you don't marry him, does that mean you can marry Ethan?"

"Oh, honey! Let's not worry about Ethan right now. Do you want to see Darryl?" When she didn't answer, Toy prodded her. "Lovie?"

"I want to."

Toy flopped on her back and rested the back of her palm against her forehead. This day had utterly depleted her. "Okay then.

I'll arrange for you to see him."

"When?"

"Soon."

"Is tomorrow okay?"

This was all going so fast. "How about the day after tomorrow?"

"Okay." Lovie turned on her side, showing her back to her mother.

Toy turned to lie like spoons with her daughter. She wrapped an arm across her body, pulling it close against her in a snug, then rested her face against Lovie's soft, wispy hair. Closing her eyes, she remembered the day Lovie was born. God had given her this gift in the midst of a fierce, roiling hurricane. When the doctor had handed her this small miracle wrapped in a pink blanket, Toy had felt then, as she felt now, overwhelmed with love for her. She knew without question that it was her love for this child that had changed her life.

She lay for a long time listening to the soft whistling breaths from her daughter's lips. Her lids grew heavy as her heart lightened, and in time, her own breathing blended into the gentle rhythm as sleep came.

17

Toy made arrangements to go into work late the following day. She dropped Lovie at Flo's and went directly to Cara's house for a confidential talk with her friend. When she arrived she was touched that Cara had set a pretty table on her porch overlooking Hamlin Creek. She'd placed a cheery pale blue plaid tablecloth over the wood table and served fresh strawberries, muffins and sweet tea.

"I'm so glad you called," Cara told her when they sat down. She began pouring tea. The ice crackled in the tall glasses. "It's been ages since you've stopped by just to sit and chat. Since summer began, there never seems to be a free moment."

Toy nodded, staring at a drop of condensation trailing down her glass. Under the table her foot wagged. She was anxious to ease her troubled mind about Darryl.

Cara flicked her gaze up from the tea,

zeroing in on Toy's face. She finished pouring and took a seat opposite Toy. "Is everything okay?"

"I just wanted to talk to you."

"Oh?" Cara asked, spreading her napkin on her lap. She lifted her glass to her lips and narrowed her eyes. "This wouldn't have to do with a certain tall, dark and handsome guy, would it?"

Toy almost choked on her tea. Across the table, Cara's dark eyes glittered.

"You know?"

"Mama knows all."

"Who told you?"

"Little pitchers have big ears."

"Little Lovie? But when?"

"At lunch the other day. She let slip that a certain man from the Aquarium was coming for sleep-overs."

Toy had to sit back and stare at her hands a moment before she put the pieces together.

"You mean *Ethan?*"

Cara's lips twitched. "Is there someone else?"

"Oh, honey, buckle your seat belt."

Cara popped a berry in her mouth, eyes glittering with curiosity.

Toy took a deep breath. "It's Darryl."

All mirth fled from Cara's face. She

finished chewing her strawberry, swallowed, then wiped her mouth with her napkin. "Darryl?" she asked with forced calm.

Toy nodded.

"Darryl?" she repeated in a higher voice. "Don't even tell me you've talked to that man again. After all these years?"

"He showed up at the beach house yesterday morning," Toy explained.

"Oh, God." Cara's hand went to her cheek. "What did you do?"

"Nothing at first. I was so shocked I just stood like an idiot and stared at him."

"Why did you open the door?"

"I didn't! Lovie did."

"Lovie?" She took a breath. "Little Lovie was there? She saw him?"

Toy nodded. "And met him. What else could I do?"

"Slam the door in his face is the first option that came to my mind."

"He'd only knock again, and keep on knocking. You know Darryl well enough to know he won't just walk away when he wants something."

Cara's face grew as hard as stone. "And what does he want?"

"He wants to get to know his daughter." She looked at her hands. "And to ask my forgiveness."

"That's bullshit and you know it."

"Cara . . ."

"You can't be taken in by him. Not again. Toy, don't look away. Listen to me, please. You've worked too hard to slip back to his level."

"He *is* her father," Toy argued back.

"He's a sperm donor. Nothing more."

Toy drew back, affronted. She was spared having to come up with a reply when Emmi came strolling out onto the porch, singing out hellos. She'd abandoned the tight fitting clothes and was wearing plain khaki shorts and a green turtle team T-shirt.

When she reached the table, she looked from Toy to Cara, very aware of the tension in the air.

"What's going on?" Emmi asked.

"Darryl's back in town," Cara answered.

"Guys like that are bad news. Take it from me, stay away," Emmi said, sitting down.

Cara nodded, gaining steam. "This man is trouble. You know he's trouble. There's a reason you broke up. Don't forget, he's the bastard who abandoned you when you'd just given birth to his child."

"I know, believe me I know," Toy replied testily. "I was there."

"I'm sorry," Cara said, reaching out for her hand. "I don't mean to jump down your throat. Well, yes, I do. But I don't want him to hurt you again. Or Lovie."

"He's changed."

Emmi rolled her eyes. "Oh, boy, here we go. I'll bet he said he was sorry, too."

He did, but Toy didn't reply. She looked at her hands.

"Did he go inside the beach house?" Cara asked.

Toy felt the same quivering of her spine that she did five years earlier when she feared Miss Lovie's and Cara's disapproval of Darryl. Back then she'd been compelled to lie and sneak. Now, she felt a rising indignation at being intimidated to the point of considering sneaking again. Or being told who could or could not be allowed into the home that she was renting. Didn't she have a voice in her own life? It was an age-old stand-off between her and Cara.

Toy was done with having to prove she was not a troubled, pregnant teen any longer. She straightened her spine and folded her hands on the table. "You might as well know it all. Yes, I invited him in. We had a brief chat. I made it clear I wasn't thrilled to see him and he did his best to be polite. Then I asked him to leave."

"Good," Emmi said.

Toy looked at her. "Then I went out to

dinner with him."

She saw the look of shock on their slack-jawed faces.

"You should have seen Little Lovie's face," Toy argued. "She was hanging on his chair, her eyes wide, just dying to know who this man was."

"You didn't tell her!" Cara said.

She nodded her head curtly.

Cara slid back in her chair with a sigh of disbelief.

"Cara, Darryl *is* her father. Like it or not, nothing will change that fact." Toy raised her hands, silencing the objections she knew were coming from Emmi's open mouth. "I was careful. I didn't want to talk to him in front of Lovie so we went to Shem Creek to discuss it. We had a nice meal and we sorted a few things out. We had left things in a bad way. I need closure on this, and apparently so does he."

"Closure?" Emmi asked, appalled. "He never opened the damned door to begin with. What's he need closure for?"

Cara swirled the tea, her face serious. "What's next?"

"He wants to come see Lovie."

"See Lovie?" Cara repeated, as though trying to get the concept to stick in her mind. "Surely you're not going to allow that?"

Toy looked Cara straight in the eye. "Yes, Cara, I am."

"Toy, what are you thinking? This man walked out on you, on his daughter. He has a very serious temper. And he's violent. He hit you before, remember. And what about Lovie? Are you thinking about her?"

Anger flared in Toy. "Of course I'm thinking of her! I'm always thinking of her! Cara, *I know* what it's like not to know who your father is. I don't want my daughter to go through what I did, or to suffer the same, crippling lack of self esteem. If Lovie doesn't answer those questions in her mind now, she'll always wonder about that other half of herself that she doesn't know anything about. She'll wonder why he never cared enough to meet her. Or to know her. She'll wonder how she mattered so little that he could've just walked away."

Toy's voice began to break and she put her hand to her trembling lips.

Across the table, Cara and Emmi shared a glance and were silenced.

Toy wiped her eyes and struggled to regain her composure. "I didn't mean to get emotional."

"It's an emotional subject," Cara replied

kindly, dispelling the tension. "What is it about fathers, anyway? God knows I certainly don't have any answers there. My father and I were always on opposite sides of any argument. Growing up, I often wished I *didn't* know him."

Emmi turned to Toy, her face softening. "Sugar, you're wise beyond your years. I'm in awe. You're right to give our Little Lovie the chance to meet her father. It's her right, as much as his."

"What right?" Cara jumped in, frowning at the path this discussion was taking. "He hasn't been her father. He hasn't paid a single dime in child support. He doesn't have any legal rights."

"I'm talking moral rights, not legal," Emmi fired back. "And besides, he just might have legal rights."

"What?" Toy exclaimed, shocked.

"You'd best find out what he wants," Emmi said to Toy. "Paternity is fatherhood in the eyes of the law. Plain and simple."

"He hasn't a leg to stand on, morally or legally," Cara argued. "That man wasn't there from the day of Little Lovie's birth."

"You don't know what you're talking about, Cara," Emmi volleyed. "The law is the law. I learned a few things in my divorce. Darryl can prove paternity and take Toy to court for custody, or at the very least, visitation rights. In many states, including the state of South Carolina, children born to unmarried parents are labeled by the law as illegitimate or bastards."

Toy sucked in her breath.

"I'm sorry, honey," Emmi said. "You know I'm not pointing fingers here. I just want you to be prepared. If you suspect he's after custody, you'd best consult a lawyer. Besides, Toy, for what it's worth, I think you're right about letting Lovie meet her father. If she doesn't, Lovie will only grow up resenting you. I should have been more like you and let my boys feel it was okay to still see their father after the divorce. In the end, my anger against Tom is destroying my relationship with my sons. I intend to back off and let them make their own decisions."

"Your boys are men. Lovie is a young, impressionable child," Cara argued back. "Tom might have been an ally cat as a husband, but he was always there for the boys. And he for sure never beat you or them. Darryl's been a no-count, no-show, sorry so and so. He says he's changed, but the jury is still out. Letting Little Lovie know who her father is — and letting him get involved with her life — are two very different scenarios."

"I realize that," Toy said in finality. The conversation was causing her such turmoil she couldn't sit here any longer. She rose then looked at the two middle-aged women sitting across the small porch table. These women were her support system, her family, the only one she and Lovie had ever known.

"Thank you. You've helped me a lot. I needed to talk it through and I appreciate you being here. But I've made up my mind."

"I can't believe you're going to let him see Lovie." Cara could not conceal her frustration.

Toy felt a small anger build in her chest at Cara's obstinacy. She felt as though her own intellect and ability to reason out a problem were dismissed. "This is *my* decision, Cara. You can't possibly understand how I feel. You've never walked in my shoes."

"I'm just trying to give you some advice," Cara said pointedly.

"I don't want your advice!" Toy cried back. "I don't want you to tell me what to do. I just wanted you to *hear* me. Can't you just listen to me?"

Cara was taken aback. She looked at Toy, long and hard. Slowly her expression softened. At length, she said, "I hear you. I'm just afraid for you, honey."

"I know what I'm doing," Toy replied.

Cara lifted her hands, implying there was nothing left to say.

Walking away, Toy was troubled that Cara was upset with her. Cara had been her role model for these past years and she'd strived to be more like her. Yet there were harsh realities about her own life and upbringing that Cara couldn't ever understand. Toy had to do what she felt was best for herself and for her child.

At the door she turned and waved. Cara's eyes were fixed on her. Toy knew that no matter what happened, Cara would be there waiting if she needed her. And that knowledge gave her strength. She also knew without a doubt what the topic of conversation was going to be on the porch the moment the front door clicked shut.

18

The following morning, the turtle tank filters were backing up, the delivery of fresh fish hadn't arrived in time for the morning feeding, and if that wasn't enough, another sick turtle was brought in to the Aquarium, this time from a beach off Litchfield.

Putting all the other emergencies on hold, Toy spent hours doing intake procedures on dark, listless "Litchfield" while desperately begging for yet another tank from other departments. Elizabeth was a lifesaver when she agreed to come in for an extra shift to help the two new volunteers, Bev and Barb, with the turtles because Ethan and Jason were out on the Scout collecting specimens for the Aquarium.

In the midst of the pandemonium, Toy's mind was struggling with finding a way to forestall a huge personal calamity. Ethan and Darryl were both scheduled to show up at her house for dinner that night.

How could she have made such a blunder? she asked herself a thousand times that day. She should have known better than to set such an important date without checking her calendar, but Darryl had been insistent and she'd been caught in the moment. It wasn't until this morning that she'd realized she'd already inked in dinner with Ethan for the same time.

She'd frantically tried to reach Ethan by telephone to beg off for the evening, but he wouldn't answer his phone. Upon arriving at the Aquarium, she'd learned about the fishing expedition and knew he'd be out of telephone range. Favel had assured her that Ethan was scheduled to dock late that afternoon, so Toy waited anxiously all afternoon. But when 5:30 rolled around without sight of him, there was nothing left for her to do but leave him a message in his office and pray.

Ethan's office was a cubicle in a long series of partitioned areas on the executive third floor. Toy peeked through the opening, feeling uncomfortably like she was spying while he was gone. Seeing the empty space, it occurred to her how much she depended on Ethan at the Aquarium. If he'd been there today, a tank from somewhere and fresh fish from his stores of food would have arrived without hesitation. Granted, she managed each emergency on her own today, but his not being there underscored how great a team they'd forged at work.

Like most others, his cubicle was barely large enough for a desk, a bookcase and a spare chair. Unlike her own cubicle, however, which was cluttered with photographs and drawings by Little Lovie, Ethan's office was void of personal effects. The only decorations were two posters on the wall: one showed different species of sharks, the other was a map of Costa Rica.

She entered the space, letting her fingertips skim along the edge of his gray metal desk. The contact was oddly sensual and her gaze devoured every detail in its path. He was a very organized man. Not a pencil was out of place. And there wasn't one personal photograph on his desk — not of family, or friends. Nor of her, she thought with a twinge of disappointment as she picked up a pen and bent to write him a short note. She set the paper up against the cup in the middle of the desk. "Please, see it," she prayed.

She closed up her own office and hurried home, focusing now on the important evening ahead with Lovie and Darryl. The inside of her car was like a furnace but she didn't delay to take down the rag top. Cranking open the windows, she squealed out of the parking lot and headed north on East Bay. The clock in her ancient VW had broken long ago but her wristwatch informed her it was ten before six. She was running desperately late for her six o'clock dinner with Darryl.

There was just too much going on in her life, she told herself as she shifted gears and turned off Palm Boulevard on to the narrow road she lived on. Mistakes were going to happen if she didn't make some decisions soon.

Darryl's Mustang was parked in her driveway. It was the same car that he'd driven back when they dated and showed its age. The front fender had a new dent, the rear tail light was smashed and the bumper bore a peeling Lynyrd Skynyrd sticker. So much had happened to her since the night he'd picked her up for the last time from this same beach house in that same car, she thought. In retrospect she saw that it was symbolic that they'd driven away into a hurricane.

She puffed out a pent up sigh and cut the engine. Instantly she was immersed in a deep island quiet. She felt suspended in time, safe from the turmoil outside the car. She longed to stay in the small compartment for a while, to be alone for a few minutes in peace to put her thoughts together. But Darryl's car was empty which meant he was waiting out there somewhere.

She hurried from the car and up the front stairs. Opening her front door, she saw that the room was empty and quiet. "Darryl?"

"I'm out here," he called back from the back porch.

Unsettled that he'd let himself into the house, she paused only to drop her purse and keys onto the front table and take a quick look around the room. God help her, but she checked to make sure the silver candlesticks were still on the sideboard. They were. Sighing with relief, she went directly to the rear porch. The screen door squeaked as she pushed it open.

Darryl sat slouched in a rocker, a bottle of beer dangling from his long fingers. One booted foot rested on the wicker table, the other was propelling the chair in its rocking motion. A fast food bag and a six-pack of beer sat on the floor beside him.

"You look right at home," she told him, barely able to conceal her irritation.

He looked up and offered her a sweet smile. "I hope you don't mind my letting myself in but it was getting right steamy in that car. I didn't think it'd be a problem if I just sat on your porch a spell."

"It's okay," she replied. She took a deep breath and tried to let go of the day's frustration. "I was held up at work. I'm sorry you had to wait."

"No problem." He lifted his hand that held a bottle. "Want a beer?"

She yearned for a beer after the day she'd had. "Not yet, thanks. I still have to get Lovie."

"Hope you don't mind I started without you. I brought some and popped them in the fridge. I was parched." He turned his head to look out over the ocean, his eyes gleaming with appreciation. The dunes looked amber colored in this light and beyond, the ocean was a purple line against the graying sky. "Man, oh, man, that's a beauty view. You got a straight shot of the ocean from here. I reckon them's the last three vacant ocean lots on the island. 'Course, someday some builder's going to come and put up more of them mansions. Then there goes your view."

"Actually, no. Those three lots are deeded for conservation. They'll never be developed."

"You're kidding? All three of them?" Darryl released a soft whistle. "That makes this property a gold mine. Ocean front. You're damn lucky."

"*I'm* not lucky. It's not my house."

"But you live here."

She thought of Palmer's comments about how much rent Cara could get from someone else if she found a new place to live. "Yes, I am lucky to live here."

"It's like they say, the rich get richer and the poor get poorer. How long do you intend to stay?"

"Not for long," she replied, uneasy. He always was nosy when it came to her affairs. "Until I get on my feet."

"Don't get on your feet any too quick, if you catch my drift. I have to hand it to them, though. That's real nice of them to let you stay here. Not many folks would do that. Is it rent free?"

"No," she answered sharply, irked that he asked. He was crossing the line. "Listen, I'm sorry, but I have to go pick up Lovie." She instantly regretted saying *sorry* to him. It was a word she'd used all the time when they were dating and anything that went wrong was her fault. "She's just next door. Will you be okay alone here for a few more minutes?"

He lifted his beer in reply. "I'm fine, darlin'. Just hurry on up so we can see the sunset together."

She hoped he wouldn't get romantic tonight. She practically ran across the path to Flo's door. Flo answered on the second knock.

"I'm sorry, I'm . . ."

"Thank goodness you're here," Flo interrupted, grabbing her arm and pulling her into the house. Once the door closed she rounded on her. "There's a strange man on your porch! I would have called the police but Little Lovie says she knows him. I tried calling you but you didn't answer your cell phone." She said the last in an accusatory voice.

"I didn't hear it," she replied, digging into her purse. Dread enveloped her as she pulled out the phone. Sure enough, the battery was dead. She immediately thought of Ethan and wondered if he'd tried to reach her. "Today of all days," she muttered. Looking up she said to Flo, "I'm sorry. I'm usually careful about charging it, but . . ."

"But you've had a lot on your mind. I *know*," she said. "And if that guy sitting on your porch is who Lovie says it is, it's no wonder." Flo's eyes were blazing.

Lovie came bounding into the room, crashing against her legs. "You're here!

Guess what? Daddy's here!" Toy could tell she loved just saying the word *daddy*. "I'm going over."

"Lovie, wait!" Toy reached for her but Lovie was quicker. She'd already pulled open the door and darted out with Flo in pursuit. "Let her go," she called to Flo. "It's all right."

Flo put her hands on her hips and watched the child run down the stairs and across the gravel driveway that separated their two houses. "I'm fit to be tied," Flo said when she turned back into the house. "What's *he* doing here?"

"Don't let's get into it right now," Toy replied, putting her palm up. "I'm already late." She turned to go but Flo put an arresting hand on her arm.

"You know what I think, and what I feel."

"It's different now. He's different."

"How is it different? Leopards don't change their spots." She narrowed her eyes and delivered the blow. "Olivia Rutledge never liked him, never trusted him, never wanted him in her house."

Her aim was true. "Oh, Flo, don't say that. It's not fair." She dropped her head into her palm. "Do you know I've said *I'm sorry* four times since I've been home? And I've only been home for fifteen minutes!" She looked up and took a stabilizing breath.

"I can't do this any more. I have to make my own decisions, no matter if you or Cara or anyone else doesn't like them."

Flo smoothed her blouse in a long silence. "Well, you're a grown woman. You're not a girl any longer." She reached out her strong hand, dotted by age, and cupped Toy's cheek. Her face softened and in her eyes Toy saw true affection and wisdom, such as she had always seen in old Miss Lovie's eyes.

Flo dropped her hand and her face grew stern again. "But don't come crying to me if he hurts you."

"He won't."

Flo wagged her finger. "And if he hurts my Little Lovie, I'm going after him myself!"

She kissed Flo's cheek. "He won't," she said softly then left, knowing full well that Flo was hawking her every move through her window.

The sky had softened to azure and the breeze held a hint of moisture. Before going to her house, Toy stole a moment to tip her head back. She ran her hands through her hair, then vigorously scratched her scalp, shaking away the tension and sending her elastic flying.

Everyone was against her decision to let Darryl near, battering against her resolve like hard wood against a beleaguered gate. No one realized how hard Darryl's return was for her or how much history was being dredged up. She closed her eyes, taking the moment to garner her strength and stay the course.

It was a quiet night, yet she didn't hear the crunch of footfall on gravel till it drew near. She spun on her heel and opened her eyes.

Ethan was walking toward her up the driveway in his steady, long legged gait. He smiled boyishly and looked carefree in baggy shorts and a pale blue, wrinkled S.C. Aquarium T-shirt. His tan had deepened from a day on the open water and the sea salt and wind had spiked his hair. In his arms he carried a cooler.

Her breath held, she dropped her hands and her stomach rose to her throat.

He stopped before her and as his gaze slowly crossed her face an expression of pleasure eased across his own. "Hello."

The word was tinged with intimacy. When she didn't reply he went on, "I hope you haven't eaten yet."

Toy struggled for her voice. "No."

"Great. I'm starved. I'm sorry I'm late

getting here. What a day!" he exclaimed, buoyant from the excursion. "You should have been there. We collected a couple dozen cutlass fish. They're amazing creatures! Long and thin, a cross between a barracuda and an eel, if you can picture it. They have this amazing, steely blue color and an enormous mouth filled with sharp teeth." He paused to grin, just thinking of them. "We didn't have any at the Aquarium and now we have a collection. It's so great. We put them in a holding tank. Toy, they're a marvel to see! They're all swimming around in a school. God, I hope I can keep them alive." His dark eyes, usually so serious, were sparkling with excitement.

"You didn't get my message?"

He looked perplexed. "Your message?"

"I left it in your office."

"I didn't go to my office. I was late getting in so I came directly from the boat."

She opened her mouth to explain when from the porch, Lovie called out, "Hi, Ethan!"

He lifted his face, grinning brightly. "Hey there, pumpkin!" Then she watched as if in slow motion as his brows knitted and his head slowly tilted. His brown eyes squinted slightly.

Toy turned to look back at the porch.

Lovie stood pressed against the screen waving, and directly behind her, with his hand resting on her shoulder, was Darryl.

Ethan blinked twice then jerked his head to look at her. In that nanosecond she thought she saw a frisson of jealousy.

"You have company?"

"I . . . I tried to reach you."

"What about?"

How could she explain so much history in seconds? She tried to find the words, but Little Lovie called out from the porch.

"Ethan! Come up here and meet my daddy!"

His gaze sharpened.

"That's what I wanted to explain. You see, Darryl, that is, her father showed up yesterday."

"Yesterday. And he's back again today?"

"Uh, yes. He came all the way from California."

"How long is he staying?"

"I don't know."

"Is he staying with you?"

She felt his gaze boring into her, mining out the truth. "Oh, no. It's not like that. He's just here for dinner."

"I see. And you forgot that I was coming for dinner."

It was a summation but to her ears, it

sounded like an accusation. "It all happened so fast. I wasn't thinking clearly." She saw a small muscle twitch in his jaw. "He got here, he wanted to see Lovie, and I . . ."

"And you said yes." He exhaled a breath. "Of course he wants to see her. It's only natural."

Moments earlier he'd spoken in an entirely different tone. Then, his voice had been warm, sharing, excited. Now, he spoke with cool indifference as though he were trying to get the situation straight in his mind. He looked off for a second, his withdrawal palpable.

"This is for you," he said, raising the cooler. "I stopped at Cherry Point on the way back. My father wanted you to have this shrimp. They're right off the boat."

"Oh, uh, thank you. Won't you join us for dinner?" She cringed after the words slipped out. It was a stupid, stupid thing to ask. She was relieved when he replied like a knee jerk reaction.

"No, I don't think so."

"Why don't you keep the shrimp? For your own dinner."

"I've got plenty. You take them." He held out the cooler.

She backed away, refusing the cooler. It felt too significant, like the passing of a parting gift. "Ethan, just wait. Please."

His gaze flicked up to the porch and she saw his lips tighten in annoyance, or was it embarrassment at being watched in this awkward moment?

"Just take the damn shrimp and I'll shove off," he said, thrusting the cooler at her.

She grabbed it stunned.

"I'll call you later," he said.

She watched him turn and walk with purpose to the door of his pickup truck. He opened the door but before getting in he looked her way once more. She felt the intensity of his gaze, as though he were taking a final snapshot of her with his mind. Her vision blurred. A moment later she heard the roar of an engine and she saw the rear of his truck, plastered with S.C. Aquarium bumper stickers, disappear around the bend in the road.

Toy was devastated but she rallied for Little Lovie's sake. She returned to the beach house with the cooler of shrimp, not knowing where she was going to find the energy to prepare a meal and get through the evening. All she wanted to do was go to her room and cry.

Darryl was sitting on the sofa watching a baseball game on the television. Lovie sat beside him, leaning against his shoulder as he tried to teach her the rules of the game. Lovie kept asking which team was *their* team. Toy knew Lovie didn't know the first thing about baseball but she wanted to be on her daddy's team. He turned his head when she came in.

"There you are," he said as he pulled up from the sofa. He came directly to her side and took the cooler from her arms.

"It's not heavy," she said.

"Don't matter. Where do you want them?"

"In the kitchen, thanks. You can just set them down on the counter."

He set the cooler down then leaned over it to get a closer look at her face. "You look tired," he said in a low voice.

"I am," she said, leaning against the counter. "It was a very hard day. Everything that could have gone wrong did." Despite her effort, her lower lip began to tremble.

He glanced out the window at the driveway, then back at her. Ethan was on both their minds, but he refrained from mentioning his name.

"Hey, you don't want to go peeling all that shrimp. In fact, you shouldn't have to cook tonight at all," he said in an upbeat tone. "I seem to recall I invited a little girl to Shem Creek for dinner. There are lots of different restaurants down there. Why don't we try out another one? With a window smack on the water so Lovie can see a dolphin? Heck, we can try a different one every night. What do you say?"

Lovie came running into the room. "Can we? Please say we can?"

Darryl swooped down to pick her up in his arms. When they both smiled back at her, waiting for her answer, her breath was caught by how their eyes were exactly the same color blue. Why had she never noticed that before?

"Just give me a minute to freshen up," she said, then laughed as they both whooped loudly.

19

Later, when they returned home from Shem Creek, Lovie was half asleep and Toy was limp with fatigue. Darryl carried the child to the door, and while Toy unlocked it, she warred with herself whether or not to invite him in. The lock clicked. She pushed the door and held it for Darryl to walk through.

"Which room is hers?" he asked in a whisper.

Toy led the way down the narrow hall to the pink bedroom. "Just set her down on the bed. Poor thing, she's had a full day. Meeting her daddy was a pretty big deal."

"Ditto. I thought it went pretty good."

Toy had to agree. She had been amazed all evening at his tireless attentiveness to Lovie and could only believe he was being sincere. During dinner, their conversation was smooth and easy, and it had dawned on her that they didn't have to go through those excruciating early stages of a relationship trying to discover tidbits of each other's past, finding out what the other liked or disliked, their habits, their choices. For all the pain they'd gone through, tonight brought back memories of the better moments when they were friends.

She pulled down the blankets then he gently laid their child on the bed. Lovie groaned as she curled up on her pillow. Toy leaned over to begin untying Lovie's sneakers.

"Do you want me to wait in the other room while you get her into bed?" he asked. "I could make us some coffee."

"Actually, I think it's best we call it a night," she said, straightening slowly. "Lovie has school in the morning and I've got a full day at work."

He nodded his head but his disappointment was clear on his face. She'd been impressed all evening that he'd not once lost his temper, despite her egging him on, testing him from time to time.

He bent to kiss the top of Lovie's head. "G'night, sweet baby. I'll see you tomorrow."

"Okay, Daddy," she murmured sleepily.

Toy's head snapped up. "Tomorrow?"

"I can come by whenever you say," he said, his face all innocence.

"Mama, what time do I get home from school?" Lovie asked on a yawn.

Toy didn't know what to say. She removed one of Lovie's pink shoes with sparkly laces. She paused and looked at it in her hand. It was so small.

"Why don't you come by at six again? We can cook up the shrimp with some grits."

"Darlin', that's an invitation I can't say no to." He was buoyant and pointed his finger at Lovie, "And you . . . Lemme hear you say it one more time. Who am I?"

Lovie lifted her face to him and she smiled. "Daddy."

"Right."

"Lovie, get in your jammies," Toy told her. "I'll be right back to tuck you in."

Toy walked Darryl to the door, acutely aware of his nearness behind her. She opened it and felt a cool ocean breeze. Breathing in, she turned to find him only inches from her. The intensity of his gaze was disarming.

"She's a great kid," he said. "You did a great job."

"Thank you. And thanks again for dinner. We both had a nice time."

She tensed, thinking he'd make a move, but he walked around her and headed out. Before he left, however, he turned. His face was backlit by the porch light.

"I meant to tell you that you look real pretty. And I don't mean just tonight. You have a new look to you."

She snorted, "I should. I'm five years older and a mother now."

"There's that," he agreed. "But it's something else. You're, I don't know, grown-up. Wiser. You've become a woman any man would be proud to call his own." He looked at her with his blue eyes shining with sincerity. "Good night now."

"Good night," she said softly. Closing the door, she knew she'd be lying if she didn't admit she'd been moved.

The sky was inky black when Toy made her way home from the beach. A heavy cloud cover obscured any glimmer of light from either moon or stars, creating a ghostly sky filled with ominous shapes. She followed the narrow beam of light from her flashlight as she walked along the narrow beach path to the street. In the surrounding field, a scuttling noise followed by a chattering high in the palm tree hastened her pace.

She'd walked to clear her mind and set her priorities after the emotional roller coaster of the past few days. Unlike the cloudy sky, her mind felt clearer now and she had to follow the course of her decisions. She undressed quickly, climbed into bed then brought the phone close. She dialed the number she knew by heart. Chewing her lip, she listened as the phone rang once . . . twice . . .

"Hello?"

"Ethan? It's me. Toy."

"Hi."

His voice didn't sound like he'd been asleep but there was a coolness to it that put her on edge.

"I was out walking on the beach and I wondered if I'd missed your call."

"No, I hadn't called yet."

"Oh. Okay. I wanted to talk to you about tonight."

"How did dinner go? Was the shrimp okay?"

"Well, actually we didn't eat it. We went out to dinner after all. I was pretty nervous so I'm glad I didn't have to cook. I would have burned water."

"What were you nervous about?"

"Everything. Ethan, I haven't seen or heard from Darryl in five years. And now he comes back to meet Lovie for the first time. Isn't that enough?"

"I didn't realize you hadn't heard from him. I guess I thought you did." He paused.

"I really don't know much about him. You rarely mention him."

"Why would I? He's not part of the life I have now, and honestly, I'm not very proud of the part of my life that includes him."

"So why do you want to see him?"

"It's not that I want to see him. He wants to get to know his daughter."

"And how do you feel about that?"

"At first I was against it. Of course I would be. I'm still so angry at him. But now . . . I realize Lovie needs to know him and, for what it's worth, I'm glad she's having the chance."

"Do you think he'll be a good father to Lovie?"

Toy had to reflect on that question. An image of Darryl kissing the top of Lovie's head shot through her mind. She thought of Darryl's tenderness to Lovie, his eagerness to please. "I think so. I hope so. But good or bad, he's her father."

"I'd hate to see her hurt. She's a good kid."

"I can't stop her from getting hurt," Toy said evenly, having given this a great deal of thought. "But I will be there to help her through. I've been a single mom since the day she was born and I've had a lot of practice. And I have my village, which has helped raise Lovie since she was born — Cara and Brett, Flo, Emmi. We're all here for her. And for each other."

"Darryl may change the balance, you realize."

"I know," she replied. "He already has."

"Oh? How so?"

"My village isn't so keen on my decision to let Darryl back in."

"For what it's worth, I agree with them."

Weary, she sighed and leaned back against the pillows, knowing she was moving into the part of the conversation that would be tough.

"Darryl coming back into my life now is very intense," she tried to explain. "I think I need some time on my own to work this out."

He skipped a beat. "You need some time? What does that mean?"

"I mean . . ." She clutched the phone tightly. "I think we should stop seeing each other, just until I settle this with him."

"Do you still love him?" he asked sharply.

"No."

"Then what difference does it make?"

"It's confusing," she stumbled out.

"Why is it confusing if you don't love him?" An undercurrent of anger sounded in his rising voice.

"I don't know! It's just too much for me to deal with. I just can't see you, is all!"

There was a strained silence where no one spoke for several seconds. Then she heard his voice, calmer and deliberate.

"Despite what you say, you seem to still have a lot of unresolved feelings for this man." His voice was low with tightly restrained emotion. "I can understand that. He's the father of your child, after all. It would be wrong of me to get in the way now. I don't want to make things more difficult for you, or for Lovie."

She wished she could explain the myriad reasons why she was compelled to isolate herself from distractions and focus on settling this one area of her life so she could move on. Except, she couldn't speak lucidly about her feelings at the moment. She only knew that if she didn't get closure on this chapter of her life she'd never heal her old wounds and be able to move forward in her life.

"Please believe me. I didn't expect him to show up like this."

"It was bound to happen sooner or later."

"As you said, he is Lovie's father. I want . . . I feel I should give her a chance to know him."

"Are you sure that's all that it is?"

She sighed, feeling extraordinarily weary. "I'm not sure of anything anymore."

"Well, I am sure of my feelings."

She paused, questioning his meaning.

"I'll respect your wishes," he said succinctly. "You know where to find me."

Toy heard a click. She stared at the phone in her hand until the high-pitched beeping told her the connection was broken.

Medical Log "Big Girl"

August 31

Turtle's appetite picky again. She spits out fish. In attempt to get her to eat anything, volunteers are skinning her salmon. Now she eats five pounds of skinned salmon per day — no icky parts like heads or tails! But her rear is floating again. Very disappointing. Chloramphenicol (oral) begun. Second endoscopy scheduled.

Why the set-back, Big Girl? What's wrong with you? Hang in there. We'll figure this out. TS

20

Summer was coming to an end. The sea oats were turning gold and crisp. They rattled in the cooler evening breeze. Cara took Lovie to the beach one last time to check on Big Girl's nest.

Cara's back was aching something fierce so she sat in the beach chair and watched the girl's willowy form rake the beach in a sweet waltz of preparation for the small nest's hatching. Such hope and joy the young had!

They'd come to this nest each of the past five nights and she had to admire the little girl for her dedication. All season, Lovie had shown up at the nest inventories with Toy, and if her mother was busy, she begged Cara or Flo to take her. The child had heart.

The trouble was, Cara knew *this* nest was not going to hatch and it fell to her to dash the child's hopes. She let her play at catching ghost crabs for a while before cupping her hands and calling out, "Come on back, now. It's getting dark!"

Lovie kicked the sand but obliged and came to sit by Cara's side.

"Don't pout, sugar. You have school tomorrow morning. Your mama wants you home on time. She'll have my head on a platter if I keep you out late."

"I don't care."

"What's the matter? Don't you like school? First grade is a big step. You're in big girl school now."

Lovie rolled her eyes, having heard that many times before. "Mrs. Cryns is teaching us to read. But I can already read."

Cara tried not to smile. "Well, sure, but there's still a lot to learn, you know."

"I guess. At least she's real nice."

Cara paused but felt compelled to ask, "Do you think Darryl is nice?"

Lovie lifted a handful of sand and let it sift slowly through her fingers. "Daddy? Sure, he's nice, too. He plays me songs on his guitar. He's teaching me how to play one, too. I like it. It's fun. He told me I have a pretty voice and maybe I'll grow up to be a singer, like him."

Cara tried to keep her voice cheery. The thought of Lovie calling that man daddy, much less growing up to be like him, was galling. "Do you want to be a singer? Like him?"

She shrugged. "It's cool."

Cool? That was a new word for her and Cara didn't have to guess where it came from. "Is he nice to your mama?"

Lovie turned to look at her like she was crazy to ask such a stupid question. "He took us to the movies on Saturday."

"Ah, well, yes," Cara replied, struggling for seriousness. "That certainly is treating a lady nice."

It had been weeks since Darryl appeared on the scene and according to Flo, Darryl had been at the house several times each week, though *just for dinner,* she was careful to point out. Cara had told Flo it was a shame she'd never volunteered her services to the CIA. Admittedly, no one was happy about his coming and going, but Cara had been watching, too, and both Toy and Lovie seemed well enough. And Toy wasn't asking for her advice. Toy was a woman, a professional and a mother. Cara had to respect her decision, even if she didn't agree with it.

"I don't think any ghost crab will dare to come near your nest tonight," Cara said.

"They'd better not or I'll smoosh 'em."

Toy had carefully dressed Lovie in a pink,

long sleeved shirt and leggings to keep the mosquitoes at bay. Lovie stretched out on the sand beside the nest and put her ear to the ground. "I don't hear anything."

Cara chuckled. "You wouldn't hear anything, even if there were a hundred turtles in there, not just six."

"When do you think they'll come, Auntie Cara?"

"You know we can't say when a nest will hatch. We count the days and look for signs, but it's up to the turtles."

"But they're supposed to come tonight, right?"

Cara sighed, choosing her words. "Lovie, you know that this isn't a normal nest, don't you? Big Girl dropped these eggs in the tank and your mama and Ethan put them in the sand with a prayer."

Lovie smoothed the sand around the nest. "I know that. But Mama says she thinks it will hatch on account of it's here on Miss Lovie's dune."

Oh, Toy . . .

"Auntie Cara, if Mama put the eggs in here, how do the other turtle eggs get in the sand?"

She stroked Lovie's silky blond hair. Even though the child had seen many turtle nests and hatchlings, she'd never seen the rare

436

sighting of a loggerhead laying her eggs on the beach.

"You remember Big Girl, of course? Well, months back, some little voice in her head, we call it instinct, told her it was time to swim home to lay her eggs in the same sand she hatched in. So she swam and swam such a long way to get here. By the time she was ready to come ashore, she had five, six hundred eggs inside of her, not just these seven eggs."

"This is her home?"

"Well, the turtle's home is the sea, not the beach. All she knows and loves is in the ocean. So to lay her eggs, the mama has to leave her home and safety and all she knows to crawl out onto land. This is scary for her. She must be very careful. She waits until night so the darkness will hide her, then she sits in the surf a while to scout things out. If she spots a person walking or a dog, or if some bright light frightens her, she'll turn right around and go back to the sea. That's why we keep the lights off on the beach at night. When she's done, at last she goes back to the sea, one very tired mama."

"What does she do then?"

Cara shrugged lightly. "Then she goes off to find something to eat. The turtles don't eat during nesting, so she's very hungry."

"You mean, she doesn't come back to the nest? To take care of her babies?"

"No. The mother does her best to hide her eggs. Then she lets Mother Nature take care of them."

"And the turtle ladies."

Cara laughed. "Yes, and the turtle ladies."

Sensing the moment, Cara drew nearer to Lovie and spoke in a solemn voice. "Remember that these eggs were put into the sand by your mother, not the turtle mother. Honey, this nest is overdue. That means we have to face that this nest is not going to hatch. There are no babies in there. It just wasn't meant to be."

"But Mama said it would hatch." Lovie's lips began to tremble.

"No, honey, your mama *hoped* it would hatch." She brought Lovie into her lap and held her close. "Sometimes, we hope for things, but that doesn't mean it will happen."

"But that makes me sad."

"I know. Me, too. It's just nature's way."

She kissed Lovie's cheek. "Okay?" When the child nodded sadly, Cara helped her climb from her lap. Then she carefully pulled herself to her feet, careful to keep pressure off her abdomen, and offered her hand to the little girl. "Come on, honey.

438

Let's go home."

Later that month, Darryl sat in the beach house at the dining table with a yellow paper clown hat on his head. Little Lovie sat at his side wearing one in pink. They were making music together on their kazoos, laughing and tooting and having a great time. Toy listened and chuckled as she stood at the table cutting into the two-tiered birthday cake adorned with yellow and pink roses, six candles, and the scrolled words, *Happy 6th Birthday, Lovie!*

This is what is must be like to be a family, she thought to herself as she sliced a piece of yellow cake for the daddy, then the mommy and finally the child. She joined her family at the table, smiling yet feeling more like an observer at this party for two. Lovie was utterly and completely besotted with her father. From the moment he walked in the door till the teary goodbye, her face was alight with joy at being with him.

And he'd been a fabulous father these past weeks. No one was more surprised than she was at this turn of events. He didn't know much about nature but he followed Lovie from shell to shell on the beach and listened dutifully while she shared with him their names and little tidbits of knowledge, some correct, others not.

What he did know was music, however, and he was teaching Lovie how to play the guitar. His early birthday gift to her was her own instrument and every time he came by he gave her a lesson. Toy was amazed to discover her daughter had inherited Darryl's musical ability, because Lovie sure didn't inherit that talent from her. Already Lovie could pick out a few songs.

As summer turned into fall, Darryl became a fixture at the house and in their lives. Toy didn't know how she felt about that. Naturally she was happy that Darryl and Lovie were getting along so well, but as each day passed, Darryl's hints at reconciliation were growing more pressing.

She looked at the man across the table. He had his lean arm stretched across the back of Lovie's chair and was whispering something in her ear that sent Lovie into squeals of laughter. Ah, Darryl . . . He always could please the ladies. He was handsome enough. She used to swoon over his soulful eyes and the way he could melt her heart with a slow smile.

But she didn't swoon anymore. She didn't even sway. She just didn't feel the same for him and she was sorry for it. It would be so much easier if she could still be in love with him. Now she was stuck trying to rationalize whether a life with him was as good as a girl in her situation could expect.

"What are you doing by your lonesome over there?" Darryl asked with the devil in his eyes. "You're thinking too much again. Go on and get a kazoo and be crazy like us."

"Yeah, Mama, be crazy." Lovie giggled, tickled by the way her daddy teased.

Toy picked up the kazoo and blew hard. It sounded more like she was giving them the raspberries than a musical note and they burst out laughing. It worked . . . Toy started laughing, too.

"Mama, you *are* crazy," Lovie said in way of a compliment.

"I guess I am," she replied, and tooted the kazoo again.

On the other side of the island, Cara and Brett sat on the sofa watching the weather report on television. A Category One hurricane was hitting the state of Florida on the Atlantic side and that prompted worry that the storm would travel up the coast to South Carolina. The advance winds were shaking the palms and heavy rains were forecast. Brett had already carried in the porch furniture and any small objects that might get tossed in the wind.

"I hate this, hate this, hate this," Cara said, clutching his hand. "Our living room looks like a warehouse."

"Honey, you're wringing my hand clear off."

"I'm sorry, Brett. These hurricanes freak me out."

"You shouldn't get so worked up. First off it's only a category one hurricane. Second, we don't know yet which way the storm's going to turn. It might head straight north and miss us completely or fizzle out after it hits land. There's no point with second guessing these things. Third, the doctor told you to take it easy."

"She also told me that spotting is normal. Especially at the end of the first trimester. I'd say you were the one getting worked up about that."

He sighed and pulled her closer to him. "I know."

She rested her head on his shoulder and put her feet up on the ottoman. She knew he was being stoic for her sake. They'd both been spooked by more than a hurricane today. When she saw that first spot of bright, red blood she'd panicked, sure that she was having another miscarriage. Her hands had trembled when she called Brett on his cell phone.

Lord, she was embarrassed now for the fuss she'd made. Brett had been out on the tour boat. Robert raced from the dock on a wave runner to the boat to relieve him of command. When Robert later called to check on her, he told her not to blame him if the motor was ruined because he'd raced flat out to the tour boat, he was so worried Brett was going to jump ship and swim back to dock before he got there.

The doctor had assured them that all was well and in the aftermath both Cara and Brett were trying to play the role of believer. They'd had a simple dinner of carry-out and had stayed in and watched television all evening.

A vicious gust of wind sent the hurricane shutters creaking and the skies opened up, dumping sheets of rain that beat against the windows like bullets.

"I'm afraid," Cara said against his shirt.

Brett tightened his arm around her and Cara knew that he understood she wasn't talking about the force of wind. When he didn't say anything, she knew that he was afraid, too.

21

The loggerhead Caretta was undeniably the star of the Aquarium's Great Ocean Tank. When the turtle had arrived in Charleston six years earlier as a juvenile, there had been a city-wide contest for school children to name the new sea turtle. The big question on everyone's mind was, *Is the sea turtle a boy or a girl?*

The Aquarium just didn't know, since it is impossible to determine the sex of a sea turtle by physical signs prior to maturity. Once it reached adulthood, the male could be identified by its longer tail. Without expensive DNA tests or ultrasound, it was the public's guess if this new resident turtle was a male or a female. So when the turtle's tail grew longer, and its testosterone level tested high, everyone assumed that the sea turtle was a male. The name Caretta was chosen, from the Latin for loggerhead *Caretta caretta.* Toy had always thought it a feminine sounding name, rather like having a boy named Sue.

Boy or girl, Caretta was beloved by everyone at the Aquarium and the state of South Carolina because he really was a character. He hammed it up for photographers, huddled close to the glass so young children could gather around him, nipped the divers — which the audience thought was funny — and was a vision of grace when he swam past the viewing window.

The star turtle's yearly physical was on Toy's schedule for the day. When she arrived for work, Elizabeth was already in high gear. She was vigorously sweeping the floor that she'd scrubbed just the day before.

"You're here, thank goodness," Elizabeth said, her blue eyes wide with anticipation of the day ahead.

"Sorry. The Ben Sawyer Bridge was up again. I swear that line of cars keeps getting longer and longer." She set down her briefcase and camera on the steel examining table. The turtle hospital still didn't have desks or files in the basement but they made do with whatever surfaces they could scrounge. She turned and gave Elizabeth a quick once-over. "Say, don't you look nice."

Elizabeth blushed slightly. She'd obviously taken extra care with her appearance. Her thick white hair was styled and she'd put on makeup for the newspaper photographer due to arrive shortly. "I just got word that Kevin wants to inspect the turtle hospital today after Caretta's exam."

Toy's face fell. "Great, just great."

She grabbed a clipboard, thinking it wasn't Kevin's inspection or the newspaper reporter that had her flustered. Rather, it was the prospect of working closely with Ethan today. Ethan had not come down to the basement since she'd told him she needed time alone.

While she walked through the cavernous basement, she made a list of things that still had to get done. There was so much potential in all this space, she thought. In her mind's eye she envisioned what she could do with all that grant money. This was the only sea turtle hospital in the state and so much depended on whether or not they got the grant.

"Everything looks great, Elizabeth. Just remember not to feed them until after the inspection, or they'll foul the water just when Kevin walks though."

Elizabeth laughed. "Especially Litchfield. He'd do it just for spite."

"Well," she said, her hands on hips. "It looks pretty darn good, if I do say so myself.

Every tank has a turtle in it. If another sick turtle comes in before the grant, I just don't know where we're going to put it."

"The grant will come through, don't worry." She glanced at her watch. "Right now, you'd better get up to the Great Ocean tank. I'll man the fort."

"Thanks, Elizabeth. I don't know what I'd do without you."

"Just be sure to include me in a picture this time. I'm always cut out."

Toy looked at her lovely, open face. Her generous spirit shone through her eyes.

"I will. I promise."

Toy took a last look around then grabbed her camera and made her way to the third floor. Her palms were damp and she tried to appear calm, but knowing she would be seeing Ethan did nothing to quell her nerves.

The dive team was already suited up and gathered on the metal platform at the tank's edge. She recognized Ethan easily by his height but his attention was on the equipment and he didn't acknowledge her approach. Favel and Irwin, also in wet suits, returned her wave. Toy walked around the top of the tank and exchanged greetings with Kevin and Jason.

The commotion at the dive platform

brought Caretta swimming by, curious and looking for a hand-out. At Ethan's signal, the team of divers jumped into the tank, surrounding the unsuspecting turtle. It didn't take Ethan and the team long to corral the indignant turtle onto the platform where a team of six stood ready to heave the unwilling and decidedly uncooperative, three hundred pound turtle out of the tank. It was quite a job. Caretta waved his powerful flippers, splashed wildly, and if given the chance, would have nipped any arm or leg within his bite radius. She saw the creamy underbelly of the turtle as they hoisted him off the platform. Ethan pulled himself out from the water and grabbed hold of the shell.

"Move off," he said gruffly to her, his focus intense. "He's too heavy."

"I can handle it," she ground out.

"I've got him," he barked, and this time it was an order.

Toy released the shell and backed away, fuming that he'd claimed rank. Although she knew that he was taking no chances with his famous turtle, it stung nonetheless to be ordered away by virtue of her sex. She watched the men struggle to get the big turtle over the tank wall and gingerly placed into the plastic crate. Everyone heaved a sigh of relief when that part of the job was done.

Downstairs in her turtle hospital, the examination went smoothly. Dr. Tom examined the turtle, took samples, gave him an ultrasound and weighed him. At the end of the exam, Dr. Tom proclaimed the turtle healthy but overweight.

"Your butterball has to go on a diet," he told Ethan.

Toy couldn't hold back the giggle that escaped from her lips. Ethan flushed slightly and said he'd look into it immediately.

The chubby Caretta behaved himself while Toy and Elizabeth scrubbed his carapace. The guys waited, standing around and talking about the possible diet changes, various Aquarium business, and "those great-looking cutlass fish." Twenty minutes later her fingers were pruned and her shoulders ached, but Caretta's shell was gleaming. The physical was over.

When they lifted the sea turtle back into his crate, he offered little argument. The turtle seemed to know he was headed back home for lunch. Favel and Irwin, still in their wet suits, came back to transport the turtle back to the big tank. They whispered something to Elizabeth that sent her squelching an outburst with her palms.

Then en masse they turned to look at Toy, their eyes bright with excitement.

What? she mouthed to them, but they just smiled and called out their goodbyes.

"How about that tour?" Kevin asked.

"Yes, sir," she replied. "I'll be right with you."

Toy washed the betadine and soap from her hands in the big sink, then tucked a fallen lock behind her ear, hoping she didn't look too disheveled after her waltz with Caretta. She was intensely aware that Ethan had not left yet, nor had Jason or Tom. They followed as she led Kevin past each of the six holding tanks and told each turtle's history. Over each tank, Elizabeth had put Toy's *Before and After* photographs of the turtle. Each picture spoke a thousand words about the miracle of the turtle's rehabilitation and was a testament to the great work being done at the hospital.

She was proud of their efforts and some of their innovative solutions. There was the epoxy seal on Cherry's broken shell and Hamlin's repaired flipper. Big Girl's weight belt drew a chuckle from Kevin. But it was Litchfield who delivered his usual coup de grace as the director walked past. Elizabeth groaned and dashed for the net to clean the tank.

"If we get the grant, we'll be able to filter the water in each tank," Toy said as they watched Elizabeth skim Litchfield's tank. "The good news is we're ready for our first release back to the ocean." She pointed to the tank beside them. "Kiawah is ready to go. We're just waiting on the final blood work results."

Kevin stopped and put his hands behind his back. Ethan, Jason and Tom gathered closer. Even Elizabeth drew her net from the tank and waited, listening. Toy sensed something was up.

"You've done a great job here and all on a shoestring budget," Kevin said. "We're all very proud of what you and your colleagues have achieved. Now, about those filters . . ." Kevin's face eased into a smile. "It's my distinct pleasure to inform you that the grant has been approved. Congratulations."

Suddenly she was surrounded by laughing and applauding and people offering congratulations. Toy's mouth hung open with shock as she tried to take the news in. Her eyes sought out one person amidst the whirlwind. Ethan stood outside the circle but his eyes were on her. When their gazes locked it felt as though everyone else in the room had disappeared. In that moment all their earlier aloofness shattered and they shared the private knowledge that this award was a result of both of their efforts and dreams.

The moment was gone as quickly as it came and she knew a profound sense of loss.

Jason called out for everyone's attention.

"Before we break up," Jason said in the tone of an announcement, "I thought you'd all want to know what we discovered today in Caretta's ultrasound."

Everyone stilled, riveted by what they were about to learn.

Jason spread out his palms. "Caretta is a girl!"

Another round of laughter rang out, peppered with several bursts of, "I told you so!" and "I knew it!" Toy had to admit, the turtle's longer tail had her fooled. Ethan and Jason bid goodbye to hurry off and escort the lovely Caretta back into the GOT.

"There's something else we need to discuss after the party," Kevin said in a confidential tone to Toy as he walked with her to a party in the conference room to celebrate the grant's success.

Flo and Emmi had the lights blazing at their house when Toy arrived. Balloons and banners shouting out CONGRATULATIONS in neon colors filled the front room, and

452

Emmi met her at the door with a glass of champagne.

Toy stepped in and looked around the front room in a daze, her eyes filling with gratitude. The whole team was here for *her* and their love was more palpable than the wild colors, the thumping music or the wide grins on their faces. Toy was keenly aware of how much each person in this room had given her and how, because of them, she had traveled far from the day she'd first walked into their lives, a suspicious, broke, pregnant teen.

There was a crush of hugs and heartfelt congratulations and plenty of jokes and stories about poor Caretta, who would be the topic of the town for weeks to come.

"The house looks great," she told Emmi.

Emmi looked around the front room and smiled. "Flo and I had a blast fixing it up. We painted all the rooms a soft palette and polished the floors. Then we just picked our favorite things, a few of my pieces from Atlanta and a few of Miranda's antiques. The rest we put in storage. It looks fresher, doesn't it? Younger?"

"It really does. The plantation shutters are a nice touch. The house feels happy."

Emmi's gaze flicked across the room shining with contentment. "We are. We get along fabulously. She loves to cook and I like to dust."

Toy chuckled. "Who'd have thought two firebrands like you could live together?"

Emmi stepped closer and said in a lowered voice, "Listen, I know you've been talking to Cara about moving. No, no," she said when Toy's eyes widened. "We're not sticking our noses in your business. We just wanted you to know that if you're looking for somewhere to move, well," she shrugged, "we'd love to have you and Lovie move in here."

Toy's breath fled from her, the kindness almost overwhelming her. "Oh, Emmi, that's so nice of you, but I don't know . . ."

"Just so you know you have an option. Not that Cara's kicking you out, God knows."

"If I did, wouldn't this be like the turtle team dorm house?"

Emmi tossed her head back and laughed. "I love that! Sure, why not. We can even get a sign made up." She laughed again then seeing Toy's uncertain expression, said, "I'm joking!"

"Thanks for the invitation, Emmi." She puffed out a soft plume of air. "I guess the summer is over and I have to start thinking about all that."

"Not tonight," Emmi said, pouring more champagne into her glass. "Tonight is to celebrate. I'm proud of you, sweetie. We all are. No one deserves this break more than you. All you have to think about is how you're going to spend all that grant money!"

Flo came up carrying a tray of cold shrimp. "Help yourself, star." While Toy took a shrimp, Flo asked, "Where's Ethan? Didn't he want to come? I seem to recall that he had a lot to do with this grant."

Toy twiddled the shrimp on the toothpick. "I didn't invite him. We . . . well, we aren't seeing each other and . . ."

"Shoot, he still could've stopped by for some champagne. He deserves it."

Emmi looked through the white window shutters at Toy's beach house across the drive. "Did you invite Darryl?"

She said Darryl's name like it was an obscenity. Toy shook her head. "I haven't even told him yet." She skipped a beat then asked, "But would he have been welcomed if I had?"

Emmi's lips tightened and she looked at Flo.

"It's your house now," Flo told her.

"I wouldn't have kicked him out . . ." Emmi said, hedging.

Toy nodded her head feeling no anger,

just a weary sadness that Darryl was still unwelcome by those she loved.

"Honey," Emmi said, trying to return to an upbeat mood, "you don't want to put Darryl in the same room with Brett anyway, especially after a few beers. I just put up my best porcelain!"

"Speaking of Brett, he's hovering pretty close to Cara," Flo said, pointing to the pair across the room. All three women turned heads to see Cara sitting in an armchair with Brett standing by her side like a guard holding a plate of shrimp. "And that's not all," Flo said bringing her head in closer. "She's drinking club soda."

Emmi's lips pursed in thought. "I noticed that! She hasn't had a drink in weeks."

"Try months," Flo said knowingly. "And look at her, she's looking a little softer and rounder." Emmi nodded in agreement. "You know what I think?"

Toy shook her head. "Oh, no, she'd have told us."

Emmi and Flo turned to look at her, both shaking their heads.

"Cara can be darn secretive if she wants to be," Emmi said. "When we were eight she had a crush on Tom for weeks before she fessed up."

"Well, I don't know about you, but I'm

456

tired of pussyfooting around. I'm going to ask her."

Toy and Emmi exchanged shocked glances, then giggled and followed Flo as she marched across the room. Cara's face lifted and she smiled when she saw the gang approach.

"Well, what's this?" she asked when they circled her chair. "An impromptu turtle team meeting?"

Emmi and Toy looked at Flo. Her blue eyes were shining like two hot torches.

"Missy, we've come to ask you a question."

Cara's expression grew rueful. "Uh-huh," she said with humor. She glanced up at Brett.

"Are you . . ."

"Hold on," Brett said firmly.

Toy held her breath. Brett was easygoing about most things, but when it came to Cara he was a bulldog of resistance.

Flo shut her mouth tight and her eyes widened with surprise. Emmi shifted her weight nervously.

Brett looked down at Cara and she nodded.

"You'll spoil our surprise," Brett said to Flo, a half smile forming at his lips. Then lifting his head he gazed at the faces of the three women. "Cara and I have some good news to share. We're pregnant!"

At eight-thirty the dishes were washed, the left-over food was stored in the fridge and Lovie was asleep in the guest room. Yet the joy of the day was still thrumming in their veins and no one was quite ready to leave.

Toy sat alone in a wicker rocker on the back porch. It was too dark to see anything but she could hear the ocean's rhythmic roar like a white noise in the distance. The hurricane in Florida had veered far northeast to dissipate in the ocean, to everyone's relief. Yet the storm's parting gift of wind and rain had pushed away the heavy humidity, leaving the islands lush and fresh. Toy was filled with languor as the off shore breezes soothed the bubbles in her head from so much champagne and good news.

She couldn't remember ever having such a day! The grant approval . . . Cara pregnant . . . Emmi and Flo settled in this house. How could she hold so much happiness? She wrapped her arms around herself and sighed. All their lives were changing so quickly. What was next?

Her gaze drifted across the driveway. Her beach house was empty and deserted. That, she thought grimly, was likely her answer.

The time had come for her to leave the beach house.

Emmi's invitation fluttered back into her thoughts. It should have been a welcome prospect, yet all Toy could feel was a shudder of dread at the prospect of leaving. She'd told Cara she would start looking for a new place at summer's end and here it was, late September, and she'd not made a single phone call. The news of Cara's pregnancy, while joyous, forced Toy to the only decision she could make. Cara would need the extra rental money now more than ever.

Yet to leave the beach house was to leave the only security she'd ever known. Toy thought of what it would be like not to live in Miss Lovie's home, surrounded by her things, embraced by all the memories. Was she ready to go?

"There you are!"

Cara came out to the porch carrying two mugs of steaming coffee. "It's decaf," she said, handing Toy one cup. "And hot. Careful! Milk and one teaspoon of sugar, right?"

"Perfect, thank you." She drew the green earthenware mug emblazoned with a turtle close to her nose. "It smells heavenly."

"Is this a private party or can I join you?"

"Sit yourself down, little mama. Please."

Cara set her coffee down on the small table and tugged another wicker rocker closer to Toy. She eased herself into the chair and sighed with contentment. "It was a great party, wasn't it?"

"I'm overwhelmed. Two parties in one day is too much for a poor country girl like me."

"You've played that poor country girl card for the last time," Cara admonished her. "You're a successful Aquarist about to launch the state's first sea turtle hospital. You're a shooting star, if you don't mind my saying so,"

Toy snorted and shook her head, but the words fell upon her as soft and welcome as the sweet scented breezes.

"How much did the grant actually award you?"

"Three hundred and fifty thousand dollars."

Cara stopped rocking and gaped. "That much?"

She nodded. "Although not all of it goes directly to the turtle hospital. The Aquarium will get a designated amount to support the facility. But we'll be receiving at least $150,000, more than enough to create a turtle hospital to be proud of."

"This was a private grant?"

"Yes. A private foundation."

"Amazing. Toy, you can accomplish so much with that kind of seed money."

"I can't wait to begin. Jason told me I will be the one to map out the facility. It will be an enormous amount of work, but oh, Cara, such happy work. I'll be able to buy most everything on my wish list. I'm still in shock. I can't believe I really got it."

Cara leaned over to hug Toy, squeezing tight, sharing all the bliss that was in her soul. Toy was small boned and baby faced. She brought out maternal protectiveness in Cara. She closed her eyes and thought this was what it must be like to be a mother and watch your child realize her dreams.

"There's more news I haven't shared yet," Toy said, pulling away.

Cara drew back, stabbed by the sudden fear that Toy was going to announce an engagement with Darryl. "What?"

"The director of the Aquarium told me that with winning this award I've been invited to attend the foundation's next meeting. It's a turtle consortium, focusing on the plight of the leatherbacks. He wants me to go, all expenses paid. Cara, it's in Costa Rica."

"I love Costa Rica!" Cara exclaimed, giddy with relief. "It's a fabulous place, a mecca for an environmentalist like you.

You'll have a wonderful time."

"But I don't know if I should go. I've so many responsibilities right now. There's my job, of course. Getting this grant will mean double the work to set up the hospital. And who will take care of all the turtles while I'm away? And of course, there's Little Lovie. I can't just up and leave her. Who'll take care of her?"

"I will," Cara answered bluntly. "And as for the turtles, don't you have volunteers to cover for you?"

"Yes, but not for the planning of the hospital. There's so much to consider."

"Don't you dare overthink this. It's a great opportunity. You've got to go."

"But Cara," Toy said, holding herself tight. "I've never been on a plane before. I've never even left South Carolina, much less the country!"

"All the more reason. It's high time. Just grab your passport and go."

"See, that's what I mean. I don't have a passport. I don't even know how to get one."

"It's all part of the learning curve," Cara replied. "Einstein said the only source of knowledge is experience."

"And there's a proverb that says experience is the best school but the tuition is the highest. Based on that, I've already been to the ivy league of experience school."

Cara sensed there was more to this fear than Toy was sharing with her. "Does your hesitation to go have anything to do with Darryl?"

"Darryl? No. Why would you think that?"

She shrugged evasively. "I was just wondering how things were progressing between the two of you. I have to admit, I was worried you were going to announce an engagement."

"An engagement?" Toy huffed out a laugh. "I'm not ready to get married to anyone."

Cara's relief was evident. "Thank God. I'm glad to hear it."

Toy sighed and stretched her legs out. Cara followed suit. They sat rocking while the pale half moon slowly rose higher over the ocean, shedding her luminous light.

"How are things going with Ethan?" Cara asked at length. "Will he be helping you set up the new hospital?"

Toy rocked back and forth then replied, "I think I've blown it. I waited too long. We're barely friends any more."

"Really?"

"It used to be so easy between us at work. He always was surprising me with his kindness." She wasn't aware that her face broke into a smile, remembering. "Like when I'd be getting soaked by splashing flippers trying to get a turtle out of the tank. Suddenly he'd be there, hoisting the turtle out. Or when Dr. Tom came to treat the turtles, Ethan would stick around to help or take photographs. And, of course, the way he volunteered to help me write a grant for the sea turtle hospital. He didn't have to do that."

"I'm sorry to hear that. I liked him."

"I did, too. I still do. But he's not interested in me, not in that way."

"Are you sure about that?"

Toy turned and Cara saw a war of emotions in her eyes.

"Things are going pretty well between Darryl and me," she said, changing the subject.

"Hmm." Cara's flat tone reflected her enthusiasm.

"It's just . . . I don't know. It's different between us. He's different, or I'm different, but it's not the same." She turned up her hands with a slight shrug. "I don't know why, but little things he does bug me now. Things I didn't notice before."

Cara started rocking, enjoying the direction of the conversation. "Like what?"

"Like when he puts his beer down on the table without a coaster, or talks with his mouth full." She looked at Cara and grinned. "Oh, Lord, and the way he laughs. He makes this guttural sound deep in his throat." She tried to imitate the sound. "It sounds like he's starting an engine, or coughing up a hair ball."

Cara was laughing so hard tears were in her eyes. "You should hear Brett snore. It's like front row seats at the Indy 500."

"Not that Darryl doesn't have good qualities," Toy was quick to add. "And he's trying so hard. He's always taking us out to eat, or bringing a little gift for Lovie. Did you know he's teaching her the guitar? She's really quite good. I would never have known that, if it weren't for him."

"Lovie told me."

The mirth fled from her face and she said more somberly, "He's had a hard time the past five years. He doesn't have much. Bad luck follows him like a shadow."

"Bad luck is what we conveniently call our bad choices."

Toy stopped talking to take a sip of coffee. Cara judiciously waited.

"This sounds really bad," Toy began again, faltering. She set the coffee on the table. "I don't want to sound conceited, like I'm a brain or anything, but . . ."

"He's as dumb as a brick," Cara finished for her.

Toy released a heavy sigh. "Well, he doesn't think things through, that's for sure. He's so impulsive and I'm just the opposite. I have to consider every side before making a decision. I was young and didn't have much schooling when we were together, so I guess I didn't notice before that he wasn't real smart, or I just made excuses. But now when I try to talk to him about my work or what I'm reading, even current issues, not only doesn't he have any opinion, but half the time he doesn't know what I'm talking about! The other day I told him I really loved the work of Henry Thoreau, and he asked what movie he was in."

Cara couldn't help herself, she burst out laughing. Secretly, she was overjoyed that Darryl was making a poor showing. Ever since he'd come back into Toy's life Cara had been living in fear that Toy would call some night, crying that she'd been smacked around again, or worse, Lovie had. Or, that Toy would convince herself she was in love with him again.

"Okay, so he's impulsive, reckless and doesn't think things through. What a prince. He might be on his best behavior now, but are you sure he isn't after the sweet situation?"

"He wouldn't come all this way just to stay in the beach house."

"Why not? I wouldn't put it past him."

"Cara, you're not being fair to him."

"How do you know? Can you really trust him?"

"I don't know," she exclaimed honestly. "What am I going to do, Cara?"

"Honey, just tell him *adios.* That's good-bye in Spanish, by the way. You'll have to start practicing it now for Costa Rica."

"I can't do that."

"Why not? He dumped you before. It's only fair play."

Toy looked off and Cara realized Toy still felt deep pain at the memory.

"You don't have feelings for him, do you?"

"Of course I do. He's the father of my child."

Toy's loyalty, while an admirable trait, was also her blind spot. Cara wasn't able to keep the annoyance she felt from creeping into her voice. "Wise up, Toy! The man used to slap you around."

Toy drew herself up in her chair. "Cara," she replied, her voice sharp with anger. "I've been slapped around by men all of my life.

Trust me. I won't let anyone slap me again. Ever."

There was such power and conviction in that statement that Cara couldn't respond without sounding patronizing. She leaned back in her chair and resolutely looked at the stars.

There was an unspoken contest between the turtle ladies while they sat at nests, night after night, over who could first spy a falling star. With her head tilted back, Cara followed a satellite as the pulsing dot moved across the heavens.

"You mad?" Toy's voice sounded soft in the darkness.

"No," she replied honestly. "I'm just wondering if this is one of those times you want me to listen."

Toy laughed lightly and patted Cara's arm, appreciating her effort.

"I have to learn I can't always make things better," Cara said. "Like Flo said."

"But you make things better just by being here and listening. And Cara, I do listen to you and think through your advice."

"Yeah, well, take it for what it's worth. You were right when you said I just don't know your feelings and the life you've lived." She turned and looked into Toy's eyes. "You're not the young kid in trouble any more. I not only hear you, Toy. I see you as the woman you've become. This is your decision."

"Thank you," she said, deeply moved by the recognition. "I'm taking it day by day. I'm not naive," she said in explanation. "I've been watching Darryl these past weeks. Every movement, every nuance. I've even goaded him, just to test him. I really believe he's changed." She paused. "He wants us to be a family."

Cara felt a panic bubble in her chest. "What are you telling me? Are you in love with him?" she asked quietly.

"Oh, Cara, I don't know what being in love is. We have a nice time together. Lovie adores him. When we're together, it feels like we're a family."

"But do you love him?"

"Love is highly overrated."

"Answer my question. Do you love him?"

"Cara, love isn't the only basis for a marriage."

Cara jerked to a stop and sputtered, "What do you think the basis of marriage is, if not love?"

Toy raised her hand and counted off her fingers. "Commitment, duty, respect, a shared life, children."

"Those are all ingredients of a successful

marriage, I agree. But if you don't first have that spark of true love, the passion, the *knowing* in your heart and body that he is your soul mate, then what are you building on? Without love, marriage is nothing more than a dreary chore."

"What about arranged marriages? They often work out."

"Darlin,' over two hundred years ago people spilled blood for the right to marry for love instead of an arranged marriage based on politics or financial advantages. Don't take a step backward."

"Being married to Darryl wouldn't be so different than what I have right now. We get along, we know each other, our good points and our bad. It would provide Lovie and me with security."

Cara tsked. "You don't get married for security." She paused as a new thought took root. "This wouldn't be because you feel you have to leave the beach house?"

"No," Toy replied so quietly that Cara knew she was lying.

"I told you that you do not have to leave."

"Cara, this is about so much more than that. A family life would be good for Lovie. She wants a daddy so badly."

"You can let him back into Lovie's life but that doesn't mean you have to let him back into yours. You shouldn't get married for Lovie's sake. This is something you do only for yourself, Toy."

"Isn't that being selfish?"

"You bet it is! *Self*-ish, in a good way. How can give you yourself to another man, be a strong half of a whole, when you don't know who *yourself* is? You need to be selfish, now."

Neither spoke for a moment. Toy brought her fingertips to her cheek. Cara wanted to grab her shoulders and shake her. It was so clear to her that Toy needed to relinquish her past and all the guilt and insecurities she harbored once and for all. Her inner wounds were as yet unhealed, despite all her outward success. Cara seized the moment. She turned to Toy and took her hands and held them so they faced each other. When she spoke, it was heartfelt.

"This trip to Costa Rica couldn't have come at a better time. It's something you should do — need to do — for you. This is not a vacation. It's a chance to do something you love, without having to worry about everything and everyone else for a change. You need this time away — from Darryl, from the Aquarium, from the beach house, even from Lovie. Mama once told me that we women need solitude in our lives to refill our well and garner strength to face life's deeper questions."

"Dear Miss Lovie. I wish she were here now."

"She is. Don't you feel her? Toy, think of how far we've both come since Mama died. She'd be so proud of you. And I know what she'd tell you. *Carpe Diem!* Honey, let go of your fears. Go to Costa Rica! Experience life! It's your turn."

Toy puffed her cheeks and blew out a stream of air. "It's a big step for me."

Cara patted her belly and said, "It's a big step for *me.*"

They both chuckled. From the corner of her eye, she spotted a fiery path arc across the sky. Cara pointed excitedly. "A falling star! Quick, make a wish!"

22

Toy and Elizabeth stood in the basement of the Aquarium facing the six tanks with looks of utter amazement. Toy had never seen anything like it.

All the sea turtles had uniformly turned in their tanks and were swimming in the same direction, their flippers stroking and their beaks bumping against the tank wall. They couldn't see each other in the tanks, so there was no communication between them. It was as if some signal in their brain, some click in their magnetic source, triggered and told them it was time to head south.

"They must be migrating," Toy said in wonder.

"Are they trying to head to warmer waters for the winter?" asked Elizabeth.

"I don't know. Look at them! They keep swimming up against the tank. They're not going anywhere but they just keep pedaling away."

"Synchronized swimming in turtles," Elizabeth joked.

Toy clucked her tongue, worried. "They're so restless. It makes me want to hurry and release them back to the sea before the water gets too cold." Her glance moved toward the big tank. "Maybe even Big Girl."

"Hopefully we'll get the okay from Dr. Tom by the time you get back from Costa Rica. Speaking of which, are you all packed?"

"Just about. Thanks again for the new swimsuit, Elizabeth. It's beautiful, but you shouldn't have."

"It was nothing."

"I know! That's the point! There's nothing to it. I never saw such a teeny bikini!"

"Just pack it. It's what they wear in the tropics."

"I don't know . . ."

"Loosen up and live a little, girl! You'll be old like me before you know it and then you'll regret not having worn a bikini like that when your figure was sexy. You've got a cute little body under all that baggy khaki and cotton. What are you waiting for? Show it off! Look what happens when gravity takes its toll." She puffed out air. "Just pack it. Trust me."

Toy chuckled. Maybe she'd toss the bikini in the suitcase after all. "I've so much to do to get off by tomorrow. If I'd known how much work getting ready for a trip was, I'd never have agreed to go."

"It's all worth it once you get there."

"Be sure to keep up the medical journals while I'm gone. I hardly know how I'll end each day without them. They're like a diary."

"If turtle meds are all you have to record in your diary, then girl, you better wear that bikini in Costa Rica."

"Could you please go fetch Jason and Dr. Tom?" Toy said with crooked grin. "They need to see this phenomenon." She grabbed her camera and began clicking pictures. She wanted proof because she wasn't sure anyone would believe her that the turtles were all voluntarily swimming in the same direction.

She was dangling over Big Girl's tank, trying to get a good angle for her shot when she heard footfalls approaching. Lowering her camera, she looked over her shoulder and was startled to see Ethan walking her way. He was the last person she expected to see that day. She slowly lifted to face him, regaining her balance, smoothing back her hair and wiping the splashed water from her face.

Her emotions were already at boiling point this final day before her trip to Costa Rica but she managed to settle herself and offer him a tight smile and hello.

"Looks like you're about to fall in," he said, trying to be amiable.

"Just trying to get pictures of this. Amazing, isn't it?"

"What's that?" he asked. His blue eyes looked puzzled.

She lifted her arms to indicate the tanks. "The turtles! They're all swimming in the same direction."

"Really?" He blinked and looked across the basement over the tanks.

"Isn't that why you're here? Didn't Elizabeth tell you?"

"Elizabeth? No. I haven't seen her." His eyes watched the turtles and a small smile lifted his mouth. "I'll be damned. What incredibly curious creatures they are. It's got to be instinct. Migration. It's the right time of the year. What else do you think could be the cause?"

"That's what I was thinking, too. I've called in Tom and Jason."

She hadn't called for his opinion in months and she knew from his reaction that he was acknowledging the same fact. "Then what brings you here?"

His hands tightened on the clipboard he was carrying and he blinked a few times, always a sign he was waging an inner struggle.

"Is anything the matter?" she asked.

"No. I just thought I'd come by and see you. Or rather, how you're doing. With the plans for the new facility, that is."

"We're busy, but handling it, thanks."

He nodded. "Yes, of course you are. Do you need help?" he volunteered. "With the design?"

"No, but thanks."

He nodded again, though she could see he was surprised by her quick rejection.

"You've released a turtle," he said, looking around. He clearly was feeling uncomfortable, grasping for things to say.

"Two, actually. Sharkbite and Kiawah. Cherry Point is scheduled to go after I get back from Costa Rica."

"Ah, yes. Costa Rica." He seized on that. "When do you go?"

"Tomorrow. The meeting is over the weekend and I'll be back here on Tuesday."

"You'll love it there. You'll be looking for an arribada, I suppose?"

"If I'm lucky. I'm really hoping to see a

leatherback."

He looked skeptical. "It's pretty early for those, I'm afraid. I wouldn't get my hopes up."

"That seems to be a failing of mine, getting my hopes up."

He raised his brows and said, "A failing? I'd call that a quality. It's one of the things I like best about you. Your unflinching optimism."

She wasn't prepared for a compliment. It emboldened her. "I wasn't aware that you liked anything about me."

"Why do you say that?"

"Why do I say that?" she exclaimed, feeling herself boil over. "Ethan, you've been avoiding me for weeks."

"I thought I was doing what you'd asked," he said in defense. "Staying away."

She shook her head, awash in hurt and frustration. "It doesn't matter anymore."

"But it does," he said quickly.

She looked at him, startled by the confession. His dark eyes were filled with unspoken words. She longed to hear each one of them and looked at his lips, hoping to see them form. The air thickened between them. Her heart beat wildly against her chest and they drew closer, as if pulled by the same magnetic force that guided the turtles. His head angled, and eyes on her lips, he leaned toward her.

From the other side of the room they heard the door slam and voices of several people as they entered the basement. "Hey, look at those crazy turtles!" called out a voice she recognized as Jason's.

Ethan and Toy took a clumsy step back. She felt herself blushing, confused at what just transpired. Looking up, she saw Jason and Tom following Elizabeth into the facility. Toy sneaked a glance at Ethan. He was standing straight, clutching his clipboard with a look of annoyance on his face.

She plastered a smile on hers and greeted them.

"I've got to go," Ethan told the group as they drew near.

"You've got a shark acting up, don't you?" Jason asked, all business.

Ethan nodded. "His habits have shifted some. I'm going in with him later this afternoon."

"Be careful in there," Tom said.

"I will." He cast a troubled glance at Toy. "I have something for your trip to Costa Rica. Can I drop it by your office?"

She answered quickly, flustered. "Of course. Any time."

"Good." With a cursory nod, he turned

and walked away.

Toy walked to Big Girl's tank and put her hand on the rim, steadying herself. To the others she looked like she was studying the turtle, when in her heart she was swimming with her, her long creamy flippers extended, nose against the obstacle, pushing beyond the pain to the other side.

Toy worked diligently as the afternoon waned to finish the mountain of paperwork on her desk before leaving. Downstairs, Elizabeth was reviewing each turtle before closing up. Jason had agreed to cover for Toy while she was gone, but Elizabeth would be doing the day to day workload. Favel, too, was spending more and more time downstairs in the basement with the turtles. Toy wasn't sure if that was because he was growing increasingly fascinated with the loggerheads or the lovely Elizabeth.

Smiling at the possible love affair blooming downstairs, she filed her manila folder and closed the drawer. She heard a soft clearing of the throat and turned abruptly to see Ethan standing at the entrance to her cubicle. She brought her hand to her throat.

"I didn't mean to startle you. Is this a bad time?" he asked.

"No! Come on in. I'm just trying to work

my way through the paperwork before I leave."

Ethan's gaze swept the cubicle which was smaller than his own. He pointed to a recent watercolor of Lovie's depicting Kiawah's release to the ocean. "That's nice," he said and a small smile eased the tension in his face. "I love the way kids draw. It's so primitive yet the details are amazing. Look at those scutes."

"She's a born naturalist."

"How is Lovie doing?"

"She's fine." She skipped a beat. "She misses you."

There was a moment's tug of silence. "I miss her, too."

Toy felt rocked by the words but could only continue to stare at the square of paper and paint stuck on the wall with a push pin. She sensed his nearness in the small space and she found it hard to keep her breathing even. When she thought she couldn't pretend to look at the little drawing any longer he spoke.

"I brought you some things I thought you'd need in Costa Rica."

She turned too quickly, almost bumping him. "Oh?"

He handed her some maps and a book. She accepted them, thanking him, and immediately dropped her gaze to the guide book. The pages were well worn and heavily notated with his thin scrawl. He'd marked which restaurants were good, which hotels to avoid, where the surf was best.

"All your personal notes are in here. Are you sure you want to lend it to me? I'd hate to lose it."

"I lived there for six years. I don't need a guide book. Besides, parts of the country are changing so fast, my notes are probably outdated. But you might find some things helpful." He pointed to the book. "There's an envelope in it, in the back."

Toy searched the book and found the envelope. Inside she found several bills of Costa Rican money.

"There's thousands here," she said, counting the amounts printed on each.

"Oh, it's not much. Maybe enough for lunch. Oh, and here."

He dug down into his pants pocket and she heard the jingle of coins as he pulled them out. Ethan opened his palm, extending his long fingers. He picked out a small black shell from the coins and put it back into his pocket, but not before Toy recognized it as the moon shell that Little Lovie had given to him on the beach.

Ethan handed her the coins. "Here's some

change. It always comes in handy."

"Thank you. I appreciate it." Her mind scrambled for words. "Can I bring you back something?"

He was looking at her intently and she had the feeling he was debating whether or what to reply. She felt herself coloring, wishing she could just blurt out what was lodged in her throat — that she would bring her heart back to him, her mind, her body, her soul, if only he'd give her some small sign that he wanted them.

He shook his head and muttered, "No, thanks. I just wanted to give you that. Have a good time."

Well, that was it, Toy thought with a sigh as she closed her desk drawer. Her work was done and she was ready to head home. Her fingers drummed the cleared desk anxiously. She so rarely took time off that a whole week away seemed like forever.

She knew it wasn't just her leaving that was making her feel queasy in the stomach. She'd been plagued ever since Ethan had stopped by. She couldn't stop thinking about him. He lurked in the back of her mind and her emotions were going round and round, endlessly, like Big Girl in her tank. Was she imagining it or did she feel the tug of magnetism between them? Did they really almost kiss? And that was Little Lovie's shell he kept in his pocket, she knew it. That had to mean something, didn't it?

She looked at her wristwatch and sighed with frustration. Time to go home, she told herself. She rose, took a last look around her cubicle then able to procrastinate no longer, she picked up her backpack and turned off the light. Her mind was still puzzling over Ethan as she rode the elevator down to the Aquarium's main floor. It was near closing and only a few stragglers remained around the large gallery tank at the entrance, pointing at the moray eel that was slowly emerging from the rocks. She walked past them, rolling Ethan's words over in her mind. She continued across the bright, airy main floor of the Aquarium, past exhibits glistening with water, glass and greenery, to the exit. Before the glass doors she stopped.

Compelled by some strange force she couldn't name, she turned and walked back through the gallery, past the cluster of people to the Great Ocean Tank gallery.

The dim, hushed room curved to encircle the bottom of the two story tank. It shimmered, alive and mystifying. She looked around the gallery, glad that the room was empty. The small exhibit tanks along the perimeter were pockets of light against the deep blue-gray walls. But it was the Great Ocean tank that lured her closer.

Toy saw Ethan in the tank and knew why she'd come. In all her rambling thoughts, she'd remembered someone saying that there was an erratic shark in the tank and Ethan replying that he was going in to check it out this afternoon.

He was near the sandy bottom, swimming slowly and deliberately around the brightly colored, rocky reef. He was wearing his black wetsuit, flippers and hood, and in his hand he was carrying a white plastic bucket. It was filled with food. A dozen big fish were swarming around him, butting their noses against the bucket. He pushed them away, his gaze trained on something overhead.

Toy followed his line of vision and saw what it was he was watching. The ten foot sand tiger shark emerged from the shadows. It swam past Ethan in its unhurried manner, a white tip on its nose and its black eyes fathomless. As the shark swam away, Toy breathed a little easier. Two more sharks, considerably smaller, also swam past and these, too, were unconcerned with the diver in black that held a food bucket.

While Ethan observed the sharks, her own

gaze was trained on him. She thought how very much in his element he was, surrounded by reef and fish. She looked upward, searching for the sharks. The silvery reflection of the water cast undulating shadows against the walls. When she lowered her head again she gasped. Ethan was looking directly at her from inside the tank. Fish swirled around him, a kaleidoscope of color, but he seemed unaware of anything except for her.

They stood for several minutes staring silently at one another. Then he slowly swam to the edge of the tank, stopping at the wall that separated them. He raised his hand and pressed his palm flat against the glass, reaching out, she knew, to her.

Her heart beat fast as she felt again the strange bond between them. It was a force of its own with the power to pull her closer to him. She walked across the carpet toward him, her arm slowly rising en route. His eyes shone in the wedge of mask. Reaching him, she pressed her hand against the cool glass to meet his. Palm to palm, the connection was visceral, as though their skin really touched. Her palm was aflame and the sensations coursed through her bloodstream, sending her heart pumping hard and her breath to come in short pants. She *knew* that he felt the same, soul stirring connection.

The sand tiger shark swam by, his long sleek body veering closer this time. She turned her head to follow the menacing path. Ethan, too, swung his head, alert to the subtle change in the shark's pattern. From above, his back-up diver was signaling for his attention.

He dropped his hand. The moment was broken.

Toy retracted hers and looked at it, still feeling the strange tingling in her palm. Something important had just happened between them. She couldn't name it but felt it as surely as if she'd been struck by lightning. Looking back at the tank, she saw Ethan swimming into the coral reef. Bewildered, Toy turned and walked away.

The sky darkened and Toy walked across the living room to the rear window to peer out at the western sky. She heard a low, faint rumbling in the heavens. A gust of cool breeze, heavy with the scent of rain, poured over her. A hard rain was coming. She could feel it in her bones.

The rumbling storm suited her introspective mood. She still felt the strange, evocative connection she'd experienced with

Ethan. She felt it swirling just under her skin. It had the power to take her breath away.

But, had it all been her imagination? Was she reading too much into it, like some lovesick school girl? She didn't need this nonsense now, she told herself. She was leaving for Costa Rica tomorrow morning.

She reached out, and with a firm push, closed the window. The old wood rumbled down the track and sealed just as the first, fat drops of rain hit the porch. It was just the oncoming storm that had brought the goose bumps to her skin, she told herself. Her moodiness was simply the anxiety of an inexperienced traveler about to embark on her first solo journey.

Again thunder rumbled, closer this time, and the rain pattered noisily on the tin roof. Toy walked through the small living room turning on all the lamps. Soon the room was bathed in soft, yellow light. She looked around, feeling secure in the warmth of familiar things. Down the hall, Lovie was tucked in bed, her story read and her teeth brushed. The airplane tickets were in her purse on the hall table, and beside it was her computer and important papers. She was packed, the final arrangements were completed. All was in order. She released a deep sigh. She was ready to go.

Outside, she heard Darryl's heavy footfall coming up the stairs. She turned her head in time to see him enter the room and wipe his feet on the kitchen mat. When he looked up, she noticed that his longish dark hair was damp from the rain.

"You're all set. I put the suitcase in your car," he said, closing the door behind him. He wiped his hands on his thighs and his pale eyes softened as he took in the dim light of the room. "It looks right cozy in here."

"Thanks," Toy replied, meaning it. He'd been a great help in closing up the house and running last minute errands. In the past few months he'd shown a side of himself that she'd missed, a caring and dependable side of someone who helped makes life easier. "Thanks for everything."

She went to the counter to the long "to do" list she'd made for herself. Picking up a pencil, she started crossing items off. She was startled when she felt Darryl's arms slide around her from behind.

She dropped her pencil and stiffened in his arms. "What are you doing?"

"I'm just getting close." His voice was a velvety purr at her ear. "You're leaving, after all. I want to say a proper goodbye."

She closed her eyes and held her breath as his head lowered and his lips feather kissed her neck.

"Darryl," she said in a soft moan, "Don't. I've got so much to do."

He turned her in his arms and his gaze was heavy and seductive. She smelled his aftershave and was struck with a sudden flash of déjà-vu. She felt once more the young girl who felt safe and secure against a harsh world in this man's arms.

His hand slid up her back to cup her head and she felt their breaths mingle as he moved her face closer to his. Toy closed her eyes, and whether from habit or inevitability, she relinquished.

Darryl's lips were full and trembled with passion. He'd always been a good kisser. Yet as he pressed against her, something was missing from her reaction. She felt cold and distanced from the kiss, as though it were happening to someone else. It felt somehow wrong.

"Darryl, stop." Toy pushed her hands against Darryl's shoulder. She turned her head, tearing her lips away. "I can't do this."

He froze, his arms holding tight. Then, slowly, he let her slide back. His eyes reflected confusion and the embers of passion. "You used to like my kisses."

"I know. I'm sorry."

"I don't get it."

"Darryl, I can't," she said softly, not wishing to hurt him. "I don't want to."

"Hey, okay," he said, but it sounded automatic. He took a deep breath and looked away, pursing his lips, like he was trying to put together what was happening. Then he swung his head back and his eyes flashed.

"Toy, I still don't get it. I've been trying real hard to please you and you keep shooting me down. Girl, you've got to offer me some hope."

She took a breath, digging deep, knowing with every fiber of her being what was the honest answer. "I can't offer you hope. I can't offer you anything more than what we have right now. A friendship. A bond with Lovie. That's all."

He looked broadsided. "Then what's this all been about?" he asked in a strained voice.

"You asked for the chance to get to know your daughter. I wanted you to have that chance."

"Are you telling me that you and I didn't have something going on here? 'Cause I felt it, babe." He pounded his chest where his heart was. "I felt it."

She swallowed hard, feeling broken. She

sought out his gaze, wanted to hold it so when she spoke he would understand that her words came from her heart. "You're right. There was something there. Darryl, I knew you wanted to get back together, the way we used to be. And I didn't do anything to discourage it. I . . . I guess I needed to find out if I still had feelings for you. I *wanted* it to work, can you understand that? I've always wanted for us to be a family. I used to dream of it. I begged you for it, don't you remember?"

His face tightened and he nodded. "I was a goddamn fool."

"I never had a family of my own and I wanted that for Lovie. You're so good with her. I thought if I could meet you halfway and we both worked at it, then maybe we could make a go of it together. We could be a family, for Lovie."

"And I want that. You know I do! You got to know I love you. Toy, I've never stopped loving you."

"Yes, you did," she blurted back. "Darryl, *yes, you did!*" She took a shuddering breath and wiped her eyes. "But it's okay," she said with calm certainty. "Because I stopped loving you, too."

He stared at her a long moment, taking her words in. Then he shook his head, as though shaking off a stupor. "Well, that's it then."

He walked to the sofa to pick up his denim jacket, his heavy heels reverberating in the tense silence.

"Darryl . . ."

"What?" His voice was sharp with annoyance.

Taken aback, she clenched her hands at her thighs, then went to pick up an envelope on the counter, and without speaking, held it out for him to take.

"What's this?" he asked, looking at it like it was dirt.

"It's a list of all the phone numbers, addresses and information you'll need while I'm gone. It's all arranged for you to take Lovie to the museum on Saturday." She spoke in a lifeless tone. "That is, if you still want to."

"Hell, yes, I want to! Why wouldn't I? She's not kicking me out of her life too, is she?"

Toy looked up sharply. She heard his hurt in his voice, and the first rumblings of his anger. "No, of course not. I'm glad you want to see her. She's really looking forward to spending the day with you."

He looked out the window, clearly anxious to get out. There was no point in prolonging this. "Lovie will be at Cara's house while I'm gone. You'll find her address and phone number in here. If you have any question, call Cara. My cell phone won't work in Costa Rica."

She lifted the envelope and held it out to him again.

He looked at the envelope like he wasn't sure whether to take it or hurl it in her face. He snatched it roughly from her hands and turned on his heel, slamming the door behind him.

23

Toy stepped from the plane into the moist, humid air of the tropics.

She'd never traveled before but now she knew what the word *foreign* meant. The airport was a vast and cleared square of grass and cement surrounded by a chain link fence and, in the distance, mountains. In the center of the square was a grey metal warehouse that was the main terminal. The tropical sun was hot and beat relentlessly upon the weary travelers emerging from the jet. Toy followed the queue through the metal gates to the terminal.

After her papers were stamped, she craned her neck in search of someone carrying a sign with her name on it. A coterie of people pulling luggage gathered in a patch of shade by the front entrance. She joined them, removing her jacket, rolling up her sleeves and slipping off her socks.

After a short wait her eye was caught by a

striking young man with dark golden skin and dreadlocks that flowed from his head to his shoulders. He wore baggy shorts, lengths of wooden beads around his neck and moved with an easy, island manner. When he spotted her, he smiled widely revealing a boyish grin that made his blue eyes brighten against his tan. He lifted a crinkled piece of paper over his head so she could read her name scrawled across it in black ink. Relieved, she waved him over.

"My name's Rafael," he said in British English. "I've come to fetch you and bring you to Playa Grande. Is that all your luggage? Right then, let me take it. Follow me."

He was very efficient, despite his appearance, and she remembered Miss Lovie telling her never to judge a book by its cover. She hoped his mama told him the same thing because in contrast, she looked like some old schoolteacher, out of sync with the relaxed island garb of the natives.

She grabbed her camera before he tossed her suitcase inside a hot, dusty Jeep with all the windows either rolled down or missing. After she buckled up, he turned his head, and with a cocky grin told her, "Buckle up. It's going to be a bumpy ride."

And lord, it was. Once they left the Pan American Highway, it was dirt roads all the way, most of them heavily pocked with huge craters steeped in mud that forced drivers to crawl around them over walkways, rocks, anything passable. September was in the rainy season and the roads were little better than mudslides. She sat by the open window and gawked, spellbound by the gorgeous and exotic country.

In the distance, mountains that Rafael told her were home to coffee plantations disappeared in misty clouds. Closer to the coast, banana plantations and small towns were carved into the rain soaked jungle. Locals were cheery and seemingly oblivious to the road conditions. Children wearing backpacks were returning home from school, skinny dogs and feral cats ran wild, and a Brahmin bull stopped traffic as it meandered across the road.

The fields were aflame with color. Tropical flowers hung from the trees, gathered wild along the roadside, and spilled from containers at the modest homes they passed. Birds soared in the sky and roosted in trees, and occasionally, she heard a strange, bellowing roar from the trees that Rafael told her was the Mono, or the howler monkey. The only thing that Toy found unsettling was the number of For Sale signs that dotted the property all along the major roads.

Rafael sadly shook his head and told her that, as far as he could tell, the whole country was for sale. She replied that she often felt the same way about the lowcountry.

Rafael was good company and seemed to know where he was going as he readily skirted the mudslides, craters, bulls and even a small river that coursed over the road. Toy had learned never to drive into fast moving water so she gripped the dashboard with white knuckles when Rafael plowed through.

"Qué hombre!" she muttered, half as a compliment, half as a tease. He turned his head, grinning with pleasure.

At last Rafael turned into a narrow, winding road that led to a cluster of low wood buildings. Beyond, she caught a glimpse of the mighty blue waters of the Pacific Ocean. Her spirits soared.

"Welcome to Villa Baulas," he said coming to a stop in the small gravel parking lot.

Villa Baulas was an ecological beach hotel made up of three low-slung, wood buildings and a few quaint bungalows on stilts, all built in the simple Tico style of mahogany and bamboo. After promising to meet Rafael for a beer later, she was led by a smiling woman past thickets of trees, a swimming pool nestled beside a thatched roof restaurant, to one of the wooden buildings on stilts that faced the ocean. As she climbed the stairs, she thought she was entering a tree house. The sun was just setting as she reached her floor and she paused to look out through the thorny trees.

She sighed with relief. Fifty yards beyond lay a serene blue ocean, only this wasn't the Atlantic Ocean, but the Pacific! Still, the sight of ocean and sand were touchstones. After driving through jungle and mountains, she felt at home.

The road dust, heat and humidity clung to her like a heavy coat. When the door to her small, dark paneled room closed, she dropped her bags to the floor with a thud and immediately peeled off her sticky clothes

"I'm really here!" she exclaimed. She stood naked with her arms spread, relishing the modest breeze from the overhead fan. The shower was tiny and there was no hot water. Still, the tepid water that trickled in a miserly stream from the dangling showerhead felt glorious and she relished each drop as it cleansed away the miles she'd traveled. Tilting her head back she imagined all the confusion and hassles and heartache and responsibilities that she'd left behind flowing down from her shoulders, swirling at her feet and sliding away down the drain.

She dressed in shorts and a cotton shirt and joined the others at the open-air restaurant for dinner. These twenty-some interns chose to stay at the cheaper, local hotel rather than the fancier hotel in Tamarindo. It was a young group and they were already sitting at the tables under the great thatched roof that spread out over the area like an umbrella. Everyone was leisurely drinking beers, laughing and eating their meals. She walked up to the restaurant feeling out of place. She didn't know anyone. Rafael came up to greet her and took her under his wing.

"Hey, everyone, this Nina Bonita is Toy Sooner from the United States. She's joining us." Calls of welcome sang out like birdsong and she was quickly introduced to the others who'd traveled to Villa Baulas to attend the symposium and work with the sea turtles.

Rafael never left her side. He was friendly and attentive, getting her a beer and finding her a seat at his table. Flirtation was an art form with him, but he was never forward. She liked him enormously and was comfortable spending time with him, intrigued by the underlying attraction between them. She guessed he was somewhere in his late twenties, as were most of the other interns. In all, with spouses, girlfriends and two children, the group filled all twenty rooms of the hotel. The officials of the Foundation stayed at the fancier meeting hotel in the town of Tamarindo, but the Villa Baulas was cheaper, and more important, smack on the beach where the leatherbacks nested.

It was a balmy night, though Toy was surprised that the weather did not cool down after dark like it did on Isle of Palms. But it was relatively bug free. Rafael advised her to skip the "American" menu and order *Tico* style. So she feasted on grilled fish, black beans and rice, all washed down with cool beer. As the night wore on she learned the interns came from all over Costa Rica, the Americas and Europe. They went to different schools, held different jobs, had different goals, but they were united by their common devotion to sea turtles.

Later, one of the men played the guitar and she dangled her legs in the pool with the others while drinking beer and sharing stories. Toy discovered that she'd just missed the *arribada* in Ostional. They regaled her with stories of the armada of hundreds of determined, scrambling Olive Ridley turtles that came ashore night after night for a week to lay thousands of eggs in a frenzy of nesting. The turtles came in waves, crushing eggs laid the previous night as they dug new nests.

"It was like Normandy Beach, man," Rafael told her. He had her laughing till her sides hurt when he did his imitation of a black vulture lurking in a nearby tree, watching and waiting to feast.

"Just my luck to miss it," she told them, then admitted what she really wanted to see was a leatherback.

"Oh, I wouldn't count on it," an intern told her. "It's early for leatherbacks."

Rafael sat beside her at the pool. His legs were thin but muscled and feathered with long, soft hair. "It's not a good situation. Last year was the worst year on record for nests. And unfortunately, they're not expecting this year to be any better. Thanks to long-line fishing and zero international cooperation, we're killing off an ancient species."

"Maybe," Toy replied. She lazily kicked her legs in the water. "But hope springs eternal, eh?"

Rafael clinked bottles with her. "So, you're an optimist? I like that. You need to be in this business."

She leaned back on her arms and grew suddenly quiet as her thoughts turned to

Ethan. What had he called her? *Unflinchingly optimistic.* She wondered what he was doing now, so far away in Charleston.

The following day was all business. To get to the symposium in the town of Tamarindo they had the choice of taking an arduous car trip through the muddy roads, or a short boat ride across the estuary that separated the town from Playa Grande. They all opted for the boat.

During the day they attended the meetings and in the late afternoon she went shopping in the charming town of Tamarindo. She fingered the coins that Ethan had given her, and on impulse bought him a T-shirt with a chart of shark species on the back. She found another T-shirt with a leatherback sea turtle on it for Lovie, and a pottery vase with a primitive turtle on it for Cara. Her shopping done, she met the group at the boat dock for a ride back to the Villa Baulas.

Everyone was talking about going out later for drinks and dancing.

Rafael hooked her waist. "Come on, Nina Bonita. Let's go."

"Oh, no," she replied self-consciously, uncoiling herself from his arm. "It's been a long day and I'm tired. Besides, I can't dance."

He laughed. "Everybody can dance."

"Not me."

"Then I'll teach you!"

Toy remembered how, when she was young, she used to love to dance in front of the mirror while the radio played. She didn't know any popular steps, but she enjoyed just moving to the music. Once, her mama had caught her dancing alone in the house. She'd hooted at her mockingly, telling her, *You dance like you've got two left feet.*

Toy shook her head, backing away. "I'm hopeless, believe me. Anyway I want to be here at the hotel in case a guide calls."

The public was not allowed on Playa Grande at night because it was a protected nesting ground of the nearly extinct leatherback sea turtles. If a leatherback was spotted on the beach, the alert came by walkie-talkie from the park rangers who patrolled the beach.

Rafael looked at her like she was crazy. "A leatherback isn't coming tonight, Bonita. They won't be here for at least another week or so. Come on, Toy," he said, seductively tugging the hem of her shirt. "Let me teach you how to dance."

"You go ahead," she said, relieved that the small boat had arrived at the dock to ferry them across the inlet.

After a shower, she decided to walk the beach before dinner. The surfers had gone for the day and only a magnificent frigate bird, with its pointy M shaped wings, soared over the waves.

Her first night had been filled with the excitement of her arrival in the foreign country and meeting her fellow interns. Tonight, however, she felt her separateness acutely. Her heart was inexplicably heavy with homesickness. She walked along the pristine shoreline, acutely aware that it was not *her* shoreline. She worried about Lovie, if she was well, happy, even if she missed her mother. Everywhere she turned she saw something that made her think of her. Wouldn't Lovie enjoy this shell? Wouldn't she love to play in this cresting surf? How Lovie would laugh at the enormous iguana that lounged by the pool!

She'd expected to face a host of things new, to feel naive, even gullible, on her first trip outside the country. But she didn't expect to feel such loneliness. The ferocity of it surprised her. After dinner, she couldn't bear the thought of going dancing. So when most of the others had driven to town, she sunk into the fiery red hammock that hung in the corner of the porch outside her room to read material from the meetings. But her gaze wandered from the page to the Pacific in the distance.

The gentle rocking of the hammock and the ocean breeze lulled her to sleep. She awoke with a start to a firm shaking of her shoulders. Opening her eyes, she was stunned to discover that it was pitch black.

Rafael raised his flashlight, his eyes bright with excitement. "Toy! Wake up! We got the call!"

"What?" she asked, groggy.

"There's a leatherback about a half mile up the beach. Grab your gear." Then with a laugh he added, "You know this turtle came early, just for you."

She felt electrified and practically fell out of the hammock in her scramble to get out. Her hands were shaking as she collected her backpack from her room then ran to meet Rafael. He led her through the deep darkness past the thicket of trees to the hotel's beach gate where a resident marine biologist and a local ranger with a large flashlight were waiting to check off their names.

Only a handful of the interns assembled, the rest having gone dancing, and they could talk of nothing but how early in the season this nesting turtle was. The dark eyed, gruff guide was fiercely protective of his stretch of beach. If someone on the list was late, he didn't care. He wouldn't allow stragglers onto Playa Grande at nightfall. Once he was satisfied that his group was organized, he ordered them to, "Pair up, stay close and keep up!"

Toy paired up with Rafael. She'd thought she was in pretty good shape but she had a hard time keeping up as they hiked at a clipped pace toward the small dot of light at the far end of the beach. She panted as she sprinted across the half mile of soft sand.

"I thought you were going dancing!" she said to Rafael, barely able to speak she was breathing so hard.

"I was," he replied, not the least winded. "But then I thought about you sitting here by yourself, and about beginner's luck, and I decided I wanted to be here when you saw your first leatherback."

"It's not my first sea turtle," she replied defensively. "I've seen hundreds of loggerheads."

Her eyes were growing accustomed to the dark and even in the minimal light she could make out the smirk on Rafael's face. "Those aren't *real* turtles," he replied. "Loggerheads are toy turtles compared to the leatherbacks."

She was affronted by this and would have said something in defense of her beloved loggerheads, but the guide flashed his light on a trail of turtle tracks carved into the beach for them to see. Toy swallowed her words and did a double take. The tracks had to measure six feet across and looked like they were dug into the sand by a bulldozer.

Rafael looked at her, his smug grin saying *I told you so.*

The guide moved up the beach alone while the biologist clustered them together along the shore. He told them that the leatherback was just ahead and that they had to wait until another guide signaled that they could move forward. No one was allowed to approach until the turtle began digging.

Toy was grateful for the chance to catch her breath. The night was hot and humid, void of wind and already she was coated with a sheen of sweat. They didn't wait long. The biologist waved his hand and whispered loudly, "Stay to the rear of the turtle, out of its line of vision." As a group they quietly made their way up the dune to gather at the guide's red light.

The beach was short and rather steep, perfect for nesting turtles. As Toy drew near, she heard the unmistakable sound of a turtle's flipper scraping the sand. The night was very black with a slender moon. Rafael turned to her and waved her closer. "Come up here," he whispered. She drew closer and hunkered low, squinting in the darkness.

Nothing prepared her for what she saw. There before her, in the dim light of moon and stars, against the creamy, glistening sand, lay an enormous, prehistoric looking black hulk. Her mouth slipped open. The enormity of the leatherback hit her first.

Then it's uniqueness. The leatherback was unlike any other species of turtle she had seen. Loggerheads, kemps, ridleys, greens or the hawksbills — all those turtles had a curved, hard shell. This gorgeous creature's shell was leathery and long with vertical ridges that curved from the tip by the head to the point at the rear. Most different, however, was that beneath the curved black shell was a blubbery body, like that of a walrus.

She knelt beside Rafael in the cool sand and he reached over to hold her hand. Looking up, she saw awe and wonder on his face as well, despite his being a seasoned intern. She smiled, grateful to share this moment with a friend. She thought of the other faces she wished could be here to share this night — Cara, Flo, Emmi, and especially Lovie.

Shoulder to shoulder they watched as the five-foot-long, at least one-thousand-pound turtle used its rear flipper to scoop out a cupful of sand. Then the other flipper repeated the motion, one after the other, in an ancient ritual. Despite her enormous size and bulk, the flippers were beautifully boned, more like human hands than the flippers of loggerheads. They lent her a remarkably feminine grace as she dug.

When the nest was over two feet deep, she rested and the beach slipped once more into a deep island silence, broken only by the comforting, omnipresent rolling surf. Then the turtle began laying her perfectly round, white eggs. They glistened in the moonlight and landed silently into the soft sand. An intern came forward to collect each of the sixty-some eggs in a bag as they dropped.

Toy knew that these eggs were collected and put into a hatchery. The species was so endangered, each hatchling survival was critical. When she looked at the turtle's head and saw the tears washing away the salt from her eyes, Toy wept her own salty tears for this gentle giant and her fragile offspring. Toy knew full well that she could be witnessing one of the final few remaining leatherbacks nesting on this Pacific beach.

Too soon, the guide signaled that it was time for them to leave. Toy was crushed, hoping she could watch the great sea turtle make her way back to the sea. She couldn't imagine how magnificent this creature would look as she slipped under the wave. The guide waved insistently, and with a sigh, she quietly left along with her group, grateful for the chance to see the leatherback at all.

As they trooped back to their inn, she lifted her gaze from the town to an endlessly vast, black sky littered with brilliant pinpricks of starlight. She slowed pace, eyes to the sky, when in a sudden flash, she caught the streaking tail of a falling star. In the time of a gasp it was gone.

She laughed as her heart lifted and she felt a sudden joy thinking of her dearest friends on the turtle team. Were they out on the beach tonight, too? Did they see this same shooting star on the shore of another ocean, waiting not for a leatherback to lay her nest, but for a nest of loggerheads to erupt with dozens of hatchlings? She felt sure they did.

She felt her loneliness dissipate like sea foam, and making a heartfelt wish, she sent it to her friends.

Darryl sat in the small bar section of a grill house on Shem Creek. The restaurant was still crowded, even at the late hour, but the only folks in the bar were himself and two pretty girls huddled at a table in the corner. One of them was crying her eyes out, causing raccoon-like black circles of mascara to ring her eyes. The crying blonde was leggy and lean with a body that made Darryl think the guy causing those tears had to be a fool. But it was the friend consoling her, a smaller, baby-faced girl with doe eyes that drew his gaze. She reminded him of Toy.

"Shit," he murmured, feeling the slam of pain again. Lifting his hand, he signaled the bartender for another beer.

This would have to be his last one, he thought, figuring out the total in his head. He was near flat broke. If it wasn't for that gig he had tomorrow night, he'd have to hit his mother for another job. Lord knew, she'd never simply lend him the money. The dust flew whenever that old lady pried open her pocketbook. When he'd come home she'd made him earn every penny she gave him. He had to paint her ratty picket fence that would have looked better if he'd just ripped it out. Then she had him fix the drywall in the front hall after her no-good, drunk boyfriend punched a hole through it after she'd kicked him out.

He brought the beer to his lips and took a long swallow. Wiping his mouth, he felt a stab of despair. All that money he'd sweated to earn was just so he could take Toy and Little Lovie out for a nice time. He didn't want them to know he was down on his luck. He'd tried real hard — never swore in front of them, watched his manners, polished his boots and sat and listened to Toy go on and on about those damned turtles.

And for what? She didn't want nothing to do with him.

"Baby, I tried," he muttered and grimaced as shame ripped through him. She wouldn't even kiss him. He took another long tug from his bottle.

The background music was country and some guy was singing about life not being beautiful. He lifted his bottle. "You got that damn straight." He cocked his ear and listened to the lyrics.

You think you're on your way
And it's just a dead end road
At the end of the day.

"Hell, I could'a wrote them lyrics," he said in a surly voice to the bartender.

The bartender only nodded, his eyes on his towel as he dried a bar glass.

Darryl sneered and shook his head. Dumb kid was too young to know shit, he thought.

He could teach him a thing or two about country rock. He'd played for some of the best country rock bands in the country. Hell, he had real talent. All he needed was one break. Just one fucking break. Hell, he thought, feeling a familiar fire in his belly. What was he doing wasting his time hanging around this nowhere town? After his gig he'd have a little money in his pocket and he was heading for Nashville. Now there was a city! His lips curled as he brought the bottle to his lips. After tomorrow, he was outta here.

The pretty girls in the corner rose from the table and crossed the bar to the door. The tall girl had cleaned up her face and even though her eyes were puffy, she was damned sexy. But it was the smaller one Darryl's eyes followed, mesmerized by the swinging of her sweet behind. She had that dark eyeliner around her pale blue eyes, making them look all smoky, the way Toy used to do.

He sneered and ripped his gaze away to his hands. She was probably a tease, too.

A low, slow burn began in his belly, the kind that he knew could grow into a simmering rage. He tilted his head and drew hard on the bottle, but it was empty. He slammed the bottle down on the bar, drawing the attention of the bartender. He was a big shouldered guy and he stopped drying the glass and narrowed his eyes in warning.

Darryl dug into his pocket for a couple of singles, laid them flat on the bar then pushed himself away. He'd sung at too many establishments just like this one and knew better than to stiff the bartender all because he was crying in his beer over some no-count girl.

24

On Saturday, Darryl pulled up along Palm Boulevard on the Isle of Palms and let the motor idle while he dug through his pockets for the address. This can't be right, he thought, pulling out the wrinkled sheet of paper that Toy had given him. He lifted his sunglasses and read the address again, then looked again at the number on the mailbox.

"Well, whaddaya know," he chuckled, looking at the modest, pink stucco house set back from Palm Boulevard. Behind it, Hamlin Creek was racing with the incoming tide.

This was what they called a doghouse coming up, though he knew any house on deep water these days was worth a world more than he'd likely ever dream of affording. He just figured the house of high and mighty Cara Rutledge would be one of them big mansions that was sprouting up all over the island. The kind that was manicured and uppity, like her.

As he walked up toward the front door, he felt uneasy about confronting Cara to pick up his daughter. He'd never actually met her, but from all the words he'd had about her with Toy, he had her fixed in his mind as a real ballbreaker. Toy used to be intimidated by her and it was always *Cara said this and Cara said that.* He chuckled as he looked down at his feet. But what kind of tough lady had stone turtles for a front walkway?

He reached the front door and checked out the shiny brass turtle door knocker, the bright green topiary by the door and the shiny clean window glass. Nice and tidy. Must be marriage softened Cara Rutldege's sharp edges, he thought. Then he recalled that she wasn't a Rutledge any more. What the heck was that big guy's name?

He smoothed back his hair, rolled his shoulders and rang the doorbell. It bothered him that he still felt so damn nervous at having to meet her. A moment later the door opened and there she was.

His first thought was that he had no idea how beautiful she was. The woman was a stunner. Not in a soft, kittenish way, like Toy, but in that sleek, glossy style that wasn't really his type. He was as tall as she was, yet she had a way of making him feel she was looking down at him.

"Mr. Duggans?" Cara asked crisply.

"That's my daddy's name," he replied. "You can call me Darryl."

"Mr. Duggans will do. I have a list here of phone numbers you can call at any time. If Lovie doesn't feel well, or if she wants to come home — anything at all — call me." She handed him the typed list.

Another list. The damn thing was even numbered.

"I'll be at work, but if Lovie wants to come home early, for any reason at all, I'll be at that number."

"She won't be wanting to come home early."

"But if she does?"

"She won't," he ground out, stuffing the envelope into his shirt pocket.

He watched her eyes narrow and her lips tighten, as if to hold in a torrent of words she was just itching to shout out at him. He waited, almost hoping she'd let loose. But to her credit she managed to rein in and put on a fake smile. He knew that face real well. It was the one the bar managers always put on right before they fired him.

"I'll get Lovie" was all she said. Then, remembering her manners, asked, "Would you like to come in?"

"I'll wait here."

He just wanted to pick up his kid and get out of here. He stuck his hands in his back pockets and paced the cement stoop of the modest house. A straggly rose bush didn't look like it was going to make it past another season. He didn't wait long. The door opened again and Lovie rushed out to greet him with a heartfelt hug.

"Daddy!"

He was surprised by the surge of affection he felt for the little girl in the blue gingham dress and pigtails. She sure did make him feel righteous and proud. She was the sweetest thing in his life right now.

"Well, let's be off," he said with a smile.

"Wait," Cara called out.

He halted and turned his head.

"I just wanted to confirm the pick-up at Patriot's Point. At the boat dock. Four o'clock. Okay?"

"Yeah, sure," he said, dismissing her. "Four o'clock."

Cara put her hand on her lower back and rubbed it absently. She looked down at Lovie and a smile sweeter than Darryl figured she could make appeared on her face.

"You have a good time, sweetie."

"She will," he said, then taking Lovie's hand, led her away.

For all that she lived on a barrier island, Toy had never surfed before. She'd been too pregnant, too shy, too inhibited to ever try the sport, even though she'd secretly admired the bronzed and buff bodies of the other men and women her age as they rode a wave in. So when Rafael offered to teach her, she readily accepted.

The waves were even and easy but Toy couldn't manage to stand up on the board. After an hour she felt beaten and tossed by the waves, she had saltwater up her nose, her eyes were stinging and sand was stuck in her teeth. She dragged the surfboard out from the water, ready to call it a day.

She was wearing the bikini that Elizabeth had given her, and over it, a tight fitting rash guard. She was so focused on remembering all the pointers that Rafael had given her that she was oblivious to the admiring glances she was getting from all the men that watched her.

"You're too stiff," Rafael told her as he trotted up to her side. "Like the board. Girl, you got to learn to relax."

It irritated her that he wasn't even winded while she could barely stand. "I'm trying," she said, but her tone was anything but relaxed.

He laughed and lifted a lock of salt stiff hair from her brow. "Maybe you're trying too hard."

"Maybe I'm just not cut out for this."

"Don't tell me you're going to quit."

"I'm not a quitter," she snapped. Then she sighed and added, "But I am a realist. I've only got this one afternoon left. What's the point?"

"Why does there have to be a point? I want you to get up on that board so when you get home to that little island you live on, you can get a surfboard and not be afraid to do it again."

"Who has time for surfing, anyway?"

"Make time! *Pura Vida!*" he called out, quoting the Pure Life mantra of Costa Ricans. "All work and no play make Toy a very unhappy girl, right?"

He elicited a smile from her and she nodded. "But Rafael, I *am* trying. I just don't get it."

"Come with me," he said, cajoling her back to the water. "No, put down your board. You can leave it there. Let's try a new approach."

He took her hand and they walked back to the rolling, white tipped surf. The water was warm but refreshing under the hot, tropical sun. He walked her waist deep into the wave.

"Okay now, put your arms straight out, like you're flying," he said. "Let the waves wash over you. Here comes one."

Toy obediently stretched out her arms, held her breath and turned toward the wave. The wave smacked full in the front, crashing and shoving her over. She rose, sputtering.

"That's how *not* to do it," he said, suppressing a laugh. "Try it again, only this time, turn your body . . . so."

Toy scowled and shoved a mop of hair from her face. Then she stood and turned her hips sideways against the waves like his.

"Arms back out," Rafael ordered. When she complied he moved behind her and slid his arms under hers. His dark tanned skin was a sharp contrast against her pale, sun-pinkened skin. She giggled and stepped away but he grabbed hold of her hips. She felt his fingers, slender but strong, holding her firmly in place. "Come on, girl. I'm trying to teach you."

"Teach me what?" she asked over her shoulder, laughing.

He had the devil in his eyes but he grinned and replied, "How to move. How to keep balance. Heads up!"

Another wave came and lifted her again, but this time her angled body sliced through the wave. His hands held firm to her hips as she slid up and down against his body with the motion of the wave.

"See how that feels?" he asked by her ear. "Relax now. Here we go."

Another wave came, and another, each time lifting her up, then lowering her in a gentle rhythm as Rafael held her steady at her hips.

"Let's go a little closer to shore," he told her. His fingers held hers at the knuckles and he led her to where the water only hit her thighs. "Now this time, querida, sway your body with the waves. Feel them. Close your eyes. Don't worry, I've got you. When the wave comes, just let go and ride it. Ready? Here comes one . . ."

He held on to her hips again. Toy closed her eyes and relinquished herself to the wave. She felt the rush of water, the powerful tug at her body. She didn't lift up this time in anticipation but allowed the water to push her hips up and to the side. It was a little frightening but Rafael's hands held her firm.

"No worry, I've got you," he said. "That was good. Feel how the water moves your hips? Put your arms out and let your hips flow with the wave. Again!"

This time she let her hips sway with the momentum, feeling the tug and pull, going with it rather than fighting it.

"Good!" Rafael said. "You got it!"

"How is this helping my surfing?"

"Surfing is about feeling the waves and having fun. Now let's try the board again."

They went back to the beach to grab the surf boards. Tired but determined, she followed him back out to the waves. Once more she lay belly down on the board and paddled. Rafael stayed close behind her, pushing her board because she was already so tired her arms were weak. Once they got past the breakers they stopped and sat on their boards, heads looking out toward the swells.

"There looks like some good waves coming."

Toy saw a swell building. As it came at them she tightened up. "Let's take it."

"No, no, not this one. You have to wait for the right wave. See how that one closed out? You want to wait for one that peels. Patience, girl."

She released her pent-up breath, and again watched the swells.

"Okay," Rafael called to her. "This one is

it! Get ready!"

"Ready!" Toy felt her adrenaline rush and turned her board to face the beach.

"Paddle!" Rafael shouted. He reached over to give her board a shove for that extra momentum. The board lunged forward in an exhilarating surge and in a splashy rush she realized that she'd caught the wave. She knew she was supposed to jump up, but wary of her balance she carefully put one foot up, then, holding her breath, the other. Up a little more, arms out . . . In one fluid move, she felt the wind at her face and an unutterable exhilaration. She was riding the wave!

It only lasted ten seconds, but it was a glorious, memorable, life altering ten seconds. When she reached the shore she was laughing from the sheer joy of it.

"You did it!" Rafael called out, running toward her. "I knew you could!"

"Thank you!" she cried out and ran to him, grinning ear to ear. Her self confidence was soaring. "I always wanted to but never thought I could!" They hugged and it was all about triumph and joy and heady success.

"Let's do it again," she exclaimed.

"No, crazy girl. You're riding the adrenaline now. We like to call it quits after the best ride."

"But I feel so euphoric, like I could ride forever."

He nodded, grinning. "That's the feeling you've got to hold on to." He grabbed her board and carried it for her as they headed back to the Villa Baulas.

"I never knew that standing in the waves could help me surf," she said, feeling as though her feet were not even touching sand.

"No one can be confident if all they do is worry and stress." He laughed. "Besides, all that wave stuff? That wasn't teaching you surfing."

She stopped short and swung her head to glare at him. "What were you doing then?"

He offered her a cocky grin. "Teaching you how to dance. Tomorrow night we're all going to Kiki's to party. You, too. No more excuses. Ticos love to dance!"

The sky over Isle of Palms was overcast and the seas choppy. There was very little business at the Eco-tours so Cara didn't feel guilty about closing up early. She rubbed her lower back. It had been aching all morning and she'd found a few spots of bright red blood on her panties. "It's only some blood," she told herself, trying to keep calm, reminding herself that the doctor said some minimal spotting was normal. It was nothing to get worked up about. She'd put her feet up on a chair all morning and it was probably sitting in that awkward position that caused her backache. There was no point bothering Brett with telling him, she thought. But just to be on the safe side, she was going home early.

On the drive home, a dull, throbbing ache bloomed in her abdomen. Her mind blindly refused to accept that it felt like a menstrual cramp. She'd been sitting funny, that was all. Her fingers tapped the steering wheel and she accelerated, wanting to get home where she could lie flat on the bed. Then she'd feel better. The cramping would go away then.

The dull ache sharpened to pain as she climbed from the car. She put her palm to her abdomen and held her breath. Her mind was screaming, *no, no, no* as she walked knock-kneed to the house, scrambling for her keys with shaky fingers. The front walkway seemed so long and each step was labored. By the time she got the door open, she felt a terrifying leakage seep between her legs.

"Please, God," she prayed. "Please let the baby be all right." But as she sagged against the wall, slowly lowering herself to the floor, Cara knew there was no more hope for the precious life she was carrying. Closing her eyes tight, she felt her dreams fading away.

Brett had arrived home not long after and found her in a fetal position on the bathroom floor in a small pool of blood. She didn't remember much about the trip to the hospital or the D&C they'd performed. By the time the hospital released her, the sky was darkening. She felt like an empty shell and wanted nothing more than to curl up in her bed and pull the blanket over her head.

She cast a glance at Brett beside her, driving them home. In profile, his face was chalky and dark circles framed his eyes. He hadn't said more than a few pat phrases to her though he'd stayed by her side, held her hand, and dealt with all the paperwork. Neither of them had uttered one word of grief or comfort to the other. To others it appeared they were being stoic. Cara knew that it wasn't courage but cowardliness that kept them mute. Neither could bear to give verbal witness to the fact that their baby, their last hope, had been lost in a sea of blood.

When they arrived home, the lights were

on. Brett hurried to her side of the car and helped her out. She was light-headed and chilled from loss of blood. Shivering in the summer heat, she leaned against him and walked in baby steps, feeling the thick pad like a diaper between her legs. Her back pain was crippling and she had desperate cramps. Pain was all she had left of her pregnancy.

Inside, Flo and Emmi were waiting for her with grief tugging at their smiles. Flo had made minestrone soup and Emmi laid out chunks of cheese and French bread but the scents only made her more nauseated. Cara accepted their kisses and murmured words of encouragement stiffly. Words of comfort rang so false in her ears. She managed to nod to everything they said until she could escape to her room with a backward wave. She rested her forehead against the closed door. The sorrow and pity in their eyes was more than she could bear.

The table lamp cast a narrow pool of light, giving the room an empty, lonely feel. Her fingers tapped her blanket. Lying in bed, her gaze swept the room — the walls, the bureaus, the open closet with rows of colored shirts, pants and terry robes on hooks. Feeling restless, she was searching for something she could not name. In the other room she heard the soft voices of Emmi and Flo and the gentle clink of silverware.

Cara could not shake the nagging sense that something was very wrong, something not connected with her miscarriage. She shifted in the bed, careful of her abdomen, to look at the clock on her bedside stand. The digital numbers were blocked by a glass of water.

"Brett?" she called. Her voice cracked. She cleared her throat and called louder, "Brett?"

She heard his footfall on the hardwood floors then he opened the door to her room. His face was etched with concern.

"Yes? Do you want something?"

"I can't see the clock."

"Honey, don't worry about the time."

"Please. Something . . . Can you move the water glass?"

Her voice was rising with urgency and not wishing to upset her, he obligingly moved the water glass. The clock read 7:42 pm.

"See? It's late," he told her. "You should try and sleep."

She dragged herself up to rest on her elbows, clawing at the sheets. Her mind fought through pain, fatigue and grief to focus on the clock. It was late. *Late.*

Then it hit her. A panic welled up inside of her and she made soft whimpering noises in her throat as she jerked her head to the left, then to the right, searching wildly.

"Cara, what's the matter?" Brett's voice was sharp with worry.

She dragged her hand through her hair, pulling it tight as her mind sharpened. "Oh, my God, Brett. Where's Lovie?"

An hour later, Brett sat on the bed beside Cara, holding her hand. She was propped up against pillows in bed, her face white with pain and shock. Flo and Emmi were pacing the floor, wringing their hands with worry lining their faces.

A policewoman in blue uniform stood in front of the bed and was writing in her notebook as she asked questions.

"You were supposed to meet this Darryl Duggans at Patriot's Point, is that right?"

Cara nodded. "Yes. At four o'clock."

"Where exactly?"

"At the boat dock. I reminded him of that when he came to pick up Lovie. Four o'clock at the boat dock." She squeezed Brett's hand. "But I didn't make it."

"Yes, ma'am," the policewoman said. "I understand that. I'm sorry." Sergeant Kim had met Cara several times over the past five years on turtle calls. She was a big turtle lover and always came running whenever she was needed.

"When did you try to reach this Darryl?"

"Not until around eight tonight. With all that happened . . ." She put her hand to her lips. "I forgot," she said, her voice breaking.

"You didn't forget!" Flo sprang to her defense. "You had surgery, for heaven's sake."

"I didn't pick her up," she said with anguish. "I didn't tell you or anyone else to fetch her. It was all arranged. I simply forgot."

Brett spoke up, his voice firmly putting the questions back on track. "We tried to call Darryl at the number he gave us, but the number was disconnected. I gave you the number we had."

"Yes, sir. It's a cell phone number. The bill hadn't been paid so it was cut off."

"Great," Brett said as a curse.

"Where could he have gone? Have you been able to reach anyone who knows him?" Cara asked.

"He has a mother," Flo offered. "She lives in North Charleston, I believe."

"We're looking into that," Sgt. Kim replied. "She claims she doesn't know where he is, either. Says to tell her if we find him because he owes her money. Seems she'd recently lent him three hundred dollars."

"Oh, God," Cara said, clutching Brett's hand. "He must have been planning to take her."

"We don't know that."

"It's a possibility we're looking into," the sergeant replied. "It's a known fact that most abducted children are taken by a parent."

The stunned silence was shattered by a doorbell and Flo sprinted from the room muttering, "At last!"

Voices sounded in the hall, Flo's high with worry and another voice, deeper and resonant. A moment later, Ethan followed Flo into the bedroom. His face was taut and his dark eyes scanned the room. He nodded in acknowledgment to Cara and Brett.

"I'm Ethan Legare," he said, reaching out to take the policewoman's hand. "I work with Toy Sooner at the Aquarium. How can I help?"

"Thanks for coming, Ethan," Brett said. "This is a terrible mess and we're trying to piece things together. First off, we have to locate Toy but we can't get through to her. No one answers at her hotel."

"It's a small, family run hotel. Tico style and very simple. It doesn't have the same amenities a western hotel does."

"Can you think of any way to get in touch with her?"

He handed Sgt. Kim the manila folder he was carrying. "That's all the information I have about the symposium she's attending in Costa Rica. I had planned to go, but I changed my mind. All the contact information you need is in there."

"Thanks," the policeman replied, taking the folder.

"We've already called the hotel that the meeting is being held at," Brett said. "And left a dozen messages for the symposium organizers. No one has called back."

Ethan looked at his watch. "It's late. The symposium will have ended for today." He sighed. "And tomorrow is Sunday. I'm not sure anyone will be in the office."

"We can't just wait around for someone to answer the phone," Emmi exclaimed, throwing her hands up. "We've got to reach her!"

"Can we call the police and ask them to locate her?" Flo asked.

Ethan shook his head. "There's only a small force with a lot of territory to cover. Look, I know Costa Rica. I lived in Tamarindo where the meeting is. I'll go get her."

"No, I'll go," Brett said.

"The roads are impossible any time of year, but in the rainy season, you'll never be able to navigate them at night. I know my way around. It's better if I go."

"It's my responsibility . . ."

The two men's eyes met in challenge.

"I love that child, too," Ethan said, his voice implacable. "And Toy. Besides, your wife needs you here. *I'm going.*"

Brett put his hands on his hips with a sigh and nodded.

"I'll catch the first plane out," Ethan said and charged from the room.

The following morning, Darryl sat on the edge of the mattress trying to focus on the numbers on the telephone. He was hung over and his brain felt like it was working through cotton candy. How much did he have to drink last night, he wondered?

It'd been a lousy gig in a small mountain town bar and from the catcalls and hollers, the patrons thought they were a pretty lousy band, too. He could usually please a crowd with his music. But last night he got stuck playing with some old-timer, local piano player who preferred classic country to country rock and a drugged out drummer who didn't know the difference.

On the wobbly wooden table was a stack

of greasy bills, his cut of three hundred dollars for the evening. Minus his bar bill, of course. He counted through the bills and frowned. Man, it was hardly worth the trip up to North Carolina.

"Daddy, can I watch cartoons?"

He turned his head and saw Little Lovie standing in front of the old television. She was still dressed in her blue gingham dress but now it was wrinkled and soiled in the front with mustard and ketchup stains from last night's hamburger. Her feet were bare and her hair was disheveled from sleep. She stood holding the remote with two hands, her little fingers madly pushing buttons. But nothing was happening on the screen.

Shit, he thought to himself, dropping his foggy head in his hands. He'd clean forgotten about her. What kind of a fool was he to drag a child all the way up here just so he'd not miss that sorry ass gig? Toy always told him he didn't think things through and this time she sure was right. Sometimes he was his own worst enemy. He'd planned to head straight on to Nashville after the gig. Now he'd have to haul ass all the way back to Charleston to deliver the kid to Cara before he could take off for Tennessee.

His mouth soured at the thought of Cara Whatever-her-last-name-was and the tongue-lashing she'd no doubt deliver. Well, where the hell was Mrs. High and Mighty yesterday when she was supposed to be picking up Little Lovie, that's what he wanted to know? She'd been such a harpy about his being on time — and he was. He'd waited at the boat dock in the hot sun for over an hour, pacing back and forth buying Lovie candy after candy till he thought she was going to puke. His damned cell phone was cut off so he had to ask around for change. Then "good luck" trying to find a pay phone these days. He finally found one near the big aircraft carrier and dialed the number she'd given him.

But she didn't answer. None of the numbers did. And after that big deal she made about giving him that list and telling him how he should call if anything happened. Then Lovie had commenced whining that she was sweaty and her stomach felt sick.

That's when he got nervous — and mad. It was after five o'clock and he had a gig in North Carolina at nine. Did Cara think he was rolling in dough and could just skip out on a job? The more he thought about it, the madder he got till he decided to just let Miss High and Mighty sit and stew. Let her feel what it was like to have to wait on him for a change. So he'd thumbed his nose at

Cara — and the whole bunch of them turtle ladies — and took his daughter with him to his gig in North Carolina.

He'd meant to drive her home after the gig was done but the poor kid fell asleep in a booth at the bar. Besides, he was pretty wiped out afterward. Four long hours of driving back to Charleston was more than he could deal with. So he'd checked into a cheap motel down the road a piece to crash.

He looked at the clock and saw that it was already 9:00 a.m. Rubbing his stomach, he burped, loud and rumbling.

"You're supposed to say excuse me," Lovie said.

"Excuse me," he complied.

"Daddy, I can't make this turn on."

He dragged himself to his feet and padded over to take the remote. With a click the television flicked on. Lovie did a little two footed jig. He chuckled and began flicking through the stations.

"That one!" she called out when a cartoon appeared. "I want that one."

"Okay. Hey, you getting hungry?"

She shook her head no.

Good, he thought to himself. He couldn't face food yet but he'd kill for coffee. "Listen, I've got to call and talk to your people. After that, we're gonna clean up and get some

538

breakfast, then head back home. Okay?"

Lovie only nodded, caught up in the cartoons.

What a dump, he thought, letting his gaze take in the cheap carpeting, the greasy paneling and the bare furnishings. He'd stayed in worse, but he'd stayed in lots better, too. It was no place to bring a sweet child like her. He sat back on the mattress and pulled the phone closer to him. Then he smoothed out the folded paper with all the numbers written out in neat handwriting. Rubbing his eyes, he squinted at the numbers, wishing to God he had a cup of coffee.

After two rings, a man answered the phone. "Yes?" The voice was huffy, like he'd run to answer the phone.

"Uh, yeah. Who is this?"

"Brett Beauchamps. Who is this?" A pause. "Is this *Darryl?*"

"Yeah."

"Where's Lovie?" he shouted into the phone. "Where the hell did you take her?"

Darryl opened his mouth to speak but he didn't have time to utter a sound.

"Do you think you can get away with this?" Brett launched into a tirade. "We've got the police looking for you so you might as well give it up right now and bring her back. You'll get off easy if you do."

"What the fuck are you talking about, man?"

"Child abduction is a federal offense. You don't have joint custody, not even visitation rights."

"I didn't . . ."

"We know about that warrant for your arrest in California. You're in deep, buddy. So make it easy on yourself and just bring her home."

Darryl felt an overwhelming sense of dread as he stared vacantly at the wood striations in the greasy paneling.

"If you touch a hair on her head, just one hair I swear . . ." Brett paused. "I'll come after you. Do you hear me? Huh? Do you . . ."

Darryl set the phone back in the receiver, feeling like he was moving in slow motion. His stomach heaved and he thought he was going to hurl. Tightening his lips, he dropped his head in his hands.

What the fuck was going on? he wondered. Was the whole world going crazy? He was just gone for one night, for crying out loud. With his own kid! What did they mean abduction?

It felt like the blood was draining from his head and he flopped back on the mattress.

It was thin and lumpy and smelled of must and cigarettes. He tried to think over the drumming of blood in his head, tried to replay the phone call in his mind — *abduction . . . felony . . . police . . .* They knew about the warrant out for his arrest? Hell, he hadn't known she was under age!

Darryl tightened his hands into fists. Shit. He couldn't go back to Charleston now. They thought he'd kidnapped his own kid. They were convinced of it and for sure wouldn't give him a chance to explain. And there was that California thing. They'd arrest him on sight. How did he get himself into this mess? He lifted his fist and hit the mattress. Then hit it again and again, all the while his brain silently screamed, *goddamn, goddamn, goddamn.*

What was he going to do with the kid now?

25

Toy heard the music from the street.

It was a pulsing, rhythmic beat against the melodic resonance of a marimba. Toy pushed back her hair and climbed from Rafael's jeep. She clutched her black shawl around her bare shoulders, feeling unsure.

"Don't be shy!" Martina said encouragingly as she climbed from the car.

Martina was a fellow intern from Brazil and already her hips were swaying to the music. Earlier that evening, Martina had seen Toy emerging from her room at Villa Baulas to join them for dancing. She took one look at Toy in her nylon sports pants and T-shirt and raised her hands.

"Aiee! No, no, no!" Martina had cried. "You no can go dancing looking that!"

Toy had looked at Martina with her flowing black hair and her tight scarlet dress that left little to the imagination. She was,

Toy thought with wistful envy, fabulously sexy.

"It's all I have. Other than a straight skirt that makes me look like your mother."

Martina pushed back her mane of hair and crooked her finger. "Come with me, little kitten. Tonight, I'm going to make you a cat."

Now, standing in front of Kiki's, a cross-roads restaurant thrumming with dance music, Toy felt sure everyone in the room would see that she was a fake, not at all the sexy girl that she pretended to be with her hair flowing, ruby lips and wearing Martina's form hugging, black halter dress. She pulled the wide pareo she used as a shawl closer around her body. It covered her like a tent.

Rafael rounded the front of the car and took her elbow. He wore a colorful island shirt and loose pants that hung from his narrow hips. His favorite beads circled his neck and his dreads flowed down his back. He fit in with the crowd of young Latinos in the open-air, circular, thatched roof restaurant.

"Ready to dance?" he asked her, his eyes already dancing.

"I don't know Latin music," she replied hesitatingly. "I thought it would be, you know, rock."

"Oh, we listen to all kinds of music," he replied in his easy manner. "But when we dance, it's the salsa, meringue, lambada. Anything and everything, as long as it's Latin." He looked down at her shawl and frowned. "What's this?" he asked, tugging at the fabric.

The shawl slipped from her shoulders and his eyes widened with appraisal.

"I just . . . Martina. . . ." she sputtered.

Qué bonita!" he exclaimed, grinning with approval. "Tonight, you are a true Tica! *Vamanos.*"

She laughed, tucking the shawl over her arm. She was in the tropics, far from home and anyone she knew. There was, she realized, an illicit freedom to being anonymous. She smiled widely and shook her hair free. Tonight she wanted to feel on the dance floor the same heady freedom she'd felt riding a wave.

When she walked under the thatched canopy with Rafael, they were greeted with shouts and waved over to three long tables pushed together in a corner of the room. All the interns and their dates, spouses and pals were crowded together, laughing and pouring drinks, celebrating the first leatherback nest of the season. Some were leaving for home the next day and others were staying on.

Randall Arauz, a lead biologist she'd heard speak at the meeting, came up to meet Rafael and slapped him on the back. Dark and robust, Randall was a native Costa Rican in full possession of the warmth and vitality she'd come to love. It didn't matter that he was a world renowned researcher. Here at Kiki's, all were equal.

"I heard about the leatherback last night. Cool, cool," Randall said, grinning broadly. "Maybe it's a good omen, eh?"

Randall guided them to two chairs at the table, greeting people that they passed, waving to others across the room, spreading his arms out in a grand gesture in response to the razzing of the Marimba band. Everyone was in high spirits, making jokes and laughing while eating grilled fish, chicken and beef, and gallo pinto, the classic dish of rice and beans.

"Let's get something special to celebrate!" Randall exclaimed, calling out an order to the waitress. The waitress returned with a bottle and a jigger. She stopped before each one and poured a jigger of the clear liquid and put it down in front of him or her.

Toy leaned into Rafael. "What is it?"

"Fermented cane sugar grown locally.

You'll like it."

She scrunched her face in doubt as she watched the drink make the rounds from person to person. Everyone at the tables cheered and shouted if you swigged it down in one gulp. If you didn't, you were jeered. When the waitress came to her, Rafael wiggled his brows encouragingly.

"Here goes," she exclaimed and tilted her head to jerk it down. The liquid burned slightly on the way down, like tequila, but it was sweet and smooth. She laughed while everyone cheered her name.

At the table next to them, a young camera crew from National Geographic had arrived in town to film the leatherbacks. They were conducting mock interviews, keeping everyone laughing till tears flowed. The band was playing local music. She swayed in her seat, enchanted by the marimba. It looked like a xylophone and sounded like a steel drum. Another man played a cylindrical gourd with rough ridges, brushing it with a stick. And Kiki, the proprietor, who looked like a Costa Rican Lionel Richie, sang folklorica while playing the maracas and swaying his hips. Folks called out songs to him, joining in and singing lyrics everyone knew, improvising with others.

As the night wore on, however, there was

more drinking than eating. More musicians arrived with their instruments — a guitar, a bass guitar, a saxophone, an accordion and the timbales. The music began to change from a gentle, rhythmic beat to a hard driving mambo with African and Spanish roots. She felt the shift in the mood viscerally. More and more people rose to their feet and made their way to the dance floor. Their bodies swayed to the Latin beat, arms in the air, hips grinding, sweat streaming. Martina was a blur of red on the dance floor. The music was infectious, so when Rafael stood and held out his hand, she took it.

She was stiff at first, afraid of making a mistake. Rafael took her hips and swayed them in time to the music. "Remember the waves," he told her as he guided her to the beat. "Let the music wash over you."

Gradually she relented and released her inhibitions. The heavy Caribbean beat was hypnotic. She swayed her hips, lifted her arms over her head and moved to the music. The floor grew more and more crowded till she was in a sea of turning, twisting bodies, all lost in the rhythm of the heavy drum beat.

Toy felt the music and alcohol combine to swirl through her bloodstream, even as she twirled on the dance floor. She felt so sexy, so alive. Around and around she turned, lifting her hair from her shoulders, laughing, feeling utterly free. "Look at me, Mama," she thought to herself with a smug smile. Yes, I *can* dance!

As she spun around, someone in the back of the room caught her eye. He was far back in the shadows behind the tables, close to the entrance. She noticed him because he was taller than everyone else and seemed out of place in his tan slacks and long sleeved white shirt.

She twirled around again then stopped dancing abruptly. Her hair slapped her face. Slowly she lowered her arms, as though in a daze, not believing who she was seeing. Her chest rose and fell as she caught her breath. Then wonder switched to joy at recognition, and pushing damp hair from her face, she waved and called his name.

"Ethan!"

He sharply turned his head.

"Ethan, over here!"

His dark eyes spotted her and immediately he began walking toward her. His gaze locked with hers as he maneuvered his way through tables and dancing bodies. As he drew nearer, however, she saw that his face was drawn and somber. Her smile fell.

All the joy she'd felt seconds ago chilled

in her veins and she pushed through the crowd to meet him. She didn't know why he was here, but when he reached her and took firm hold of her arms, she felt a rising panic.

"Toy . . ."

"What happened?" she shouted over the sound of music.

"We have to go."

"What's wrong?"

"I've got you a plane ticket."

She searched his face, strained and taut, and his eyes, dark with worry. "Tell me what's wrong!" she cried. Then in a flash, she knew. Clutching his shirt she cried out.

"Oh, God, is it Lovie?"

26

No sooner had Ethan's truck come to a stop in the driveway of the beach house than Toy pushed open the door and ran up the stairs. The front door was locked and she hit it with the flat of her palm in wild frustration before digging in her purse, tossing its contents to the porch floor before she pulled out the key. Her hands shook violently as she tried to maneuver the key into the lock. Ethan, coming up behind her, took the keys from her hand and readily opened the front door.

Toy exploded into the house. "Lovie!" she called out, turning her head from right to left. She raced from room to room like a madwoman, calling over and over, "Lovie! Lovie!"

Ethan stood in the living room and watched, knowing she had to go through the motions, to see for herself that Lovie was gone. She hadn't cried. Nor had she slept or eaten in the twenty-one hours it had taken them to wait in the airports, to fly to Charleston and to drive to Isle of Palms. He knew she'd dissolve soon and he planned on being there when she did.

Toy came stumbling back into the living room, her eyes wild with despair as she glanced around the familiar room that had always felt so comforting and was now empty and cold without her daughter in it. She had a dazed look on her face, as though she'd been hit by a bullet, felt the sting, but had not fully absorbed the blow. Her gaze finally fell on Ethan.

"Ethan," she said in a hollow voice. "Where is she? Where is my Little Lovie?"

Her voice broke on the last word, as did her balance. In three strides he was at her side, collecting her in his arms before she collapsed to the floor.

Cara sat in a chair facing the window, staring out. Across the bedroom, Brett was on the phone with Ethan. He spoke in low, even tones that revealed the depth of his fatigue. She'd always thought that in times of crisis, she was the strong one, the clear thinker who could make quick decisions and act on them, efficiently and effectively. She sighed wearily. Not any more.

She looked out at the sunny sky over the glistening marsh. The bucolic scene mocked the misery she felt inside. She sat riddled with self loathing, of no use to anyone — not to Toy, not to Little Lovie and least of all, not to her husband.

Brett hung up the phone. She heard his heavy sigh and knew that he was also carrying the burden of worry for Toy.

"How is she?"

"They got back from the police station. Ethan's hoping she'll sleep some now. She's pretty wired. He's going to stay with her tonight."

"That's good. She shouldn't be alone."

"She's going to the station again tomorrow morning. I hope she can think of something we've missed."

"I should go see her."

"I wouldn't go just now," he said in a hurry. "She's probably exhausted."

"She doesn't want to see me, does she?"

"She doesn't want to see anyone right now. She needs to rest. She'll want to see you tomorrow."

"No she won't. She's angry at me, I know she is. And I don't blame her. I'd be angry, too."

Brett moved to her side and reached out to put his hand on her shoulder but Cara pushed it away. "She is not angry at you," he said slowly and with deliberation. "She's not angry at anyone. She's only worried about Lovie."

"Of course she's angry. I lost her child!" Cara put her hand to her head and shook it in disbelief. "How could I have lost her child? How could I have lost your child?"

Then Brett was there and she was pounding his chest with her fists. "I *lose children*. My God, Brett, I lost two children!"

He managed to get his arms around her and hold her still. "You didn't lose any child, Cara!" he said close to her ear. "The children, both of them, were taken from you. You're not to blame."

He held her tight until her sobs subsided and she felt limp in his arms. He loosened his arms, but still held her.

"It's a sign," she said wearily. She turned her head to rest her cheek against his chest. The fabric of his shirt was damp with her tears.

"A sign? Of what?"

"That I'm just not cut out to be a mother," she said, her voice cracking. "Maybe this was for the best."

Brett's sigh trembled as he squeezed her. "Oh, honey, what good is it to talk like that?"

He was right. She knew he was, but it did not stop her pain. She looked over at his hand on her shoulder. It was a large hand, strong and firm. She rested her lips against his skin.

"I am so sorry," she said, a broken woman.

The following day Toy rose with the sun to find Ethan slumped and asleep on the sofa. He was still dressed in the tan pants and long sleeved, white shirt he'd worn on the plane and dark stubble shadowed his jaw. He looked exhausted and she knew it was all for her.

She tiptoed past him, so as not to awaken him, to slip out the back door. In October the morning air was cool and damp. She gulped deep mouthfuls of it as she followed the narrow, winding beach path to the ocean. The wildflowers were closed tight and dewy, not yet opened to the sun. Toy broke out from the high dunes on to the beach and walked at a heady pace from the dune to Breach Inlet and back. She had to get outside. She needed to feel the sand of her beach between her toes, to see the detritus rich waters of her Atlantic Ocean. She needed to feel grounded when her whole world was tilting out of orbit.

When she returned to the beach house

she found Ethan awake, pacing at the door.

"Where've you been?" Worry made his tone sharp.

"On the beach," she replied. Her own voice sounded dead.

"Please, let me know if you're going out."

"Why?"

His eyes pulsed with frustration and he turned to the counter. "Want some coffee?"

"Yes. Thank you."

His went through the motions of making a pot of coffee and as it brewed, Ethan prepared breakfast with the same neatness and attention to detail that he had at the Aquarium. He chopped neat piles of mushrooms, green peppers and scallions, beat eggs in tight circles with a wire whisk and flipped the omelet with a professional turn of the wrist. Pulling out a chair at the table, he set the beautifully prepared plate before her.

Toy sat woodenly and stared at the omelet congealing on her plate. She felt her stomach turn at the rich scents. "Where did you get the food?"

"Flo and Emmi stopped by last night and brought food. Cara was here, too. You were asleep and no one wanted to disturb you."

"Cara was here?" She pounced on this. "Was there any news?"

"No, nothing."

The light that had momentarily sparked in her heart was snuffed out. She felt cold — in her body, her heart, even in her soul.

"I'm sorry, I can't eat this," she said, pushing the plate away.

"You've got to eat something to keep up your strength."

"Maybe later."

"You haven't eaten in . . ."

"I'll be sick. My stomach . . ." She waved it away, shaking her head. Instead she sipped some water, feeling the cool liquid moisten her lips. "Should I call the police again?

He shook his head. "They said they'd call you if they learned anything at all."

Her fingers tapped the counter restlessly "They wanted a recent picture of Lovie."

Seizing on this, she stood and walked to the bookshelf to retrieve a gray cardboard box. Bringing it back to the table she emptied the contents. Dozens of photographs spilled to a pile on the table. She began to sort through them, one by one. Ethan came near to look, leaning over her shoulder.

"These are the pictures I took this summer," she told him.

She'd taken photographs all summer of

the turtle nesting season. Some of the photos were taken with her cheap instamatic camera. Some were sharper and had better color. Those were taken with the camera that Ethan had given to her for her birthday.

Using her index finger, she pulled out a photograph of the remarkable turtle tracks that had gone around Lovie's sand castle and another of Lovie sitting beside the turtle nest, curious. Lovie proudly carrying the orange nesting sign up the dune. Lovie packing turtle team supplies into the backpack. Lovie bending over to inspect a sea shell. Lovie following a hatchling crawling to the surf. Hers and Lovie's footprints, side by side, in the sand.

"They're good," he told her.

She picked up a close-up photograph of Lovie in her favorite turtle team T-shirt. Lovie was smiling ear to ear, revealing a missing front tooth.

"She was so proud to be a turtle lady," Toy said in a soft voice, remembering each incident in the photographs as though it were yesterday.

"A little turtle lady," Ethan said, reading the words on the T-shirt.

Toy was struck by a thought and bolted down the hall to Lovie's bedroom. She went straight to the white wicker laundry hamper, and opening it, tore through the clothing in it, dumping them on the floor. At last she found it and pulled out Lovie's pale green turtle team shirt. Her breath hitched at seeing it and she buried her face in the soft cotton. She could still smell Lovie's sweet scent in the fabric.

"Lovie, where are you?" she cried and dissolved in tears. She felt as lost and frightened as the child she had once been. Then she suddenly stopped and wiped her eyes with determined strokes. Clutching the shirt, she rose and walked to the kitchen counter to fetch her pocketbook.

"I need to see my mother."

She found her keys, and closing her purse, walked quickly to the door. Ethan followed her and grabbed her arm.

"Wait, I'll come with you."

She stopped at the front door and turned to face him. He was tall and strong and his eyes shone with determination to help her. She thought for a moment that it would be comforting to have him with her then shook her head.

"This is something I have to do alone." She held her breath then said, "In fact, Ethan, I need for you to go home."

He looked hurt, his eyes bruised with

fatigue. "You're asking me to stay away again?"

She nodded. "Yes."

Toy turned off busy Rivers Avenue in North Charleston onto a narrow street of box-like houses with squared off, scraggly lawns, gangly oleanders, unclipped hedges, and older cars parked in the street. She had to go slow to navigate around potholes so big she'd lose a wheel if she drove through one. She passed a few kids riding bicycles and an old woman in her bathrobe rocking on her front porch. She continued on to where a twisted fence partitioned off a trailer park. A jungle of weeds and vines writhed through the rusted chain link and partially obscured the sign: *Charleston View.*

Toy shivered as she drove through the gate. Memories dappled her homecoming like the light that struggled to pierce through the leaves of the ancient oaks that grew between the trailers. The road here was little more than a graveled rut but the day was dry and her car reached what looked like the oldest trailer home in the park.

She closed the car door and faced the house she grew up in. The rickety trellis that she'd painted forest green still bordered the bottom of the trailer, covering the cinderblocks it sat on. She'd painted it over ten years ago. There were big gaps in the fencing where it had rotted or just fallen off. She followed the gravel path and climbed the wood stairs. Rust ate at the hinges of the front door like cancer.

She took a deep breath and exhaled slowly, trying to calm her nerves. She'd not stood at this threshold since she was kicked out six years earlier. Her mother had shouted unspeakable things to her, words that could not be recalled without sharp stabs of shame. She'd sworn she would never return and remembering, she had second thoughts. Then she thought of Lovie and raising her fist, she knocked on the door.

A moment later she heard footfalls approaching and steeled herself. The door swung open and a heavyset woman in a pink cotton floral bathrobe stood before her. She had thin, mousy blond hair pulled back in a ponytail, revealing gray at the crown and temples. It was a rough face with smoker's skin. Pale blue eyes very much like her own stared out from under a greasy shock of bangs.

Mother and daughter looked at each other a moment as they marked the changes that six years wrought.

"You're the last person I expected to see

today," her mother said without a smile.

"Hello Mama."

"What do you want?"

"I'd like to talk to you." She peered over her mother's shoulder. "Are you alone?"

Her mother's eyes hardened. "He's gone. Come on in."

Toy released a quick sigh of relief that her step-father wasn't in. She'd hoped that he still had his job at the foundry that meant he'd be at work by six.

She stepped inside the closed, dimly lit room and was assailed by the scents of mold and the stale sweetness of spray starch that had always lingered in the air for as long as she could remember. She shuddered at the memories the smells triggered, even though the trailer was stifling hot.

Nothing much had changed. The same dingy brown furniture sat in the same places in the room. Several cloth laundry bags lay on the floor beside an ironing board in front of the television. Her mother must still be taking in ironing, she thought. A rotating fan whirred in front of the ironing board, stirring the stale air. Across from it, the television had been muted, but on the screen a tele-evangelist in a long black robe was pacing a stage, raising his hands and preaching.

Her mother stood in the middle of the room. She didn't ask Toy to sit down or offer her so much as a glass of water.

"I seen you on TV," she said. "With them turtles."

"Oh, really? That must've been the release of Kiawah. A television crew came out to film it."

"So you work at the Aquarium now?" When Toy nodded, her mother said, "I hear you went to college?"

"I graduated last year."

Her mother made a face of surprise. "What do you know? You must be the first one in the family to graduate from college."

Toy felt a blossoming of pride before her mother added with a snort, "Who'da thought it would be you?"

Toy was surprised that her mother still had the power to hurt her. She bent her head to open her purse and pull out the photograph of Little Lovie. "Mama, have you seen Darryl?"

She looked surprised by the question. "Darryl? Hell, no. Why would I see him? He knows better than to show his face around here."

"He came back from California. He was playing music out there for the past five years. Anyway, he came by my place saying

562

he wanted to get to know Lovie better." She took a breath, realizing the magnitude of the moment. She held out the photograph for her mother. "That's her," she said "That's my daughter. Your granddaughter. Her name is Olivia Sooner, but we call her Lovie."

Her mother took the photograph and drew it close to her eyes, studying it. Toy braced herself for a torrent of accusations that she'd not brought her daughter to meet them, not once in all these years. So when her mother's face softened, Toy was caught off guard.

"She's the spittin' image of you at that age."

Toy was deeply moved. No one in the new life she'd carved for herself had known her when she was young. It was the kind of observation a young mother hoped to hear from her own mother. Toy brought her hand to her mouth. "Really?"

"She's a pretty thing." She handed the picture back to Toy. "You ought to bring her by."

"Mama, Darryl took her!"

Her mother's face screwed up in puzzlement. "What do you mean, he took her?"

"I was out of town and he took Lovie for the day. It was all arranged. But he never brought her back! He's been gone for three days and we don't know where he went. That's why I'm here. I was hoping you might've seen him, or heard something about him. Maybe his mother called you or . . . I don't know. Something. I thought maybe even he'd dropped Lovie off with you."

"No, I haven't seen hide or hair of either of them. He wouldn't likely come by here anyhow, knowing how we feel about him. Who was taking care of the child when you was out of town?"

"Cara, my friend."

Her expression hardened again, so fast that Toy wasn't sure she'd seen the softening in the first place. When she saw the flash of anger in her mother's eyes, she felt herself reverting to the insecure teenager again.

"What business do you have leaving your child with friends when you've got family who'd take care of her? You should've left her with me."

"No," Toy blurted out, finding her strength. "I'd never leave my daughter with him."

Her mother swiped her hand in the air with her lip curled in disgust. "You're not going to start in on that again? He didn't do nothin'. He swore on the bible he never touched you funny. You were just imagining it. Or lying. You never cared for Roy."

The image of Roy's hands on her breasts rose up in her mind and she shuddered, bringing up her palms and backing away. "No. I'm not going to get into this. It's not why I'm here."

"Your father is a God-fearing man and he'd never do anything to hurt you or that child."

"He's *not* my father," she screamed back.

Her mother appeared stunned by her outburst and, to Toy's surprise, backed down a bit. "He's the only father you have. And I'm your mother. You should've left that baby here with me, not some stranger. I never would've let anything bad happen to her."

"Like you did with me?"

"You have no call to come here and say those things," she said, very angry now. "I didn't ask you to come."

"Mama, I didn't come to fight. I only came to see if you heard about my baby."

"You came home because you're in trouble again," she said with a sneer. She waved her arm at her, shooing her away. "Go on, get out of here. You haven't changed. You're still in trouble. You're always in trouble. Your kind always is."

Toy sucked in her breath, turned and hurried to the door. Her mother followed her, shouting cruel things at her back as Toy fled the trailer. She slammed the door of her car shut and started the engine, eager to escape.

She looked back to see her mother standing in her housecoat on the front stoop, her face scowling while clutching the railing. It was, she knew, the last time she'd see her. Ever. As she pulled away her mother leaned over the railing and shouted, "It's your fault your child is gone. Your own damn fault!"

Toy held Little Lovie's T-shirt close to her breast as she drove. She desperately wanted to drive past these lines of cheap strip malls and gas stations, straight back to the Isle of Palms where she felt safe.

But she had one more stop to make. One last hope for some clue to where her baby was. She clutched the slip of green fabric like a security blanket and pressed on.

This house wasn't much bigger than her mother's trailer but it was in a nicer neighborhood with paved streets lined with trees and sidewalks that crossed tended lawns. Though the houses were similar, each reflected the personality and care of the owner. A cement walkway, hugged by marigolds, led a tidy path as straight as an arrow to the front door of the beige vinyl-sided house. Toy stood at the front door, clutching her purse close. This door was freshly painted and the louvered glass sparkled. She peeked through but couldn't see anything more than a wall.

The doorbell chimed and shortly afterwards a woman about the same age as her mother opened the door. She looked a lot like Darryl, small-boned and trim. Only her hair wasn't dark brown like his but dyed a white blond. She took a lot better care of herself than her own mother did. Her face was madeup and she was dressed in bright green plaid shorts and a green polo shirt with a horse emblem.

Toy struck a smile. "Hello, Mrs. Duggans. It's me, Toy. Do you remember me?"

Mrs. Duggans narrowed her eyes and her penciled-in brows furrowed. "Toy Sooner? Of course I know you."

"I don't mean to bother you but I need your help."

Mrs. Duggans pursed her lips and moved her eyes in a way that made Toy think she was nervous.

"I won't take but a minute."

"All right. But just for a minute." Reluctantly, she opened the screen door and stepped aside.

Toy entered the Duggans's front room. It was painted a green near the same shade as Mrs. Duggans's shirt. Even the carpet was the same green. The furniture was white wood but the cushions had that green in the swirls of paisley. Artificial flowers in milky white vases were on both sides of the sofa and more flowers curled along the white iron chandelier in the middle of the room. There was a funny smell in the house and Toy must have crinkled her nose because Mrs. Duggans said in an apologetic manner, "I'm cooking greens."

"Oh."

"Sit down, won't you?"

Toy sat stiffly in one of the paisley chairs. After her disastrous encounter with her mother, Toy knew better than to start chit-chat.

"Mrs. Duggans, have you heard from Darryl?"

Mrs. Duggans sat in the chair opposite Toy and smoothed out the fabric of her shorts. "Why, Darryl's been home for over two months now. You know that, Toy. He's been at your place more often than mine. The only time he comes here is to eat or borrow money. I reckon some things don't change. But I'm his mama and I'm glad to help him when I can. Last time he was here he kept talking on and on about you and your little girl. Little Lovie, right?"

"Yes ma'am. We just call her that. Her real name is Olivia."

"That's a pretty name."

Toy opened her purse to retrieve the picture of Little Lovie and handed it to her. Mrs. Duggans took it then rose to walk to the table where her glasses lay on top of the newspaper. She put them on and looked at the picture for a long while.

"What a pretty child. She favors Darryl, doesn't she?"

Toy raised her brows. She didn't think she looked like Darryl at all, but she didn't say that.

"He sure does love his little girl," Mrs. Duggans said.

"That's why I'm here, Mrs. Duggans. He didn't bring her back after their last outing. He's been gone for three days."

She slowly lowered the picture and frowned. "He hasn't called you?"

Toy's attention sharpened at her question. She shook her head. "I was out of town. But he called Cara. Brett talked to him but Darryl didn't tell him anything, not where he was or why he'd done it. He just hung up. Mrs. Duggans, did he call you? Do you know where he is?"

"I don't know anything," she replied icily, returning the photograph to her. "Why would he call me?"

"I don't know," Toy replied, bringing her fingertips to her forehead. "I'm just grasping at straws. The police are trying to find him but we don't have much to go on."

"The police?" Mrs. Duggans asked, her voice rising in alarm. "The police are involved?"

"They have to be. We filed a missing person report. They're calling it a kidnapping."

"Good Lord!" she exclaimed, extremely agitated. She walked closer, wringing her hands. "Toy, what have you done? There was no need to involve the police. My son did not kidnap your child!"

"He's had her for three days!"

"No one came to pick her up! He had to get to his job, is all!" she cried. Her eyes widened when she realized what she'd said.

Toy jumped up. "He *did* call you! You talked to him. Where is he?"

Mrs. Duggans retreated, shaking her head. "I can't say."

"You have to! If you know where he is you've got to tell me. Please!"

She backed away. Toy grabbed her hands

and held them tight. "Where is my little girl?"

"I don't know!" she exclaimed, looking into Toy's eyes. She saw that Mrs. Duggans was truly upset. Yet she also saw that she knew something that she wasn't telling.

"Tell me what you do know," Toy replied, her voice hardening. "Tell me — or tell the police."

"No! Don't call the police." Mrs. Duggans pulled back her hands and wrapped them around herself in a self-comforting gesture. She averted her gaze and spoke in a low voice. "He said he had to get to his job in . . ." She brought her trembling fingers to her lips. "Oh . . . Boone, or Brevard, or Baileyville. I don't know where exactly, some town that begins with a B. Somewhere in North Carolina."

"North Carolina? He crossed state lines?"

"He wasn't kidnapping Lovie. Don't you see that? He was just going to some job he had there. To play music. That's not the kind of thing a man does when he's kidnapping a child!"

"Then why doesn't he bring her back?" Her voice was filled with anguish.

Mrs. Duggans brought her hand to her throat. "I don't know. That fool child never did have any sense."

"Well," Toy said, turning on her heel. "I can't wait for him to come to his senses."

"Toy, please! One day. Give him one day to call. If he calls me, I swear I'll have him call you. One day, that's all I ask. My boy might be impulsive, but he's no criminal. You have to trust him."

"Trust him?" She shook her head. "I'll never trust him again."

The rain that had threatened all morning began in fat drops on her windshield as Toy raced from North Charleston to the Isle of Palms police station. It was still falling three hours later when they sent her home. They were polite and had let her sit in the waiting room of the Town Hall while they followed up on the North Carolina lead. A nice woman who worked the phones brought her a cup of coffee and told her, "I just know they're going to find your little girl now."

Toy sat on the uncomfortable chair for hours with her hands clasped tight in prayer. At four o'clock the door of the Town Hall opened and her head darted up, hope shining in her eyes. When she saw Flo coming through the door, her heart sank. She'd been sure it would be the policeman and that nice lady, bringing in Lovie.

"I've come to bring you home," Flo told her.

"I can't go. I just know they're going to find her. I've got to be here."

"They know where you live. You're not doing Lovie or anyone any good just sitting here."

How could she tell her she didn't want to go back to the beach house and see how empty it was without Little Lovie in it? "I'm okay. I want to stay here."

"Honey, they're closing up. You've got to go now."

When she stood she felt light-headed, tottering on her feet. "I'm okay," she said, regaining her balance. "I'm just dizzy from all the candy bars I've been eating from the vending machine."

"Come on," Flo said, taking her arm. "I'm taking you home."

27

As the sun slowly descended in a gray sky, Toy grew increasingly restless. She couldn't face the reality that another day was slipping away and another torturous night without Lovie was beginning. She paced the floor, going from room to room, wringing her hands and waiting for the phone to ring.

On the third pass through the house she grabbed a yellow slicker from the hook by the door and took off again for the beach. The rain had diminished to a fine mist and she could hear the storm waves thundering at the shoreline. Summer was over. She saw the changing of seasons in the yellowing of the sea grass and the dulling color of the trees. Everywhere she looked the landscape appeared gray and lackluster.

She climbed atop Miss Lovie's dune and stood buffeted by the strong winds. The waves looked wild and tumultuous with white crests curling and crashing in all directions. The incoming tide sent foamy fingers scaling the dune and sending bits of froth into the air with each insistent gust of wind.

She remembered the last time she'd sat on this dune as the waves crashed. Little Lovie had been with her, sitting on her lap. They'd thrilled to the ferocity of nature together.

Her eyes wildly scanned the empty horizon. I am a mother, she thought with anguish. I'm used to having my child with me. Without her, I'm done.

"Lovie!" she cried out. She filled her lungs and cried out again. "Lovie!"

The ocean's roar seemed to mock her insignificance. She fell to her knees in the damp sand and wept great, heaving sobs.

Toy didn't know how long she'd cried, but when she'd finished the sky had darkened to a leaden gray and her hair was wet from the mist and ocean spray. She felt exhausted and spent, at her lowest point. The cool wind pierced through her damp clothes and shivering, she brought her knees to her chest and wrapped her arms around them. She sat facing the sea.

Somewhere out there the turtle mothers were once again on their solitary journey.

She imagined them swimming in the great current, their long, creamy flippers gracefully stroking the water. Their season's nesting saga was completed. Their eggs had been laid, their scores of hatchlings — a new generation of loggerheads — had joined their species in the sea. The mother turtles had abandoned their nests, she knew. But they'd followed their maternal instincts and obeyed a far greater force.

Now the turtles had gone. Miss Lovie was gone. Little Lovie was gone. Only the slender hope that her daughter would return kept her from following the turtles into the sea.

A wave crashed against the dune, sending a cold spray stinging her cheeks. Toy closed her eyes and heard her mother's bitter accusations in her mind. *It's your fault.* They battered at her soul as cruelly and with the same consistency as the fierce waves battered at the dune. She was defenseless against the onslaught of memories she'd kept at bay for years. Toy put her palms to her face, lowering her head to her knees. Shrouded in darkness the memories came alive.

She was thirteen and back in the trailer. She smelled again the mold in the walls, the grease from the kitchen and the noxious scent of spray starch. A rangy black cat slept on the sofa. Her mother was standing at the ironing board, dressed in gray sweatpants and a ratty old maroon Citadel sweatshirt she'd found at a flea market. Half a dozen men's shirts hung from a metal rack beside her but the cloth bag on the floor wasn't even half empty.

"Mama, I'm hungry."

"Go git something to eat then."

"There's nothing to eat." She'd already gone and looked in the fridge and found a canister of ground coffee, some bruised apples and several bottles of beer.

Her mama set down the iron and sprayed the shirt with the aerosol can. The mist tickled Toy's nose in the steamy air.

"Then go get something from McDonalds."

"I don't have any money," she replied in a teenage sulk.

Her mother tore her gaze from the television. "Then you're out of luck. Go on, get out of my way. You're bothering me."

Hunger and frustration gnawed at her belly, making her reckless. "I'm hungry!" she screamed. "You're my mother. Aren't you supposed to feed me once in a while? I haven't had anything to eat all day!"

Her mother's face colored and contorted,

and with a sudden move, she lashed out. Only this time she didn't hit with her hand. Toy felt a fierce, white-hot burning on her flesh and lurched back, screaming. The cat leaped to disappear under the sofa. She continued screaming, hysterical, running around the room and collapsing in the corner, clasping her arm where the pointed edge of the iron was burned into her flesh.

Toy whimpered at the memory, still feeling the burn of insult that her mother could have done such a thing to her. How could any mother do that to her child? All her life she'd rationalized, even accepted as normal, that there were no meals on the table, that her clothes were dirty and smelled of body, that family shouted and swore at one another. But she'd always told herself that her mother loved her. That child's faith got her through the tough days.

So when she was thirteen and her stepfather began bothering her, she was able to tell her mother. There'd been a fierce row when Roy came home, with broken furniture and bruises. In the morning her stepfather was gone. Toy had felt safe, believing for sure that her mother loved her.

But Roy came back a few weeks later. Her mother told her then if she lied about him again then *she'd* be the one to get kicked out. Toy started having more sleep-overs at her friends' places and coming home whenever she wanted. When she found her mother didn't care, she stayed out longer. At sixteen she met up with Darryl. He was older, had his own apartment and took good care of her, buying her meals, clothes, even CDs. He never let anyone say anything bad about her and with him she felt safe. When she found out she was pregnant it just made sense for her to move in with him. It didn't seem her mother even noticed. But she must've been mad because when Darryl had started smacking her around, Toy was afraid for the baby growing inside of her and ran home seeking shelter with her mother.

Toy tightened her grip around her knees and rocked, reliving the shame. Her mother had been no different that day than she had been today. She'd barred the door with her loathing and beaten her back with her words. She'd hurled insults at Toy that hit hard, knowing where to aim.

It had always been so, Toy could see that clearly now. Her mother had no maternal instincts. Quite simply, her mother did not love her.

Toy lay down on the dune, stretching out so she could place her cheek on the wet sand. The dune comforted her. It was like she was lying on Miss Lovie's grave. She dug her fingers through the sand like a kitten pawing at its mother's chest. One thing she felt sure of. If she'd stayed in that trailer or if she'd stayed with Darryl, she would have become someone very different than the woman she was today.

The Fates had been kind when they guided her to the path of another mother.

Miss Lovie had, without question, saved her. That gentle woman had changed her life, not with grand gestures but with simple consistencies. She'd taught her the simple tasks of cleaning her room, setting the table, preparing a meal, sewing on missing buttons. Miss Lovie had taught her to pay attention by paying attention to her. She had tended her own nest, faithfully and with kindness, as she had tended the turtle nests on the Isle of Palms for so many years. And when she died she'd passed on this pattern of consistent tending to Toy. Because of her influence, Toy went to school, got a job, and most important, became the best mother to her daughter that she could be.

Toy pulled herself up to sit Indian style on the cool, damp sand. She brought her hands to her wet hair, pulling it back from her face and clutching a fistful at her neck.

But was that enough, Toy wondered? *What*

kind of a mother was she?

Did genetics win out? Was the tending instinct something that was learned? Or was it inherited, a toss of the dice on the X chromosome? How could she have been so careless a mother? she thought, berating herself. She'd been thousands of miles away, surfing and dancing carefree while her daughter was being kidnapped! She should have been home. She should have been paying attention. Did a good mother make such mistakes?

Her hands raked through her hair as she searched her memories for answers. She thought again of her mentor. Miss Lovie had been a good mother, but she had made mistakes, too. She had stayed in a loveless marriage and had been estranged from her daughter, Cara, for years. So perhaps good mothers did make mistakes. No one was perfect. But Cara and Miss Lovie had reconciled. They'd made peace before Miss Lovie passed on. The difference was, she knew, love and the act of forgiveness.

Toy shivered, feeling the wet cold clear to her bones. She felt unloved and unforgiven. Her head was heavy with her thoughts and the sky was darkening. There were no answers here.

The wind tugged and pushed at her in the

dark, but she made her way over the twisting path more by instinct than sight. Ahead, soft yellow light flowed from the windows of the beach house. One foot after the other, she followed the light home.

Toy stepped into the shower and let the hot water warm her numb body. She changed into flannel pajamas and wrapped herself in a thick chenille robe. Then she checked, for the hundredth time, the telephone answering machine, hating the nasal recorded message that told her, "You have no messages."

Drawn again to the photographs, she picked up the gray box and spread them on the floor. Kneeling beside them, she began picking through them once again. She'd diligently taken photos all summer. There were pictures of the tracks, nests, eggs and hatchlings. There were pictures of Cara, Emmi, Flo and herself, doing the typical duties of the turtle ladies. There were countless pictures of a bright and inquisitive Lovie involved in each phase of the nesting saga.

Toy felt a sudden sense of urgency and began putting the pictures into piles in chronological order. May June July August. September. Then she divided these into pictures of turtles and pictures of people, gathering them in a circle around her. She scooted closer, getting drawn into the stories. As she arranged the pictures, memories of the events came alive in her mind — words that were spoken, jokes shared, secrets revealed. Her hands worked quickly as the jumbled pile of memories was gradually arranged in some semblance of order. Hours sped by as the cool air of night settled around her. When she finished she stepped back and looked at the table, astonished.

There before her, in a neat succession of moments in time, was a beautiful, poignant, and revealing pattern. The succession of photographs created a story of one glorious summer on the Isle of Palms. It was a story of the nesting saga of the loggerheads. It was a story of duty. It was a story of friendship. It was a story of a mother and daughter.

Looking at the images she saw that she was there when Lovie built the sandcastle. She was there when her daughter collected sea shells. She was there when her baby sat in her lap and thrilled to the sound of waves crashing against the shore. Just as she was there when Lovie was sick, and on her first day of school. She'd sewn her missing buttons, made her Halloween costume, cleaned her clothes, read her books, prepared her meals and served them on a clean table with a fork, a knife and a spoon. She'd kissed her soft sweet face every night before sleep.

"I was there . . ." she said aloud.

Toy brought her hands to her lips and tears filled her eyes, blurring her vision, turning the photographs into a kaleidoscope of color.

This was her pattern of consistency. She may have made mistakes. She certainly was not perfect. But there in the series of images she found her answer.

Yes, she was a good mother.

It was very late when the front doorbell rang. Toy startled, dropping a photograph as she climbed to her feet. Opening the door, she found Ethan in the narrow halo of light. He wore a black slicker and his dark hair was plastered to his head, like he'd been walking in the mist for hours.

He didn't wait to be asked in, but marched past her into the living room. When he got there he turned on his heel, his eyes blazing.

"I'm not going away," he said. "I know you're hurting. You think you don't need anyone. You think you need to be strong, to do this on your own.

"But you're wrong. It's times like these that you do need people. People who care about you. People who love you."

He paused, his mouth working. "I love you, Toy," he blurted out. "I'm going to stay right here and get you through this. And when it's over, when Little Lovie is back, then we can talk about the future. We have a lot to sort through. But goddamn it, Toy, don't tell me to go away again. Because I won't." His mouth was set in a straight line and his fists were bunched like a pugilist's ready for a fight.

Toy stood stunned to silence. She'd never heard Ethan sound like this before. She let the door slip shut behind her and quietly walked across the room to him.

He was watching her, his eyes burning with intensity from under dripping locks of hair, waiting for her response. She remembered that first day she'd brought Big Girl into the Aquarium. He'd been standing on the platform, his hair was dripping down his face as it was now. He'd heard her call and turned toward her.

And he was here now. She heard a click in her mind, the sound of a final tumbler of some complex combination falling into place. Gingerly she reached up to remove the wet slicker from his shoulders. He did not move to help her. She dropped the jacket on a nearby chair then reached up to stroke a damp lock from his forehead.

He looked into her eyes and his face relaxed. A half smile played at his lips. One familiar gesture evoked far more memories than words.

"Then don't leave," she said simply.

Something deep and abiding sparked in his dark eyes and his long arms slid around her waist, holding tight, not letting go.

28

The police told her all she could do was wait, so Toy waited.

The following day was overcast and blowy as the storm front slowly crossed over the barrier islands on its way to the ocean. The weekend visitors to the island were undoubtedly mumbling in their hot drinks about ruined golf games and rotten luck but Toy was glad for the rain. The somber clouds inveigled her to sit at the table with her photographs, a journal and an artist's pencil.

She was a woman with a mission. The night before in a flash of brilliance she'd decided to create a journal for her daughter using the pictures she'd taken. She was restless like the sea outside her window, tossing in the night. She woke at first light and went directly from her bed to plunge into her project. Ethan found her hours later leaning over the table to sketch in the journal and make notations, writing feverishly. While she wrote, she talked aloud to Little Lovie, telling the great story of their summer together as turtle ladies on the Isle of Palms.

So it went on during the morning. Ethan sat on the sofa reading, but on occasion he let his book fall to his lap as he listened, a bemused smile on his face, to Toy as she spoke aloud the words she was writing, as though Lovie were there.

"You are my helper on the Island Turtle Team," she told her. "One night we saw a loggerhead come ashore." She laughed. "You thought the eggs looked like ping pong balls!"

As the journal took shape, Toy gained strength and purpose, feeling a connection with Lovie. She worked diligently, believing fervently that when her journal was finished, Lovie would be home and she could read it to her.

As the day grew long however, and still no word came from the police, her faith began to waver. The journal was bulging with pictures and scraps she'd glued to the pages. It was a scrap book of memories. Toy closed the cover and rested her hand over it, feeling the shadow of restlessness creep again into the quiet room.

The sound of a book hitting the table

ricocheted in the stillness. "Come on, let's go."

She turned her head to see Ethan rising to a stand.

"Where are we going? To the police station?"

"Nope," he said, shaking his head and reaching out his hand to take hers. "To the Aquarium."

Ethan was right. The Aquarium was exactly the right place for her to go. She'd missed the bright and airy halls with the gleaming tanks, the exotic fish and the stunning views of the harbor. A choral group of children were singing songs from The Little Mermaid and she paused to listen. One little girl looked a lot like Little Lovie. She had a bright orange bow in her hair and was stretched out low on the floor to go eye to eye with the nurse shark. When the child turned her head she spied Toy staring. Toy smiled. In response the girl offered a tentative grin before turning back to the tank. Toy felt a pang of longing for her daughter.

When she entered the basement, the strong smell of fish and salt assailed her and the thrum of engines filled her ears. To her, it smelled and sounded like home. Behind the heavy metal doors, the small turtle hospital was empty save for Ethan, herself, and of course, the turtles. Ethan hung back, giving her space as she walked from tank to tank, greeting each turtle as she passed — Hamlin, Litchfield, Cherry Point.

"Each one of them is a teacher," she said to Ethan, looking over the tanks. "I've learned more from them than I can ever thank them for."

She walked beyond them to the largest tank set far in the back. "And you're the best teacher of them all, Big Girl."

The big sea turtle swam gracefully across the big tank to the plastic window cut into the wall of the tank. Toy climbed the three wood steps to look down into the tank. Big Girl's almond turtle-eyes were watchful, patient, as she breathed in gulps. Her neck had filled out from its emaciated state to fill out the curve of her carapace.

"You're so beautiful," she told the turtle, bending closer to meet her gaze. "Look how fat you've gotten. And your shell is gleaming. Ah, Big Girl, the water in the ocean is getting colder. If you're going to be released home, it's got to be soon. Are you ready, huh? Are all your wounds healed?" She reached out to pat the turtle's shell. Big Girl dove and took a turn around the tank, gaining speed. Toy leaned back, lest she'd get splashed. But Big Girl only swam around once more then drew near again, her nares spouting droplets of water as she noisily exhaled.

Toy felt a surge of affection for the turtle mother who had journeyed with her through so many lessons this summer. She was her first rescue turtle of the hospital, the turtle that presented challenge after challenge, as though to test her. She was the turtle who taught her not to give up.

"I don't know who saved who," she told her in a soft voice. "Oh, Big Girl, I don't know if I am ready to let you go."

As Ethan and Toy drove home over the Ben Sawyer Bridge, Toy felt listless. She leaned her head back and let her gaze wander out over the vast marshes that stretched out to the ocean. The spartina grass was yellowing and the air was heavy with the pungent odor of pluff mud. Thousands of fiddler crabs were burrowing in that mud, preparing to hibernate for the winter.

They were crossing Sullivan's Island when her cell phone chimed. Toy dug into her purse, her heart pounding, scrambling for the phone. When she pulled it out she saw that it was an Out Of Area call.

"Ethan, pull over!" she cried and flipped

the lid of her cell phone. "Hello! Hello!"

There was a pause and she listened hard, closing her eyes to hear something over the beating of her heart.

"Hello, Toy?"

She could have wept. "Darryl!"

Ethan pulled the car into the parking lot of Christ Our King Episcopal Church and cut the engine.

"I'm here," she shouted into the phone. "Thank God. Darryl, where are you?"

"I'm at a phone booth, so don't be tracing my call."

"No, I won't. I swear. I'm in my car on my cell phone. Please, where's Lovie?"

"She's fine. She's here with me. Hell, Toy, I didn't kidnap her!"

"I know. I know you didn't."

"How do you know that?" he asked with suspicion.

"I talked to your mama yesterday. Didn't she tell you?"

"No." He paused. "What'd she tell you?"

Toy licked her lips and wondered how much to say. "She said you'd gone off to do a job and that you never meant to kidnap Lovie."

"Yeah, you got that straight. No one came to pick the kid up. I waited in the sun for over an hour."

He sounded angry. "I know," she said, placating him. "Cara was ill. It was an emergency. She couldn't come."

"Well she should'a sent someone. She left me standing there. I had to go, man. I couldn't lose the gig!" His voice was rising. "So I brung her with me."

"Yes, okay."

"Do you believe me?"

"Yes."

"Well, that's a switch," he said, his voice menacing. "Them others don't. Cara and Brett. They called the police. Shit, why'd they do that? I'da brung her right home if they hadn't gone and done that. Now I'm fucked. I didn't kidnap Lovie and I didn't rape no girl in California. I ain't going to jail, Toy. That girl told me she was eighteen and I swear she was willing."

"I believe you." She was trying to keep her voice steady to calm him. He spoke in rushed sentences like a man at his breaking point. "Darryl, where's Lovie?"

"I told you. She's right here."

"Can I talk to her?"

"Better not. She's been crying all day for you and I just got her settled. When she commences crying, I swear, I'm at my wit's end."

"Bring her home, Darryl. Please."

"Don't you think I want to?" he blurted out. She could envision him raking his fingers through his hair in an agitated swipe. He sounded calmer when he spoke again. "I'm not cut out for this daddy business. She ought to be with you. She wants her mama."

She clutched the phone, squeezing her eyes tight. She wanted her daughter in her arms so badly it hurt.

"Toy, what do I do now?"

His voice told her he'd had his Come-to-Jesus and was desperate. "Bring her home," she said, trying not to plead. "I won't cause you any trouble. Just bring her home."

"Right. The minute I show my face they're going to arrest me. I'm damned if I do and damned if I don't."

"Then I'll come get her. Just tell me where."

He sighed into the phone. Toy held her breath. Looking at the cross on the church steeple, she began to pray.

"Okay then," he said. "Listen good. I've got an idea. But you're going to have to follow it to the letter, hear? If you don't and I see a policeman anywhere, even one strolling by, I swear, Toy, I'll take off and you'll never see Lovie again."

Her face paled and she nodded in agreement. "I'll do anything. Just tell me what to do."

"I'm in a town called Baileyville, in North Carolina, just across the border on Highway 26. There's this park in the middle of town, with a big white gazebo in the middle. If you drive through on Main Street you can't miss it. So here's the deal. I'm going to leave Lovie sitting in that gazebo at eight o'clock. Got it? Eight o'clock tonight."

She looked at her watch. "But it's already four o'clock and it'll take at least four hours to get there. I don't know if I can get there by eight."

"Shit." She heard him pound the wall. "I don't want to leave her in the dark. She'll get scared."

That he had thought of that gave Toy hope. "I'll be there by nine. I swear."

"No, that won't work 'cause I won't be. Tell you what. You be there by 8:30, even if you have to fly to get here. But at 8:35, I'll be gone. I swear, Toy, I'll leave her sitting there alone."

The phone went dead. She stared at it a moment, trying to take it all in. Then she looked across the seat at Ethan, breathless. "Ethan, turn the car around. Hurry! We've got four hours to get to North Carolina. Drive!"

■ ■ ■ ■

They drove north like a bat out of hell. Toy's knuckles were white but she didn't utter a sound as they whizzed up Interstate 26, across the Carolina border into the mountains. She was too busy praying and checking her watch. Traffic was mercifully light and they made it to the town of Baileyville by 8:28 p.m.

The sky was already darkening and the street lamps clicked on as they started driving up Main Street. Toy opened the window of the truck and stuck her head out, craning her neck as they meandered up the narrow street at a snail's pace. Baileyville was a classic Southern town plucked from time. Main Street was lined with mature trees with gracious overhang, crooked sidewalks and low, red brick shops. She thought the town looked like it had weathered hard times since the closing of the textile mills. Still, there was a sense of pride evident in the fresh paint on the trim. And in the middle of the park, just as Darryl had described it, sat a pretty white gazebo.

"Pull over there, Ethan," she told him, pointing to an open parking space parallel to the park. "This isn't too close to the gazebo. Darryl can't see you. Now remember, stay here. I'll be back as soon as I can." She reached for the door handle, but Ethan's arm shot out to restrain her.

"I'm not letting you go out there alone."

She spun around in the seat to face him. "Ethan, please!" she cried, brooking no argument. "Don't do this. We discussed it over and over. I know him. He won't hurt me. But he'll do something stupid if I rile him. So please. Just stay here. I've got to go alone to get Lovie."

Ethan's eyes were tortured as he mulled this over. "All right. But I'll be watching. One false move . . ."

"Okay." She burst from the car and took off running for the gazebo. The yellow bulbs of the movie marquee were glowing, guiding her. Only one other person was in the park, an elderly woman walking a small brown dog.

She slowed to a fast walk as she drew near the gazebo, not wanting to come up too quick and scare anyone off. She squinted and spied a small head and two short legs dangling beneath a bench, kicking with impatience. A lump grew in Toy's throat. She knew that kick, recognized those chubby legs. She thrust out her arms and cried out, "Lovie!"

The child turned her head and peered through the white wooden slats. "Mama!"

The next few seconds went by in a blur. Toy bolted to the gazebo, her shoes leaden and her breath coming short. She saw Lovie's face, her outstretched arms, her blue eyes bright with excitement. "Mama!" she called out again and this time the voice was tearful.

Toy leaped up the stairs and with a cry of relief, scooped her baby in her arms and held tight. She buried her head in her daughter's neck and held her close to her breast. She felt her daughter's slender arms around her neck, her heart beating against hers. Toy was laughing and crying all at the same time. Lovie began crying, too. She'd been brave for so long, but now that she was in her mother's arms she could hold the tears no longer.

"What took you so long?" she cried, angry at her mother. "Where were you?"

"I'm here," Toy crooned, tasting the tears on her cheek. "I'm here," she murmured, smelling the scent of her hair. "I'm here."

Around Lovie's neck she saw a chain of silver with a silver ring hanging from it. Toy recognized it as the ring she'd given to Darryl years before, the one he'd worn around his neck. She heard an engine rev, and clutching Lovie to her breast, she swung her head to the left. From the corner of her eye she saw a red Mustang parked down the road partially obscured by an overgrown shrub. A man was sitting in the driver's seat. She squinted but couldn't make out the features but she knew it was Darryl. The car rumbled in place.

"Thank you," she whispered.

As if he'd heard, he stuck an arm out the window and waved. Just one single salute of his arm, then he pulled the car from the curb and roared away.

Toy didn't judge him nor did she blame him. She understood where he came from and who he was. She merely sighed in relief as the car disappeared around the corner. She knew she would never see him again.

"Come on, baby," she said. "Let's go home."

It was past midnight when they reached Brett and Cara's, but the lights were blazing in the pink stucco house along Hamlin Creek. When they pulled off Palm Boulevard into the narrow driveway the front door of the house burst open. Brett, Cara, Flo and Emmi rushed from the house, hands high in the air, their calls of welcome piercing the darkness like the dawn song of birds.

Little Lovie was kicking her legs and pawing at the window when the truck came to a halt.

"Auntie Cara!" she cried, struggling for release. As soon as Toy unbuckled her seatbelt and opened the door, the child scrambled from the truck.

"Where's my baby?" Cara called back, her voice breaking.

Lovie took off across the yard in a beeline for Cara. Cara bent to one knee and flung open her arms. Lovie ran into them, wrapping slender arms around Cara's neck. Cara hugged the child to her breast, clinging to the life in her arms. Her eyes sought out Brett's.

"There's your sign," he told her, his eyes pulsing with meaning.

Cara's grin trembled and she nodded in agreement, then she kissed the child's face. "You're home," she said, her trembling hands smoothing Lovie's hair from her face.

"Did you miss me?" Lovie asked.

"Oh, yes," she replied with a watery laugh. She squeezed Lovie tight. "We missed you."

"My turn!"

Lovie released her and ran directly to Brett. With a joyous "Whoopee!" he lifted her high into the air and swung her around, eliciting squeals of delight. Everyone laughed, relief ringing in their voices.

The sight of Brett with a child was bittersweet for Cara. She rose slowly, her hand on her back and grimacing at the cramping. Looking up, her gaze met Toy's. There was a moment of silent commiseration. They had not seen each other, not spoken one word, since Lovie's disappearance. Cara's breath caught and she lowered her hands to her side.

Toy smoothed the hair from her face and walked with a steady gait up the driveway toward her. Cara was aware that Brett had stilled, holding Lovie in his arms, watching. Emmi and Flo silenced as well. Cara's fingers twitched at her side and her eyes pulsed. In her mind she'd said "I'm sorry," so many times that she wasn't even aware she'd spoken the words aloud as she took a faltering step forward. Toy flung open her arms and Cara stepped into them.

Flo clapped her hands and stepped forward. "Now that's what I call a homecoming," she exclaimed, her blue eyes shining as she wrapped her arms around the pair. Emmi joined them, grinning wide and uttering words of support. They formed a united circle. Little Lovie wiggled free from Brett's arms and ran to join them, pushing her way between the legs so she could be part of the circle of turtle ladies. The women cooed their welcome as Toy lifted Lovie up to their presence.

Ethan strolled from the truck to Brett's side, his hands in his pockets and slumped-shouldered, not sure of his position in the tight group. Brett stretched out his hand in welcome and Ethan reached out to grab it.

"We owe you," Brett said, tugging him closer and delivering a few firm slaps on the back.

"Hey, no you don't," Ethan replied, stepping back. "That's my family."

Brett's eyes narrowed as he studied the man. "Is it really?"

Ethan nodded firmly, crossing his arms. "You bet."

"Well, hell!" Brett shook his head, laughed and stuck out his hand again. "Congratulations."

Ethan shook his hand again, joining in the laughter. They were of equal height yet now Ethan had achieved equal status.

Brett drew back and his hand indicated the group of women. They were clustered together, heads bent close and arms intertwined, talking with animation. Their voices were high with excitement. From the outside it was clear this was a tight, devoted group.

"Those are our women. Are you sure you're ready for this?"

Ethan's eyes kindled and he nodded. A grin stretched from ear to ear. "I've been ready for a long time." Then he scratched his jaw and said in a wry tone, "But if you think this is a tight group, wait till you meet the Legares."

■ ■ ■ ■

PART 4

■ ■ ■ ■

*Dive in! Enjoy the feel of water
washing over you.
Let go. You are swimming now!*

29

For Toy the most beautiful time on Isle of Palms was October, when the evening air cooled and the wildflowers bloomed purple and gold, bringing color again after months of sizzling heat. The busy tourist season quieted and the residents relished the peaceful off-season with less traffic.

She would miss it here, she thought, pausing in her cleaning to let her gaze sweep the quaint beach house that she'd called home for the past five years. Each rafter, each mullioned window, each stick of furniture was precious to her. Over there under the front window was Miss Lovie's favorite chair. If she let her mind wander, she could still see her old mentor sitting deep in the cushions reading her bible and sipping tea. Miss Lovie would tap her hand on the ottoman, indicating for Toy to come sit by her for a moment to chat.

What would she tell her, Toy wondered?

She had so much bubbling inside of her to share.

Surely Miss Lovie had witnessed from heaven all the trials she'd endured in these past months, she thought. Such a journey it had been! In hindsight she saw now that the past five years of struggling to stay in school, establishing routines for herself and her daughter, working long hours, and her unwavering focus had all been preparation for the events of this past summer. They'd formed her armor as she'd come to terms at last with the ghosts of her past — Darryl, her mother and the legions of insecurities and self-doubt.

Her musing was interrupted when Cara walked into the room carrying another box in her arms. She set it down on the floor by the door with a thump.

"I swear, I never knew a child could have so many toys."

Toy laughed and scolded, "You gave most of them to her so no complaints."

They had been working steadily for all of the morning and most of the afternoon cleaning the beach house and loading up Toy's possessions into Brett's truck. It had been a day of bonding again. They'd scrubbed and polished this place that they both loved and that harbored so many of their most precious memories. Perhaps it was because their hands were busy vacuuming and washing that their tongues loosened and they'd been able to talk as they hadn't been able to since Lovie's disappearance.

"That's the last of the boxes," Cara reported. "The bedrooms are cleared."

Toy removed the rubber gloves and tossed them into the bucket. "I just finished the last of the windows. Once I get the cleaning supplies put away and set the trash at the curb, we'll be done." Toy looked around the room one more time, feeling a tightening of her heart. "I guess that's it, then."

Her voice broke and her lip trembled. Embarrassed, she brought her fingers up to cover them. But she was too late. Cara had seen them and came quickly to her side.

"I didn't think I had any tears left," Toy said with a broken laugh. "I about cried a flood last night."

"Are you sure you want to leave? You know you don't have to. You and Ethan can live here."

Toy stepped back and wiped her eyes. "Don't think I wouldn't love to. It's going to be a little crowded in Ethan's apartment. But he's all ready and it's only for a little while. I can't wait to move into that sweet house on John's Island, even if it is a stone's throw from his mama's." She rolled her eyes and Cara nodded in understanding.

"I'll be fine," Toy said resolutely. "It's time for me to move on."

"You know what Mama always said. A long journey begins with the first step."

"Imagine me, getting married. Oh, Cara, I'm afraid of such happiness."

"Don't be. You've earned every bit of happiness that comes your way."

"So have you," Toy said.

Cara's face sobered to reflect the depth of her emotions. "Filling out the adoption papers was our first step. I suspect it will be a long journey. Not too long, I hope. We are so ready to have a child."

Toy linked arms with Cara. They stood together in the middle of the room, each lost in her thoughts as the ocean's salty air whisked in through the open windows. Outside, the palm fronds bent in the wind, scraping the frame. Beyond, the sea oats clicked. Toy thought how another turtle season was over and the loggerheads were swimming off for a winter of foraging. She was swimming off, too. And tomorrow, Big Girl was scheduled to be released back to the ocean to follow her sisters in the great current.

"Things are changing so fast," Cara said

wistfully.

Toy felt a sudden sadness at the prospect of Big Girl leaving. That, coupled with her own leaving, loomed heavily over her.

"Sometimes I wish things wouldn't change," Toy said. "Why can't things stay the same?"

"Because they can't," Cara replied simply. "Look at your little girl. If you want to mark the passage of time and changes, just take a picture of her every year."

"I'm thinking of Big Girl. It's going to be hard to let her go."

"I know. But it's time for her to go home, to be with her own species where she belongs. We have to know what we can let go of, and what to hold on to."

"You're right, of course. I want her to go home and be free. But looking around, I'm finding it hard to let go of so much all at once. It's all very emotional, you know?" she asked with a sniff. "Just before you came in I was thinking of Miss Lovie again and the good times we had here, in this room, together."

"She always created such magical times for us. She had a gift for making people feel at home and welcomed."

"Sometimes, I just want those sweet moments back again," said Toy.

"We all want them back But it's our job now to be the good mother, and to create that magic in our own lives. With our children."

"I'll always be grateful to Miss Lovie — and to you — for all I've learned while living here."

"There's something about this place," she said looking around the room again. "The older I get, the more I understand what my mother meant when she said that the beach house was not so much a place as a state of mind. So you see, Toy? You're not really leaving, are you?"

Toy shook her head as tears threatened and they hugged exuberantly.

"Time to go!" Cara said, separating quickly, not one for gush and sentiment.

They began piling Toy's last remaining items from the house into the truck. Their heels clicked loudly on the polished floors. After a final quick, perfunctory walk through the house, Cara closed the front door. Standing beside her, Toy thought it closed with a whisper of wind. But she heard the click of the lock as a ponderous clamor in her heart.

As she walked down the wood stairs, Toy turned her head to look once more at Primrose Cottage. A tremulous smile played at her lips. "Oh, Miss Lovie," she whispered. "Thank you for being there for me when I needed you most. I may be leaving the beach house, but I'll always carry you and your words in my heart."

Medical Log "Big Girl"

Oct. 22

We pulled sea turtle for final weight check and pit tags. Blood culture came back negative. Plan for release off Isle of Palms.

Weight: 266.1 lbs.

PIT tag #43490001

CASE CLOSED

Goodbye, Big Girl! Good Luck! TS

30

It was a glorious day for a release.

The rain had finally stopped and the sun shone high in the late October sky, warming the ocean's water and the faces of all who had come to Isle of Palms to observe the return to the sea of a turtle rehabilitated at the South Carolina Aquarium.

Toy drove in the Aquarium's pickup truck with Ethan. She looked over her shoulder for the hundredth time to check on the large sea turtle bundled under damp towels. Big Girl was unmoving, nestled securely in a white crate. Toy bit her lips, trying to keep her composure as they passed over the marshes toward Isle of Palms. Looking out, she was amazed at how much more yellow had tinged the grasses in the few short weeks since her return to work. Time was passing by so quickly, she thought. Some days it seemed like only yesterday they were driving in the opposite direction with a sick

Big Girl in the back of the truck on her way to the Aquarium for rescue. Other days it seemed like years had passed.

There was no denying that this turtle was special. With Big Girl, she'd battled with her personal attachment versus the scientist's neutral detachment. The reality was that her blood work came back clear and the waters of the Atlantic were cooling. It was time for Big Girl to go home.

Ethan reached out across the seat to pat her hand. Toy turned her head to look at his face. He glanced from the road to offer her a smile of encouragement, knowing how hard today was for her. She returned a watery smile and they both set their gazes on the road ahead without needing to say anything.

Ethan drove the truck up the vehicle path directly to the beach. A small crowd had already gathered at the water's edge, many of them readily recognized as turtle volunteers by their T-shirts. Stepping out from the truck Toy saw a television crew as well. A man with a microphone was interviewing Flo. Toy smiled, thinking that no one could answer their questions more colorfully.

She turned her attention to the turtle and climbed to the back of the truck. Ethan was already there, directing Favel, Irwin, Brett and Elizabeth into position. On his cue, the six of them carefully unloaded the large white crate to the sand. Immediately the crowd drew closer, eager to see the turtle. Children pushed past the barrier of tanned legs, pointing and crying, "Look! Mama, look at it!" Volunteers guided the crowd back, instructing them all to form a wide, inverted V along the sand, opening up a wide space at the surf for the turtle's final trek to the sea.

When they were in place Toy stepped forward with a microphone. She looked over the crowd dressed in swim suits and casual clothes and saw true affection for the sea turtle shining in their faces. Feeling a bond, Toy's nervousness fled and she spoke with warmth as she told them Big Girl's story of rescue and recovery. When she finished, she turned and walked to the crate.

The excitement built as the damp towels were removed from the shell and Big Girl was lifted from the crate. Toy felt a hitch in her throat when she watched the great sea turtle touch sand for the first time in many months.

Once again, the crowd edged closer. Big Girl lifted her head and looked around, her beak open, trying to make sense of what was happening. Emmi, Flo and Elizabeth sprang forward to walk the line and kindly but firmly nudge the crowd back into position. "Give her room," they called out.

Toy turned to Cara. "Would you help us escort Big Girl home?"

Cara's hand flew to her chest. "Who, me?"

"Of course. You spent that hellish first night under the porch keeping guard over her. It seems only fitting that you act as her honor guard today."

"Why, sure! I'd love to. What do I do?"

"Same thing you did that first day. Pick her up and carry her. Only this time in reverse. This turtle is heading home."

Cara wiped her hands on her shorts and bent over to grab hold of Big Girl's side next to Brett. Toy and Ethan took hold of the opposite side.

"I'm warning you," Toy said. "She's a bit heavier than the last time you carried her. We only have to carry her a little way. We want her to walk herself to the water. Ready? Let's go!"

They hoisted the big turtle, straining at the task. With synchronized steps they carried Big Girl to within several feet of the ocean then gently lowered her to the sand. Big Girl rolled her almond eyes back to look at them.

"It's okay, Big Girl," Toy told the turtle.

"You know what to do. Don't you hear the ocean calling? Go on, now. Don't be afraid. You're going home!"

Her voice broke and she tightened her lips, willing herself not to get too emotional, especially not on film. Her job was to heal sea turtles and each release marked a success for the Aquarium. But sometimes the job was bittersweet and she couldn't stop the tears from blurring her vision of Big Girl's first, tentative moves toward the surf.

This was not the weak and listless turtle they'd rescued from the sea months earlier. This was a healthy female turtle in her prime and she moved like an iron tank, slow but deliberate, to the sea. Her powerful flippers dug into the sand, creating the turtle tracks that volunteers searched for every morning from late May through July. The closer she drew to the water the more determined she stroked, pausing only once to raise her head, straining, sniffing the salt air. The surf rolled in, white and foamy, and Big Girl dug in with renewed vigor, propelling herself forward.

Cara and Toy were her honor guard, walking behind her to the water's edge. Big Girl pushed into the sea without pause, her beautiful dark eyes focused on the horizon where sea met sky. Cara stopped at the water's edge but Toy continued forward, feeling the warm waters of the Atlantic swirl at her ankles. A white crested wave crashed over Big Girl, washing her shell. Her gorgeous, reddish brown coloring glistened in the afternoon sun. Toy sensed the turtle's awakening as she tasted salt water. Her own heart quickened as Big Girl's clumsy struggle grew graceful in the deeper water.

Onward Big Girl swam, far beyond Toy's reach. Toy pushed clumsily against the waves but she could not catch up to the powerful turtle in her element. When the water reached her thighs Toy stopped. Her heart lurched as she watched Big Girl dive into an oncoming wave and disappear.

Standing alone in the swirling waters of the ocean, Toy thought again of her recurring dream. She saw again the great mother turtle, journeying through the dangers of the murky waters, following the call of instinct and knew with sudden clarity that she was the sea turtle in her dream. It was herself pushing through the crashing waves, propelled through the great current, swimming forward to find her way home.

She heard the crowd behind clap and cheer at Big Girl's return to the sea. Toy knew a sudden sense of loss and took a few more steps into the depths, wildly searching the horizon for one more glimpse of the sea turtle. She'd rescued this loggerhead from the ocean, helped her to heal and grow strong. She wanted just one final chance to say goodbye.

For several minutes she stood in the water watching the horizon, feeling a growing despair. A long line of pelicans flew low over the water. A gull circled overhead, crying out its mocking laugh. She stood shivering, staring out. But Big Girl was gone.

With a heavy heart, she turned back toward the beach. The crowd had already begun dispersing, walking off in groups along beach paths. The television crew was packing up. She saw Emmi and Flo walking shoulder to shoulder back to their beach house, Flo's hands gesticulating in the air as she spoke. Not far behind, Cara and Brett strolled hand in hand.

Her gaze landed at last upon the tall man standing at the water's edge with his hand resting firmly on a little girl's shoulder. Suddenly Lovie raced off across the beach to climb the dune. Perched at the top, she stretched out her arms to the sea in a heartfelt embrace of sea and sky. Wisps of her blond hair caught the wind to sail above her shoulders and she cried out with all the joy and exuberance and hope of youth.

"Goodbye, Big Girl! Goodbye!"

Toy swung her head around to scan the horizon once more. With a gasp she caught sight of the large glistening brown head of a loggerhead rising high from the water, far off in the distance. Toy's heart lifted with joy and she brought her hand up in a wide, arcing wave.

"Goodbye, Big Girl!" she whispered. "Thank you!"

Then she watched as Big Girl dove a final time and disappeared under the dark water.

She turned back toward shore and saw Ethan standing at the shoreline, waiting. He stretched out his hand to her.

With a sudden brilliance her heart expanded with light. She waved her arm and quickened her steps as she moved toward shore. Lovie jumped up on tiptoe, then ran back to the shoreline calling out to her, "Mama!"

Toy felt herself carried by waves, gliding through liquid wind, propelled by love. She pushed on through the surf, stroking with her long, slender arms, reaching out to her family, finding her way home.